IMPEACHMENT

Anjali Deshpande is a freelance journalist who has dabbled in the women's movement and the struggle of Bhopal victims for justice and other such lost causes. Eclectic, an iconoclast to the core, she is never at a loss in any debate – the noisier the better. She manages her world without much discipline, any sense of design or patience, and cultivates the virtues of laziness. She lives in Delhi with her husband and without cats or children.

IMPEACHMENT

ANJALI DESHPANDE

First published in 2012 by Hachette India
(Registered name: Hachette Book Publishing India Pvt. Ltd)
An Hachette UK company
www.hachetteindia.com

SRD

ISBN 978-93-5009-276-7

Hachette Book Publishing India Pvt. Ltd
4th & 5th Floors, Corporate Centre,
Plot no. 94, Sector 44, Gurgaon 122003, India

Typeset in Janson Text LT Std 10.5/13.75
by InoSoft Systems Noida

Printed and bound in India
by Manipal Technologies Limited, Manipal

MIX
Paper from
responsible sources
FSC™ C104740

To the late Dr Heeresh Chandra
The unsung hero of Bhopal

PROLOGUE

Hally arrived a little past 9:30 a.m. at the gates of the Supreme Court and was pleasantly surprised to see Avidha and Suguna already there.

'Where are the brooms?' asked Suguna, almost in a whisper.

Hally laughed. 'Did you expect me to come here waving them above my head? I left them at Ajit's last evening and he will get them.'

Ajit would park outside the Law Institute and the volunteers were to go to his car and secrete the brooms under their shawls. The sweeping time was 10:30 a.m.

The three went down to see Ajit drive in but they still had to wait for the press to arrive.

'And I thought we were the press,' said Avidha to Ajit.

The press was not happy about the timing but representatives of seven dailies and two agencies arrived on time to crowd Ajit. They were sent off to wait in the veranda of the court.

Nine of the volunteers walked to the court with the brooms under their shawls, seven of them women. They climbed the flight of stairs to the veranda outside Court Number One.

'Down with the Bhopal Settlement. It stinks. Down with the justices, they stink,' they shouted in unison as they threw their shawls open, took out the brooms and began to sweep the veranda outside the court. Other protestors stood at the bottom of the stairs raising slogans. 'Supreme Court ne kya kiya? Hatyaron ko chhod diya, Carbide ko chhod diya. Adalat me gandagi, nahi sahenge, nahi sahenge!'

Lawyers paused in their brisk walk towards the courtrooms. People waiting in the lawns for their cases to be heard rushed to the scene of activity. It took no more than twenty minutes but the impact was stunning.

The volunteer-sweepers came down the stairs and stood in front of the semicircle of slogan-shouting protestors in what appeared to be a choreographed scene, though it was a coincidence.

'We are waiting for this court to haul us up for contempt,' Suguna told the waiting press people. 'Let them arrest us if they dare.'

The court disappointed them once again.

Chapter I

A TIME OF CONFUSION AND HOPE

The middle class often confuses traversing the middle path with being centre stage.

One balmy February morning, Avidha got up to some decisive actions, not to clear that confusion, only to tamp it down. She woke up early, in defiance of her avowal never to, damaged her track record by making herself a bad cup of tea, and tried hard to think when she had last seen the sun rise. All this, in a deliberate attempt not to dwell on the unknown place the detour she had taken was leading her to. She roamed the terrace fronting her *barsati* and watched the bands of early sunlight change from a deep red to grey concrete – defined and ugly.

When Suguna, her flatmate of four months, saw these extraordinary events she was convinced the world was about to change. Avidha's assertions of independence and self-reliance had never included mundane things like making tea. When she offered to make another round, Suguna knew something really special was on the menu. *Must be that man Avidha keeps locked in her bottom drawer.*

'The world is so interesting,' Avidha said.

To Suguna's solidly pragmatic eyes the world was exactly as interesting as it had been the night before. The day was as it ought to have been in February, when the air in Delhi is still free of dust, the power cuts few, the petunias in bloom, the sun's fleshy vulgarity concealed in a light chiffon wrap. True, it was election year, the ruling party had seen some high-profile defections and charges of corruption in high places and anti-national conduct were making headlines, but that had been the case even a month ago.

She, however, nodded in agreement.

Avidha could not have found anybody as suited to her privacy and comfort as Suguna. Suguna did everything in the house – bought the gas cylinder on the black market; kept track of the cumin and turmeric, rice and dal; hoarded candles for powerless nights, and was so singularly devoid of curiosity that Avidha often wondered, perversely, what had made her a journalist.

'I am going to CP today...'

'That awful party's press conference is in Connaught –?'

'– in the Press Club. I am meeting someone for lunch in CP. I wish I didn't have the press meet before that. Bloody fascists. They give me hypertension.'

Avidha was known to fly off the handle at press conferences, a must-see spectacle for her colleagues who ridiculed her behind her back but gleaned new angles for their stories from her haranguing all the same.

Avidha dressed with extra care in a red and blue top, black trousers and the blue leather jacket her brother had sent her from Canada. Looking at the mirror, she wished for glossier hair once again, thinner lips and a slimmer figure, attributes owned, she imagined, by all the females *he* could and would see in CP – the favourite shopping haunt of the flamboyant female. Once again, her perfectly shaped features, set in her dark face, were not enough. She tugged her comb through her unruly short hair, hurting her scalp. No amount of brushing gave it the bounce she wanted. Nor was she in the mood she needed to be in today. Considering how she had everything else she wanted this was an incomprehensible catastrophe.

A rendezvous with Prashant, Avidha noticed, always came her way on particularly bad days. Today she had the press conference, then an afternoon appointment and a feature piece to put together for the Sunday supplement.

Avidha arrived at the press conference just as the national leader of a belligerent right-wing party took the mike from her flunkey. A minor saffron-robed functionary of the party had been arrested in a small town in Uttar Pradesh for raising passions to such a pitch with his incendiary speeches that a crowd of his supporters had torched some shops. He had been remanded to judicial custody by a trial court and the party had launched an agitation for his release. The family members of the arrested leader wanted to serve him hot home-cooked food even at night and objected to being searched by prison guards. His supporters had been blocking railway tracks and stoning buses for interrupting the flow of his vitriol. They had vociferously protested against all the rules that the hapless district and jail officials tried to implement in a politically charged atmosphere.

Now one of the top women leaders of this growing and predatory organization was condemning the arrest. She asserted that it was a shame that the administration ill-treated men of faith and denied them the freedom of expression.

Avidha had come prepared to ask her one question and then leave and waited impatiently for the briefing to end. She was the first to raise her hand.

'Mrs Vindhya Devi,' Avidha began, but before she could complete her sentence one of the people on the dais prompted her to address the leader as 'Rajmata'.

'Why?' asked Avidha hotly. 'There are no kings and queens in this country.'

'Call her Rajmata,' said another of the supporters loudly. There was an uncomfortable silence as three supporters of the leader closed in on her. Avidha looked around at the other reporters, all of whom sat staring at the dais avoiding eye contact with her.

The feeling of being hounded brought her defiance to the surface. 'Mrs Vindhya Devi, how can you demand constitutional rights for your party members when you won't recognize my right to call you by your name?'

A clamour rose demanding that the press show 'proper respect to the Rajmata' from all corners in the room where numerous hangers-on stood in small groups.

The leader pursed her lips and turned her glance to another part of the room with arrogant self-assurance.

Undaunted, Avidha raised her voice. 'Did his arrest violate any law? If it did will you file an appeal in the High Court?'

This was too important a question to be ignored so the leader turned to her and said in a deliberately slow tone: 'Faith is above all laws. How can you not understand it? Our campaign for building a temple is like a prayer and nothing should interfere with a prayer. No law, no history, nothing is above faith.'

Avidha had her quote and got up to leave. As she was walking out one of the junior leaders came up to her and asked her for her card. She handed him one.

'You are very-ill mannered. I will call your editor,' he told her as he pocketed it.

'Please do. Give me your number, I will remind you to call him,' she said haughtily and walked out.

Seething with rage Avidha walked briskly to CP thinking of the threat the leader had held out, the slavish attitude of her colleagues, and their indifference to her predicament.

She arrived at the restaurant five minutes before the appointed hour hoping he would surprise her with his punctuality but knowing he would be late as usual. In the foyer she combed her hair, and walked slowly down the stairs to the basement, her heavy shoulder bag swinging dolefully. She picked a table in the dark, having negotiated the obstacle course to it in the crudely suggestive subdued lighting, and sat down. Five minutes turned to eight, ten, then fifteen. Could her late afternoon meeting be postponed?

Prashant had made it a habit to arrive late for his meetings with her that she found dissonant with his old-world manners. Avidha had come to view it as the subtle exercise of power by a lover who knew she would wait.

A waiter came up to check if she was the one waiting for 'Prashant Sahab' and told her he had called the restaurant to say he would be late and that she should place the order. She felt a hollow in her stomach. The waiter spoke of him

7

as if he knew him. How many women had he played footsie with here? She made a show of studying the menu, placed the order, pulled out her notebook, and stared into it without taking in a single word.

She saw him enter the restaurant and stop, waiting to let his eyes adjust to the dark. When he saw her she turned her face away. 'Sorry, sorry. The boss called me at the last moment.' He shook her hand, holding it tight for a moment giving it a slight squeeze. 'Don't I get even a smile?'

Her face lit up. She asked him if he was a regular at the restaurant as he turned to wave to the waiter who came with his favourite drink, Limca, and glasses on a tray.

Her face clouded over again. 'Why can't you tell me minor things?' asked Avidha.

'Like what? Like why I am late? With Parliament in session you know how much work we have to put in? Yet I still found time to meet you,' he said, put off by her tone.

'Where did you go last week? You were away for three days.' She was here to assert herself; high time she did.

'Lucknow,' he said curtly as the waiter came with the plates.

'Lucknow? Why?' she pursued when the waiter left.

He ignored the question and her old grouse resurfaced. His obsessive secrecy always made her uneasy. He treated even minor bits of information like classified data.

'I will tell you why, because you have a girlfriend there and you went to meet her,' she said testily.

He poured the Limca, offered her a glass, pushed his chair back a little and took a sip. 'No,' he said. 'Not one. I have three girlfriends there. That is why I went for three days.'

She laughed in relief. 'You sadist,' she said.

'Oh! Why do you love me then?'

'I am a masochist!'

He laughed. 'You are simply crazy.'

It was his stock phrase for her and she had herself come to believe that this terrible self-destroying passion she had for him was a form of madness. What else could explain this overpowering desire of hers to have all of him, even his past, because of which she could no longer face Nirmala. Till Prashant sauntered into her inner world it was Nirmala's perception of her that Avidha measured herself against. She could not bear the thought that she could fail the image Nirmala had of her and had driven herself underground to avoid Nirmala's condemnation. What did Prashant know of the depths of her passion for him?

'I was very close to Lucknow last week,' she said. She had travelled to three small towns in its vicinity to cover the political meetings of the leader who had begun to pose a serious challenge to the ruling party. The press had christened him the 'Supreme Challenger'.

He was silent.

'We could have met,' she said.

He did not even look up from his glass. No regrets that they had missed out on a golden opportunity. It confirmed to her that he had been with someone else.

'Why do you make an issue of such minor things?' he asked her.

'Because I am what I am,' she said. 'You know what I did before I came here today? Many would say it is a minor thing I blew out of proportion.' She told him about the press conference.

'You see what I mean? How does it matter what you call her?' he asked. 'These people can be dangerous.'

'I will be damned if I use feudal titles. It is unconstitutional,' she said adamantly.

'Improper,' he corrected her.

The waiter came up with the food and hovered around placing the dishes on the table.

'By the way, I need some information...' Avidha said after he had left.

'Sorry. I won't, even if I could. If the government has decided it is classified there must be some reason for it.'

Avidha looked at him in surprise. 'What do you think I am asking for?'

'The same Bhopal ICMR reports, what else. As if you will let me forget.'

Avidha had been thinking about the new hospital purchase policy for a story she was planning, not about Bhopal. But this was the first time he had commented on the issue and she could not let it pass. 'What could be the government's reason? Can you tell me that at least?'

The waiter lifted the lid off the bowl of rogan josh and was about to serve it when Prashant dismissed his service rather imperiously. 'The information can get into wrong hands. It can be misused.'

'You truly mistrust people, don't you? What did the bloody government do with all the data it had about the chemicals inside the factory? It could not even prevent the disaster,' she said, raising her hand to stop him when she saw him open his mouth, 'which, by the way, was preventable. *Fully* preventable. Now they don't want to tell people what they are suffering from and how long they will suffer. They collect data about their lives, their health, derive conclusions and keep them locked up. Does that make sense?'

He dug the serving spoon in the curry for a satisfying piece of meat without answering her.

'But like you said, people can't be trusted,' she said again.

Prashant began to laugh. 'Of course the government was at fault in the gas leak. Not here, though. You think those victims of the disaster will read ICMR reports? You people will. And Carbide will when these reports are made public.' He shook his head in disbelief. 'How can you be so naïve?'

'I love you,' she said impulsively.

His eyes lit up. 'Let us go out next week,' Prashant said abruptly, changing track. 'Not on a Saturday like we do. On a working day. The hotels are less crowded then.'

'Oh, my! How will Parliament function? Who will prepare answers to all those earth-shaking questions?' she asked, eyes wide in mock surprise.

'You take precedence over people's rights, ma'am,' he said, deliberately training his eyes a little below her neckline. She looked at her plate and blushed, suddenly unable to eat.

Reporters were postponing marriages, having abortions, and sharpening knives to slit each other's throats, just to get into the Supreme Challenger's convoy; it was not a good time to annoy editors with absences. At the rally last week, the Supreme Challenger had pulled out a slip of paper from his kurta pocket and waved it at the crowd declaring, 'On this paper I have the names of the top people who took money in this deal. You will know all this when these people are made to pay for their crimes.' Reporters scrambled to take a peek at that chit.

Avidha sighed. Even reporters can get the flu.

As they walked to his car, parked a little distance away, Prashant asked, 'Why didn't you wear a sari?' Under the cover of her sari *pallu* his hands were free to get inside her blouse and find plump flesh to grab on the ride back in the car; she blushed.

'Don't go to work. Let us go to your place for a while,' he said.

She had to tell him that her landlady would be out in the garden, maybe even sitting in the lane outside, soaking up the sun. That was not an option at all.

'What a bore she must be,' he said, but he did not look sullen or sound too disappointed. Her smile faded. His equanimity disturbed her.

'I knew I would forget something. Avi, be a darling and fetch some imli will you? Vineeta said she must absolutely have my *saru*,' Suguna said to Avidha as she walked in late in the evening, surprised to see cauliflower, peas, potatoes, tomatoes and even fish on the table. They seldom had anything elaborate to eat.

'People coming to dinner, I see,' said Avidha.

'Mukta called and I had to ask them over. Can't keep putting them off. Even ran across to tell you but you were not in.' Suguna's office was in the same building across the corridor.

'Oh, that's all right,' said Avidha as she carried the fish into the kitchen not wanting its overpowering smell to invade the room further. 'But you know those two alone will be so killing. Vineeta is dumb as a cow and Mukta forgot to laugh when her soul was waiting for a rebirth. Must have waited long, poor thing.'

'Don't be mean,' said Suguna, laughing despite herself. 'Have you and Nirmala fought? I have not seen her around in months. We could have asked her over.'

Avidha did not like the idea of whiling away an evening

with friends when she wanted to finish stitching together the patchwork sheet she had been embroidering for six months now. She wanted to take it along on this trip. 'I thought you didn't like Nirmala' said Avidha.

'I find her a little extreme in her views, but I don't mind her,' said Suguna.

'*That* is true. Didn't I tell you she said horrible things about journalists?' asked Avidha peeling off her jacket and fishing in her bag for a cigarette.

'Ho, you took that to heart? Didn't know you had begun identifying with the profession so closely.'

'Let's invite Zintac. I can call to check if she is free,' suggested Avidha.

She decided to phone Zintac from the market.

Avidha and Suguna did not have a phone yet. At first they had wondered if they should even bother applying for one. They were sure – given that their uncertain hours did not match her notion of decent jobs girls could have – that the landlady would ask them to leave before the year was up. 'To think that we fled the shadow of parental control, only to end up with this self-appointed custodian of our morals! Can't imagine how we will cope with the killjoy, Mis*suj* Kapoor,' Suguna had commented sourly, when they had first moved in. Once they had become comfortable with each other though, and decided that the landlady was, after all, not much worse than many others, they had wondered if they should humour her with a little chatter once in a while so she would let them stay on. She was a lonely widow, after all. Any way, they decided, it did not hurt to own a phone. Finally, after much discussion, Suguna had applied for one. Despite press priority, they had been waiting for over a month now to hear from the telephone department.

After she had finished shopping Avidha called Zintac.

'House-warming, finally? You bloody women! I thought I would never get to see the inside of your house,' Zintac trilled.

Then, on an impulse, she dialled Prashant's home number. A female voice answered and handed the phone to him.

'Who picked up the phone?' asked Avidha.

'Hello, what a surprise, how come you are calling?' he said in response.

'You wanted to come to my place, didn't you? I wondered if you could come by this evening. I mean now,' said Avidha

'Are you going to be alone?' he whispered. 'I thought your landlady didn't allow men in the house.'

'She doesn't. But some friends are coming over and, well, you could too. That way it would be perfectly all right.'

'Oh! Sorry, but that's too short notice for me. I am going somewhere, *haan*? It was so nice of you to call me. Some other time, then?' She heard the click of the phone in disbelief. Could he not spare her an extra minute?

They were fiddling with the tableware when their first guests arrived – the perpetually frowning Mukta and the radiant Vineeta in an extra long, pale pink woollen cardigan with red flowers embroidered on giant patch pockets.

'How do you manage to carry off such confections?' asked Suguna as she hugged her with genuine affection. Vineeta's lustrous waist-length hair, shining black eyes and perfectly arched eyebrows were enough to turn heads, but it was her unfailingly good nature and open smile that made her truly attractive and repulsed any feeling of jealousy her good looks might arouse. She handed Suguna a packet wrapped in shiny red paper. 'We were roaming around in CP and picked this up for you two,' she said. This was a lie; her notions of propriety always clashed with Mukta's more informal style so she had learnt to make every formal gesture appear like an impulsive act.

'Of course,' said Mukta with a tolerant smile. 'We *never* buy gifts on purpose.'

Mukta looked away as Suguna opened the packet and extracted two single bedcovers from it. Only Vineeta could have picked bright orange sheets with green camels printed on them.

'They are beautiful. I am going to use mine immediately,' Suguna said, noticing Mukta's disapproval.

'Perfect colour for the winter, isn't it?' Avidha said.

Vineeta turned around and looked at the house, much impressed by its austere beauty. There were only two rooms, both opened to the terrace and into one another. One was sparsely furnished with a bed, a small wooden cupboard and a stuffed chair covered in bright tapestry. This was Avidha's room. The bigger room was Suguna's. Avidha had insisted she take the room that could fit in the work table which doubled as the dining table. She was too lazy to do all the cleaning that more furniture involved.

They sat in Suguna's room, partitioned unevenly by a book-case behind which was her bed. The shelf was a true antique. It had belonged to Avidha's grandfather and her father had given it to her when she had left home. The small rectangular table had been laid with care. Three sunny chrysanthemums stood in a narrow vase without any green fronds to temper their brilliance. A decanter, glasses and a glass bowl with three lemons cut into halves stood alongside the plates.

Suguna took Vineeta to the back to show her the small kitchen. The two had grown close ever since Suguna and Avidha had moved into their own flat. Before Suguna had bought all the necessary paraphernalia for the kitchen and a gas cylinder, they had frequently dined at Vineeta's.

'Why do people in big cities have small kitchens?' Vineeta asked.

'We don't spend much time in it, not as much as you people would in Bhopal, perhaps,' said Suguna.

The bell rang and Avidha ran out to open the door. Zintac breezed in with a potted cactus in her hands: 'Hi-ya, meanies! Never as much as a come over, have a drink, for the months that you have been here! Hi, Viny love, God, you grow more beautiful every time I see you! Hello, Mukta,' she said.

'Take a breath, darling,' said Suguna.

Zintac was a bundle of energy with laughter in her voice. Her small thin frame made her seem almost insubstantive. Two enormous eyes, the irises of which seldom remained still, dominated her thin face. She carried off a rag like a princess and wore any colour she chose without any thought to whether it suited her dark skin. Zintac was more than beautiful; she was an original. Her cheerfulness and eternal desire to stay off the beaten track, her surprising lack of envy and her pathological hatred of turbulence made her a social antacid and it was a matter of time before she was christened Zintac.

She handed Avidha the cactus, a pale green rotund ball with serrated ridges running down its side. In the furrow of every serration stood a cluster of brown needles like a spider sheltering from the sun. 'It's quite old, it will flower soon,' said Zintac.

'You brought only one cactus?' asked Vineeta in her ingenuous way.

'Oh dear, do you think they might fight over who will water it?' asked Zintac.

'What if they decide to rent separate flats next year? Who will get the cactus?' asked Vineeta.

'Oh ho. Let them fight. I will at least know my present was important to them!' said Zintac.

'Mukta can draw up a pre-nuptial agreement right now,' said Suguna, warming to the subject.

'Is it like *that* between you two? I mean, you two are not...? You are only sharing a flat, like me and Viny here, right?' Mukta stammered.

There was an uncomfortable silence. Mukta always reacted seriously, even to a remark made in jest.

'We need to lubricate our throats or I shan't be able to laugh anymore,' said Zintac, rushing to the rescue.

Suguna turned to Mukta. 'I know you like whisky but we thought gin was a safe choice – just in case Mis*suj* Kapoor comes in to check...'

'That's why we poured the gin into this decanter,' Avidha said pointing to what Vineeta had thought was a jug of water with a stopper.

'And I thought it was your style!' said Zintac with her infectious laugh. 'Are we waiting for someone? Any guys?'

'No boys! Jailer's orders!' said Avidha. She measured and poured the gin into three glasses and brought out some lemon squash for Vineeta from the kitchen.

'So much for freedom,' said Mukta.

Vineeta had wearied of the never-ending discussion on freedom for women. When she had first arrived from Bhopal and seen the way Mukta and her friends lived she had been shocked. She knew Mukta smoked but she had not expected all of them to have completely lost all sense of morality or form. Men and women hugged each other with abandon, women smoked and drank and swore like men, lolled on the floor on durries and held intense discussions on subjects she had no clue about. Vineeta bought a sofa to replace the narrow mattress thrown casually on the floor, organized the kitchen and designated the sitting room for friends who had the awful habit of walking straight into the bedroom and sprawling on the bed. She began to keep the door to their bedroom pointedly closed.

Mukta's friends commented on how her *adda* had become a proper house. This made Mukta squirm and Vineeta beam. She never thought there was any irony in those comments. She was incapable of suspecting that friends could be cruel.

'You have all the freedom you want. In our Bhopal, women would never be allowed to drink openly like this. And living on your own when your parents live in the same town would be unthinkable.'

'Freedom is an addiction. The more you have the more you want,' said Avidha, raising her glass.

Watching Suguna and Vineeta chattering away Avidha began to feel glad Prashant had not come. He would not have spared her a glance with these two beauties around. Suguna was not an acknowledged beauty like Vineeta. Seen individually all her features were a little off centre. One eyebrow was too arched. The lips curled upward, distorted by a perpetual smile. Her left shoulder drooped a little, seemingly weighed down by the pallu of her sari. Her long straight hair hung in a loose plait that she never unbraided. She looked what she was – an unfinished work of art.

Avidha wondered where Prashant was at the moment and with whom. What would he do if she appeared before him all of a sudden? Drop everything, forget whoever he was with and turn to her with open arms?

Mukta was talking earnestly: 'The Supreme Court has been hearing the Bhopal case on a daily basis for three months now and we are still not close to any decision.'

Avidha looked at her, struggling to pay attention. Why was Mukta always playing the serious lawyer? Why could she not let her hair down? *Not much of it to let down*, she answered herself drolly, looking at Mukta's closely cropped hair and began to giggle at the silly conversation in her head.

'You think that is a joke? Maybe it is. Still, it is necessary to think of some way to get rid of all these delay tactics the Carbide lawyers are using,' Mukta said.

Avidha felt ashamed. She had been involved in the campaign to seek justice for the survivors of Bhopal right from the beginning. That was how Mukta and she had become friends. They had partied hard the night they had heard of the trial court in Bhopal ordering Carbide to pay some money to the gas affected till the case reached a final decision; Mukta had warned them Carbide would file an appeal and they should not celebrate too soon.

'What case is this? The appeal they filed against the order to pay interim compensation?' asked Suguna.

Mukta began telling Suguna about it. 'Do you know when some of our great lawyers told the American court that our judicial system is fully capable of handling such a complex case, they never pointed out this escape route litigants have in India? Keep delaying the case till there is no need for a verdict. They use the tiniest pretext to file appeals in the higher courts...'

'Being asked to pay before being proven guilty does not seem a pretext to me,' Suguna said reasonably.

'It is just a matter of a few crores of rupees, peanuts for Carbide, isn't it? Why don't they want to pay it?' asked Zintac.

'Because that will prove they were guilty,' said Avidha.

Mukta wanted them to do a report on the tactics Carbide was adopting. 'The story is in the details. Look, the High Court orders Carbide to pay interim compensation. It does not pay. It does not even ask the Supreme Court to stay the order of the High Court. Without a stay it must obey the order. It does not. So it actually stands in contempt of the Jabalpur Bench of the High Court. It is said,' she paused and sipped at her gin, 'that Carbide officials told the press in New York they will ignore the High Court order and the court can't do anything to them. You people can check on this. It is a sensational story, isn't it?'

Suguna sighed. The Bhopal gas disaster had been one of the biggest news stories in the world but there was a sense of fatigue in the press now. They did not want to cover the daily grind of the case. That angle of Carbide being a contemner was too hard to sell to editors. 'Don't nitpick. They have filed an appeal in the SC. Let us wait for the outcome,' her bureau chief had told her last month when she had suggested an article after Mukta had told her these details.

'So why doesn't the High Court put them in jail?' asked Avidha. That would be a sure front-pager.

'And complicate the case further? Higher courts don't function like that. They have to take the survivors into consideration so they are swallowing everything. To make sure Carbide does not cry foul.'

'She is very deeply concerned. She only talks about the Bhopal case,' said Vineeta sounding a little tired. Actually Mukta hardly talked to Vineeta about the case. She talked in her presence to others who came by and Vineeta found the discussions too abstruse.

'Have you been going to the hearings?' Suguna asked Mukta.

'No. Ajit keeps me updated.'

Vineeta went red in the face and glanced furtively at Mukta. Avidha noticed the flush and wondered if she was having a fling with Ajit.

'Maybe Avi can do a story. Her paper is from Madhya Pradesh. Mine is a Karnataka paper,' said Suguna

'Aw, Mukta, please don't talk business,' said Avidha.

'Yeah, spare us, you career woman! Even the *hai-hai* society has had a lean season this year,' said Zintac.

'High society?' said Vineeta perplexed.

Avidha looked meaningfully at Suguna. Oof, these two bores, one talked of work all the time, the other never understood a single witty line, the glance said.

'Those people who go around doing *hai hai* all the time. *Jhola uthao naaraa lagaao*! People like us, *yaar*!' explained Zintac.

'How is Nirmala? I thought we would see her here,' Zintac asked, trying to change the subject.

'Seems like she is spending a lot of time with Hally,' said Mukta

'Or it could be the other way round,' said Suguna tartly.

That annoyed Avidha. She had not expected Suguna to make that kind of remark about Nirmala's sexuality. 'Hally is very committed. Like Nimmie. Not like us who only flirt with causes,' said Avidha.

Suguna got up to fix another round of drinks ignoring Avidha's jibe that had been aimed at her. 'Who wants a refill?'

Zintac aided the distraction. Holding out her glass she said, 'I shall have the beautiful Viny mix my gin and water. A beautiful *saaqi* makes a difference to the intoxication levels of the *jaam*, does she not?'

Vineeta blushed again, very pleased. 'I think it is not important to be beautiful. It is important to have brains. Like Mukta has.' She corrected herself quickly, 'Like you all have.'

Later, after they had all left, Suguna said to Avidha, 'Did you notice Mukta said, "you two are not like that..."'

'Did she hope we were?'

'Must be rather stressful for them, to not be able to be open about their lives,' said Avidha

'I don't know. They think nobody guesses. They are a little weird, those two,' said Suguna.

'And I would think,' Avidha added with a naughty smile, 'you would get tired of a finger after a while.'

Chapter 2

AN UNUSUAL TRYST

That was exactly what Ajit thought: that Vineeta must be tired of a finger and must be taught that it cannot stand in for the real thing. He had worked hard for an opportunity to teach her.

Ajit Khanna had met Vineeta at an NGO where she had been employed for some months. It was a small women's group Ajit did not have much respect for but he was on its board of directors. He sometimes helped organize funds for them and held meetings to review their activities. In the world of deceptive equality that Ajit inhabited, all the workers in the organizations he associated with were introduced to him and were, in theory at least, free to talk to him, even question his motives. Ajit would have treated such dialogue as a whetstone to hone his skills but the workers had little or no confidence to engage him in such full-blooded discussions. Their stance was defined by their need for financial security. They brought with them the visceral experiences and earthy tongues of the vast multitude that lived in the working-class colonies, unorganized and insecure. There was an insatiable demand for that experience – like guano from Peru whose buyers paid top dollar for it. It was a world that rested firmly on the cloudy foundation of declarations and protestations and it appeared to need nothing else.

Ajit was popular. He was generous. He threw sumptuous parties. He kept an open house and loved the idea that all kinds of people active in a variety of movements ran free through it, raided his fridge and cooked their own things in his kitchen. Like a great patriarch heading a large family dependent on his munificence, he enjoyed being surrounded by retainers. He kept his eyes open for volunteers who needed money, finding work for them – as translators, editors or short-term consultants – or hired them as resource persons in training sessions, just about anything for a little money, and gently broke their resistance to foreign funds. He was well placed to help, being on the board of several NGOs and in contact with many others. He also helped people personally.

When Vineeta was introduced to Ajit she did not say anything to him beyond a namaste.

'Only an NGO as dense as this would employ a girl as raw as that,' he had thought.

She had been hired to arrange files systematically but had naturally begun counselling women. Ajit sighed. He noted that this new recruit was exceptionally pretty, but callow young girls, especially those with exaggerated femininity, the kind that came from smaller towns, who wrapped their dupattas around their fingers and never looked a man in the eye, left him cold.

He would have completely forgotten Vineeta had it not been for a coincidence. One day, dropping by at Mukta's house to discuss the legal points in the Bhopal case, he was surprised to find her there. Vineeta had given him a spiel about how she was in Delhi to take some private coaching and gain some experience in social work so that she could find a job.

On one such visit he had asked her if she had a boyfriend. 'There are many boys in the institute I go to, but I am not interested in boys,' said Vineeta with refreshing candour. Ajit took it to mean she was interested in experienced men. His interest piqued, he began paying more attention to her.

Soon he began courting Vineeta. It did not take any special effort. He realized she was not too shy, never flirted and was slightly embarrassed by compliments. She behaved with him on a footing of equality which intrigued him. She could discuss the Bhopal disaster with some information if not knowledge. He also discovered she was a great cook.

'I like you,' she told him simply. '*Aap bahut achche hain.* In Bhopal, grown-ups don't talk like this, to girls. They treat us like we are children. You talk as if I am mature.' After that it became easier to flatter her.

His house was not far from Mukta's DDA flat in Hauz Khas. He believed sufficiently in the rights of women to buy off his two sisters' share which, if anybody had cared to enquire, gave him a firm certificate of belonging to that minuscule community that respected women's rights. Nobody did given the code of polite circles in which the sanctity of matters of income and property was never violated. His upper floor was vacant and occasionally used as an office with two bedrooms reserved for outstation guests. When Avidha and Suguna had a tough time finding a flat they had even asked him to rent out a portion of his upper floor to them.

'Rent out? My dear, the house is yours, come and stay as long as you want, just don't talk about rent,' he had replied.

'Which is as good as saying I won't give it to you,' Suguna had commented to Avidha.

Moved by his friendliness Vineeta had confided in him after much hesitation and many promises of confidentiality that she and Mukta were, 'you, know, like, more than just friends.' By that time Ajit had gathered as much. It made the conquest a greater challenge and he laboured to make Vineeta bend to his pleas. She had eventually succumbed.

Mukta had to help her mother sort out some tax matters and was to be away the whole day but she had woken up so late that Vineeta was afraid she would not leave home at all. She was expecting Ajit today for the promised trip to a new experience. She began to feel uneasy. Mukta left after a leisurely breakfast and Vineeta had just begun combing her hair having bolted the door behind her when the bell rang. She froze. He must have run into Mukta. She opened the door with trembling fingers. For Ajit to dash up to their place in Mukta's absence was not unusual and she chided herself for feeling so guilty. Mukta stood on the doorstep. She had forgotten some important papers. She left again five minutes later.

Now Vineeta began to regret having invited Ajit home. She picked up the phone to cancel the invitation, asking herself why she had let his continual phone calls and persistent flattery get to her.

The bell began ringing impatiently. She replaced the receiver and opened the door. Ajit was on the landing. He was early. He came in, kicked the door shut and pulled her into his arms.

She tried to pull back. 'I have waited too long. Too long,' he muttered in her hair preventing her from getting away. She pushed down her panic. He was kissing her hungrily, sucking on her earlobe – too slurpily, she thought – as she tried to move his face away from her own. He paused, and held her close, stroking her back sensuously, moving down to her hips and squeezing her butt. Then he pulled her closer till she could feel a strange bulge straining to get out of his trousers. She pulled back, almost gasping for breath.

He had to remind himself to be gentle. He stroked her neck lightly, moving his fingers upwards into her hair. But he had imagined this tryst too long for the gentleness to last. Suddenly tightening his grip on the roots of her hair he pulled her violently to himself and bent to press his lips on hers. She was trembling now and trying to wriggle out of his arms.

'I must stop this now,' she told herself.

She wanted to sit him down and tell him that she now had a foretaste of the unknown and did not want any more. She did not know what she had consented to; he must forgive her for having asked him to come like this, for this.

She watched in disbelief as he began to unbutton his shirt. She looked on impassively, as his body emerged from under his clothes, unable to think how she could get out of the situation without hurting him. This was a flat chest, so flat, it could only squash her. She had to make an intense effort to hide her revulsion. His trousers were now coming off. She ran into the bedroom, but he came after her.

Nothing she did could drive him away. It only provided an opening for him to inch closer. She later thought her flight to the bedroom and the lying down in bed was her ultimate folly. He took that as an invitation and lay down beside her, unbuttoning her cardigan with practised fingers. She pulled the quilt to cover herself and he slid in gratefully into the warmth covering her legs with his and drawing her closer. His hand moved down, fingers getting to where he thought he would find a dewy welcome. There was instead a rigid resistance in her taut muscles and a fuzzy dryness.

She pushed him away, sitting up and gulping air. He lay there watching her back on which her hair stood on end like a strange fern on an unbending tree trunk. Her disinterest was clear to him now.

'Don't you like me?' he asked, disappointed and feeling a little tired with all the effort.

Her caring nature then became her undoing. She came down on him, hugging him impulsively. 'I do,' she said.

She actually did. The hug brought her in touch with the hair on his chest, the gorge rising to her throat as he took hold of her hand and moved it below to the groin to what he had come to boast about. She felt a strange ooziness lick at her finger amidst coarse hair. Feeling sick she pulled her hand away.

'I am just nervous. This is the first time for me,' she explained.

The first time! He suddenly felt an upsurge of power. How could he have forgotten that whatever experience she had till now was like a bad rehearsal with an incomplete dummy.

'Don't be afraid. I won't hurt you,' he said and took over, smothering her dissociation and her lack of enthusiasm.

He pushed her off himself, made her lie down on her back and parting her legs with one violent move, got onto her, as much to prevent her from running away as to ease his now unbearable tension. He inched in closer, looking into her eyes steadily.

She felt strangely detached, as if she hovered somewhere above their bodies. She waited patiently, having written off this moment in time from her life. She seceded from her existence and handed him the residue.

He took much longer than he thought he could. It was his ego that propelled him and the more he wanted it to end, the longer it took. He began to pant with the effort.

A drop of sweat dropped on her forehead and she opened her eyes to look at him hanging above her, a naked accusation in his eyes. He slid away onto the bed and threw an arm over his eyes. Finally it was over!

He felt curiously empty. The subtlety of her betrayal and his inability to avenge himself angered him. Had Vineeta resisted he would have at least had the relief of being acknowledged. It was her lack of response that left him shaken. No woman had ever made him feel so redundant like this small-town girl with nothing but cooking skills to her credit. He had no intentions of ever exchanging another word with her.

Dressing himself as fast as he could, he told her he had to leave.

'The bitch,' he thought furiously. 'Why couldn't she simply say no?'

Ajit could not work at all that day. He went home in a foul mood and locked himself inside his bedroom. He took his son's football and went out in the park, kicking it furiously, imagining it to be Vineeta's face. He hit the bottle early that evening, giving his wife, Kamini, some anxious moments. She put it down to work-related tension. It was unlike him to be in such a bad mood. He found fault with the food, screamed at his son for turning up the music too loud and wasting his time recording 'some stupid rock' from a cassette he had borrowed from a friend. He screamed at the maid for letting the tap run too long while doing the dishes. It was all Kamini's fault, he said aloud, spoiling the maids with her generosity.

He drank till he passed out in an alcoholic fugue. Around midnight, he sat up in bed sweating inside the quilt. He felt cold and a sudden pain constricted his chest. Kamini sat up too, some instinct in her waking her up to the discomfort of her husband.

'Are you having a heart attack?' she asked him, alarmed and trying not to show it.

He held her hands and said, 'No, I just... felt a little... breathless.' He struggled to get the words out. His throat was raspy and he spoke with difficulty for the pain gripped him like an iron band tightening across his chest.

Kamini called the doctor. She began describing the symptoms once he came on the line. Putting down the phone she told Ajit they must go to the doctor. 'Relax,' she said as much to calm her own frayed nerves as to soothe him. She helped him out of bed and drove him to the doctor's house nearby. The doctor was a friend of the family and had actually asked Kamini to take him to a hospital instead of his house where he could at the most only give an opinion and some preliminary aid.

He made Ajit sit down, felt his pulse and asked if the pain had gone. It had not. The doctor slipped a sorbitrate under his tongue. The pain did not go. He decided there was nothing very serious though Ajit did seem to be in acute discomfort and quite out of breath. It did not appear like a heart attack, only an attack of spondylitis perhaps. For precaution's sake he sent them to AIIMS.

In the emergency room an ECG confirmed that his heart was beating without any interruption. The doctor gave him a painkiller and a lecture on the virtues of regular exercise, less drinking and less stress. It was a bad night.

Back home in the wee hours of the morning Ajit fell into a fitful sleep. He woke up late, still drowsy and tired of the agitation of the day before. He told Kamini he needed rest. Kamini was sure there was more to it than an attack of spondylitis but no amount of questioning got her to loosen Ajit's tongue.

'Tell me,' she said to him tearfully. 'You know you can tell me anything.'

Ajit toyed with the idea of discussing it with her. How could he tell her what he felt? How could she help? He told her there was nothing a little rest could not cure.

'Someone you want who said no, is that it?' she asked him.

He scowled at her. 'I wish she had said no,' he thought.

By the time Mukta had got home Vineeta had put on fresh sheets and soaked the dirty ones. Mukta grew alarmed to see her puffy eyes. She noticed the soaked sheets too. It was not like Vineeta to soak sheets and leave them unwashed. 'What is wrong?' she asked.

'I have a horrible headache,' said Vineeta.

Mukta switched off the lights in the bedroom and sat in the faint glow that filtered in from the sitting room where she had left a single overhead lamp on. She pulled Vineeta's head to her lap and pouring some drops of eau de cologne on it began rubbing it in gently.

Mukta's concern made Vineeta even more miserable. She lay listlessly, unable to decide whether to tell Mukta of her act of deceit or not. Would she hug and comfort her?

More likely she would be angry and ask her to get out of her life.

Chapter 3

A SETTLEMENT

Hally missed Mukta as he sat on one of the back benches of Court Number One of the Supreme Court presided over by the Chief Justice of India. The courtroom looked crowded, though there were not many people inside. Most of those present were lawyers, some directly involved in the case and others who had drifted in to watch renowned seniors present arguments in a famous case. Carbide had a battery of black robes headed by a most venerable old man from Delhi, Sohrab Daruwala, known for his low profile, his sealed lips and his exorbitant fees. The Attorney General represented the government with his own assistants in tow.

The survivors had a smaller team but in Chand Cawasjee, they had a legal luminary whose presence in a courtroom never went unnoticed. When he rose, adjusting his gown and bowing slightly towards the bench, a respectful silence filled the courtroom. Hally acknowledged the brilliance of his mind and the value of having him on their side but he was not someone you could walk up to and seek interpretations of every objection raised and every argument made.

Mukta was used to doing that, deciphering the arguments of the lawyers and the remarks of judges but she could not spare the time for the hearings every day. She had many cases to argue in the trial court. Hally had been listening to the interminable arguments by all three teams for months now and had even stopped paying attention to some of the more involved ones. To him they all seemed to harp on the single issue that the trial court in Bhopal had no power to grant any interim compensation. The arguments had continued unabated and now it was being heard daily because Cawasjee had pushed for an early decision but they seemed nowhere near a verdict.

Hally almost switched off from the tedious legal speak, wondering instead why Ajit was so unusually glum. He had not reported to office or come to the court for a few days. Today when he finally made an appearance, he looked drawn and irritable. It was close to lunch recess and Hally was beginning to feel hungry. For months now they had always broken for lunch at exactly 1 p.m. and he cursed the Pavlovian conditioning that made his stomach rumble punctually.

The five judges sat frowning with concentration in plush red chairs embossed with the Ashokan Lions. When the clock struck one, orderlies in smart uniforms pushed aside the heavy burgundy velvet drapes, stepped inside the room and stood ramrod straight behind the chairs, waiting respectfully for the judges to get up. Once the justices got up the orderlies pulled the chairs gently behind to make space for them to leave. Everybody in the room stood up. They had been watching this ritual every day now for months and Hally still found it difficult not to laugh at this clockwork precision of the breaking up of the court for lunch and the ceremony surrounding it.

The canteen adjacent to the library had become quite a favourite with Hally, who liked to eat while reading the titles of the books displayed in the glass cases. What a daunting task, he thought; lawyers had to bring up precedents from so many dusty volumes. He repeated what had become his habit, 'I wish it would be over soon.'

'What's your hurry?' asked a junior lawyer with a laugh. 'This is only one small part of the case. You can bring your grandchildren to hear the verdict when the case is fully decided.'

'Our only consolation is that Carbide is paying heavily for this delay,' said Cawasjee. 'My friend Sohrab will be much richer than he already is.'

Hally laughed politely at that. Ajit grunted. Hally turned to Ajit to ask him why he was so off colour.

'Only an attack of spondylitis,' said Ajit shortly.

After lunch Ajit told Hally he wanted to leave early but was persuaded to stay back for half an hour. There were no gas victims in court; they were standing in for them and could not deprive Cawasjee of an audience. He also wanted a lift back to the office in Ajit's car. They entered minutes before the justices were ushered in with some pomp. The curtains were pushed aside sharply; the orderlies came in, pulled the chairs back and waited deferentially for the justices. Everybody stood up again when the justices came in and resumed their seats after the orderlies left. The lawyers bowed to the bench and looked at the papers in their hands.

Hally was wondering which lawyer would resume the interrupted hearing when one of the justices said, 'We have an announcement to make.'

Comprehension dawned only after the first few sentences and everyone listened in stupefied silence as the justice read out a settlement order. Final compensation to the victims was granted. All cases pending against Carbide were snuffed out. The case was over in less than ten minutes. 'The case is fully and finally decided,' said the justice as he placed the sheet he was reading from on the table.

Daruwala bowed deeply to the bench saying, 'Thank you, Milord.' He was too dignified to look triumphant.

Hally could not believe what he had heard. Cawasjee turned back to look at them, eyes wide open in astonishment. He turned to the bench and slightly inclining his head, muttered, 'Your Lordships.' He walked out of the room from a side door into the ante chamber reserved for lawyers as Ajit and Hally hurriedly left from the main door. They met in the veranda outside the court.

'Could they have written this order in the lunch break?' asked Hally.

Cawasjee looked angry. He was terribly upset that he had had no inkling of what was to come. The Bar Association grapevine, usually a reliable indicator of things to come, had given him no clue that such an operation was in progress. The Carbide counsel had lived up to his reputation of confidentiality and loyalty to his client. Cawasjee was acutely aware that he too was a party to the case, an equally important party, the only one that was truly fighting Carbide. He represented thousands of victims. The court had not even bothered to consult him, the representative of the victims, a party so directly involved in the case.

Hally had a point; this order could not have been written in a hurry. It may have been written in the morning. It may even have been drafted elsewhere, the justices scrawling their autographs on it over lunch. He felt personally humiliated. 'Such treachery,' he said under his breath.

Daruwala walked out of the ante chamber and past them, down the short flight of stairs, followed by a bunch of lawyers, towards the court lawns. Cawasjee did not envy the high-level parleys he must have been involved in to hammer out this settlement but his professional respect for his opponent went down. He would have urged his client to consult the victims, not cut a deal behind their backs. He found Daruwala's conduct unacceptable to his finely tuned principles of fairness and justice. Could this man have done such a thing in an American court? Even in India, could he have ignored the claimants had they come from palatial homes with ranks and titles to their names?

'Why did they do this?' asked Ajit still recovering from the shock.

'Don't ask me. He is the one who knows,' said Cawasjee, pointing to the receding back of the stout Carbide counsel, and walked away. His juniors explained to them what the order contained. It did not sound good to them.

Ajit turned to Hally saying, 'We have to do something. Call the press, call all our supporters. We must prepare a statement.'

The first demonstration of protest against the settlement took place that afternoon around four outside the Supreme Court, even as the state-run radio had begun broadcasting the news. It was small, yet a sign of things to come.

Only after the demonstration did Hally call Ali in Bhopal and caught him minutes before he was going to release his statement. Arshad Ali, the leader of the Bhopal Gas Affected Women's Committee, the largest and most militant group of survivors, he learnt, had prepared a note welcoming the decision.

'*Haley bhai*,' Ali said, excitement in his voice, '*Mubarak ho*! What a good judgment. We are finally going to get compensation. The judges of this country are great. Otherwise the case would have taken I don't know how many years.'

Stunned, Hally asked him to tear up the note and to never mention it to anyone. Then taking a deep breath to calm his nerves, he told him what the 'judgment' meant. 'It is a compromise between Carbide and the government, it is not a judgment. It means those who were responsible will not be punished. It means that your children cannot take Carbide to court tomorrow if they are born deformed. It means you will get some measly amount. Is that what you want? Does an Indian's life come so cheap?'

'But what can we do now?' Ali asked.

'Many things,' Hally said. 'Many things.' He himself had no idea what could be done. 'They will have to be considered. The order will have to be studied. We will hold a meeting to decide what can be done,' he said, playing for time.

Hally then called Mads, short for Mahadev Mahapatra, and told him about Ali's reactions. 'What did you expect of that opportunist?' asked Mads, laughing his head off before saying he would go round and make the fellow see sense.

It had not occurred to Arshad Ali to ask the questions Hally had asked. He tore up the press note and went out to tell his group that the court had actually let them down and they were to hold meetings to think of ways to go ahead with their battle. He would never report his blunder to anyone, especially to that highbrow Mads. So when Mads came to look for him and discuss a joint press note Ali showed him a short note.

'We have condemned the settlement and said that we will think of ways to carry on the fight,' he told Mads without a clue that Mads knew of his first reaction.

Mukta went over to Ajit's house in the evening to get an account of what had transpired in court.

'The order said "fully and finally", did it? Those words are so important,' she said.

Ajit and Hally looked at her questioningly.

'They are crucial because the American court had subjected Union Carbide Corporation to the jurisdiction of the Indian courts till a full and final decision was reached. Those were the exact words,' she said.

They looked at each other as the import of the order began to sink in.

Hally thought back to the months he had spent in the court. The negotiations must have been going on while he sat there every day. The Carbide lawyers and the attorney general had all behaved as if they were contesting the case vigorously. 'They had all continued as if the hearings mattered,' he said. His nerves went cold.

'Do me a favour?' she said, looking straight into his eyes.

'Yes?' he said.

'Tell me a lie,' she said, running a light finger down the side of his face.

'Lie?' he asked, laughing, a little surprised.

'Yes. Tell me you love me!'

He felt trapped.

They were lying in bed, thighs intertwined. He shifted one slightly, his fingers paying homage to the dying erection of her breasts. He rested his head on one elbow. She lay on her back, tired with the effort to control the fury of his movements as she had pressed down on him just a while ago, watching his face, tortured by the want of emotion in it.

He slumped on the bed disentangling his thigh. Annoyance replaced his surprise. He usually liked the surprises she sprang, in bed and outside it, the way she made innocuous phrases resonate with deeper and sensuous meanings, openly inviting him to naughty pursuits even in public, with nobody able to crack their code, her eyes crinkling with humour.

'I don't lie,' he said, cocking an eyebrow in mock humour, trying to wriggle out of the situation.

Avidha sat up. 'Really?' she asked. Had he told his wife that he was going to the hotel to be free from all disturbances, to indulge his passion for another female in bed?

He pulled her back.

'I love you,' he said mechanically.

It left her devastated, that simple sentence devoid of emotion. She was better off earlier. Now it was over. She pushed back the tears. She knew she should not have asked.

The next day, she woke up with the resolution that she would insist on leaving early, not wait till after lunch. He was fast asleep. It occurred to her that had she not had that officious old woman for her landlady he would be visiting her at least thrice a week for a quick roll in bed. How that would have cheapened me, she thought as she quickly got into the bathroom to cry secretly, under the shower.

She came inside the room and opened a window for fresh air. She now felt ashamed of everything, even her embroidered coverlet that was now thrown over the hotel quilt. The clear morning light stole the haziness of its colours and the uneven stitches stood revealed for what they were, crooked with no harmony, no symmetry, not even delicacy. She had spread it on this impersonal hotel bed with expectantly trembling hands the night before lining it like a bird would line a nest. He had made no move to help her.

'Where did you get that?' he had asked.

'I made it,' she had said, laughing awkwardly. 'Bad, isn't it?'

'No-o... It is nice. Very nice,' he had said.

Nice! His etiquette galled her. If he had simply laughed or told her she had done a truly bad job, that he couldn't imagine someone like her doing something so conventional, the sheet would have become an heirloom for her. She wiped her eyes.

'Where are you?' she heard him ask. She had not even noticed that he had woken up.

'I just remembered I had an assignment to complete. Can we leave early?' she asked him.

'Certainly not,' he said.

They left after a very late lunch as they had planned. Delhi was no more than a two-hour drive.

When she began to pack she wondered if she should leave the coverlet behind. She could throw away her work, the long hours of hunting for patches of embroidered cloth to put together and the small midnight blue square of silk as her centrepiece to display her needlework, but not the rolls of fantasy woven into every stitch and her imagined conversations with him as she threaded the needle, and saw how there was just that tiny little part where the patchwork and the sheet ends did not meet perfectly. She folded it and stuffed it in her overnight bag.

They heard the news on the car radio, crackling through a lot of static. She missed out on the first sentence, but a small part of her brain automatically went on the alert and she latched onto the rest of the news as something to fill the void that rode in the car with them. She turned up the volume. The newsreader mentioned a sum and said the order had come after four years of waiting and would be a great relief to the victims of the Bhopal gas leak disaster. Nearly the entire bulletin was devoted to the case after that. The Supreme Court had just made the final decision in the Bhopal case.

Avidha found the bulletin completely unreal. Baffled, she turned to Prashant to ask if he had heard the news. He nodded. She asked him what the newsreader had said.

'I thought you had special interest in this case,' he said. 'The Supreme Court has finally given the gas victims compensation and concluded the case.'

'How can the Supreme Court do this? The whole case was not in the Supreme Court,' she said perplexed.

'The Supreme Court can do anything,' he replied. 'You people should know. You are the ones who are rushing to it for everything.'

'Well, we did not take this case to the SC,' she said with some asperity, her annoyance overlaying her pain of impending separation. This was a separation, she knew it.

'My God,' she added, 'that is a shame. They have said that Carbide has no criminal liability anymore. That really is a shame.'

He knew instinctively this would be a major headache for the government and it was best to not offer any comments.

Avidha looked out at the fields by the roadside. The season of sunny mustard blooms was over and slim green pods moved reluctantly when the breeze pushed them.

'Why is it a shame?' he asked her after a while. 'I know you always criticize anything the government does but the courts are your friends, are they not?'

She was not interested in raking up that old discussion again. A writ petition in the Supreme Court against a contraceptive was the reason they had met for the first time.

'You think it's okay that Carbide be let off the hook like this, Mister Prashant Kumar Mishra?' she asked, pronouncing his full name as she did when she was angry with him.

'Oh ho, don't start being the journalist so soon,' he replied.

Now she wished she had paid more attention to what Mukta had been saying just a few days back. There had been rumours earlier of Carbide reaching a settlement with the government but they had never materialized.

'They will at least get something after five years,' Prashant said finding her unusually quiet.

'Four years,' she corrected him. 'Is that all that matters? The money?'

'Maybe not,' he said tactfully. 'But look at it this way. So many innocent people died and the least their families can get is money.'

'I dare say there were some thieves and molesters and wife-beaters among them. So what? Did they deserve to die while the innocent didn't?' she asked, infuriated.

Prashant drove on silently.

She knew as a ministry official he could not afford to talk loosely. She also found his lack of trust in her bothersome. With her unwillingness to push beyond a limit and his hesitation to be seen with her, it had destroyed the easy friendship they had had for a while before he began making suggestive remarks to her. It seemed like a long way back to

Delhi, a journey they had made many times from different places. She used to feel ridiculously happy if he ever took a wrong turn telling him it would give her a few more moments with him. A journey in an official Ambassador car with a hand buried in her lap had till yesterday been her definition of adventure and romance. That was how they had driven to the hotel, like always, he at the wheel, one hand on it, the other playing with her. She had even worn a sari to please him. That was how they used to return. Today, his hands firmly clutched the steering wheel.

As Prashant neared the Dhaula Kuan roundabout and turned onto the Ridge Road, she asked him to drop her off. He usually dropped her a little away from her flat.

'I am going to my parents' house,' she said. That was in the university area where her professor-father lived.

'You should have told me,' he said. 'I will take you there. No problems.'

She protested. It would be too long a drive for him.

'No problems,' he said. He drove all the way to the college in North Campus where her parents lived. She needed a walk to sort herself out before she went in to face her parents and she insisted on being dropped off at a distance. He paid no heed and dropped her at the college gate.

As she opened the door of the car, he got out and gave her hand a tight squeeze. 'Will call you,' he said without the usual meaningful wink. She slung her heavy overnight bag over her shoulder and waited on the sidewalk. He got back behind the wheel, let in the clutch, made a U-turn on the road and sped past her. She waited to see if he would wave at her. He did not.

❖

As Avidha entered the college gates, she asked herself what had brought her to the house she had impatiently wanted to be free of. Would her mother guess she had brought a broken heart for them to soothe? Would she dare tell her mother? She wondered whether she should go back to her flat. It was dark already but she could get a bus to CP and from there she could get home. Suguna would be waiting; she had not told her she might extend her absence.

Loneliness surrounded her like the ague. She began to shiver. The bag in her hand suddenly felt heavy. She put it down under a tree and leaning against its trunk began to weep. She heard footsteps. The guard was coming to check on her. Wiping her eyes and picking up the bag, she turned once again onto the path that led up to the house.

She saw her father through the lighted window sitting by his table reading a book. Her mother must be inside in the kitchen giving instructions to the maid. The house was silent, the oppressive silence of two adults whom convention had forced to remain tied to each other. It had been like this for as long as Avidha she could remember. This was the silence she had populated with visuals of a different life with companions that defied reality. Her brother had grassy fields to escape to. They had both simply waited to run away.

She opened the gate to the small garden and said, 'Baba?' Her father looked up and saw her through the window. The delight that shone in his eyes and the arms he opened for her as he stood up from the chair suddenly made her feel secure.

'Sushi, see, Avi is home,' her father called out.

Her mother came in from the kitchen. 'Why, girl, what a surprise!' she exclaimed, then turning towards the kitchen she said, 'Leela, you will have to make four more chapattis.'

45

'Ma, I am not hungry, not much,' said Avidha, prompting her mother to amend the order: 'Leela, make paranthas.'

'I want some tea, Leela, your *adrak ki chai*,' said Avidha.

Her mother took her bag and sat down with her on the sofa. 'Have you been out on an assignment?' she asked. Then she noticed her moist eyes and her wet cheeks. 'What is wrong?' she asked placing a hand on her head.

'Just tired, Ma. I stumbled against that tree. It was dark out there,' she said.

Her mother understood. Her father looked concerned. Avidha felt a pang of remorse for bringing her troubles to them. They were old and lonely and she had left home when they could have done with her help and her company.

Then she remembered to call Suguna. As she dialled Mrs Kapoor's number, a corner of her brain nudged her to call Mukta or Nirmala for the details of the verdict but the fog of despair and confusion prevailed.

'Tell her I had to come to my parents' house,' she had to scream thrice into the phone.

'What do you think brought about this verdict?' asked her father. 'The news is that the judges came back from lunch and sprang this surprise. Were you in court when this happened?'

She knew he was talking about Bhopal. A sharp image of herself prostrated on the patchwork sheet rose in her mind. That had been the lunch recess for her. The disconsolate submission to his desire and its aftermath, the dull headache. That is what Prashant had done to her, taken her away from what she was, taken her so far that she felt almost no interest in something she had been involved with for years, an issue that had also brought her some professional prominence. He had got what he wanted. And she? Where did she stand?

46

She quickly left for the bathroom without answering, and when she got back her father was fiddling with the radio to search for some light music, clearly admonished by her mother for bringing up heavy subjects when the girl was obviously exhausted and in trouble.

Avidha's father Sudheerendra Chaturvedi taught English and wrote learned pieces of criticism on Hindi literature. He had named her Avidha telling her it meant she was free of all genres, free of form. Her mother was fond of classical music, and had to have her dose of *khayal* every day. Avidha and her brother Kaustubh, had waited impatiently to get to college before they could play their English pop. Kaustubh had left for Canada some years back much to the Chaturvedis' delight. Much to their disgust, however, he had refused to get married to a nice Allahabadi girl.

When Avidha decided to become a journalist her father had offered to talk to an editor in a national daily. She refused to use her father's influence and he was proud of that. Avidha had grown up alternately making excuses to not invite her more 'wild' friends home while feeling proud of the good education and the learned opinions of both her parents. Her mother, for all the housework she had to put in before they were comfortable enough to have a maid, was quite well read and could surprise with her understanding of politics and culture. She had known of her husband's affairs with at least two PhD students. The first one caused a rift that took nearly a year to heal. After the second affair she saved her marriage by letting him know that she was staying on only because of the children. The arrangement continued and she had severed all physical relations with her husband.

After Avidha had graduated they had invited a young man to 'see' her. 'He comes from a good family,' her mother had

47

told her, 'a family full of doctors and professors. And he is a good boy. Does not drink or smoke.'

She had later gone out with the 'boy' into the park of the college under the beaming permission of her parents and told him she did not intend marrying him or anyone else for that matter. 'I don't know what you have to say about marrying me, but please say no to my parents. That will make it so much easier for me,' she had told him.

He had then told her parents that they should not force their daughter into marriage. That had led to a storm in the family.

'Imagine, telling a stranger instead of telling me,' her mother had fumed. 'What will he think of you and of us? Have you any regards for the prestige of this family or not?' Her brother had stood by her, though. After that fiasco her parents left the question of marriage alone, not sure what the girl would do next time a decent boy came to meet her. 'What will people say' had been the governing principle of the household.

When she had left home to be on her own, her mother had told her firmly, 'I know you will do what you want to. But do not ever bring disgrace to our family. This is a great family.' That almost provoked Avidha to want to do something disgraceful immediately like streaking in the college lawns during the recess.

Sushila had taken Avidha's nonconformity as a slur on her own capability to bring up children. From fighting her father, who blamed her for Avidha's insubordination and took all the credit for her writing skills, to total resignation, her mother had eventually given up on her.

Earlier, she used to ask her for favours. 'Don't do this, Avi, for what will people say about me,' she would plead with her recalcitrant daughter. 'Come back home by six, Avi, don't stay out late please. Just imagine what people will say about me?' Avidha never argued with her mother. She simply lied.

Even when she left home to share a flat with Suguna, she had made it sound like a favour to Suguna. 'Suguna can't live alone, Ma,' she had said. Her mother did not argue with her. Her father had. 'Why is she leaving home if she can't live alone?' he asked, to which Avidha had no answer.

Her mother had guessed that she was having an affair and had tried many times to find out who it was and had even asked Suguna. Today the prodigal daughter had come home.

'So tell me what it is,' she said to Avidha, sitting on the bed beside her once they had cleared the table after dinner. Her father had retired to bed knowing the daughter had something to tell her mother.

Avidha was silent for so long her mother wondered whether she would ever open up. 'Is there somebody?' she asked prompting her.

'Maybe, maybe not,' said Avidha relieved that finally it was out.

'What does that mean? Are you afraid that we won't approve? Does he belong to a lower caste?'

'Oh, that never even occurred to me. No it is not that... I have met someone I like but I don't know if he cares for me,' said Avidha improvising, falling back on her habit of fibbing to her mother except this time a large part of the fiction was fact. Despite herself she began to cry.

Her mother grew alarmed. She looked distraught. 'How far have you gone with him? Have you crossed the limits?' she asked, sounding more frantic than she intended to.

Avidha felt like asking her if there are any limits in love.

Then she began to ask more questions realizing Avidha would not volunteer information though she had clearly come to do that. What does he do? Work in her office? Were his parents against the match?

'His parents don't come into it at all,' Avidha told her, having composed herself. 'Listen, Ma, I really don't know what this is. I met someone and am not sure what is happening. That is all.'

'I hope he will marry you,' she said.

That brought Avidha's defiant nature to the fore. 'There is no marriage in the picture so stop talking about it.'

Her mother's response came after a long silence.

'A relationship without a name has no future,' she said.

Chapter 4

MUKTA IS ANGRY

Vineeta rarely read newspapers but she was an incurable radio addict. She kept the radio on all the time she was at home letting Mohammad Rafi and Asha Bhonsle sing to her while she worked. She paid little attention to news bulletins but the mention of Bhopal made her turn up the volume and that is how she heard of the settlement in the case. She immediately called Mukta's chamber but she was away with a client.

She fervently hoped this would put an end to Ajit's continual visits. For a whole week now she had felt unwell and waves of nausea invaded her at the thought of what had happened. The long agony she had suffered made the incident seem very remote to her at times. Mukta took her to a doctor who diagnosed a viral flu and prescribed antibiotics and vitamin C. Mukta insisted that she stay in bed. A final argument in one of the cases Mukta was defending had kept her busy but she worked from home to look after Vineeta.

Ajit had not come to their house since that day and now he would not even have to. The Supreme Court had ensured that much.

Vineeta felt light and full of vigour. She cooked rice and dal as a standby just in case Mukta came back too late, washed her hair, painted her nails, and pulled out her *jamdani* shawl.

'Have you heard the news? In the Bhopal case?' she chirped the moment Mukta got home. 'I thought we could go out for dinner.'

Mukta gave her a curious look.

'All dolled up to celebrate, are you? What else could I expect of you?' she said with down-curled lips. 'Tell me, have you even understood what the court has done?'

Indeed, what had the court done? Vineeta thought the court had done a very fine thing. 'Listen,' she said, 'those poor victims will get some money. They are dying, waiting for it.'

Vineeta really thought it was a good order. She did not know the details but the amount Carbide had been asked to pay sounded good to her. A full 450 million dollars which meant 705 crore rupees! Good. She knew the rich never paid for their misdeeds and if so many thousands had not died and the news had not made it to the international media Carbide would not have shelled out a penny. Now because of intense pressure Carbide would have to cough up something. She however did not have the courage to hold on to her opinion before the might of Mukta's intellectual prowess or her obvious anger. Words cascaded from Mukta's mouth without allowing her time to even grasp their meaning.

Tension returned to claim its place between them and Vineeta curiously felt the burden of her secret lift from her brow. She mildly suggested to Mukta that what was done was done, hoping to close the argument, hoping to go back to the comfortable zone in which she had no opinions, only smiles. 'The Supreme Court is the final court, isn't it? Now what can you do? You can only ensure that the right people get the money.'

Mukta was too angry to argue it out. 'It is people like you who have sent this country to the pits,' she said, losing control.

The rejection of her attempt angered Vineeta. The Bhopal case was the one thing she had definite opinions about and Mukta would hear it if she insisted on continuing the argument.

'Why? What is wrong with the order? They have given over 700 crores as compensation. What else do you want?' she asked.

Mukta poured herself a drink, walked into the kitchen to cook and noticed the food Vineeta had made. She carried her drink into the bedroom. They sat in different rooms, Mukta with her whisky and taut face, Vineeta with her thoughts and face burning with humiliation.

At dinner Mukta, slightly drunk and contrite, tried to explain the order to Vineeta. 'Viny,' she said, 'the court has said nobody has to go to prison for killing thousands. You think that is justice?'

'All this business of getting justice may be important to you, it is not so for the poor. They need money to buy food and medicines. Do you know our *kaamwali* had borrowed 5,000 rupees in one year for her treatment? What do you know about it?' Vineeta said bitterly. 'I met some of those American lawyers who came to Bhopal. They said in America people get millions from corporations. They promised millions to those victims and made them sign documents. It has been more than four years now and what have these people got? Zilch. Not even money to buy medicines. It is God's grace that the Supreme Court has taken some pity on the victims. You people think that the life of an Indian is equal to that of an American. It sounds good but it is not true, you know. *Aise nahin hota. Yeh anpadh gareeb bechare. Mungiyon ke jaise mare the. Kaise kaise to jeeye hain bechare.* At least the Supreme Court knows more,' she continued. She was convinced that in the next few days money would reach the survivors.

'Really?' asked Mukta unable to keep quiet. 'You would know what those American lawyers did if you paid more attention to reading the books here than to dusting them.' She walked to the bookshelf and threw Dan Kurzman's book on Bhopal on the table. 'Read it, you will know what has been happening in the case. You are saying that any bloody American company can come here, kill our people and pay some pittance and walk away? That Indian life is so cheap? That Indian life has no value? That their murderers won't be taken to task?'

'Yes. Indian life is cheap and the sooner you accept that reality the better a lawyer you will become,' Vineeta retorted. 'Anyway, now that the SC has decided the case, it is over, so why are we fighting about it? The SC's order is final. There is no court above it. Only God's court and God has given *sadbuddhi* to the justices. You can't do anything now,' she said triumphantly.

'Stop crowing. *Sadbuddhi*, my foot. Have you thought how much it will mean to each individual? There are millions of survivors to share that money. It won't come to more than 20,000 a head.'

'Not if you people will not insist that two thirds of Bhopal was affected. If you distribute the amount to only the one or two hundred thousand people who were affected, there will be enough for all,' Vineeta shot back.

'Oh, is that so?' asked Mukta in a dangerously quiet voice.

'Yes, I know enough arithmetic to do my calculations,' said Vineeta, unmindful of her tone and thinking she had scored a point.

'Shame on you,' spat Mukta and carried her plate into the kitchen.

Vineeta had become quite accustomed to being called an idiot. All endearments seemed to have been replaced by this one word. She knew how involved Mukta was in the case and even though she did not understand her objections to the order or agree with it she could sense her pain. She also realized she had gone too far in doubting Mukta's intentions who had consistently claimed that the government had under-reported the numbers of affected.

'What can you do? The Supreme Court is the final court, isn't it?' Vineeta said in an effort to pacify Mukta.

'It is and it isn't.'

'It isn't? How can that be?' asked Vineeta, amazed.

'That is why I have a degree in law. To try seek justice, not lie down prostrate and say *huzoor mai baap* whatever you do is acceptable to me,' Mukta replied sarcastically.

Vineeta was silenced for a moment. Then she began to make guesses. 'Oh, you will go fight in the US now?'

Mukta gnashed her teeth. 'Spare me your ignorance.'

'You know in Bhopal they say whatever you do you should never go to court for the courts are not meant for the poor,' Vineeta said.

That further infuriated Mukta. 'I suppose if I got murdered you wouldn't go to court,' she said illogically.

'*Tumse to baat hi nahin ho sakti,*' Vineeta screamed at her. '*Har baat ka tedha matlab nikaalti ho.*'

Mukta knew she was right. She had begun snapping a lot recently.

The next morning Vineeta took Hally's call. He said there would be a demonstration in front of the SC that afternoon around lunch time and asked them to be there. 'What do you have to say about this settlement?' he asked Vineeta, who replied that the milk was about to boil over so she must dash off.

She passed on his message to Mukta who did not even ask her if she would attend the demonstration, breaking her own rule of always dragging her to such protests and meetings. Vineeta felt left out even though she was not opposed to the settlement.

After the protest as Nirmala, Mukta, Hally and Suguna walked towards Mandi House, Nirmala asked Hally what the reaction in Bhopal had been 'before Mads stepped in'.

'Why, they condemned the settlement or the decision or whatever it was,' Hally said feigning surprise.

'That is what we heard here. My question is what happened before?' insisted Nirmala.

That infuriated Mukta. As a member of the legal group that was set up in Delhi to follow up on cases concerning Bhopal, Mukta had spoken to Arshad Ali late in the evening, who had clearly told her that he was disappointed with the settlement. Nirmala appeared to think he could not take a stand without someone propping him up.

'This must not get out,' said Hally stopping in mid-stride

and turning to look at them. He then told them how Arshad had reacted and how he had asked Mads to go talk to him.

'He did not understand the other parts of the settlement. He had paid attention only to the compensation amount,' said Hally. 'I told him about the rest. And he tells me, *"Haley bhai, unko phansi dene se yahan dawai ke paise to nahin milenge."*' He imitated Ali's distinctly Bhopali accent

Nirmala laughed. 'That is true,' she said. 'They really have nothing, poor things. For a year they lived on dole, now they live on debt. So you made them change their stand. I wonder what Mads told them.'

Mukta felt ill at ease and her anger burst out again. 'How can they forget the murders of their children, their husbands?' she asked.

'The same way the elite ignore the way politicians kill thousands of children every day with their corruption and their skewed policies,' Nirmala said angrily.

Nirmala found Mukta a deadweight with her eternally serious attitude and her incapacity to appreciate that people with other opinions could be as committed as she. Mukta found Nirmala's readiness to laugh and her preparedness to justify anything people did as a serious flaw in her character.

'If the poor started being content with some money we may as well incorporate the concept of blood money in our laws and forget bringing criminals to justice,' Mukta retorted hotly.

Avidha did not attend the demonstration outside the court that day. Her head seemed to have divided itself into clearly demarcated portions, each one of which hurt differently. The

morning papers had not helped her headache. Her father had read out an editorial to her condemning the settlement as a sell-out. 'I don't care, my head is not here,' snapped Avidha tying a dupatta tightly around her head.

She knew how furious her chief would be that she was away on such a crucial day. She swallowed two aspirins one after the other, refused breakfast, lay down in bed and was unable to sleep. Late in the afternoon she went to office, knowing she must, trying to retain her professional reputation at least. She cursed the Supreme Court for piling on her the responsibility of analysing the order in the Bhopal case when all she wanted to do was sleep and forget even her existence.

In office she learnt that Ajit, Hally and Mukta had all called her about the settlement. The call she had come to hear about was the one nobody mentioned till one of her colleagues, who had been out when she arrived, told her in the evening that Prashant had called and had asked her to call back. Her heartache eased a little. She did not call him back.

She also felt bad that Nirmala had not called her. She had completely forgotten she had brusquely dismissed Nirmala only three days ago because she was in a hurry to get home and feel rested for her early morning trip with Prashant.

'I am a complete fool,' she told herself as she dashed off to Suguna's office across the corridor to gather news about the demonstration. Suguna was shocked to see her condition. Avidha said she felt like she had caught some bug, but work was waiting so could she tell her what happened in the demonstration and what plans were afoot?

Suguna also told her about Ali's reaction. 'It must be kept off the record. I promised Hally I would not mention it to anyone. These things create such problems, Avi. As insiders we get to know so many things and we censor ourselves.

Don't you feel any dilemma? About this conflict of interest?' she asked Avidha.

'I don't care,' Avidha snapped, immediately regretting her impatience. 'Suguna, I am so unwell. Just want to finish the article and leave,' she said. 'Was Nirmala there?' she asked as an afterthought.

Avidha took very long to write her piece and even then it did not have the expected bite. Her deadline was drawing close and she struggled to rescue her mind from its intense engagement with a man and the way he had driven away without a glance at her. Words seemed to have suddenly fled from her. 'Everybody is angry with me,' she thought, 'my mother, Prashant, Nirmala and now I have made even Suguna angry with me. I am a worthless woman.'

She had not counted the bureau chief, B.L. Joshi, who had come to her table twice to check if she had finished writing and was furious with her for coming in late, not even going to the court to cover the demonstration and then handing over an indifferent piece after hours bent over the typewriter.

She reached home to find Suguna waiting for her with a hot lemon and ginger.

'There was no honey so I put in some sugar,' she told her. 'It helps when you have the flu.'

Her concern made Avidha even more miserable.

'I just want to be alone,' she told Suguna.

Avidha picked up the half-empty bottle of gin, offering some to Suguna, who refused. She bolted herself inside her room and slugged the hot lemon and ginger with a large portion of gin.

Chapter 5

A DEMAND FOR IMPEACHMENT

The Supreme Court had sullied its own reputation with such wanton abandon that even those who had long turned to it as their messiah were too shocked to feel betrayed. Anger stalked the room of the All India Law Institute, where people dragged their heavy feet, nodding gravely at the reflection of their own disbelief and in the eyes of the others. Few understood the ramifications of the settlement order and nobody seemed to know what to do now. They were all sure of one thing alone, that this injustice must be set right. Their need to do something, anything, was so urgent, so physical, they did not stop to ask who had organized the meeting or what would be discussed in it. The many shades of ideology were subsumed in the desire for subversion.

The long regulation tables had been moved to the back;

many were perched on them and many were slowly making their way inside the room to find a spot to stand.

For the first time since that cold December night in 1984 when people had been gassed in their sleep, the theatre of action had shifted from Bhopal to Delhi and the liberal middle-class intelligentsia had arrived to seek answers and accountability.

Ajit Khanna was addressing the meeting, a mike in hand, when Avidha dragged herself in. It seemed natural that he should take the lead in giving some direction to the people assembled.

Ajit headed the Delhi group, a small one that was set up a few months after the gas disaster. The group pooled information, fed it to the press, and kept in touch with organizations in Bhopal and officials in Delhi connected with the case. It worked closely with lawyers representing the survivors in the many cases filed on issues related to medical and economic relief and rehabilitation and extended logistical support to the three major survivor groups. Hally and he had spent the last four years organizing many meetings and conferences, including some international meets in Bhopal and some in the US and Europe.

'Yesterday there was a follow-up order on the settlement. We are waiting to get hold of an official copy and only then can we examine it closely,' Ajit was telling the meeting when Avidha arrived. 'I can only tell you that there had been attempts at an out-of-court settlement when the case was filed in Judge Keenan's court in New York. Those attempts failed. This time there weren't even rumours that some sort of an agreement was being negotiated. We had no suspicion this would happen. We had been following the case as closely as we could. Every day, at least one of us was present in the court to watch the proceedings. We are not even sure what it is. Is it an order of the Supreme Court being passed off as a settlement? Or is it an out-of-court settlement between Carbide and the Government of India that has been sanctified as an order of the Supreme Court? We cannot wait for such detailed examination to launch a campaign. For three days now we have been holding demonstrations outside the court and tomorrow we must show up in good numbers. Let us not fool ourselves that this will be an easy battle. It won't be. Let us make this our priority number one.'

The mood in the room shook Avidha out of her prostration. She knew almost everyone in the room but not one of them commented on her obvious ill health. She spotted Nirmala in the front row, waving to a seat by her side. Avidha nodded and quickly turned away pretending to look for someone else.

Hally took the mike as Ajit stepped down from the podium, and said, 'I demand the impeachment of the justices who handed us this shameful verdict.' Ajit looked at him, surprised, as he continued: 'We need advice about it. But I am sure nobody in this room will object to the demand for the impeachment of all the five justices, including the Chief Justice of India who headed the bench that handed us this settlement. This settlement has made India look ridiculous in the eyes of the world. This settlement has sanctified the murders of our people as a sacrifice to corporate profits.'

A roar of approval filled the room. 'Impeach them,' said someone loudly and people began thumping the tables on which they sat.

'Don't we need some legal advice on this?' asked Ajit but only Hally and some others close to him heard him in the din.

'We don't,' said Hally in an aside to Ajit.

'We may need advice on how to go about it but we must

keep the Supreme Court in focus from now on,' he continued on the mike. 'Every day we must come here and stand before the court and show the court that the people are angry. We may or may not discover its motives. But there can be no justification for what it did. No justification in law or in realpolitik. This court was the one institution we all looked up to and it has let us down in the most ignominious way. We must let the justices know that if this is their notion of justice we cannot let them continue in their positions. That is the least we owe ourselves, our resolve to fight for justice, our determination to never tolerate injustice. Do we demand that these justices be impeached?'

'Impeachment, impeachment,' some people began chanting in the back rows and soon everyone had taken it up.

The meeting then got down to practical details. A register was being circulated for people to write down their names, addresses and phone numbers. A small group for planning the strategy and the daily campaigns was urgently required and Hally began asking for volunteers. Ajit wanted to find a place to hold daily meetings and was asking whether the institute would spare a little room when Harjit Singh offered his house along with the unlimited use of one of his three telephones to the group. He lived on Sikandra Road, about a kilometre from the Supreme Court.

'We must first decide on a name for the group,' said Nirmala. She was not part of any group. She was an individual volunteer, 'lancing free' as she liked to describe herself. Grabbing the mike she said loudly, 'Let us remember, all of us, this is the struggle of the Bhopal survivors. They have fought till now while we sat in our homes and they will continue to fight. We did not and we cannot fight their fight. We must be clear about this. We are only a support group.

Don't get carried away and make a commitment you can't keep. The name we give to the group must also reflect this.'

Ajit felt irked by this intrusion of sanity. Hally smiled. They were always at loggerheads, these two. They knew the wave of energy that confronted them would lose its tide soon. Ajit liked to harness the wave when it came and Nirmala wanted every droplet to think before it joined a wave.

'There is not much to think of. We can call it the Settlement Virodhi Sangharsh Samiti. After all that is the tradition, isn't it?' asked Suguna.

Mukta suddenly felt angry. She wondered why she was always cross nowadays. This was not the wrath against the court order or Carbide. It was a deeper discontent, more like a persistent annoyance that seemed to underline all her interactions.

'Something a little more creative will be better,' said Hally. They began thinking of names for the group.

'Wouldn't Friends of Bhopal be appropriate?' asked Latika, one of the more dedicated volunteers in the campaign, who had even spent nine days in prison after an aggressive demonstration in Bhopal. She was a virtual storehouse of information on the case and Carbide, much of which was sourced from abroad.

Friends of Bhopal came into being to the sound of slogans denouncing the Supreme Court in the biggest room of a law institute.

'Brilliant, the short form can then be FOB. Good, that sounds good. Fob off the settlement,' said Harjit excitedly.

The meeting broke up and some left, some milled around the podium volunteering for the daily drudgery of the campaign.

Avidha realized Nirmala was standing close to her asking, 'Won't you? I am sure you will.'

Avidha said yes, without knowing what she had assented

to, and clutching at her throat ran out of the room, feeling suffocated and nauseous.

For Avidha the settlement could not have come at a better time. Her relationship with Prashant had brought her proof of a singular weakness that dented the image of a strong and capable woman that she had assiduously cultivated. She was ashamed to feel like a tick mark on Prashant's private scorecard of the women he had taken to bed. Did she have at least a special place in his harem? If she now turned her back on him would he remember her as an unforgettable woman? Would he miss her, not in the way he must miss all those other women but as a very special experience he had had? That was what she wanted to know now.

She had an urge to run and increased her pace going around Connaught Place, not caring whether she walked all the way home. She ran away from herself, ashamed that she fell short of the expectations of her most intimate friends, her parents and absurdly even the man who had brought her to this pass.

She asked herself repeatedly why she had asked that fatal favour of him, to tell him he loved her when she was sure of the nature of his passion. He would find someone else for the forays he liked to make into the worlds of others. If only there was some sign that he would forever regret not being able to leave everything for her, her pain would be much lesser. She looked into the debris of that relationship to salvage something as a keepsake.

The bitterness of her disappointment painted her past in sombre colours of needless sacrifice and consensual exploitation. Distraught, she went to bed without dinner. Later, Suguna switched off the light in her room. They had not spoken a word to each other that evening.

Chapter 6

VINEETA REMEMBERS BHOPAL

'You are a caring person. God will bless you,' the Sister had said. Vineeta still remembered her name, Sister Philomena. 'If this is the way God had to bless me I was better off without his blessings,' she thought.

She had woken up with a heavy head. Mukta had left early without bothering to tell her where she was going. Vineeta was tired of the way Mukta treated her. She went about the housework like an automaton and soon gave it up. Sitting at the dining table she began to cry softly, despair clutching at her heart with icy fingers.

She had come to love Mukta with a fierceness that drove any possibility of walking out on her, or worse, Mukta dumping her, out of her mind. She tried hard to meet her expectations and demands but Mukta seemed to dislike whatever she did. Vineeta could not imagine how anybody could live like Mukta did. She could not understand how a phone could become a substitute for meeting people.

She had handled so many things without letting Mukta know. Did Mukta think they would have been allowed to live here in peace without the whispering campaign getting louder had she, Vineeta, not adroitly told everyone they were cousins?

The repression of her nature began to give her headaches. She sometimes could not believe she was the same girl who had fought her parents and run away from home to come live with Mukta, leaving behind a letter and not even an address for them or their letters to follow.

People in Delhi seemed very cold and formal to her. She wondered how many here would do what the people of Bhopal had done in those terrible days when the gas had leaked. The whole city had poured out. Chemists had emptied their stocks of medicines and eye drops. Students had rushed to the Hamidia and Kasturba Hospitals and fetched water from hand pumps and people's houses. They had started a collection drive and bought fruits and milk to feed the sick lying in the hospitals.

The gas leak had silenced the crows in Bhopal and Vineeta was among the first to come out and help those who were sick and dying, who had lost their children and their hopes to the gas and who went wandering like lost souls looking for lost children and lost house keys when they left the hospitals. She had then been a final year BA student at Nutan College.

Overnight her lazy laid-back Bhopal had turned into a city of intense activity. The roads were full of stretchers and vehicles. The air was rent by the cries of the bereaved. She still had vivid memories of that horrible Monday when she had woken up to find the town trembling in fear with the radio broadcasting news of some poisonous gas that had leaked from the most famous factory in Bhopal. She had stepped out into her front yard and watched unbelievingly as people ran clutching cloth bags, screaming in terror. The day before had been such a beautiful Sunday. Her aunt had come down from Indore to invite them to her daughter's wedding and to order some ornaments from the reliable family jeweller. They had gone to New Market to shop and eat pastries. She had left late in the afternoon and they had been up till ten at night waiting for her to call their neighbour to let them know she had got home safely.

Her mother had woken her up rudely in the morning with the news of the gas leak. Her parents were debating whether they should immediately leave for Indore when her neighbour called out to them to say her aunt was on the phone. 'Come away,' her aunt had urged. 'Brother, please come away for a few days. Even the chief minister has left the city.'

Her father, Harish Saklecha, had refused. 'There is nothing to worry about,' he said. 'The gas leaked at midnight and it won't stay in the air permanently.'

Her brother Vipin walked up to the main road and came back to report that buses spilling with people were speeding towards Misrod. Taxis were overcharging people like there would be no tomorrow.

'*Koi daya maya nahin bachi kisi mein,*' her mother had said in disgust, adding almost involuntarily: 'Maybe we should go see if we can help people.'

Soon Vineeta and her best friend Uma, who lived three houses away, had found their way to their NCC trainer Aslam Khan's house. There were two more students there. Khan suggested they go to the Hamidia Hospital to see what they could do. Auto rickshaws were refusing to go in the direction from which people were fleeing and they had walked to the railway crossing to take a bus but the conductor said the bus would halt at the entrance to Jehangirabad only to pick up those who were leaving the town. They could not take too much of a risk.

From the bus they saw shattered bangles and stray clothing scattered on the road leading to Jehangirabad from MP Nagar, markers left behind to indicate the route people had taken out of the poisoned town. But nothing had prepared them for the desolation of Jehangirabad. It was so quiet they could hear their own footfall. A crow lay dead on its back, its beak open in silent protest against the unknown poison in the air. Though the place was crowded with small houses separated only by thin walls, the area was deserted. Vineeta felt a flutter of fear pass over her heart.

Khan wondered if they should check the houses for people but one look at his students' petrified faces decided it was better to go to the hospital and seek professional advice about the kind of help needed.

'We must go back,' Uma had begun screaming suddenly.

Vineeta stood rooted to a spot, where, just in front of her, lay a dupatta and a single sock, a child's sock, frayed and threadbare. Perhaps it had slipped off because the foot was thrashing too much. Next to it lay a green dupatta and a heap of shining blue and red pieces of bangles. That silent testimony to the agonies suffered by an unknown woman and the child in her arms spoke volumes to her. Buses in Bhopal would normally wait for a woman to lock the house, retrieve the fallen shoe of her child and pick up a kilo of potatoes on the way before she could cross the road to board the waiting bus. What had driven all such unhurried habits from the terrified woman's heart? What had made her run leaving her dupatta behind and her child's foot unclad on this winter morning? Vineeta had shivered and looked at Uma, her teeth clattering with fear.

'Yes, yes, go back,' Khan was telling Uma, holding her shoulders, trying to calm her down. Uma began to run towards the bus they had gotten down from. Then she turned back and holding Vineeta's hand began to pull her too.

Vineeta shook off her friend's hand.

The other two students, both boys, stopped a few paces ahead of them uncertainly. Khan asked one of them to escort Uma home. She was his responsibility and on this day when even buses were scarce and too overcrowded he could not let the girl go back alone.

As Vineeta and the other boy walked on with Khan towards Hamidia Hospital, they saw the first victims. They lay on the bank of the lower lake vomiting and drinking water from the lake. A nun held the abdomen of a young woman as she doubled up to retch. She then made her sit up and lovingly cleaned her mouth with a small towel and moved on to help a little boy up the bank.

'Only Christian missionaries can do this to total strangers. I have always marvelled at their spirit of service,' said Khan to Vineeta.

As the three of them turned into the lane that led to the hospital a strange noise drummed at their ears. It was the sound of thousands of throats coughing together in an irregular rhythm as if the devil's choir was practising a new dirge. Shrieks punctuated the funereal chorus. The road was slippery with vomit, urine and globs of spittle, green and yellow. Three goats lay dead on the road, their bellies swollen and bulging as if they had drunk too much water.

Cattle were careening as if they had gone mad, seemingly blind. They tottered and walked with a swaying gait as if drunk. A cow lowed loudly till she could stand no more and lay down on the road in mute protest against an enemy her instincts had never prepared her for. She turned over and claimed the release of death.

Bravely, Khan smiled and said, 'We have come where we are needed.'

Vineeta was aghast at the sight that met her eyes. The hospital was like a war camp. Outside the gate people lay coughing, covered with inadequate sheets in the cold. Dead bodies lay in the compound that led to the emergency room. People walked from the gate to the hospital, holding the little hands of small children who could hardly see for the tears streaming from their eyes.

The three of them stood there confronted by the enormity of the tragedy, feeling utterly helpless. What were they here for? What could they do? What was there to do? Tears sprang to her eyes. 'Sir, I can't bear this,' she said. Khan took charge of the situation. As a young officer used to teaching young boys and girls some drill and shooting 12-bore rifles from behind sandbags in neatly laid out camps Khan himself had no experience to handle this onerous task. However, he was a trained officer. He knew he must seek the doctor in charge and seek directions. 'Talk to them. Get them water or help them take medicines and wait for me,' he told them as he vanished inside the hospital. The boy went out to help orderlies unload stretchers.

Volunteers were handing out fruit and bread. Vineeta had helped a woman sit up and eat two slices of an apple. The woman told her how she had run out without her shawl and had not felt cold at all. 'My lungs are burning,' she said, taking Vineeta's hand and laying it on her chest. 'Can you feel the heat?' She continued to talk incoherently, telling her how she had been running, following the backs of people who had begun the race before her believing it was the direction to safety.

Then a number of people began talking to her, asking her for water, asking her to fetch the doctor. An old man told her he had lost his transistor radio on the way when he fell down and passed out.

'Why were you bringing the transistor with you?' asked Vineeta.

'I thought they would tell us on the radio what to do, where to go,' he said. Instead, there had been nothing. Silence. Static. Strange music. But no news, no instructions.

Vineeta slowly gathered that they had followed a jeep speeding out of the factory blindly believing it was taking a route to safety and had instead walked straight into the cloud of gases that came whooshing in from the factory and rushed into their eyes, their open mouths and their lungs, its toxic drops clinging to the alveoli in their lungs, hopping from branch to branch of the breathing tree and into their tissues and their blood.

'The only way to escape was to stop breathing,' said the old man.

Another woman came up to her, crying that her husband and child were missing. Vineeta took her around the hospital, the woman leaning on her arm, looking for her husband and child. There were patients lying on the cold floor. The image of the nun wiping the vomit from the woman's mouth at the lower lake kept coming back to Vineeta. Could she do it? For her mother she could have done it, but could she do it for a stranger?

She began to cry softly. The woman looked at her touched by her empathy. 'Don't cry, child,' she said. 'I will look on my own. You don't have to come with me.'

'It is not that,' Vineeta had said. 'I will come with you.' She walked with the woman out of the front door of the hospital to take her up to the gate where she had seen many patients lying and sitting around helplessly.

There were three long rows of dead outside the morgue as there was no space left inside. The tragedy hit her then with its full force. Taking the woman firmly by the hand she said, 'Are you strong enough to go looking on your own? I must help other patients.' The woman wandered away. Vineeta turned back inside the hospital and asked an orderly to give her a broom, a *chilamchi* or a pan to collect all the filth lying on the floor and throw away. The floor was reeking of vomit with the liquid flowing away from the half-digested mess lying in piles.

'This is so filthy. People will get sicker,' she had told him.

The orderly looked harassed. '*Kya karein*,' he said to her, 'all the *safai* karamcharis are affected. Four are lying in the emergency room. There is nobody to clean the place.'

'We are here. At least I am here,' she said. She went to find something to collect the filth in. In the bathroom she turned back repulsed by its state, about to contribute to the mess. With teeth clenched she went in and collected a flat tin pan, a bucket and a broom. She began to collect the vomit and dump it in the bucket and moved from the emergency to the OPD area and then to the wards, coming out finally in the courtyard wondering where to dump her bucket full of filth. Nothing would take her back to the toilets with their backflows. As she stood there some sisters of Asha Niketan came up to her. One of them suggested that they dig up a

73

little hole, empty the bucket and cover it with the soil. The sister and Vineeta got to know each other as they dug a pit under a tree. Her name was Sister Philomena, and it was then that she told her, 'You are a very caring person, Vineeta. God will bless you.'

God certainly does not seem to be in a mood to bless me, thought Vineeta as she sat listlessly at the breakfast table. All her caring seemed to be going waste on Mukta. Sister Philomena herself would not bless her today if she knew Vineeta's nature. Her best friend Uma, who had later come to the hospital and watched her in open-mouthed admiration cleaning the place, had rejected her for being what she was. She had not replied to any of her letters. Vineeta had for long lied to herself that Uma had never received the letters. Her mother must have read them and thrown them away. But she could not fool herself forever. Something in her bones said Uma was ashamed of her now. What did Mukta know of this loneliness? She was used to being on her own and did not have many friends to lose.

Vineeta had been a constant volunteer in Bhopal not caring with whom she worked. It did not matter to her who led which campaign. It mattered to the others though, and some people, to her eternal confusion, even fought among themselves. She had done what was required. With the Scouts, with the Marwari society, the Jain society, the Waqf Board, the NCC and also the Bhopal Gas Leak Virodhi Nyaya ka Sangharsh Morcha, the front of citizens formed to fight for the gas-affected that now seemed to be dead. What a mile-long name that organization had. She had translated for some of those American lawyers too who had come to Bhopal and made people sign their *vakalatnamas*. She had made many friends and she had lost all of them.

Vineeta sat at the dining table crying silently. She resolved, once again, to keep her opinions to herself, not express them, never to interfere in anything. She valued peace at home above anything else and was now beginning to feel scared of saying anything. She had begun to feel that the relationship was doomed.

The bell rang. The help had arrived. 'Why do you have to come so late? Just because I don't say anything to you does not mean you will come any time you want to,' said Vineeta to her sullenly.

Chapter 7

THE CAMPAIGN BEGINS

onnaught Place was going about its business when a man on stilts sauntered onto the grassy dome of the underground Palika Bazar, wrapped in a black silk cloth with 'Carbide' emblazoned across it in huge red letters. A tall hat painted with stars and stripes was perched on his head. He played a happy tune on a *dhapali*. A few girls and boys followed him dancing and singing joyfully with cymbals and *chimtas* in their hands. Suddenly the man stopped. He turned to the crowd following him, sucked in air till his cheeks were distended and began to exhale hard in their faces. The children dropped their instruments, waved their hands in front to clear the air, opened their mouths wide, clutched at their throats, began to choke and slowly slumped to the ground.

'Hear, hear,' said the man, 'all of you hear me carefully. I am an American Bakasur. I demand the sacrifice of thousands.

I am glad to know that your rulers have conceded my demands. Now I can eat people without fear. Long live the rulers of democratic India. All of you were born to feed me. All of you say with me, *Dhanya bhaag hamare...*'

The boys and girls lying on the ground in what appeared to be death throes responded in a chorus, '*Hum Amrika ka khana banenge.*'

The man in stars and stripes said, '*Dhanya bhaag hamare...*'

The chorus responded lustily, '*Hum unka munafa banenge.*'

A crowd began to build up as the man in the hat roamed around playing his *dhapali* and describing a small circle that the actors lying on the ground occupied. When the crowd was sizeable Avidha stepped into the small circle and began to address it.

'What you have seen is a very poor imitation of the Bhopal disaster. Yes, this is how people died there. Have you ever sprayed insecticide on insects at home? Seen them run helter-skelter and choke to death in the open air? That is how people died, people of India, our own people. They died like insects, choking in open air, breathing in poison, starved of oxygen. And the poison turned slowly into cyanide inside their blood. It killed them slowly. That happened more than four years ago. You will all remember that December in 1984 when India became the site of the worst industrial disaster in the world.

'We all know why it happened. It happened because Carbide had come here to make and sell pesticides. It began to make losses. You know what they did when that happened? They simply cut down on safety measures. To save some money. They knew that they had lethal poisons in their tanks.

77

But they did not store it safely. Their gauges and valves and who knows what else malfunctioned. They said no problems. What will happen? Only some poor Indians will die. Who cares?

'When people died you know what the government did? They took a dishcloth and wiped away all the traces of blood and vomit.'

The boys and girls lying on the ground began to swab the grass.

'Our government, as you know, has always been weak in arithmetic. They did not keep an accurate account of the dead and the affected. That is how they destroyed evidence...' Pointing to the boys and girls on the ground she continued, 'You can see there are four dead but the government says only two died.'

Two of them sat on the prostrate figures of other two. It was a smooth performance even though they had had only two days to rehearse it.

'This week the great Supreme Court of India proved that what the Carbide people thought was right. The great court said there is no need to try Carbide for murder. Over five thousand people died when the gas leaked out. They are still dying. At least one person dies a day. It was not an accident. It was a result of not implementing safety measures. It was a result of looking upon Indians as insects.'

A white Ambassador car stopped on the road and Avidha was immediately distracted. She looked at the car as the driver got off and opened the rear door and a woman stepped out, gave some instructions to the driver and walked towards the entrance of Palika Bazar. It was not him. The man in the hat prodded Avidha who shook herself.

'But what does our Supreme Court say? It says there is no

need to punish Carbide and its officials. All criminal cases against them are erased. Like something written in pencil and rubbed out with an eraser. It says a few thousand rupees are enough to compensate people for losing their fathers, their mothers, their little ones. You know why this has happened? Because our government became the agent of Carbide. They treated our own people like they don't matter. Indian life is cheap. Now any multinational is free to come to India and kill us all. And when there is an international uproar they will pay us a handful of rupees. Finish. They are free. We are free to suffer. We are free to die. They are free to kill. They are free to make profits. Simple rules of this game.'

She continued in that vein for another five minutes. As the crowd scattered she turned to Hally and asked, 'Why did the police not arrest us? Section 144 is in force here.'

Hally laughed and began folding the silk wrap. They were moving to another location in CP for the next performance.

That evening the FOB met at Harjit's house to chalk out a long-term strategy.

Harjit Singh's two-storeyed red sandstone house on Sikandra Road was a highly suitable address to run the campaign from. It was close to the Supreme Court. It was a spacious house with a big enough lawn to hold meetings and above all it was an address that kept the police at a distance.

With a big departmental store in Connaught Place and a crockery shop in Fatehpuri, Harjit could afford to hang around like a maverick messiah. He kept the two shops, the milch cows of his affluent life, hidden like a dark secret, preferring to be seen in his identity as the trustee of a charitable school that provided, not free education, but education for a small fee. 'People never value what they get for free. You must always charge them. Even if they part with a *chavanni* they will value what they get in return,' he said. He looked down on the habit of distributing printed leaflets. 'People just throw them away. They don't read. It is a waste.'

The 1984 genocide of Sikhs had shaken him deeply. After that his house had become even more open to those who were intolerant of religious bigotry. Harjit seldom lost the opportunity to point out that he, a Sikh, had rooms stinking of tobacco smoke in his house. 'Where will the smokers go to argue if they cannot come here?'

A year earlier he had become a legend in the press club with his gut reaction to the popular jingle that the Doordarshan had begun telecasting on national unity. From classical musicians to popular film actors and cricketers, many stars ran for unity in natty dresses, holding aloft a torch, telling India with moist-eyed smiles that if only 'you and I sang the same tune we would all be one'! *Mile sur mera tumhara*, they sang.

'*Aur mere jaise besuron ka kya hoga*?' asked Harjit Singh. 'Democracy is meant to protect the *besuras*. *Mile sur mera tumhara* indeed. This is the language of Hitler. Bloody fascists! Even our progressive poets are writing rot. Shame on them.'

Harjit stood hardly two inches above five feet, had a ruddily fair complexion with whisky bags under the eyes. He affected the style of a careless dresser who lived in jeans. He had many of them, one older than the other, one a very old pair from before the time Levi's had zippers. His one overriding passion was to remain engaged in a state of permanent discussion about the state of affairs in the country.

Harjit Singh was much liked.

He welcomed the discussion on Bhopal into his house with a warmth that brought relief to the tortured passion of the people involved in it. He was hospitable and non-interfering. He sat in on the meetings some days, keeping away most of the time.

To Harjit's eternal dismay he was not present at the first FOB meeting in which the most dramatic plan to embarrass the Supreme Court was hatched. It emerged from a light-hearted remark that Avidha made.

'Isn't this settlement really a dirty one?' asked Zintac.

'Makes you want to sweep the dirt out of the court, doesn't it?' asked Avidha.

'Let us do it, *literally*. Let us take some brooms inside the court and sweep it,' said Nirmala.

It was not such an impossible task after all. The SC was open for anyone to walk into. It was winter and the women could easily carry brooms inside the courtroom tucked under their sweaters.

'Are you people out of your minds?' asked Mukta. 'You can't do this. The court will not stand it for a minute.'

'We can't stand the court either,' said Nirmala hotly.

'This is truly contemptuous. You will all go to prison,' said Mukta amazed that such a preposterous suggestion could even have been made.

She pointed out that they would only end up making the courts more security-conscious. All they needed to enter the court now was a pass signed by any of the lawyers and lawyers who signed their entry passes could get into trouble if they indulged in such frivolous acts. The court could even impose restrictions on the numbers and kinds of people allowed inside the courtrooms. 'This is not a joke. Is it not enough that for days now we have stood before the court raising slogans against it, demanding impeachment? They have not hauled us up for contempt. That does not mean we go overboard. This is truly abuse of liberty,' she said.

'The court hasn't had us arrested because the judges have a guilty conscience. Don't make it sound like they are doing us a favour,' Avidha told Mukta.

'You are impossible,' hissed Mukta.

'Your faith in the system is very touching. Please explain the basis of this faith when all that the SC has done is to betray the trust of the survivors of Bhopal,' said Nirmala.

Finally they worked out a compromise. They decided to sweep the veranda outside Court Number One presided over by the Chief Justice. They could have the press waiting there and grab a few pictures. That way no lawyers would be involved.

Mukta protested once again but she was overruled.

As they walked out Avidha looked at Nirmala wondering if they could get back to their old comfort levels.

'That was good, wasn't it? It had become so much of the same thing, raising slogans outside the court every day,' she said to Nirmala,

'I hear you have moved into a flat of your own,' said Nirmala.

'Yes, you should come over someday,' said Avidha. The old Avidha would have asked her to come and sleep over that very night and they could have planned more dramatic acts of protest.

Chapter 8

SWEEPING THE SUPREME COURT

Hally had a broad face that gave the impression of being long because of his sharp features and the pointed chin that seemed to have been pulled down a little, leaving a deep hollow between his lower lip and chin. When he arrived a little past 9:30 a.m. at the SC gate he was pleasantly surprised to see Avidha and Suguna already there.

They went to the Law Institute canteen for coffee. Hally asked Suguna what she would tell the press if they asked her for a quote.

'Ask Avidha,' she said.

'She is usually ready with a response.'

'You think I am a moron, don't you?' she asked.

'He is teasing you, silly,' Avidha said.

'I think you are a coward to not join us in the sweeping,' said Suguna.

'I am. What can you do about it?' he asked laughing. She was surprised by his good humour. They had finished the coffee and went down in time to see Ajit drive in but they still had to wait for the press to arrive.

'And I thought *we* were the press,' said Avidha to Ajit.

The press was not happy about the timing but representatives of seven dailies and two agencies arrived on time to crowd Ajit. They were sent off to wait in the veranda of the court.

Nine of the volunteers crossed to the SC with the brooms under their shawls, seven of them women. They climbed the flight of stairs to the veranda outside Court Number One.

'Down with the Bhopal settlement. It stinks. Down with the justices, they stink,' they shouted in unison as they threw their shawls open, took out the brooms and began to sweep the veranda outside Court Number One. They went down the flight of stairs sweeping each stair on the way. Over a score other protestors stood at the bottom of the stairs raising slogans. '*Supreme Court ne kya kiya? Hatyaron ko chhod diya, Carbide ko chhod diya. Adalat me gandagi, nahi sahenge, nahi sahenge!*'

Lawyers paused in their brisk walk towards the courtrooms. People waiting in the lawns for their cases to be heard rushed to the scene of activity. It took no more than twenty minutes but the impact was stunning.

The volunteers came down the stairs and stood in front of the semicircle of slogan-shouting protestors in what appeared like a well-choreographed scene though it was a coincidence.

'We are waiting for this court to haul us up for contempt,' Suguna told the waiting press people. 'Let them arrest us if they dare.'

The court disappointed them once again.

'I wish it had occurred to us to have someone sitting inside the court. We could have got to know how the judges reacted,' said Suguna to Hally as they left the court premises.

Mukta could have done it but she did not come to even watch them sweep the place.

Everybody was scared of Mukta.

They turned serious when it was time for her to arrive. She was punctual like the seconds hand of a clock and was late only when a judge sat late on her case. Many were sick of her but they admitted she brought discipline to the campaign committees and groups she sat on. None of these groups was ever formally disbanded even after it became defunct and Mukta took serious note of such things. She had gradually restricted herself to participating in only a few campaigns steering clear of the protests that popped up in reaction to any incident that caught the imagination of the media or the intelligentsia. 'Popcorns,' she called them. 'Either do a thing properly or don't do anything.'

It was past ten at night by the time Mukta got home. She knew even as she put her key in the latch what she would see inside: a table, with two white china plates on it, two big steel bowls and the salad in a small plate. The idea infuriated her.

For two days now she had wished she could tell Vineeta about the way she had been sidelined in the meeting and how Nirmala had humiliated her but would she even understand? She longed for a companion with whom she could dissect the finer points of her differences with the group, especially today when she felt left out. Vineeta felt the weight of

Mukta's depression burden the atmosphere and had a strange foreboding. The Bhopal case had grown to be a bigger challenge but she had seen Mukta thrive on challenges, not sink like this.

Mukta quietly changed her clothes and sat down at the table to honour Vineeta's efforts at cooking and serving. She felt absolutely lonely and desolate. She broke a piece of the roti and dipped it in the potato curry. It tasted like cardboard. She swallowed it with great difficulty and bending her head began to eat slowly, sipping water with every bite. All of a sudden tears began to spill down her cheeks. She began to cry softly, pushing the plate away. Vineeta was astounded. She had never seen her cry before, not even when she had told her about her father and his death and how she had felt so guilty about being relieved at it. 'Sometimes the death of others liberates you. I took a long time to come to grips with that,' she had told her, dry-eyed.

'What has happened? Tell me,' said Vineeta getting up from her chair and rushing to Mukta. She was sure Mukta had discovered that the settlement was final, nothing could be done to overturn it and that knowledge had devastated her. 'Don't take it too much to heart. Whatever it is,' she said, not wishing to name the settlement that now seemed like the fuse of a bomb.

'You won't understand,' said Mukta to her. 'You are so involved in your own stupid world. Just cook and feed. What do you care how many things I have to handle? I have nobody to even talk to. I feel so lonely.'

Vineeta felt cold with disappointment and her own sense of incapability paralysed her. She stood near Mukta, desperately wanting to comfort her and not knowing how to. As Mukta gave a small sob and wiped her eyes, Vineeta could bear it no longer and placing her hand on her head, she said, 'Don't cry please.'

Enraged at herself for having displayed such unforgivable weakness and Vineeta's predictable response, Mukta picked up her plate and flung it across the room, breaking it and splattering the wall with the yellow of the dal. She stood there stunned by her own reaction. Not trusting herself for another moment in the room, she quickly ran into the bedroom and slammed the door shut.

She opened it after a few minutes. 'Don't come in here. Leave me alone for at least one night, okay? I will clean your precious wall in the morning. I'll even have it painted. Just leave me alone!' she screamed.

Vineeta sat stunned, afraid to even blink. She sat motionless for almost an hour, eyes glued to the closed bedroom door, afraid it would open, then hoping it would open and wishing she had some place to run away to and then hoping fervently that Mukta had gone to sleep. She stirred after a very long while having sobbed silently and softly till she could cry no more.

She stored the food away, picked up the broken pieces of the plate, took a wet mop and diligently wiped the wall as much as she could. She was emotionally exhausted and wanted nothing more than to collapse in bed but she would have to spend the night on the sofa. She finally swept the floor as quietly as she could. The sound of more sweeping was the one thing that Mukta could not have borne tonight.

Arriving early at the FOB office the day after they had swept the Supreme Court Zintac noticed the police constable hanging outside Harjit's house. She felt sorry for the man. He looked truly out of place here. She had noticed the presence of the police the day FOB began its meetings. Mostly it was just this one constable, but on some days there were three or four others who came in uniform and stood across the road. They followed the women who walked out, walking in the same direction across the road or even openly behind them. They followed them right up to Connaught Place as she had discovered the day before when she had walked with Avidha and Suguna chatting about the success of their programme. In a sense it was good to have them around. At night they provided some protection from the molesters who roamed the streets.

The police constable on guard dared not go inside though he watched many walk in and out freely. The house was too imposing for him. He had a duty to perform in a place he was not comfortable with. He had discovered that people came to the house whenever they chose. Some came at eleven in the morning and usually a large crowd came in around five in the afternoon. Sometimes they stayed there beyond eight at night. The evenings were still quite cold and waiting for the last of the group to leave, he fervently wished he could at least have a cup of tea. There was not even a roadside tea stall close to the house. He surreptitiously counted the number of people who went in and counted them again when they left and wrote down the numbers in a little notebook he kept in his hip pocket. That was all the information he managed to gather. Sometimes he walked up and down the road, loitering near the bus stop which was some little distance away but from where he could see people going in or coming out of the house. Zintac wondered how the police knew that this place had become the FOB office and concluded that one of them must have attended the meeting in which Harjit offered his house.

She thought the police were truly stupid. Had she been one

of those officers in charge of gathering intelligence, she would have got a young presentable cop to pose as a volunteer and join the campaign. Instead they had sent this poor constable who could not, or would not, go in, and who, even if he did manage to get inside, would not understand the language they spoke. Zintac roamed around the front lawn, waiting for the others to arrive, watching the gardeners deadheading flowers when she noticed the constable come close to the gate. She stepped out of the gate and smiled at him.

The constable did not know how to react but here was an opportunity to chat up this girl and he had to take his chance.

'Madam,' he said as if he had just stopped near the gate to take a leak and had hung around. 'Is there some function here? I see many people coming every day.'

'So you are here every day?' she asked throwing him off kilter and enjoying his confusion.

Realizing his mistake, the constable smiled at her. 'I work at the Himachal Bhawan as a guard,' he quickly improvised.

'That is far from here,' she said to him. It was across the road and some distance away.

He looked sheepish. 'Duty *khatam*, madam. I am going to ITO every day to catch bus at this time,' he said. He was after all not as stupid as she had thought him to be. He could think on his feet.

She cut through the pretence. 'I know who you are and what you are doing here,' she told him. He kept quiet. 'I feel bad to see you roaming around like this. It is cold too. I will send you some tea when we have it.'

That was welcome. 'What is your name?' she asked him.

'Suresh,' he told her, 'Suresh Malik.'

She did not know if he was giving her his real name but that did not matter.

89

'Whom do you report to? I mean to the police station here at Tilak Marg or the police headquarters?' Most likely the headquarters she thought, considering the slip he had made about going to ITO to catch his bus.

'How can I tell you?' he said. He was still smarting at the dressing down he had got the day before. After what had happened in the SC yesterday the DCP had summoned him and had scolded him in very foul language.

'They are gentry, sir, they don't talk to me at all,' he had told the furious DCP.

'Madam,' he said now to Zintac, taking his chances, 'my life is so difficult. You know I am standing here all the time. My duty is bad.'

'How long does your duty last?' asked Zintac, curious.

'It depends on you people, madam,' he said. 'When you leave my duty ends. If you stay here till midnight I also will have to stay here. I am here in the morning at ten.'

'That is tough,' she said to him sympathetically.

'Madam, you know, people above me, they don't believe that I am coming here regularly. They say I am not coming.'

Zintac laughed at this. Considering the amount of information he must be carrying back she did not blame them for thinking he whiled away his time elsewhere.

Then, struck by an inspiration, she told him, 'I can help you. Every day we give out a press release. So what we can do is give you a copy of the press release. That will be your proof that you came here. Will that be all right?'

He beamed at her. 'You will give me, madam?' he asked her. 'What is your name?'

'That I won't tell you. But I will tell everyone here to give you a press release and they will. But I am not asking you to stop doing your duty,' she told him firmly. They may as well have a policeman following them at night.

That evening he got two rounds of tea and his first press release. So what if it was after the event that he was expected to inform the police about? He at least had proof that he had been to the house. He did not know that some people were expected to arrive from Bhopal to join the protest. That was not in the press release. The meeting had decided to keep every plan close to their chests and take only some reporters into confidence.

Mads was arriving earlier and some of the gas-affected were to follow. The arrangements for their food and a discussion about where they could stay dominated the meeting that day. Harjit promised to get in touch with his rich friends and raise some money.

'The gas victims will stay in Delhi for at least a week,' Ajit told the meeting.

Chapter 9

THE DOCTOR OF THE DEAD

As a reporter Avidha had seen the worst days of Bhopal when everybody in power had turned their faces away from the worst accusations against Carbide. She had seen what one maverick dissenter could do to find, record, preserve and collate evidence and how ruthlessly he could be defamed and dumped.

She had landed in Bhopal two days after the scrubber vent of the factory that had never been used to wash down any leaking gases became a subject of photographs that identified the crime scene. She still recalled her confusion and incomprehension with some amount of embarrassment. Avidha prided herself as a weatherworn reporter but she was out of her depth when confronted by such a massive tragedy.

She had watched with growing disbelief the official under-reporting of the magnitude of the accident, not so much of the numbers of the dead that most people confused for under-reporting, but the other dimensions of it. She had seen how officials and senior doctors obfuscated the case with their diverse interpretations and had found herself incompetent to hack her way through their technical and impenetrable verbiage. She watched the government disparage its own experts by bowing to the versions of Western scientists and look away red-faced when those white scientists confirmed what some Indian doctors had said the day after the leak.

Above all she had lost her faith in the medical profession as she watched junior doctors grapple with the symptoms of the victims without a coherent treatment plan while the seniors got down to preparing contesting diagnoses angling for promotions and posts. A bitter fight had broken out in the medical community and with mounting horror she had watched the denigration of the head of the forensic department of the Hamidia Hospital who had first handed in his verdict on the cause of death within hours of the gas leak.

'The bodies have cherry-coloured blood. People are dying of cyanide poisoning,' he had said categorically and had immediately prescribed the antidote to it, injections of sodium thiosulphate. The dominant faction in the hospital had denied the diagnosis.

'He is a doctor of the dead. He has no business diagnosing and recommending treatment. It is our job to diagnose and prescribe, his job is only to confirm or refute our diagnosis,' the head of the medicine department had told her. Then he had gone on to assert that there was no cyanide in the victims' system, sections of their alveoli had burnt out, their oxygen intake had gone down and people died because they already had TB or were otherwise sick.

'Sad,' he said. 'Malnutrition kills a lot of people. It wasn't the gas. That may have hastened their demise but it was not the main culprit.'

The forensic scientist had told her calmly, 'The dead have no reason to hide the truth. They talk to me. They have made the accusation that methyl isocyanate breaks down into cyanide in the body. They told me what they died of. Let these agents of Carbide disprove the evidence.'

She had watched the ruthless refusal of the antidote to cyanide poisoning in government-run hospitals and had been perplexed about the stance the government adopted. The head of the medicine department had said it was to protect people from side effects of sodium thiosulphate to which the forensic scientist had replied with bitter sarcasm, 'And push them into the trap of one sure after-effect – death'.

She had not understood why the denial of treatment was in the interest of the government. She had laid the blame, then, at the door of the politicians' lack of understanding of medical issues. Her ears burned to think of the many mistakes she had committed in her reporting, the many leads she had not followed because they had seemed insignificant to her. It was only later that Nirmala had told her that the efficacy of the antidote could be proof of cyanide poisoning and Carbide and the government must have been keen to prevent the accumulation of such evidence.

The forensic scientist had insisted on terming the gas leak an 'aerosol disaster', refusing to accept that methyl isocyanate was the only gas that had leaked from the factory. She could not recall when the press had veered round to the consensus that only MIC had leaked out of the factory, forgetting that there were other gases too, forgetting that in the first few days they had always said that a mix of gases had leaked, some of which remained unidentified. She had herself begun addressing it as a MIC disaster. Was it for the sake of convenience, the urge to simplify, leading inevitably to simplistic descriptions and finally to acceptance of that reductionist explanation? She now wondered if they had been gently edged into accepting this simplified version by sarkari scientists and babus who constantly talked about the 'killer MIC gas'? Nirmala had been very angry with her for succumbing to it.

'In all this confusion Carbide probably spoke the truth when it claimed that MIC does not kill,' she had told Avidha. 'That was an indication that there was something else that leaked, something else that killed.'

MIC had killed and that did not exclude the possibility that other gases too had contributed to the slaughter. Avidha had not thought in these clear terms then. She had assumed that Carbide was lying.

The scientist had intervened at every turn. When the government planned to neutralize the remaining MIC he had demanded that he be allowed to examine the tank that had exploded and had later petitioned the High Court asking that samples of the residue be preserved.

'In that tank are the ashes of the disaster, in it is the weapon that killed the people of Bhopal. It must be conserved, analysed and used as evidence,' he had told her.

He had been lambasted then for straying beyond the post-mortem room though he insisted that the examination of the tank was every forensic scientist's right.

Even some of her colleagues had begun deriding him as a mad man and ascribed motives of self-aggrandisement to him ignoring his heroic efforts. By then the doctor of the dead had begun to shy away from the press. Avidha still remembered her last meeting with him. She had called him for days on end till he had agreed to meet her on condition that he could change his mind at the last minute and she could get no interview. When she had arrived his Labrador bitch ventured out and Avidha bent to pat her head. The dog was all over her wagging her tail furiously.

'They say dogs have a sixth sense, they know whom to trust. I will talk to you because my dog likes you,' the doctor had told her.

She had lost that trust almost immediately.

He told her how when he went to collect the results of the analysis of the tissue samples and compounds he had isolated from tissues he had found no mention of cyanide in it.

'"Was there no cyanide in it?" I asked the scientist. He tells me, "Oh, very little. Not enough to mention." Now tell me, how much cyanide do you need to kill a person? As much as there is oxygen in the air? And forget that, is this science? A scientist must mention even a single molecule of a substance he finds; he can't say, oh it is negligible, I won't list it. That is the level of science education in our country. You think your editors will let you write all this?'

She had recounted this story to many and every time she did people simply said that the company of the dead had affected his head.

'Do you know, these great professors of our IIT could not even identify two of the 28 compounds that I had isolated in the tissues of the dead?' he told her.

She had then asked him how everybody else could be ignorant and wrong. He had thrown her out.

Soon afterwards he had withdrawn into a stubborn silence refusing to trust anyone.

Avidha prided herself on her political insight but even that aspect had eluded her grasp for a long while. When the chairman of the Union Carbide Corporation was arrested she had failed to see it for what it was – a cynical ploy of a discredited chief minister, used unabashedly in an attempt to reclaim moral high ground – but had hailed it as an assertion of Indian sovereignty and her blood had pulsed like the rousing drumbeats of a war dance. She had even had a showdown with her business editor who had told her that such irresponsible conduct could make India lose all industry.

She, along with scores of reporters and photographers, had stood guard for half a day at the front gate of the Carbide Guest House, while the chairman had been in custody inside. She could not forget the anger in the press, the way one of the local reporters had dared the armed guards at the gate and rushed inside the guest house with some of them in tow and how they had been politely asked to wait outside for the chairman to make a statement.

They had waited and waited, typewriters perched on the low boundary wall of the building, notebooks in hand, hungry and thirsty but not daring to move away, trying unsuccessfully to hound the cars that brought in US embassy officials, till agencies flashed the news that the chairman had left Bhopal. Even the fact that he had been smuggled out the unused rusty back gate, taken off its hinges after the padlock hung on the thick iron chain refused to cooperate with officials desperate to let the man in their custody escape, rowed across the lake in a boat and taken to the airport to be flown to Delhi by the same chief minister who had paraded his courage before them only hours ago, and from there to the US, had not dimmed her pride. She had seen it as only a legal right he had to bail and had no doubts he would be facing trial soon.

She had grown up with a distrust of the government, its lethargic reactions and its mammoth inefficiency, but she could see no reason for it to scramble to cover evidence in a case in which she saw it as an inefficient bystander, not a vicarious participant. Gradually it dawned on her that officialdom had done its best to lose, destroy, ignore and obfuscate the evidence of Carbide's culpability.

The attempt had been so sophisticated she now marvelled at the instinctive manner in which they had all closed ranks in a cover-up that few could see through. This went beyond the street-smartness of politicians. It had the unmistakable stamp of technical experts trained in the best institutions of the country. There had been misreporting and under-reporting by deranging the diagnosis, playing down the after-effects, not creating a record base of evidence, inefficient filing of case details, and ultimately by floating hypotheses that she and her colleagues were ill-equipped to crosscheck or challenge. The other evidence of violation of the factory's safety rules and the chemical properties of the gases and eventually even the number of gases that leaked was too dry a subject with no human face for the press to follow closely.

The real disaster, she thought now, was the way the aftermath had been handled. The only living evidence of the gas leak – the people who had survived it – had been destroyed systematically. Their lives were made to depend on charity. Their right to rehabilitation was never properly recognized, planned or implemented. She had seen local leaders of political parties corner contracts to supply doles siphoning off large parts of the rations. Even the communists had fallen prey to philanthropy and ran charities, fighting only for proper distribution of the full amount of rations and cash to the victims, incompetent to examine the deeper politics behind it. Eventually, even the right of survivors to take the culprit to court had been taken away from them, the press giving a standing ovation to the government for agreeing to become the representative of the resourceless.

She had gradually begun to realize that no matter which party came to power the people would remain unprotected and disempowered and the culprits would remain immune. Before the catastrophe, two parties had come to rule the centre and the state had seen an alliance of several small parties but it had made no difference to the way industry functioned. The weapon of state power was never raised in favour of the weak and the resourceless, only against them.

Avidha still could not understand how from being an essential part of the economy, industry had come to be viewed as a blessing and industrialists came to be vested with divine rights. Employing people was never seen as a necessity of industry but as a favour done to them by kind-hearted investors.

It was now clear to her that even in those initial days the political instincts of the leaders were alive. At payback time they had proved their loyalty. The foundations of the settlement had been carefully laid in the way they had obliterated the evidence of culpability and she now felt acutely guilty for not having been able to understand and question it fully. It required too much time and she was interested in too many issues.

She had told Nirmala straight, 'Honestly, I don't see myself doing only this. I don't feel up to it.'

'How does honesty matter to the world?' Nirmala had asked her.

Avidha had to admit it did not make much difference. That could be the reason why things never seemed to change. Even the faces in the several campaigns did not change. There were just those five hundred of them – growing older, more cynical, less optimistic, a little tired – who led and populated all the campaigns and protests. There seemed to be something missing in their campaign for people remained as apathetic as ever.

Now she tried to incorporate some of these thoughts in her articles. Her articles began to grow in length but were devoid of the outspokenness she was known for. Joshi told her tersely to not ramble and to confine herself to the current issues. 'Save your historical analyses for your memoirs,' he told her.

A job not done satisfactorily added to her despondence. She was trying hard to not lose her perspective and her fighting edge, but a man had got into the line of her vision and had stolen its focus. The daily skit became routine. The exuberance of the dramatic performance outside the SC did not last long and the intimate theatre of her love life began to claim her attention again. The campaign had got into full swing and Avidha was buried deep in work. They used the skit, which had improved considerably with daily performances, to attract a crowd. Avidha spent the mornings going from one market to another with the performers, making speeches that got bolder with each passing day. Then she had office and her evenings were now spent at FOB meetings. It gave her little time to mope but she was not at peace with herself. She did everything that she took on, but her mind was not fully focused.

The more she tried to concentrate on work the more her errant mind sought relief in memory and the more she wallowed in memory the more her mind berated her for neglecting her responsibility to the cause she espoused. She felt relieved when she faced a crowd and launched into a diatribe against the court, the government and Carbide.

'Carbide is a foreign company, out to make profits. What could we expect of them? Nothing. This government is ours, we elect these people. This court is charged with the responsibility to protect our rights, protect us from the excesses of the government, and get us justice. Look how they have bartered away our rights. Would the court have done this had the victims been rich? The government and the court, they stand before us as our culprits and they must be punished,' she said in her speeches.

She read the papers every day and began her speeches with every new development in the case moving on to the terms of the settlement and the reasons to reject it. The more her speeches were admired the more she wished for Prashant to hear her speak on the issue. She sometimes argued with him in her imagination thinking up things he would say in defence of the settlement and tackled them in her speech.

Chapter 10

AN EXTRAORDINARY WOMAN

Mukta was an unusual woman in many ways. She knew she was strong but she also fought many of her weaknesses without letting anyone into the secret of that struggle. Vineeta was one of her weaknesses and she constantly asked herself whether her ability and her desire to take on all the burden of the inane matters of life made Vineeta weaker than she had been to begin with. Mukta handled everything in the house – from problems in plumbing, trips to the electricity and telephone offices to pay bills, to dealing with taxmen. Her own mother, she had seen, had become so helplessly dependent on her lawyer-father to take care of such matters that even years after his death she could handle nothing and called Mukta over if she had to as much as write a cheque for the premium of the life insurance policy her father had bought her.

Mukta had changed her name from Lata the moment she became an adult, filing an affidavit and placing ads in three newspapers, even though the rules required ads in only two. No parsimony in such things. If proof is needed, give an extra one was her axiom. She did not like anything about Lata. Imagine being named a creeper, dependent on the support of a tree, a pole, a wall. Really, what were her parents up to, thinking up such a weakling's name for her!

After some thinking she had chosen Mukta. She liked the way it matched Mathur. She had even toyed with dropping that surname and adopting a new one. In Bihar they had begun adopting a name that would denote another religion. The trend was for Muslims to adopt a Hindu-sounding name and for Hindus to adopt a name that Muslims would have had. Mukta Meherunnisa would have sounded too heavy, though. She thought of Mukta Mahjabeen. But Mahjabeen was too moony. A friend had suggested tagging on 'Gauhar' to it. Gauhar was Urdu for pearl. 'I am not some Gauhar jaan,' she said haughtily. Eventually she had decided to retain her father's surname. A tribute to the father she loved.

She liked to imbue her new identity with the connotation of a free woman, a *mukt* woman, Mukta. To honour the name she had bought herself a double string of pearls, small strings of small rice pearls, to clasp around her slender throat. They underlined her name. They gave her a style. She always wore those pearls. Painfully thin, with a heart shaped face and a slightly tip-tilted nose, Mukta was no pretty woman but she had extremely good taste in clothes. She dressed impeccably in trousers and shirts and coats and jackets and occasionally a cotton sari, stiff with starch.

Her prosperous lawyer-father could have bought her any number of pearl strings. He did not resent the fact that Mukta had worked to buy her pearls although he would have loved to have her come to him asking to be pampered a little. J.P. Mathur loved this serious daughter of his, his third child, to distraction.

His three sons, one born after Mukta, did not show the intellectual depth that his favourite child seemed to possess. None of them had wanted to follow him into the courtroom. Mathur was one of those rare people who could make their distinction between education and degrees and diplomas. He knew intellect was beyond and above the recognition universities granted people.

Only Mukta had measured up to his strict standards. He had watched her grow, besotted by the books in his library and asking her father with a straight face to leave his library to her in his will. That is all the girl wanted, his most precious treasure, books.

'You should draw up my will,' he would say to her with a twinkle in his eyes. 'You would know exactly who deserves what!' He bought a flat for her in Hauz Khas, a flat built by DDA which was, compared to the flats built by private operators, inexpensive.

'This girl will make the family proud,' he had told his wife who had given up trying to teach her daughter how to pickle mangoes.

'How? She does not even want to keep the name we have given her?' she had said, miffed at what Mukta had done.

'She knows what she wants. Only such people can achieve great heights. How would you know?' he had asked his wife.

He was always a little derisive of his wife and her low ambitions for their daughter. He also knew that had he had an intellectually endowed woman for a wife his life would have been miserable. He knew he would not have been able to take a career-oriented wife. In his own way he liked his wife, though he did not love her much.

What he did not expect Mukta to have was a body of her own. It belonged to him, the frail body that belied her fiercely strong mind, to be given to a man of his choice or at least one he approved of.

Mukta had always known what she wanted and also how to go about getting it. But the one thing she wanted above all she did not know how to get. Like a terrible secret she hid it in her bosom, sure that even her broad-minded and doting lawyer-father would not understand that his daughter, his favourite child, could have been born like this. She loved her father. His pride in her, in her abilities, her sharp intellect and her disregard of, what he called, girlish behaviour. Her total indifference to boys was what he took absolute pride in, confident that she would never bring shame to the family, falling in love with some chap who could even belong to another caste, and defying her parents to run off and sign a register in court.

He was sure that is how Mukta would be married. In court. Not for her this religious ritual of going around the fire. He had heard her argue against *kanyadaan* and seen her buy badly printed booklets on marriage rituals and read them avidly. He would find her a boy who suited her intellect and her beliefs, he promised himself and her. He was blissfully unaware of the unbearable burden this love of his placed on her shoulders.

The idea that someday she would have to disappoint her father appalled and scared Mukta. She knew he was liberal enough to let her establish herself in her career and confident enough of finding her a very good match when the time came.

Mukta had joined the civil liberties movement as a final year student of law and had held long conversations with him when the organization split and she had found herself gravitating to the splinter group.

'A civil liberties group should be as broad-based as possible,' he had told her, gently egging her to stay on with the bigger group.

'The smaller group has more depth and is addressing many more issues,' she had said. 'The bigger group has all sorts and they don't do a thorough job of anything.'

'To have all sorts is the essence of a civil liberties movement. Civil liberties are meant for everyone, whatever their political views. A smaller group is only better at research. Its reach is limited,' he responded.

He saw her gravitate towards the splinter group and still maintain her relations with the bigger one with great interest. He respected her decisions and watched her grow through her dilemmas. Above all he liked the fact that the girl would not blindly follow any advice, even if it was his.

When it came to choosing which section of law to specialize in Mukta had been confused. While she loved the romance of presenting evidence and building up a case from before the charge was made, she also loved to argue on a higher plane, in a philosophical vein, on constitutional law.

She had had numerous discussions with her father in his room, dark and cool with its book-encrusted walls. The light from the table lamp on his big table would be shining on the little copper *kadahi* he used to keep his pins and clips in. That *kadahi* was the only thing she took away when she left home. The books would come later.

He had heard her out patiently. 'Why can't I do both?' she asked. 'Argue in Tees Hazari and the High Court?'

'Nothing to prevent you. Except for the distance between the High Court and Tees Hazari. Soon you will be spending more time shuttling between courts than arguing in them,' he told her.

She had eventually chosen the higher courts as he had hoped she would. She needed experience to start practising in the High Court. He had seen her get involved with the Bhopal case. She had been working with him for six years as his junior then and had recently begun working independently on cases, some of which she did for free.

Mukta knew that in the near absolute male space of courtrooms it was her father's hand and chamber that had launched her. He had wanted her to specialize in criminal law like him but was quick to sense her deep interest in human rights. Perhaps that was the best he thought, for the girl could soon go to practice in higher courts and be spared the petty-minded small-time lawyers who dominated the stinking Tees Hazari courtrooms. He had nothing but contempt for most of them, though he hid it behind his calm face just as he hid his contempt for the younger judges who sat before him.

He never worried that her interests would prevent her from making money. Money he had enough. Money he knew she would rake in the day she wanted to. He valued fame above that. One day Mukta Mathur would be a great lawyer. Perhaps even a justice of the Supreme Court. Perhaps the first woman justice. Yes, he wanted that.

Choosing which court to practise in had been a difficult choice, but to suppress her nature, her natural liking for the touch of a woman's hands, was more difficult for Mukta. She fretted about what would happen the day she told them about herself. Her father's face would burn with shame. He would throw her out of his house, but that did not matter to her. It cleaved her heart to think that he would throw her out of his affections. He would pluck the pride he had in her from his heart like a thorn, throw it away and turn away his face.

To let down such a father was beyond her imagination. She would sit distressed in the back veranda of her father's house in New Rajinder Nagar, looking out onto the ridge, thinking hard what she would or could do. The dilemma sapped her energies, sucking out any capacity she had for pleasure. Her father wondered what it was that the girl wanted, why she was so sombre and quiet at times. He put it down to moodiness.

Just when she had prepared her first petition for the Madhya Pradesh High Court on an issue emanating from the Bhopal case and gone through it with him (he was always included in her activities) he had suddenly collapsed in his chair. A massive heart attack had claimed him.

Even in the overwhelming despair that she felt on his death a sense of relief had lifted the gloom from her brain. Now she would never have to tell him her terrible secret.

Her father's death had liberated her. Her widowed mother had little say in her life. She watched silently as the girl moved into her own apartment that her father had bought to find the life she wanted to live. She had told her mother that the house haunted her, she could not work in it and it was true.

Mukta soon discovered that she would have to go on living a lie even among the most liberal-minded. She longed to live like other couples, acknowledged by going unnoticed, but she had been left with no choice. Perhaps someday she would be able to win that recognition. Right now there were many battles she was waging. She was fighting to be a good lawyer. She was fighting a giant multinational company that was reputed to have bought over a large number of politicians and professionals and was prepared to buy more.

On the personal front she was fighting the hardest of

battles, to get Vineeta to become more than just a housewife. She could not imagine a variation of the life her father had lived, with a caring wife who had a life of her own only within the confines of her family and her kitchen. She wanted a companion who had her own friends, her own opinions, her own pleasures and her own work to give her a distinct identity. She had begun wondering if she had been carried away by her attraction to Vineeta's beauty. Not that Vineeta had given her much choice, running away from Bhopal to land on her doorstep one morning. How could she have condemned her to the life being planned for her by her parents? But the inequality between the two burdened her with a responsibility she found repulsive.

This house is becoming more and more conventional, Mukta thought, as she climbed the stairs to her house. The appetizing aroma of fried garlic that emanated from the house made Mukta's stomach feel like a hollow pit. After the way she had exploded and flung the plate at the wall a few days ago Mukta had tried hard to keep her fury in check. She had apologized the next morning.

'I will hate you, Viny, if you forgive me. I will hate myself if you don't,' she had said, feeling wretched. Vineeta had broken down. Mukta hugged her and they had both cried a long while.

'I don't mind any differences in opinion. It proves the group is a living organism. But they make me feel as if I am not part of that organism. I feel outside it. Do you understand this, Viny?' she had asked.

Vineeta had stared blankly at her.

Mukta found it painful that her anguish did not seem to move Vineeta at all. For some days they had carried on in an uncomfortable silence, Mukta driven to tenderness born of guilt and Vineeta pretending to be normal but tiptoeing around her sensitivities. Her annoyance resurfaced soon. Cooking, cleaning, serving, the woman was driving her crazy and she now blamed her for driving her into a frenzy. If Vineeta would only try to understand, she would walk her through the nuances of the case. Instead she had stopped talking to her about Bhopal and continued to do her household chores as if paying for her keep. Today she had cooked Mukta's favourite dishes, cauliflower with a generous amount of peas in it and *arhar* dal tempered with shredded garlic and chopped green chillies fried in oil. She waited to hear the key in the latch.

Mukta arrived just as Vineeta had settled down to listen to some Hindi film songs. Mukta gnashed her teeth so hard pain shot through her head. Here she was in her house, the dishes on the table and Vineeta smiling at her like it was another day in a middle-class couple's life.

Hunger, exhaustion and despair asserted themselves after a day spent in endless argument. 'Will you *ever* do anything more than being just my housekeeper?' Mukta asked in her fiercest voice.

Vineeta quickly switched off the tape. 'You are angry with Carbide. Don't take it out on me,' she said escaping into the kitchen to find something to do.

'I am not angry with Carbide, I am angry with the Supreme Court. I am angry with the way things are going. You would know if you paid more attention to what I think and say instead of what I eat.'

Mukta felt the anger demanding to be let out in an explosion. She had loved the style and the care showered on her to begin with, but three years later she had begun to resent it. It was not as if she hadn't heard the whispers about how she was the husband in the relationship.

Every time she mentioned the possibility of a career to her, Vineeta would pull a sad face and say, 'Yes, I must earn.' That infuriated her even more. 'It is not about money, you can go out and work as a volunteer. It is about evolving a personality,' she would try to point out. She had begun to dread bringing it up now for she could not bear the idea that Vineeta thought herself a financial burden. Mukta had never treated anyone as a financial burden. Her attitude to money was straightforward. One should always have enough and if one did not one should make do with what one had. If she had extra she gave it to whoever needed it.

She flung her lawyer's coat on the bed and began taking off her trousers trying to work out her fury through brisk movements, petrified she would break something in the house again. Then she poured herself a whisky, pulled out a copy of the settlement order she had procured and pretending to study it told Vineeta that she would eat about an hour later.

Vineeta did not respond. When Mukta had told her about the loneliness she felt in the group she had shuddered to think how much lonelier she would feel if she knew about her and Ajit.

Mukta looked up at her drawn face and felt contrite.

'You know some people are coming from Bhopal to hold a dharna in front of the Supreme Court,' she said to her. 'I guess you wouldn't want to go there and help out with the arrangements?'

'I will come,' said Vineeta. She was a little apprehensive about the questions that Bhopalis would ask – she knew many of them from before – but she knew that if she now spoke of any doubts Mukta would once again spin out of control. She was being given a chance to help her out. Ajit was sure to be there. She did not want to see him again. She dreaded it but more than that she dreaded the thought of not standing by Mukta when she needed her. She thought it was unfair of Mukta to expect her to help in a campaign she did not even agree with.

Vineeta's willingness to come to the dharna helped cool Mukta's anger a little. She piled the *gobhi-matar* on her plate and with two chapattis folded on it began to roam around the room telling her excitedly that once the people from Bhopal arrived they could consult and get down to finally talking about challenging the order legally.

'Till now we have only denounced it, we have not thought of what to do,' she told Vineeta.

Chapter 11

ARRANGING FOR A DEMONSTRATION

Gossip refuses to go away even after relationships are over. Nirmala's intimacy with Hally had been over for months now. But the gossip it evoked lasted longer than most of her affairs. Hally was a few years younger which Nirmala was sure must have added to the tattle. She was too possessive of her independence to let anything pose the slightest threat to it. The idea of a single partner seemed a derivative of the institution of marriage. 'It appears to me like flagging every sperm,' she had told Hally. 'So remember we have fun as long as we both want it and either of us can end it.'

'Do we have to give each other a notice and stick out the notice period?' he had asked, optimistic that he would change her perceptions.

'No, we just have an extra session in lieu of notice,' she had replied.

The parting, like with most men in her life, had been bitter.

One evening, after Nirmala, back from Bhopal, had finished tabulating some data in Ajit's office, Hally had asked her as usual if he could come to her house.

She had refused.

'Someone else coming?' he asked.

'I don't owe you any explanations,' she replied stiff with anger.

'I know... was only asking... for information,' he had replied, miffed at her tone.

'I owe you no information either.'

That had been the end.

The end of what people called an affair. Hally had not expected it to end just when he thought they were getting to know each other better, which is exactly where it should have ended for Nirmala. Emotional comfort was what unerringly signalled to her the need to put a stop to any more demands on her intellectual life. It was like a new beginning of a new and enriched relationship where sex did not matter anymore. It had run its course and could now be tucked away as a pleasant memory.

'No love can give you freedom, no lover can tolerate the freedom of a loved one,' she had told Hally, who had refused to understand. 'Look at Ajit and his wife,' he had responded. Those two were brought up without fail in every discussion on relationships. If only people would put ideas and values at the centre of discussions on possessiveness, not the physical part. She felt let down that even Hally had demeaned the sense of possessiveness that people struggling for an alternative value system had to guard against.

Nirmala did not regret it. Hally did.

The campaign on the settlement had brought her together with Hally again and she was relieved to see no rancour in his behaviour towards her. In the meetings they continued as if there had been nothing special between them. She found it strange that all the commonality of thought and perception was not considered special; only physical intimacy was thought to make a relationship special.

'The invasion of dominant perception is so insidious you have to fight it every moment of your life,' she thought, as she waited for him to arrive at the Regal building. They had some errands to run for the campaign.

'Let us first book the water,' said Nirmala to Hally when he arrived. They had volunteered to inform the police about the demonstration and to book water tankers for the gas survivors who were to arrive the next day. Three others had gone to the Nizamuddin station to order tea for them. They had no clear idea how many people were coming. Their estimate was about 500. They actually expected only 300 or 400 people. Nizamuddin *basti* could easily provide sabzi rotis for 400 people and it would be cheap too. Hygiene wasn't fashionable. Slumming was.

Nobody was too worried about funds. Enough money had been raised through donations and individual contributions to pay for everything. More could be raised. Nobody wanted to talk of funds at this moment and Hally knew that like him Nirmala had pushed her own discomfort about the funding of the campaign to the back of her mind in the interest of raising a strong fist to shake in the face of the establishment. He still marvelled at the way the government and the judiciary had closed ranks with the criminals and it wouldn't do for protestors to fight among themselves. Both were aware that sooner or later the issue of funding would come up and the group would break up, go their individual ways, each feeling lonely but very sanctimonious and righteous. It was the norm in all campaigns. Nirmala and Hally walked up Parliament Street towards the grey concrete building of the NDMC. 'The government spends so much money on creating ugliness,' commented Nirmala as they went up a spiral staircase in a neglected corner to the section where water tankers had to be booked.

'Where do you want the tanker?' asked the rotund clerk, Ram Babu, pulling a thick bill book and inserting a sheet of blue-black carbon under the topmost leaf. Endless cups of sweet milky tea showed as much in his belly as on the blotter on his table printed with faded brown marks of the round bottoms of generations of glasses.

'Nizamuddin station,' said Nirmala.

Ram Babu's pen paused. 'Not possible. The tanker cannot go to Nizamuddin station. That is MCD territory,' he told them with relish. He liked underscoring the ignorance of middle-class people who spoke English like they knew no other language and behaved as if they lived in this garbage-ridden country only as a favour. They underlined the education he wished he had and he disliked them intensely.

'Do something, please,' said Hally. 'We want the tanker to come to Nizamuddin station and then go with us to Tilak Marg.'

Ram Babu advised them to go to the Town Hall in Chandni Chowk, to the MCD office, and book a tanker there.

'We will send our tanker to Tilak Marg,' he said.

'Why?' asked Hally, 'The MCD tanker can come there too.'

'No,' said Ram Babu leaning back in his broken backed chair, 'it can't. That is NDMC area!'

That meant booking two tankers in two places when they probably did not need even one full tanker, considering it was not so hot yet. That led to an argument. Nirmala said surely they had some provisions for exceptions. Someone could overrule the rule.

'We want the tanker to follow some people as they walk from the Nizamuddin station to Tilak Marg. It can't come and stand in one place, that won't do,' said Nirmala. 'Suppose you pretended that you are going from one part of the NDMC area to another and the people got in the way and you are moving slowly. This can be done. That will solve our problem.'

Hally and Nirmala had come here with the decision to not tell the authorities that they wanted water for protestors. Who knows they may find some excuse to refuse water? They knew the administration did it all the time, refusing permission to hold a sit-in, or walk as a group on the roads.

They began to argue. What Nirmala and Hally had thought would take ten minutes was now turning out to be a job that would gobble up hours. The clerk would not budge. They asked to see the officer.

'Which officer?' asked Ram Babu, cocking an eyebrow.

'The officer in charge,' said Nirmala, mental teeth gnashing at his presumption that she would know the whole hierarchy of this slothful organization.

'Why?' asked the clerk, infuriated. Did they think officers knew more about rules? 'I am sitting on this chair from morning. I am doing all bookings. I am knowing rules,' he told them firmly.

Hally suddenly hit upon a happy idea. 'Tell me, where does the NDMC area begin? Suppose we are coming from Nizamuddin station?'

'You must look up the map,' said Ram Babu, sulkily.

'You must have the map in your head,' Hally said, trying to placate him.

Ram Babu, a little mollified, turned to his junior at the next table, 'See what they are saying? That I have the map in my head.'

'Of course you do. Everybody in the office asks you for such details don't they? *Arre madad kardijiye becharon ki,*' said the junior who did not like the way his boss threw his rule book around.

Hally gave Nirmala a meaningful look checking to see if they could take this man into confidence. Nirmala shrugged.

'Listen,' said Nirmala to Ram Babu, 'have you heard of the Bhopal gas disaster? Victims of that disaster are coming here. They will be walking from the station to the Supreme Court. They get tired easily. They need water.'

Ram Babu went silent. Hally wished they could take the words back. Their plan had misfired.

Ram Babu looked at both measuring them up.

'Madam,' he said, 'you are doing something good. But rules cannot be changed. That is MCD area.'

'Please help us,' said Hally.

Ram Babu relented. 'The NDMC area begins near Sundar Nagar,' he said. 'What we can do is we can send a tanker to Mathura Road near Sundar Nagar. From there it can come with you up to Tilak Marg. It is up to you to make its progress slow. You understand? I am doing this especially for you, because you seem like nice people,' making sure they would know whom to thank.

It took another ten minutes for the clerk to get the spellings of the organization right. They spent another two minutes pleading with him to send the tanker on time. The time was a difficult target for them to set. Many trains came from Bhopal, the earliest around six in the morning, and they had been told that it would bring survivors. It would still be dark then. They deposited Rs 1,100 for the tanker and left.

They were now running late. Their plan had been to walk up to the IENS building on Rafi Marg, to Avidha's office to use her typewriter to write the application to the police. Just a two-liner, a mere formality, to inform them that gas survivors were to arrive and they would hold a dharna in front of the SC. They were not seeking permission. That, they knew, would never be granted. They were not planning the sit-in in any area around the Parliament where Section 144 of the Indian Penal Code was routinely clamped the day the Parliament began its session.

They were not sure if Avidha would be in office. They stepped out of the lift on her floor to find her walking listlessly towards the staircase on her way down. Avidha dropped the idea of going wherever she was headed. She heard the story of the territorial division between NDMC and the MCD with so much concentration it was obvious that she was making an effort to follow the details.

'The Parliament Street police station may not be the right place for informing the police. Should it not be the Tilak Marg station for the Supreme Court?' Avidha asked, aware that Nirmala had guessed her absent-mindedness.

They decided to take two applications, one each to both the stations. While Avidha hammered them out they sipped on the extra sweet tea served by the canteen downstairs. The window panes darkened with the evening as another day passed by. Lights came on and traffic saw a sudden increase. Nirmala asked her to come with them to the police station but Avidha declined.

'If you don't have much to do after this, we can have dinner together,' said Hally as they turned onto Parliament Street. Nirmala knew what that meant. Either they would eat bread and eggs at her place or some place in CP, nowhere very expensive, the English Dairy perhaps, which, notwithstanding its name, sold not a single pint of milk but greasy Punjabi food. Hally never invited anyone home. Despite all his candour about his humble origins, he kept his house and his old mother out of the sight of his friends.

'No hidden agenda?' she asked.

He laughed. 'We shall talk about how I changed from being a cup of poison to a glass of honey, okay?'

Nirmala laughed, 'You will have to doss down on the sofa,' she said to get any carnal expectations out of the way.

Hally looked away.

Hally was not a name he liked. One of his college mates had given him that name. He called him *hala*, Hindi for poison. 'You are always spouting poison,' he had said to him and the name had stuck because the unimaginative friend was so enamoured of his one act of imagination that he went around telling everyone how he had thought up this name for that bitter pill, Heeralal. From Hala to Hally was a short step.

'Tch, you are too touchy,' she said placatingly.

'No, Nirma, I am practical,' he said hitting back with the nickname she disliked.

'Don't call me Nirma. I am not a soap.'

'You are,' he said, his good humour reasserting itself at her obvious annoyance. 'You wash the accumulated dirt of life from all souls.'

They reached the police station. Hally took out the application from his *jhola* and handed it to the constable who glanced at it and asked them to wait.

'Just receive this and we will leave,' he said, smiling.

'I will get the stamp,' said the constable ignoring the fact that the inkpad and rubber stamp lay in full view in front of him on the counter.

'The stamp is here,' said Nirmala deliberately, picking up the flat tin box with its squishy bed of ink. The constable scuttled away.

'For heaven's sake this is not an FIR that he is refusing to take it,' said Nirmala. 'We all know that the police has the right to refuse to lodge a first information report.'

They stood there impatiently, expecting to be kept waiting for a long time. Surprisingly the man came back almost immediately, beaming a smile at them. 'Please go inside,' he said. 'The DCP wants to meet you.'

There it is, they thought, now he will want to know the programme. He will insist that we seek permission which will be promptly refused. We will be sent to Tilak Marg police station.

'This is what we pay taxes for,' she told Hally irritatedly, 'so they can be paid to harass us.'

'Relax. We can't afford to fight,' said Hally to her.

Bracing themselves for an argument they went in.

The Deputy Commissioner of Police sat behind a gigantic desk almost eight feet in length, with a sheet of glass on the table top framing some colourful prints underneath. His name was engraved in capital letters on a sheet of brass wrapped around a triangular block of wood: T.R. Balagopal. He was stout, and whether he had a paunch or not was difficult to tell because the desk hid him from below the chest. His jowls and bloodshot eyes spoke of a well-fed man fond of the good things in life. Four colour-coded telephones sat on one side of the desk and a chart of all the DCPs who had blazed the trail before him hung on the wall behind his chair.

He motioned them to sit and asked them politely if they wanted tea or coffee. Nirmala thought he was truly a sophisticated one, offering them tea before a refusal.

Before Balagopal could open the assault Nirmala said to him with her sweetest smile in place, 'We came here only to tell you that we shall be holding a demonstration on the Bhopal issue. Some people are coming from Bhopal to attend it. Just receive the application and we shall be on our way.'

'We do not want to waste your time, you must have plenty to do,' put in Hally for good measure.

'Oh, no, no problems. I have read the judgment too. I mean I have read the reports about it and the comments in the press. I am shocked. Like the rest of the nation. I am truly shocked. It is horrible,' said Balagopal, 'I agree that what has happened is very bad. My uniform prevents me from owning it up but I must tell you I am on your side.'

'Are you?' asked Nirmala. 'Then take off the uniform and join us.'

Balagopal smiled a sad smile. 'That is not so easy, you know that. But let me tell you I can help you from where I am sitting.'

The constable came in bearing a tray laden with three cups of tea and a plate of biscuits. Porcelain cups, brought out on special occasions for special people in this *sarkari* place full of tiny chipped cups of cheap china and thumb-sized glasses found at every roadside *chaiwalla's*.

They waited till the constable had left.

'Believe me, I can help you. I know you are angry. You are right. Any sensible person would be angry with what has happened. I want to help you.'

They remained silent. They had not expected him to take this line and did not know where he was leading.

With his left hand hovering over the telephones, Balagopal looked at them and said, 'Tell me which minister you want to meet. I can call and fix an appointment for you. Right now. Just tell me.'

'We do not want to meet any minister right now. People are coming here to protest against a Supreme Court order. What can any minister do about it?' asked Hally, taken aback by this move.

'I understand. Really, what has happened is terrible. People are coming all the way from Bhopal to sit on a dharna. I wish they did not have to. I wish it speedy success. In fact I am trying to aid its success. Tell me, what is the dharna aimed at? To change the situation, isn't it? And how can you do it without talking to the government? If you won't talk to the government who will you talk to?'

'We are here only to make some arrangements for the people from Bhopal. We are not running their campaign. It is their struggle. Let the survivors come. We will consult them and decide. We are not the Supreme Court that can decide without consulting affected parties. We are ordinary citizens,' said Nirmala.

Balagopal smiled at the jibe she had made at the court.

'Even then, is it not good for you to discuss with the government? I think those poor gas victims should not suffer much. It cannot be easy for them, coming here, sitting on the roadside. Wouldn't it be good if you opened talks now? It would save time.'

They sipped the tea in silence. They were unprepared for this approach and had no time to consult with each other. It was obvious Balagopal had instructions to facilitate discussions with protestors, make sure things did not get too hot for the government. They had not thought the pressure would get to the government so soon. It hadn't even been a week since their protests had begun and here was a DCP offering to fix an appointment with any minister at the centre. The alacrity of the system astonished them as did the fact that a low-level officer had been given access to people in top echelons should protestors come calling. Things did not move in this country so fast. Or were they wrong? Was the DCP playing a game of his own? Pretending to be a good cop trying to elicit as much information from them as he could? They were not sure what the DCP was aiming at but they were in no mood to engage in a lengthy discussion with him.

They did not even know which minister would be in charge of this imbroglio now. If it came to negotiations which minister would they really want to meet? Was it possible now for any ministry to do anything? They had not even thought what they would do after the dharna was over. What did they want to do? How would they overturn the settlement?

'It is an order of the Supreme Court. What can any minister do about it?' asked Hally, trying to wriggle out of the situation.

'I am sure the government will know how to find a way out of this situation. Otherwise what will you do? Just demonstrate outside the court and go back?' Balagopal asked reasonably.

'We will have to consult our group first. Let us hold the protest, hold some meetings. After that we can talk about meeting officials or ministers,' said Nirmala.

'No problems. We will only fix an appointment now. You don't have to go meet the minister immediately. You can talk to your group and meet the minister the day after. But I think we should resolve this as soon as possible. I feel bad that the poor gas victims have to go through all this trouble. They must be so unwell. I feel terrible about this. You can spare them all the trouble,' pursued the DCP.

They sipped the tea quietly, even munched on biscuits to gain time to think.

'You mean you can fix an appointment with any minister? In the Union Cabinet?' asked Hally.

'I can. Any cabinet minister. So tell me,' said Balagopal suddenly alert, 'which minister do you want to talk to? The law minister? Home minister? I can call right now. '

'Call the prime minister,' said Hally.

Balagopal's smile thinned. 'I can't call the PM. You know I can't.'

'He is the only one who can help. This deal has been made at the highest level,' said Hally, watching his transformed face with great interest.

Hally had either called his bluff or defeated whatever strategy this officer had devised. They went on arguing for a while, the DCP continuing to persuade them to talk to someone high up in the government. 'Meet one of the ministers. Perhaps the minister can take you to see the PM? How about that?' he asked, regaining his composure.

Finally realizing they wouldn't agree he gave up, smiled and wished them luck. 'You know we would love to discuss this issue with you but we have many other things to do,' said Hally.

'If you change your mind please come to me. I will put you in touch with any minister,' said Balagopal.

Outside, the desk constable received their application.

As they walked away Hally said, 'I am getting a little anxious.'

'That if the numbers who arrive are just a handful what face will we show to our friend Balagopal? Or the government?' said Nirmala. 'Yes, I am worried too.'

'We still haven't thought where we will take this struggle. What will we do once the demonstrations are over?'

'I am clear about that. We have to go beyond Bhopal, turn this into a wider fight. But the FOB is not meant for that,' said Nirmala.

She thought of Mukta and her discomfort with some parts of the campaign. She had tried to plead in the FOB to think beyond the denunciation of the settlement. They probably would have been better prepared and who knows they could also have wrangled some minor concession today if they had discussed her proposal instead of being carried away by their anger.

Chapter 12

A BREAKDOWN

Avidha finally called Prashant after waiting in vain for him to call her. 'Were you upset I did not call earlier? I have been very busy,' she said.

'I know. I have been reading the papers... seems you people are out on the streets all the time. I am surprised you find the time to go to office,' he said cheerfully.

'Did you call that day for anything special?'

'Nothing,' he said. 'Campaign going well I see.'

She began telling him about it. 'Do you agree with us? Or are you for the settlement?' she asked.

'Personally, I agree with you people though I don't agree with some of the things you are doing.'

'You can send us a contribution. There are so many expenses we have to bear,' said Avidha.

'Sure. You people got a bank account? Or do I send cash?'

Avidha knew Prashant was very helpful but she had not expected him to contribute to the campaign. She was surprised and told him he could drop by any day at the SC around lunchtime and give the cash. He said that would be tough for him.

She began telling him about how they had swept the court.

'I read that in the papers,' he told her cutting her off. 'Rather silly, wasn't it? Those are the things I don't agree with.'

That made her angry. 'The justices did not think so. One of them cried in court,' she told him.

'That was reported too,' he replied. 'It does not make your action less sillier.'

'You will remain a stuffy bureaucrat,' she told him.

'Maybe,' he said not arguing.

'When can we meet?' she asked feeling sick at her weakness.

'We'll see,' he said.

She replaced the receiver reluctantly, only because the line had gone dead. She decided to flee office and was on her way out when she met Hally and Nirmala.

Avidha walked out of the office as soon as they did. She even neglected to tell her chief she was leaving. She had been restless the whole day, hoping for one phone call, just one word before finally making the effort to call him. She had called twice to be told he was in a meeting. When she managed to talk to him the sound of his voice had made him real again.

Avidha forgot that Prashant always spoke like that on the phone, even in the first few weeks when the affair had just begun. Those days she put it down to his self-control, finding it irresistible. Now she could slap him for his businesslike tone.

She turned towards Parliament House and walked with rapid strides, oblivious to the dangers of walking alone in the

dark on a deserted road in a city full of molesters. Snatches of all the conversations she had had with him dogged her. It seemed to her that she had used every stratagem to keep him interested in her. Like the word she had given his fixation with her breasts. Inspired by the way he pressed the tips of his thumbs on her nipples, spreading the palms to cover them or running his fingers around them like a compass tracing a circle on paper, she had christened his fixation 'trigonometry'.

'So that is your specialization. Trigonometry,' she had told him the first time they had made love, as she watched the backs of his hands covering her breasts like a vulgarly designed bra.

'What?' he had asked, surprised and distracted by the word.

'That is a branch of mathematics,' she told him, explaining the allusion to trigonometry.

'You are amazing,' he had said to her then. 'What a way with words you have!'

Later, sitting across him in his office she had said to him casually, 'Do you think you could spare some time for a class in trigonometry?' He quickly glanced at his secretary who was arranging some files on his table. A smile crept upon his face.

She wondered if she had used that demeaning invitation subconsciously to keep him interested in her. Every touch of his, it now seemed to her, was motivated with a single desire and she had encouraged it with a single-minded passion of tying him to herself.

She did not have the moral strength to share this pain with even her best friends and her screams swirled inside her, suffocating her. A love that she had herself branded as illegitimate had left her with nothing to complain about, robbing her of the relief of justified grievance. She came to

understand that emotions have no rights. Their rights depend on the recognition of the loved one and he had always refused to recognize any right of hers.

Never had he hugged her close, only her body. His arms had never moved naturally behind her shoulders pulling her close in an embrace; they always went to her hips, pulling her lower regions to his stiff desire. She had always tried to steal that embrace from him, to feel his chest caressing her body with tenderness.

In her imagination there lurked that embrace, her one desire that was never fulfilled. Not even in the most intimate of moments, when his face hung above her and she would rise, her heart propelled by the desire to be in his arms, he would push her down, his hands on her shoulder and come down on her not to meet her yearning but only to press his hot dry lips on the breasts. 'I will never have that embrace now, never ever,' she thought.

She wanted to sink into the bosom of her mother and cry, let herself go, ill-formed words pushing their way up her swollen throat. 'Ma, ma,' she said out aloud without even realizing she had said it.

Her mother had told her that such relationships have no future. Nirmala would ask her to let the past go. Avidha resented that everyone around her had so many principles. They oppressed her, made her feel as if people who did not live up to those principles were low lives, and their emotions were not worthy of consideration.

She stumbled on the road, one memory fading into another. 'I only have a past, I have no future,' thought Avidha, suddenly bursting into tears. 'Ma,' she said, 'Ma, help me, Ma. Help me. You made me weak. It is because of you that I am in this condition.'

An auto stopped near her and the driver leaned out towards her. He was from the stand near IENS and had taken her home many times. She took some time to hear him. He was asking if she was unwell. She awoke to reality with a shock. Ram Manohar Lohia Hospital was close by. She looked bewildered. Then collecting herself she said no, she wanted to go to Patel Nagar.

She hopped on for she was tired and had suddenly been brought to her senses. He said he thought her mother was in hospital and wanted to help for he had heard her call out to her mother.

'Yes, she is,' she said. Then she said she had to go home to fetch important things for her mother. She would go to the hospital later.

She began to sob. 'Take me home, please, take me home.'

He did. He knew how people reacted when their parents were dying.

'Don't worry, madam,' he told her. *'Waheguru sab theek karenge.'*

Chapter 13

AN UNEXPECTED CHALLENGE

Ajit was relieved that Vineeta had not joined the FOB and had not come to the meetings at all. He had slowly resumed his normal routine when the settlement was announced and gave him something very urgent to do. In every meeting he looked around apprehensively to check if that woman was around.

When news came from Bhopal that some gas-affected people would arrive to protest against the settlement he knew he would soon have to face the cause of his humiliation. Mukta told him Vineeta would be helping out. He sighed. The settlement had given him a reason to not go to Mukta's house anymore. He thought it best to not go to the railway station. That way he could at least postpone what he could not totally avoid.

His worries now lay in another direction. Like Hally he was anxious that at least 500 should come from Bhopal. He had asked Mads, who had arrived a day earlier, how many were expected. It would have helped to know even for the amount of food to be ordered.

'Who knows how many that Ali can round up,' Mads had said with infuriating vagueness. Sometimes Ajit thought Mads enjoyed placing them in a quandary.

Hally and he had had several discussions and called Ali several times to check how many were expected. 'I am trying to bring thousands,' Ali had told them, 'but we are not booking any tickets. We are all travelling without a ticket so I won't really know how many are coming till the last moment.'

Ajit doubted if thousands would come. Eventually, Hally suggested ordering food for 500 and then splitting the food into two batches for lunch and dinner just in case fewer than 500 arrived. Ajit agreed. The food had been ordered and money had been paid in advance.

Many volunteers stood on the platform with three drums of tea to welcome the survivors of Bhopal.

The first train brought less than a hundred. The second brought so many they could not count. Within an hour, nearly 8,000 people from Bhopal had landed in Delhi. Nizamuddin station reverberated with their slogans. Most of them were women and many had small children with them. The tea ran short and many had to go without it.

The march began from the station to the Supreme Court after nine, an impressive crowd rarely seen on those roads. The police presence was low and unobtrusive and Nirmala was surprised to see a water tanker standing outside the station. She went up to the driver and asked him where he was from, the MCD or the NDMC? He told her he was from the NDMC and had orders from the police to follow them.

She told Hally that they would at least not have to worry about water anymore for the police seemed rather helpful. 'So the police has the power to overrule all those divisions of NDMC and MCD,' she told him.

'You think we should send the DCP a thank you note?' asked Hally as he saw the survivors pour out onto the road with little bundles of clothing in their hands. Most of them had not slept the whole night on the journey, taking catnaps when they could, crowded as they were in a few compartments. That did not seem to have affected their zeal and as Hally watched them all marching to the court to tell the judges that their voices must be heard, his heart swelled with pride. He had no time to bask in his glory though. There wasn't enough lunch.

He split for Nizamuddin *basti* to review the arrangements, annoyed that Ajit had absented himself on such an important occasion. Where was he to find the money to pay for the extra food?

Other volunteers had begun mentally counting the amount they had raised. They needed an emergency meeting to discuss the changed situation and when the march began to converge on the SC some of them rushed to Harjit's house. There they found Mads, sitting in the veranda. He laughed at their concerned faces.

'Did you really think there would be just 500 of us coming to Delhi? May I remind you that 600,000 were affected by the leak,' he said, rubbing weed on his palms. He then meticulously mixed it with the tobacco without looking up. The others were checking the list of donors and asking each other if someone could lend a few thousands, for the food would have to be paid for immediately. Ajit had yet to arrive and he was the only one with the resources to handle this.

'The money can be found,' said Zintac. 'Think about where these people will stay. The tent we had thought we will put up won't be enough now. It is too cold for them to sleep in the open.' She was the treasurer and knew exactly how much money there was in the kitty.

Harjit said, 'Think out of the box, people, think of other avenues of support.'

Mads strolled out into the garden to smoke his joint in peace. He did not make a secret of his marijuana habit but he avoided doing it in dharnas where he stuck to plain cigarettes.

Eventually it was Harjit who found a solution to the problem of accommodating so many unexpected guests. 'Mads, come with me to the Bangla Sahib Gurudwara,' he said. He got the keys to his car. As Mads dragged on his joint and considered his words, he asked him impatiently, 'Do you think you must take a bus? Does riding a car make you less revolutionary?'

Mads laughed. 'No, I think people like you and your cars have their uses. I was waiting to finish my joint.'

Harjit said to him, 'Be my guest. Smoke in the car. Hurry up.'

An hour later they were back with the news that the gurudwara management had agreed to let them all stay in its premises and would even give them breakfast and dinner. They could not provide lunch though, for they had no arrangements to send food outside the gurudwara. If the people could come back for lunch they could get it.

Ajit had had a trying day. After the frantic call from Hally he rushed to the bank, withdrew a large sum, went to Nizamuddin to pay for the food and the transport, and went to FOB office from where he made a trip to the gurudwara to see if they had enough blankets or he would have to arrange some. He came to the SC only for a short while and left soon to see to other things like the press release that was being typed in his office. Hally too arrived late having stood around the *basti* making sure the extra food was being cooked and as hygienically as possible.

Vineeta was as scared of facing Ajit as she was of facing the people from Bhopal. She had avoided going to the station but had later arrived at the site of the dharna. She soon realized that nobody remembered her as a volunteer of old. She did not recall having met anyone before. When she talked to them she realized most of them were not from JP Nagar and Qazi Camp where she had earlier gone to help as a volunteer.

The small stretch of road between Mathura Road and Tilak Marg had been blocked for traffic by the police. Over 10,000 people were spread out in that space, a traffic stopper visible from far away surrounded by red banners.

'*Carbide ne kya kiya? Hazaron ko mar diya*

'*Sarkar ne kya kiya? Hatyaron ka saath diya,*

'*Supreme Court ne kya kiya? Hatyaron ko chhod diya!*'

The slogans filled the air. The public address system had not been used at all. The slogan shouting continued without a break till lunch arrived.

The food arrived in a tempo well past noon and the driver parked in Tilak Lane. He looked around to find the guy who had hired him. Nobody seemed to want to listen to him. One would point him to another, till he ran into Ajit who told him to wait.

'I can't wait. You never told me the kind of function you asked me to bring the food to. Just unload the stuff and let me go,' the driver said.

'This is not a function...'

'Hurry up, whatever it is...' the driver grumbled.

Ajit decided to ignore him. They would have to make space to unload the food which took nearly half an hour and the driver swore he would not come to the spot again. 'Find someone else tomorrow,' he told the volunteers.

Vineeta offered to distribute the food. The newspaper that covered the *khamiri* rotis was clinging soggily to the upper layer of the bread. She began to clean the rotis when a woman nearly snatched it away from her hands. Soon the volunteers were struggling to serve the surging crowd. Overcome by the near-stampede Vineeta gave up in ten minutes. The women would not wait in a queue. They seemed to have forgotten what they were here for. They all rushed to the *degchi*, holding children in their arms or dragging them along. The little ones appeared to be in real danger of being crushed under their feet as they clamoured for food. Vineeta watched horrified as the noise rose to a deafening roar. Unable to handle them she plonked the rotis back into the basket and quickly moved away.

As she made her way to the pavement she saw some women tucking roti sabzi inside their cloth bags. They then rushed back to get more, hands spread out for a second helping. Vineeta did not know they could fall short of food or money; still the behaviour of these women infuriated her. She caught hold of one of them and told her, 'You got your share. Now let others get it. Go eat what you have.'

The woman protested. She said she had still not got any food, and waved her hands in front of Vineeta's face to prove she had no food on her. Vineeta pulled her to the side of the pavement where she had seen her hide the rotis inside her bag. She pulled out the roll and showed it to her. The woman got angry. 'That is for the night,' she said to her.

'There will be more food at night,' Vineeta shouted at her. Then she spotted Arshad Ali sitting on the pavement smoking a beedi surveying the scene. She walked up to him briskly.

'Why are these women behaving like this?' she asked him.

'They always do,' said Ali dragging on his beedi.

She was truly angry. 'We have enough food to feed them all twice if they want to and they take food and hide it in bags. Why can't they go get food in a line? Would they behave like this if they were in a *baraat*? They would not,' she said to him. Then carried away by her anger she wanted to know why they were treating the agitation as if this was something that did not belong to them. She struggled to find a word for it. She did not want to say, 'as if this is their own function'. It was not a wedding party after all. 'Why are they behaving as if this is not a joint effort but as if they are here because they have been forced to come? Why are they behaving as if they have been hired to come here?' she asked furious at Ali's calm response.

Ali threw away the beedi he was smoking, got up in a huff, went to the side of the road where the public address system stood. Grabbing the mike he stormed into the middle of the road and said, 'You people who are distributing food, please stop the distribution.'

Then he began to harangue the crowd. 'Are you people beggars? Do you know these rich people in Delhi have got enough to feed you all for several months? What have you come here for? The food? Or the campaign? What impression are you leaving of your city? Are Bhopalis beggars? Or so poor anyone can pay them a few pennies and bring them here to raise slogans? So desperate that the moment they see food they forget the purpose of coming here? You are here to raise demands for justice, not to stuff your stomachs. I have just been asked if you have been hired to come here. Shame on you. You have shamed Bhopal. You have shamed our struggle. Now if you do not sit down properly to eat we will all board the train tonight and go back. You deserve the shabby treatment the court has meted out to you. The government, the court, Carbide – all of them have treated us like beggars and now you have proved them right.'

A hush fell on the crowd. Some women began trotting back to the pavement where they sat down wearied. Some began to feed their children. A plump woman got out from the crowd around the *degchi* and began trying to organize the crowd into a queue.

'If we start making a line to sit down we will be here eating till evening. Don't be stupid,' screamed a man at her. There were very few men among the agitators.

Vineeta turned away, tears in her eyes. Why did she have to throw such a fit about such a small thing? Why had she come here at all if she could not stand a little noise and disorder?

She walked across the road to the Law Institute and sat down on its steps. There were small groups of people in the narrow dusty strip of a lawn of the institute eating the cold food, a mix of potatoes and cauliflower yellow with turmeric, with the rotis serving as plates. The thick rotis were now cold and rubbery. This was their first meal of the day after hours of slogan-shouting. Their throats must be parched. They stood in queues waiting for their turn at the tanker for a few sips of water. Some had bottles to fill; most cupped their hands under the taps of the tanker. They had walked from the station to the Supreme Court after a night spent in an uncomfortable journey. Vineeta did not know that most of them had had no breakfast either, not even tea. She had shamed them when it was time for them to eat their first meal, a cold meal in this cold weather. The food distribution was now slack as the women got their food and scattered away. Ali's words had worked. But what a thing to be told? To be called beggars just when you held food in your palms.

Mortified and tearful, Vineeta thought she should go back home. Mukta was right, she was too stupid. She felt a hand on her shoulder and looked back. Latika stood behind her.

'Hi, you waiting here to use the loo? Go into the library. That one is clean. Most people do not know about it,' she said to Vineeta who shook her head.

Latika noticed her tears. She sat down next to her and asked her what had upset her. 'I am a very bad girl,' said Vineeta. Latika looked at her as if she was a little touched in the brain. Vineeta told her what had happened.

'So that was the reason for Ali to take off like that? Don't worry, these things happen in an agitation. Relax. Come, we must eat too, let us go to the canteen. That is where the Delhi people are,' Latika said to her.

Vineeta told her she would join them later.

'Cheer up. And chin up!' Latika said to her and left.

Vineeta was struck by this incongruity. Everyone said that the lives of people of Bhopal were as precious as the lives of Americans and here they were unequal even among their campaign comrades. The Delhi group was eating in the canteen, seated on chairs. The affected were out there on the road tearing at rubbery rotis. She went up to Ali who was smoking a beedi and said, 'Ali bhai, I am sorry. I should not have said what I did. Come let us eat.' Ali looked away. 'You are angry with me. I know that, but don't take it out on the food,' she said.

He pursed his lips and asked her to go away.

'Should I get some food for you too? I am going to get for myself,' Vineeta continued.

At this Ali looked at her. He lit another beedi. 'You go eat with your friends,' he said.

'We will eat together,' she told him. The crowd had thinned around the *degchis* but it parted the moment she arrived, not because they knew she had been responsible for what Ali had said to them, but because she was obviously middle class with a right to passage. She smiled futilely at their sullen faces, got the cold food from the *degchi*, carried it to Ali, and eating with him began to apologize again.

'Everybody thinks they are a burden,' he told her. 'It's not your fault. For the first year after the tragedy the government gave them free rations. They had to fight to get them. First they stood in a line at the hospitals, then they went and stood in a line for their rations. It was sickening. They were all people who lived with dignity, who worked, who had homes of their own. Then they became beggars. Everybody treats them as beggars. Carbide also thought that is what they are and gave them so little. It is not Carbide's fault. Our government also treats them like beggars. They all think, just throw a few rupees at them and that will be enough to shut them up. That is how things are.'

'I am from Bhopal,' Vineeta told him about the time she had been a volunteer. 'I never met you,' she said. Ali told her he had been very unwell for a whole year. He had joined the struggle later. They began talking about Bhopal. She told him she was here to do a course, feeling bad that she had to lie to him. 'You must come to our house. I am staying with Mukta,' she told him.

Memories of Bhopal came back to her. For as long as Vineeta could remember Bhopal had been a Carbide town. People took pride in that factory. It was big, its compound even bigger. It provided jobs to many, not just to those who worked inside it. There were many more who ferried their stuff in trucks and tempos. They drove their officers' cars. They rented their houses to Carbide officials. They did all sorts of things she did not even know about. They even talked about the effluent that flowed in the drains that burnt away suppurating sores. 'This company town will now die. The factory will shut down and thousands will lose their livelihoods,' her father had said after the gas leak.

She remembered how her father always compared Carbide with the BHEL complex near her house. To her it had all sounded so useless. 'BHEL has beautiful gardens people can take walks in. What does Carbide have?' he would ask the engineer who worked for Carbide and was a family friend. The engineer invited them to visit the factory and see the kind of machines and facilities they had. 'Just look at the building on Shimla Hill, our guest house, our research laboratory,' he would say. 'There is no building as beautiful as that one in all of Bhopal.'

Vineeta felt a sudden yearning for the hot sweet samosas of Bhopal and the *sabudana khichri* they sold on the road. You couldn't find such samosas anywhere in Delhi. Soon a woman joined them and introduced herself as Sumitra. They talked of New Market and the trees with red flowers, each one with an orange fringe. Nobody knew the names of those flowers but near the BHEL colony, there were rows and rows of those trees dripping vermilion when they were in bloom. Ali promised to find out and write to her.

Going up to CP with Hally in the late afternoon to get the press release photocopied Vineeta told him about what she had done. He looked at her with interest. 'You are very romantic,' he told her. 'You know what Nirmala said the first day we formed this group? She said this is their fight and we are only providing some support. We must be clear about that. We are doing what we honestly can.'

She felt uncomfortable. 'I am less idealistic than you people are,' she said and told him what she thought about their assertions of the equality between Indians and Americans.

'That is political equality. It is equality before the law. Even all Americans are not equal just in case you think they are,' he told her.

'You don't even eat with the victims...'

'Makes no sense falling ill. We can't afford to at the moment.'

Vineeta did not reply.

Chapter 14

ROMANCE AT WORK

Running a campaign is headier than rum and a relationship forged in the sweat and grime of politically loaded campaigns has a romance unequalled by roses and perfumes. Suguna had volunteered to help out in the logistical part of the campaign that few wanted to do. Her practical mind did not look down on money as filthy and unworthy of attention. She and Hally had begun making numerous trips to the small printing press in one of the dark lanes of Paharganj where hardly any sunlight penetrated.

'How do you manage to find your way in this maze?' she had once asked Hally. He told her he had grown up in the area.

Now they sat at an ink-stained table in the press under a naked light bulb watching the workers painstakingly assemble letters of the alphabet on the frame and gingerly pick out a single comma or a letter to be replaced with another after the proofs had been read, as two others wielded the machine that clamped on plain paper rhythmically, staining it with the carefully formed blocks. She was fascinated by the letter press that seemed like the blocks used for printing patterns on clothes. The smell of ink mingled with that of urine reeking from the lane outside made her sick till she became oblivious to it. She always refused the tea the press manager offered. She could not think of drinking anything in this stinking place. She and Hally read the proofs and sat talking while the corrections were being made.

'They should have magnifying glasses,' she told Hally. 'It is such tough work. Look at the thick glasses they wear. Must be going blind, all of them. Do you think they are paid minimum wages at least?'

Hally laughed.

After having seen them work Suguna's sympathy for people who complained of proofing errors in the leaflets went down.

With her pragmatic approach to life, Suguna had not expected to get along with Hally, who, she thought, was too idealistic. This was the first time they were working in such close proximity and Suguna was pleasantly surprised at the ease she felt working with him. For all his lofty talk he appeared to have his feet firmly planted on the ground and displayed no derision for people with less clarity of concepts.

She also made daily trips to Nizamuddin *basti* with Hally very early in the morning to order lunch. Ajit did not understand Hally's insistence on this. They could easily order food for a week. Hally said the vendors would slip up on the quality and cheat on the quantity if nobody checked on them. On the very first trip he understood the difference Suguna made to the work. She berated the vendor for not washing the vegetables properly. Then she bought a packet of salt and told him to wash the vegetables in salted water. 'If I find one worm in the vegetables I will get the food from somewhere else,' she told him.

'Worms from vegetables come to the surface if the water is salty. You get rid of most of them,' she explained to Hally on the way back.

She asked the man who baked the *khamiri* rotis why they went so rubbery.

'When they are cold they are like that,' the shopkeeper told her. 'We cannot keep them hot. The weather is cold.'

She asked Hally to think what they could do to keep the rotis warm.

'Wrap them in quilts,' said Hally to her laughing.

'Not a bad idea,' she replied seriously.

They waited till the market opened and bought two garishly coloured bed sheets and two shiny synthetic blankets, the cheapest ones.

'We can wash and keep them as campaign property to be used again,' she told Hally.

They had handed these to the tandoorwala and made him line his basket with the blanket first then cover the blanket with a sheet. The tandoorwala laughed at her which made her angry.

'I have brains. I use them,' she told him angrily. 'You probably burnt yours in the tandoor.'

Hally stepped in to ask the shopkeeper if it was too difficult to wrap the rotis the way she asked. 'If it is too much work, don't do it, we'll find someone else,' he said.

The shopkeeper said he was only joking '...but sister gets very angry.'

The rotis stayed a little warm and the ones deeper inside the blanket stayed the softest. She peered into the *degchi* to inspect the vegetable, stirring it with the long ladle to go beyond the thick layer of fat. Suguna then began testing the results. She never ate the food, for her digestion was delicate, but she would break off a tiny piece of the roti and chew on it.

Hally began looking forward to being with her early in the morning. In the beginning they met at the Nizamuddin bus stop walking into the *basti* behind it but three days into the campaign Hally began to meet her at the bus stop near her house in Patel Nagar. Suguna noticed this change but did not comment on it.

While Suguna was busy with these chores Avidha wrote and translated leaflets and kept clippings of the news reports about the campaign. Prashant kept his word and sent 5,000 rupees, wrapped inside some routine press releases and stuffed in an envelope that one of the peons from his office delivered to Avidha at her office.

That afternoon Ajit asked her, 'Who is this secret admirer of yours, Avi, who is being so generous?'

Avidha laughed. She felt nice that Prashant had not been miserly with his contribution. That contribution made her absurdly happy, as if he was by her side in the campaign though he never showed up there or called to ask her about the agitation. The Bhopal campaign had kept her from going insane with grief.

One morning Avidha woke up with an intense desire to hear his voice. It was a craving as physical as the craving for a cigarette she had after a day spent in forced abstinence. She went to the market and called his private number in office. She called again from another shop and then another. No luck. She left a message with his secretary. He did not call back. The secretary promised to pass on the message and told her he was away with the minister, in her office.

'What is up?' she asked, pretending professional interest.

'Routine things,' the secretary told her noncommittally.

Not wanting to arouse suspicion she later went from one office to another in her office building. She dialled his private number to avoid her number being identified in case they had some system of tracing the caller but replaced the receiver the moment the secretary answered the call. Mostly however, nobody answered. For sure he was not in the office. She tried till late in the evening and then gave up, went home giving FOB a miss, collapsed in bed, beating the pillow in deep despair and screaming loudly.

After that Avidha went to the dharna in front of the SC every afternoon. Suguna's and Avidha's parents came to the demonstrations on different days. Suguna's mother told her about the wild rumours floating around about the motives of the ruling party for having agreed to the settlement. 'They say the ruling party took a lot of money to finance its election campaign and paid some to the justices too. The more honest thing would have been to get more money and charge the victims a commission like touts do.'

Suguna's father warned her against saying such things in the open. 'You can't prove it, you know,' he said.

'There is no smoke without any fire,' said her mother.

Avidha wondered if Prashant would come by, out of curiosity, like the thousands of others who had come from all over the city to take a look at the impressive protest. Every time a white Ambassador car drove past she would look carefully at it. She threw herself into the campaign with unusual vigour. She spent at least half an hour in the dharna listening to the stories of lives shattered by the gas leak and began to feel that only the well-off had the luxury to mope like she had been doing.

She felt humbled when she saw the way in which the women and men from Bhopal put up with the many inconveniences of coming to Delhi in this cold weather. They sat the whole day shouting slogans, holding small marches on the road outside the court, up Tilak Marg and back to the gates of the court. They did not complain that the food was cold and their children were cold or ill. A steady stream of political leaders began to arrive to address the dharna.

Avidha's public speeches grew bolder by the day. She had begun by questioning the principles on which the settlement was based and progressed to questioning the motives of the court. What she could not put down in her articles she boldly stated in her speeches, naming the justices and the ruling party and its leaders who were responsible for negotiating the deal and claiming they were being or had already been rewarded handsomely.

The volunteers violated the prohibition imposed on the assembly of more than five persons with impunity. Every day, winding up her speech, she thought it would be her last for surely the administration would put a stop to it; they would be arrested or the court would send them a notice of contempt. Nothing of the sort happened. Avidha even began to complain against such inaction.

The question had been on everyone's lips. Why did the court permit them to abuse it openly? Was the ruling party, embattled by charges of corruption in a defence deal with a multinational arms manufacturer, waiting for the effervescence of this protest to die down?

'Why don't they arrest us? I have a very bad feeling about it,' she told Ajit one day when he asked her to tone down her allegations against the justices.

'The government is not acting because the judiciary is taking all the flak. Try targeting the PM and you will see what happens,' said Latika.

'That only means power is on our side at the moment. We can lose it, Avi, if you don't take care. Don't say things we can't prove,' Ajit cautioned, aware that she had begun naming the PM in her speeches.

That made no difference to her. Gradually the agitation began to impact her self-esteem. As crowds heard her out and clapped, and people struck up discussions with her on the issue, Avidha began to feel more confident.

The FOB meetings in market places stopped after a few days. They began to address more organized groups. Small teams went to colleges and to schools and eventually to trade union meetings at factories organized by the left parties where Avidha's speeches met with their greatest success. Nirmala accompanied her to these meetings and appealed to the workers to join in the protests. They strove hard to turn Bhopal into a workers' issue. The working class did not turn up in support of the agitation even though they called the union leaders several times to remind them that the campaign before the SC would not last forever.

That led to a loud discussion in the FOB where Latika forcefully advocated the need to mount a legal challenge to the settlement as the only way out of the impasse and not depend on the working classes to turn Bhopal into a wider issue of challenging industrial policy.

Hally scoffed at the unrealistic expectation of involving the working class with such an ad hoc approach. 'One speech and you think they will jump through hoops to support you. Get real. We have to work harder for that to happen,' he said.

Suguna found herself agreeing with him. She had not been very involved with the Bhopal issue but she was now attending FOB meetings with a regularity that matched her attendance in office. She waited for Hally to arrive and paid close attention to every contribution he made to the discussions.

In the middle of this two men from the telephone department landed at their door one morning and announced that they would install the telephone that day. Suguna asked Avidha to handle it for she had an appointment with Hally. They had ordered a fresh batch of pamphlets and she was going with him to pick them up.

'Why don't you say you want to see him? I can collect the pamphlets. You booked the phone, they might need your signature,' said Avidha.

Suguna smiled and said she would let her know if she got involved with Hally. 'You will see, I won't hide my man.'

As she and Hally walked through the winding narrow lanes towards the press she asked him directly, 'Tell me, are you going around with Nirmala?'

'As far as I know I am going around with you at the moment. Round and round the lanes of a city,' he said laughing.

'Basically, you are saying it is none of my business?' she asked.

'Basically, I am saying, I don't know what going around means. My English is not good,' he said.

Suguna laughed at that. 'I heard that you were sort of... close to Nirmala. That you and she are having an affair.'

Hally was quiet for a while.

'Sorry. There was no way of finding out except asking you, or asking her. I am not that close to her,' Suguna said.

He liked what she had implied about feeling close with him. He had been feeling the strong pull of her attraction for days now. 'I do not know if I want to call it an affair. That sounds so casual. We are very close even now. But that other part is over... the physical part, I mean,' he said. 'It never lasts with Nirmala. I have got over it too.' He was glad it was off his chest. In the speaking of those words he had shaken off the ashes of that pain.

Every time Avidha managed to push Prashant to the bottom of her mind something or the other brought him forcefully back. It was the phone this time. After two men spent hours fixing a telephone in her house and telling her that the line would take another ten days to work – after the file had shifted from their part of the office to another room where the worthies who controlled the lives and deaths of phone cables sat – they stood around congratulating her for having finally got a phone. Tired of her obtuseness, one of them brazenly asked her for 'chai pani'. Not wanting to delay the time when the phone line would spring to life Avidha gave them a hundred rupees. She seldom argued about minor bribes. Prashant, she knew, would have told her she shouldn't have tipped them. She knew how strong his views were on financial corruption. Had the phone been working she would have immediately had a vigorous argument with him.

To escape her drooping spirits she forced herself to go to the FOB meeting and ran into a harassed looking Mrs Kapoor who asked if Avidha worked for the government press. Any journalist accused of working for the government would feel humiliated, she told the old woman, who was flummoxed by this dismissal of a secure government job as a disgraceful one. The government press was only a printing press that published gazettes and results of board exams. It dawned on Avidha that Mrs Kapoor's misunderstanding of their employment had probably helped them rent her flat.

'Then you can't help me,' said Mrs Kapoor rather despondently.

Mrs Kapoor had a major problem on her hands. Her phone had been dead for nearly two weeks and she had been calling from the market every day to remind them to set it right. Today she had made a trip to the telephone office with her complaint and had been told that all the linemen were busy and that she was not the only one with a dead telephone. Half the city had filed complaints and they could not tell her when her phone would ring again.

'Is that all? Leave it to me,' Avidha said breezily.

To Mrs Kapoor's surprise her phone woke up with a shrill ring early next morning. The department called Mrs. Kapoor every morning for three days after that to check if her phone was working. The landlady was very impressed by her influential tenants and sent up a bowl of khir she had cooked the next day.

Chapter 15

RUMOUR OR TRUTH?

Shekhar Singh was filming the campaign to make a documentary. Every morning he would position his 35mm camera and would hope that he would get something more dramatic than slogan shouting. The funds had come too late for him to have recorded the sweeping of the Supreme Court. He and his assistant Radhika Garg interviewed survivors, identified after brief chats, to capture some personal emotions. They had identified Sumitra, one of the more vociferous protestors, for an interview and Radhika began, as always, by asking how it felt when the gas hit her.

'Get a packet of red chillies and stuff it into your eyes. All of it, *poora* packet, you will know how it felt,' said Sumitra Devi, nostrils flaring, lips pursed, turning away from the camera.

'Damn good shot,' Shekhar remarked from behind the camera poised like a bloated assault rifle. 'Try to get her to talk more.' Sumitra Devi refused to turn her face to the camera.

Shahina Khan, another protestor who was watching the interview, stepped in front of the camera without realizing what she was doing.

'They are only trying to find out how it felt, poor things. Why are you so angry?' she asked. Then she smiled pityingly at Radhika and said, 'It was like what she said. Like somebody had stuffed red chillies in our eyes.'

'Where do you come from? JP Nagar?' asked Radhika, deciding to interview Shahina instead.

'Is that the only place in Bhopal that was affected? Not Ibrahimpura? Kabit Pura? Jehangirabad? I live in Kabit Pura,' said Shahina.

'Where are these places?' asked Radhika.

'In Bhopal,' said Shahina and burst out laughing. She was a plump matronly woman. 'Do you see my stomach?' she said patting her voluminous abdomen. 'It is swollen with all the gas I swallowed that night. Then I began eating kilograms of pills, all kinds of tablets. That added to my health. Am I not healthy?'

'Don't laugh,' said Nasreen, another of the survivors pushing forth with her son Guddu in her arms. 'If these people want to interview anyone they should interview Ali bhai.'

But Shahina was warming up to the subject. 'You do a proper interview with me. Here, let me sit down near that tree. You should have a good background for the picture,' she said as she plonked herself under the tree by the roadside in front of the institute.

'You know, those Carbide people killed us on purpose. They were doing some experiment to see how many people that gas could kill. So they let out the gas and afterwards they took away the bodies,' said Shahina.

'They did?' asked Radhika. This was a new one, certainly. She had never heard of anyone from Carbide taking away dead bodies. In fact Radhika had no clear idea of what had happened in Bhopal and had been reading the leaflets avidly to educate herself.

'Yes, they did. They took many dead bodies inside the factory and cut them up. They did post-mortem to see how these people died. They are going to make weapons with the gas,' Shahina said assertively.

'Nobody stopped them from taking away the bodies?' asked an astounded Radhika.

'We were all in the hospital. Some had run away from Bhopal. There was nobody. All of them, the sarkar and the police and the big people, they are all with Carbide. So Carbide took away the bodies. They have big rooms in there, inside the factory, with air conditioners. They kept the bodies there to study. Later, they burnt them. We saw them burning the bodies. That is how we got to know that they had taken away many bodies,' said Shahina, feeling very important.

Radhika did not know how to proceed. There certainly was a theory of experimenting in chemical weapons, but the burning of bodies inside the factory premises sounded too outlandish to her.

'How do you know they were burning bodies? When did this happen? What did you see?' she asked disbelievingly.

Shahina took a deep breath. 'They burnt the bodies ten-fifteen days later. They burnt them inside the factory grounds. To make sure nobody could see what they were doing they draped the fence with lots of jute cloth. You know, cloth they make gunny bags with? We could not see what was going on inside. The whole press was there. They were also not allowed to go in. They stood outside. Nobody was allowed to go in.'

'So you could smell the bodies burning? That must have let out quite a stench,' asked Shekhar, intrigued by this narration.

'They had thought of everything. They had helicopters sprinkling perfume on the factory. Ask any press people who were there. You will know I am telling you the truth,' Shahina said, swelling with pride and throwing a challenging look at them.

Sumitra had wandered close to them and was watching the interview.

'Yes, they did. They killed us. They cut us up,' said Sumitra. 'This Shahina has no sense. Why are you laughing, you idiot?' she screamed all of a sudden. Then she began to gnash her teeth. 'They are all laughing at us. The Carbide people are laughing at us. I want to smash their teeth. They will never laugh again. They laugh. They are laughing,' she said repeatedly.

She sat down and began to hit her head on the ground. Alarmed, Shahina held her head and began rubbing her back vigorously. Radhika ran to fetch water for her. Sumitra began to wail loudly. A small crowd gathered around her. Mads arrived just as Radhika got back with a bottle of water.

'Let her breathe. Move away from her. Give her some space to breathe,' he said, pushing people out of the way. Shahina held the bottle to Sumitra's lips but she pushed away the bottle and said, 'We will smash their teeth. They killed my child. My little Kanta. They have no right to laugh. I want to smash their teeth,' she screamed.

'*Carbide ne kya kiya? Hazaron ko maar diya. Sarkar ne kya kiya? Katilon ka saath diya. Supreme Court ne kya kiya? Katilon ko chhod diya,*' rang out slogans from thousands of throats as the dharna began in earnest.

That evening in the meeting Radhika recounted what Shahina had said on camera. 'Listen, a lot of things happened in Bhopal. But this definitely did not happen,' said Latika.

'There must be some explanation,' insisted Zintac who also found the story difficult to believe.

Latika shrugged. 'Rumours, perhaps.'

'She gave details,' said Radhika recounting what Shahina had said about the draping of jute cloth and aerial perfume sprinklers.

'Now I get it. There is an explanation. I can explain this,' said Avidha.

'We have to discuss tomorrow's programme,' said Latika.

They argued about that for a while till someone realized they could spend the entire evening discussing the desirability of an explanation that would perhaps take much less time.

'It won't take much time,' said Avidha. 'The factory had three tanks full of MIC. After the gas leak, the authorities realized that the gas in the other tanks could leak too and must be neutralized. After much discussion the government decided that the best way out was to use it up to make Sevin. That was the brand name of the pesticide Carbide produced. There was a lot of panic about more accidents. You know, there was again an exodus from Bhopal.

'The government made elaborate arrangements to contain the leak if other tanks also exploded or the gas leaked. They draped gunny sacks on the fence. The whole administration stood by. The army was put on high alert. Water is supposed to neutralize MIC, so they doused the gunny sacks with water and the helicopters made their rounds sprinkling water as another precaution. I saw it all. I was there. It was quite a joke. The best part was it was called Operation Faith. You know what they did with the Sevin they produced? They gave it to Carbide. It was their property after all!' said Avidha winding up her explanation in less than five minutes.

'Very interesting. And people don't know all this? Shows that despite being so active in the struggle they are still ignorant. What does that say about those who are leading this struggle?' asked Suguna.

'Shows they know the truth. They may not know the facts. But they have grasped the truth, have they not?' asked Nirmala.

'Really?' asked Latika.

'People know that Carbide wanted information about how people died. The leak may or may not have been an experiment but the information is of great importance to them. It has implications for chemical warfare. Carbide was associated with the Manhattan project, was it not?' said Nirmala.

When the meeting broke up Nirmala asked Avidha if she would like to hop over to Bengali Market to eat something. 'I am starving,' she said and giving her no chance to reply she turned to Ajit for help. 'May I exploit your prosperity? Come drop us to Bengali market.'

'That is hardly exploitation, Nirma. I have been waiting so long for you to exploit me!' said Ajit. The double entendre was not lost on Nirmala who chose to ignore it.

In the sweet shop Nirmala ordered a dosa. Avidha stubbornly refused to order anything. 'I am feeling a bit queasy,' she said. Nirmala had always been the domineering one and Avidha generally gave in to her, even in little matters like choosing what to eat in a restaurant. This time when she suggested fresh fruit juice with lemon squeezed into it Avidha refused stubbornly.

'We used to be such good friends. What has gone wrong?' asked Nirmala coming straight to the point.

'Nothing,' Avidha looked away.

'Running away, Avi? When will you learn to deal with reality?'

Avidha squirmed. 'I am sick, really. Can we talk some other day?'

'You can't let criticism bother you so much. Do you expect me to apologize for it?' asked Nirmala, purposely to demolish any excuse she may begin making.

Avidha looked flummoxed. 'What criticism?'

'The things I said about your article. The one you wrote after Judge Keenan's order.'

Avidha began to laugh. That was such a long time ago. Nirmala had called her ignorant and had said that she should have called her or Mukta to understand the judgment before heaping praise on an American judge. 'Journalists do at least that much, talk to people. They hardly have anything original to say though they get the credit all the time. The byline is all the public remembers,' she had told her, face burning with anger.

Avidha had exploded at that. 'Spare me your blind anti-Americanism. You were the one who was opposed to taking the case to the US and now you can't stand the judge who sent it back to India. Do you even know what you want?' Nirmala and she had then had a real showdown. Nirmala had said that unthinking journalists misled people all the time. She had said that if intelligent people still read the papers it was because despite themselves reporters slipped in some information. 'I read the papers to entertain myself. To laugh at the ignorance of people like you,' she had added for good measure.

Avidha had asked her why activists needed journalists.

'To give them something to write about. Or how would they keep their jobs?' Nirmala had said, her voice dripping with sarcasm.

'Oh, stop doing us the favour,' Avidha had said. She had a healthy irreverence for the profession and could take swipes at it but Nirmala's comment had felt like an insult to the whole tribe of journalists. Journalists, she had pointed out, based their opinions on the sturdy foundation of facts and information, not on abstract ideas that Nirmala appeared to be so enamoured of.

'Had we not been around, doctors would have butchered patients with impunity. Between the media and the medical profession you are the more ignorant and the more unethical one,' she had shot back angrily.

'Hah! Journalists always have this arrogance of thinking they are changing the world. In fact they don't even record the changes accurately and properly.'

Avidha had forgotten many details but she still remembered how the fight had ended. She had eventually said to Nirmala with great fierceness, 'If journalists still go to activists despite all the contempt they face it is because journalists are better creatures, their hearts are in the right place.'

After a spell of speechlessness, just when Avidha was about to say sorry Nirmala had made her reply. Leaning very close to Avidha she had said, 'Let me tell you, it is not good intentions that change the world. It is an understanding of what governs self-interest and how to overcome it that changes the world. But how can a journalist understand that? They don't understand abstraction. They only understand examples. That is why they are always looking for a "story". A "story idea". Not for an idea. Never.'

Now Nirmala was bringing up that conversation to underline her ignorance. Avidha intensely disliked this habit of Nirmala of putting people in their place before opening a conversation.

'We will talk when we can get away from Bhopal,' she said sullenly losing her sudden urge to confide in her.

Chapter 16

WHAT WAS THIS CASE?

Like all spontaneous formations FOB revolved around an axis. A core group emerged and its members took all decisions that gave a definite shape and direction to the campaign. Sumitra's inventive elucidation of the neutralization of MIC prompted Ajit to ask Mukta to prepare a small presentation recounting the significant turns the case had taken.

The talk was to be held at the Law Institute. Mukta agreed reluctantly. 'There are so many differences in approach. I think we should take them all into account,' she told Ajit.

He refused to listen to her pleas. 'Don't confuse them. Just keep to the facts,' he had told her.

'The facts are what I am talking about,' Mukta hissed at him. 'There have been different approaches right from the beginning. There was the stand that India should never have gone to the US to file a case. That is a fact. What am I supposed to do with it?'

Ajit sighed. Some of these differences would have to be presented, else a question could derail the discussion. He asked her to decide.

Avidha was up past midnight translating the speech that Mukta was to deliver. Her respect for Mukta grew as she translated. 'I wish she was not such a sourpuss,' she said to Suguna.

On the day of the talk, Avidha was surprised to see Mukta trembling with nervousness as she walked to the podium. With an understanding as sharp as hers and the experience of arguing in courtrooms how she could be anxious escaped her comprehension. She took a seat in the front row and smiled in encouragement at Mukta.

'I am here to give you the facts of the case. There are many who wonder how the case came to be in the Supreme Court and was concluded so fast. So I will begin at the beginning,' said Mukta and sipped water from a glass, shuffled the papers before her and looked at the attentive faces in the room.

'I know all of you remember the terrible day in December 1984 when gas leaked from the Union Carbide of India Limited factory in Bhopal. But many things have happened and some details may escape memory. I am going to recount the main events so please bear with me. You can seek explanations or ask questions later. Avidha will tell you in Hindi what I am now going to say in English so those of you who can't follow English, please have patience.

'February 14, 1989, will go down as the most disgraceful day in the history of the Indian judiciary,' began Mukta. 'The settlement order that the Supreme Court passed that day has been condemned all round as a sell-out and a betrayal of the people of India.

'We all know what happened that day. The survivors of Bhopal are incensed that they had not even been consulted before their rights and the rights of their unborn children were bartered away by the one agency they looked up to, the judiciary.'

She suddenly realized that she was extemporizing. She would try now to keep to the written text for she knew Avidha was to read out a translation.

'On the night of December 2–3, 1984, a few tonnes of poisonous gases leaked from the UCIL factory in Bhopal. UCIL is a subsidiary unit of the multinational Union Carbide Corporation. The Indian Government was, and is, part owner of the UCIL factory. Thousands died that night and in the following days. There are at least two opinions and two hypotheses about everything that happened in Bhopal from that night onwards.

'Within two days of the gas leak many American lawyers came to India. Nobody respects these lawyers much even in their own country. They are known as ambulance-chasers there. Whenever there is an accident these lawyers follow ambulances carrying victims to sign them up as clients. They charge no fees, they bear all expenses and if they manage to get compensation they take a third of the amount as their fees.

'Many such lawyers signed up people in Bhopal as their clients. In fact, the first case against UCC was filed in USA on December 7, 1984, only four days after the gas leak, by one of these lawyers. Later many of them filed cases in 145 different courts in the United States representing over five lakh victims. They asked for over a billion dollars as compensation.'

Mukta suddenly spotted Vineeta sitting at the back with Ali smiling at her very happily. Mukta smiled back at her and waved to Ali.

'In January 1985 all these cases were bunched together and handed over to the District Court in New York. This was the court of Judge Keenan who is now as famous as Warren Anderson. These American lawyers were in no position to fight a giant multinational and possibly did not even want a trial. They wanted an out-of-court settlement so that they could pocket their commission. To prove that UCC was directly responsible for the accident or that it was a case of sabotage was not an easy task.

'In India the Central Bureau of Investigation began investigations on December 3, 1984, the morning after the gas leak. It was and still is a highly complex case and the evidence too is very complex. We needed to prove that Union Carbide Corporation was responsible for the design of the factory and was therefore directly responsible for the accident. Only then could we launch civil cases against the corporation for compensation. Otherwise we would have to fight cases against UCIL alone.

'It is also a fact that most survivors of Bhopal do not have the resources to fight a multinational like Carbide. Besides, in India, we don't have a law under which all these victims could file a single case. Each individual would have to sue Carbide separately. Courts would have to try at least two lakh cases. All in all, the situation was unimaginably bad.

'Something had to be done to meet this unprecedented challenge. A new law was required to consolidate all the cases. So the Union Government passed the Bhopal Gas Disaster (Claims Processing) Act in March 1985. I will call it the Bhopal Act.

'The Bhopal Act made the Government of India the one and only representative of those who died or were injured by the gas leak. It made it impossible for victims themselves to file cases against Carbide. There were two opinions about the Act.

'One lobby said the government had no right to become the sole arbitrator. This lobby said the constitution gives citizens the right to nominate their representatives and the government had abrogated that right. They challenged the Bhopal Act in the Supreme Court questioning its constitutionality. That case has still not been decided. Carbide did not challenge this Act though. It accepted the Indian government as the one and only representative of the victims. The other lobby said even if there had been some curtailment of citizens' rights, it was necessary. The numbers affected were huge. The amount of compensation would be massive and its distribution would be a tough challenge. Only the government was capable of handling all these tasks.

'In April 1985 the Indian Government filed a civil case for compensation against UCC in the court of Judge Keenan as the sole representative of victims. It asked for three billion dollars as compensation.

'Again there were at least two opinions on this move. Some said the government had brought shame to the Indian judiciary by openly stating that we were incapable of handling the case. Others said only American courts could try UCC and do it fast enough before all the survivors died of old age and illness.

'The government gave three arguments in favour of going to a US court. One, it said that the Indian law of torts was too undeveloped to handle a case of this magnitude. Two, it argued that the judicial system in India is very slow and would not be able to deliver justice speedily. Three, it said that UCC was responsible for the design of the UCIL factory in Bhopal and all the evidence is in the US. Since UCC was not subject to the jurisdiction of Indian courts India wanted to fight the case in the US to get to the evidence. The evidence involves the processes of production and storage of hazardous chemicals, complicated technological safety systems and standards of safety and their monitoring. The CBI wanted to examine all the evidence to determine UCC's responsibility. India was trying to prove that UCC's corporate policy had led to the disaster, not just the working or non-working of its subsidiary in India.

'In July 1985 UCC asked the court to dismiss the case in the US on grounds of *forum inconveniens*. What it meant was that the accident had taken place in India and the US was not the right forum to fight the case. UCC provided affidavits of some of our best legal brains to support its argument that Indian lawyers and judges were capable and creative enough to meet any challenge.'

Mukta paused. Was this getting too heavy? She turned to Ajit with a questioning look. He was listening to her with deep concentration and asked her if she wanted a glass of water.

'I hope this hasn't become too heavy,' said Mukta uncertainly.

'No, of course not. Please continue,' said Latika who already knew all this about the case but was impressed by the way Mukta was presenting it, sidestepping all the intense arguments that had accompanied each stage of the struggle.

'Some highly respected constitutional experts of India told Keenan's court that Indian lawyers and judiciary would handle the case very well,' resumed Mukta. 'They did not tell Judge Keenan that the Bhopal Act had itself been challenged in the Supreme Court in India. They kept quiet about legal procedures that make it possible for lawyers to drag cases for decades.

'Judge Keenan also did not want the case to be tried in the

US. There are many opinions about why this was so. Some say that American courts could not have awarded low levels of compensation because they would have been lambasted for double standards. International pressure then was very high. Even in the US people were supporting the struggle of Bhopal survivors.

'It was also said that trying UCC in the US would be a political blunder. It meant making American multinationals answerable in the US for their acts overseas. American multinationals have subsidiaries operating in many of the less-developed countries. If they did something there and their parent corporations were hauled up before American courts they would suffer heavy losses to their pockets and to their reputations. Sometimes what these corporations do in other countries is, strictly speaking, not illegal in those countries. In the Bhopal case, for instance, India had permitted Carbide to bring and store MIC in huge quantities. Carbide would not be allowed to do this in the US. It is not allowed to do so in France. So why should they answer to an American court? This was not acceptable to US multinationals or even US courts. Another argument was US courts would not be able to compute the value of Indian life.

'The judgment that Judge Keenan delivered makes it clear that he did not want to try the case in the US. He could not dismiss the case. That would have led to an uproar and tarnished the image of the American judiciary. He first tried to work out an out-of-court settlement.

'You won't believe it but UCC offered only 100 million dollars in the beginning. It had to raise the amount later. At one point a settlement was nearly reached and UCC agreed to pay 350 million dollars but the Indian government refused to accept it.

'When it became clear that a settlement would not come about, Judge Keenan passed an order in May 1986. It has been lauded as a great piece of penmanship. I think everyone must read it for its beautiful prose. He said that the Indian judiciary should not be denied an opportunity of standing tall before the world and passing an order on behalf of her people. He said he had full faith in the judicial system of India. He also pointed out that to try the case in the US would be an act of imperialism. It was so well written that even some well-intentioned people in India were mesmerized by it.'

Avidha felt her face beginning to burn. She had showered praise on the order and had asserted that the American judge was far more alert to imperialism than the government of a former colony like India that had defamed its own judiciary in an American court. She looked at Nirmala, who was sitting at the back on one of the tables, trying to catch her eye. Nirmala however was looking at Mukta and did not turn towards her. Avidha felt a sharp pang thinking she was deliberately avoiding her. Nirmala definitely did not need to listen to Mukta's speech to refresh her memory.

'He sent the case back to India,' Mukta continued, 'with some conditions. One, he made UCC subject to India's jurisdiction and said that UCC must give India access to documents, etc., meaning evidence. This was the only gain we had from the case we filed in the US. Otherwise UCC was under no compulsion to obey any of our court orders or summons or produce any documents.

'However Judge Keenan also laid down the condition that the Indian courts would have to satisfy minimum standards of due process.

'I won't go into the details of what is meant by due process. I don't know it so well either. In the US they have

something called the "due process" of law and something
they call "discovery process". It relates to the way evidence is
presented. There, the prosecution has to give all the evidence
to the defence so that they have a fair chance to rebut it.
In India we do this differently. We have something called
the procedure laid down by law. So here we have to follow
rules laid down when presenting evidence. When Judge
Keenan laid down the condition that Indian courts must meet
minimum standards of due process, that was also imperialism
but nobody noticed this contradiction.

'Two, Judge Keenan also said that Carbide could file an
appeal against any decision of the Indian courts in the US if
due process was violated. What this means is he was willing
to safeguard a multinational's interests in the US for acts of
omission and commission overseas but he was not willing to
protect the rights of people overseas so brutally victimized by
an American corporation.

'In May 1986 the case came back to India.

'In September that year, the Indian government filed a
case in the district court of Bhopal against UCC. Mind you,
this was not a case against UCIL. This was a civil case filed
for compensation and punitive damages against UCC, the
parent corporation. We had already lost about two years by
then. The condition of the victims was worsening and many
more had died.

'We all know that the case would drag for decades. So a
group of survivors asked the trial court in Bhopal to order
Carbide to shell out some money as interim relief. That
amount could be adjusted against the final amount later.

'In December 1987, district court judge W. Deo in Bhopal
ordered Carbide to pay Rs 350 crore as interim relief.
Carbide challenged that order in the High Court on some

technical grounds and said many objectionable things against the judge.

'Carbide said that Judge Deo's order to pay before the trial was over was equivalent to declaring Carbide guilty before trial and said that the judge was biased and he should no longer try the case. The Jabalpur Bench of the MP High Court ruled that the lower court had the power and the right to order payment of interim relief. The High Court then ordered that interim relief be paid but it reduced the amount to 25 crore rupees. The government filed a case of contempt against Carbide and its lawyer. Carbide simply refused to obey the High Court's order. Its officials made statements in the US saying they wouldn't pay and the Indian courts could do nothing, they were powerless before them.

'Carbide then came to the Supreme Court in appeal against the High Court's order. The whole case was not before it. We must always remember that the civil case for compensation was not before the Supreme Court. The criminal cases against Carbide officials were also not before the Supreme Court. It also did not stay the order of the High Court to pay interim relief. Carbide did not even ask for such a stay order.

'All of you who wonder why this court,' she said pointing backwards, in the direction of the Supreme Court, 'has not hauled us up for contempt must remember that Carbide is guilty of contempt of court but the SC has been hearing it patiently.'

She paused as the assembly broke into shouts of 'shame, shame'.

'Okay, to continue, from November 1988 the Supreme Court began hearing the appeal on a daily basis,' said Mukta. 'Of course, behind the scenes, the SC was trying to reach an out-of-court settlement. That settlement was read out after lunch break on February 14 and that is what we are protesting against. That is where we stand today.

'There are many questions that remain to be answered now. Why did the SC transfer all criminal cases against Carbide and quash them? And what was the need to extinguish future liabilities? And why now?

'There will be many hypotheses about the hows and the whys. Whether any of these hypotheses can be or will be proven is for the future to tell. Perhaps we shall never know the truth. Perhaps we shall never know why and how this happened. We shall all make our guesses. For the truth goes beyond facts. The motivations and intentions of all the people involved are intangible but are an integral part of the truth. It is not for me to go into them here. A lot is being said in the press. A lot more is being said on the streets.'

Mukta realized she was digressing again. She took a deep breath to calm her nerves.

'My job here was to recount only the case facts in brief. There are only two more facts that I want to mention here.

'Many are asking why and how the court settled on this amount of 470 million dollars? As one of our members of Parliament has pointed out in the Lok Sabha, UCC is insured for 350 million dollars and that is what it had offered to settle the case for earlier. Now it has only added interest to that amount and that has brought the sum to 420 million dollars. The other 50 million has to be paid by UCIL.

'Another fact that I want to mention here is even more interesting. CBI had applied for permission to examine the UCC plant in Virginia and inspect their documents. On February 13, 1989, just a day before the settlement was ordered, that permission was finally granted. CBI was to go to the US to examine the evidence. Now it won't go there. The case has been "finally decided".

'Technically speaking, UCC is no longer subject to the jurisdiction of the Indian judiciary because Judge Keenan had made it submit to Indian courts only till the full and final decision has been made.

'Of course, the way this case has been decided violates due process but UCC is not going to rush to an American court to crib about it.'

There was a wave of laughter and the tension broke.

'Finally,' said Mukta, 'I come to the question that has been haunting us all for days now. If this is the full and final decision what can be done now except lobby our Parliament to impeach some of the justices? Is there any way to have this settlement cancelled?

'We have to evolve a consensus and decide. In a recent judgment the SC said that if a verdict is patently unfair and amounts to denial of justice it can be reviewed. The SC can open the question again. We can go to the same court again. Somehow we must unsettle the settlement. How to go about it is something we shall decide. Thank you.'

Mukta sat down with relief. There was no applause. The meeting was thrown open for a discussion but there were not many questions. 'Okay,' said Ajit, 'if people want to ruminate and get back with their suggestions, no problems. There is time to formulate a strategy.'

'We shall overcome,' said someone and some broke into that famed song.

'Shall we?' asked Nirmala as she walked up to where Mukta and Avidha stood near the podium.

Mukta shrugged. She was suddenly aware of Vineeta beside her.

'That was such a good speech you made,' Vineeta said, pride dripping from her eyes.

Mukta knew she was about to tell her how sorry she had been about her views. Acutely embarrassed by the adulation visible in her eyes she quickly turned away to find Zintac approaching her. The bubbly girl looked unusually subdued and disturbed.

'What I can't understand is, didn't the Supreme Court *see* all this? I mean you can see it, now we can also see it, why could the SC not see it? It had to meet such a historic challenge, it failed the survivors. It failed us, who trusted it so much. But what bothers me is, it failed itself, its own image and reputation. Did it not?' asked Zintac.

Mukta said, 'Don't ask me how it could do it. The Supreme Court has philosophical powers.'

Nirmala overheard the conversation. 'How well put, Mukta. We will have to answer philosophy with philosophy.'

Chapter 17

THE SMUTTY HANDS OF REALITY

Mukta and Vineeta left the group soon after the meeting broke up, refusing Ajit's offer for a lift home. Mukta had noticed that he had not spoken to Vineeta at all while they were all hanging around near the podium.

Vineeta did not give her a chance to talk about it. 'You were wonderful. I did not even know anything about the case, you know, and I just feel that I was so wrong,' said Vineeta to Mukta, hugging her thin arm close to her breasts.

'Stop being so effusive in public,' admonished Mukta, smiling with pleasure.

That night they went out to dinner, both hanging out around Connaught Place and tucking into Chinese food. That was Mukta's definition of a good dinner – greasy noodles and mutton balls.

When they got back home Vineeta went to the bathroom to turn on the geyser. 'We must first have a bath,' she said.

'We will, after we have sweated a little more,' said Mukta, kissing Vineeta full on the lips. They sank onto the sofa pawing each other and giggling. Mukta began to undress her slowly, stripping off her kurta then taking off her bra. She ran a light finger down her midriff close to the skin but not quite touching it. Vineeta turned, and taking off Mukta's shirt, bent to kiss the back of her shoulders, then jumping up she said, 'Eek, salty. I need that bath,' and ran into the bathroom turning on the shower.

'Wait for me,' Mukta called after her and throwing off her trousers she joined her under the shower. They giggled as they soaped each other and Mukta pinched Vineeta's breasts hard. They stepped out dripping wet into the bedroom.

'Don't wet my clean sheet, pleeease...' said Vineeta as she grabbed an extra large towel. She threw the towel around Mukta and drew the ends to pull her into her own dripping body in one deft move. They danced inside the towel and out of it falling on the bed and on each other laughing till deep throated moans took over.

As her body pulsated with contentment, Vineeta began to shiver. She hugged Mukta close and as her consciousness emerged from the deep forgetfulness of bliss, her being expanded, radiating out into space, light and soaring, and as her breathing returned to its normal pace she found herself crying. The memory of that other time when she had left her body to escape from the egotism of the male organ sent a shudder through her.

'What is it, Viny, what...?' asked Mukta pulling up the quilt.

'Don't ever leave me.'

The next morning the phone trilled shrilly. Avidha took the call. The telephone department was calling to tell them their instrument could now be used. Their line had started working. Suguna was out on her morning errands.

Avidha dialled Prashant's office. She caught him in.

'Hey, how are you, busy babu?' she said cheerily.

'What a surprise, free of the campaign?' he asked.

'Why? You planning anything special?'

'No. You must be very busy,' he said.

'Not too busy if someone really wants to meet me,' she replied.

'Not now, am overworked, not even getting enough sleep,' he said.

'No time even to meet the press?' she asked half jokingly, feeling sick at being rebuffed again.

'Anything special you calling about?'

'I thought everything I said was special. Sometimes you should also say something special,' she complained.

'I am busy. Can I call later?' he asked

'When?' she asked almost as a reflex.

'I don't know when,' he sounded annoyed.

'I have a feeling something is wrong,' she said dropping the pretence of normalcy.

'Nothing is wrong. Listen, I have to go.'

'Where?' The word slipped off her tongue before she could check herself.

'Somewhere,' he said testily and banged the phone on her.

Avidha detested the responsibility thrust upon her to respect an institution she did not believe in and yet she saw herself as an encroacher in his marriage. Encroachers, she knew, have no right to complain. The denial of this right was her punishment to herself. For him to punish her for it was unbearable.

Avidha had gone to her assignation with him determined to get squatter's rights or threaten to walk out.

He had evicted her.

This power she had given him began to haunt her and she thrashed about to find some way to avenge the humiliation.

Two days later she dialled his number again promising herself she would disconnect if he picked up. She got his secretary who told her he was out.

'Out of station?' she asked him.

'No, he is in Delhi,' the secretary told her. He promised to pass on her message, that she wanted to discuss the Bhopal issue. Prashant did not return the call.

Avidha thought of going to his office and confronting him. She could call his home and insist on talking to him. She did not do so, not only out of her sense of self-respect but also because she did not want to get him into trouble. She told herself that if only she could have a normal conversation with him just once, she would put him out of her mind.

Chapter 18

A DEMONSTRATION GONE WRONG

It was the day of the final demonstration of the campaign which had continued unabated for three weeks now, the grand finale of the first phase. It was the first programme they had formally informed the police about. The day chosen was International Women's Day and most women's groups in Delhi had decided to make Bhopal the theme of their protests that day.

Nobody thought that the rally on Parliament Street would end the campaign but the symbolic move from the judiciary to the representatives of the people was a good way to make a grand show before moving on to the next phase. The people from Bhopal were to leave Delhi after this march, handing the baton over to the FOB.

The fight had come to Delhi.

Avidha had accompanied Ajit, Hally and Nirmala to meetings with three members of Parliament to explore the possibility of the Supreme Challenger addressing them.

In a press briefing by the Supreme Challenger Avidha had asked him for his views on the settlement and he had replied with a glum face, 'People are saying everything that has to be said. What can I add to it? I am not shocked. I had not expected anything better of this government.' Avidha had asked repeatedly if he would, someday, address the survivors but the Supreme Challenger had only smiled vaguely. 'We will see. I have many engagements to keep.' Avidha was disappointed. Ajit asked her to have patience. Leaders of his stature had to consider many things before making a commitment, he said. Many leaders of his new party had come to make speeches to the survivors earlier and were to attend this rally too.

For three days the FOB had been in a tizzy. A petition to MPs, a booklet detailing the judgment and its flaws, banners, placards and cameras were all readied in their arsenal to be aimed at the insulated portals of those who exercised sovereignty. Protestors assembled outside the SC around ten in the morning as usual and headed out from there.

Springing surprises had become the style of FOB and the main contributor to the campaign's success. Descending on a marketplace to start speeches, unexpectedly starting a play on the street lampooning judges and ministers and hanging an effigy labelled 'Carbide' with a tall hat painted in stars and stripes had prevented the protest from becoming a monotonous display of angry faces and fists.

The success of the campaign eventually resounded in the Supreme Court. A judge from the bench that had sanctified the settlement as an order of the court had nearly wept complaining that people were dragging their names through mud on the streets and nobody had stood up to protect the dignity of the court. The protestors had been thrilled when they read the report in the press and several placards proclaimed their response to the complaint.

'Deserve the dignity before you demand it, Supreme Court!' said one placard in bold black letters emblazoned under a cartoon of the bench with five judges wringing their hands.

The FOB was not going to give up its style. A small part of the demonstration had been kept from the police and the larger numbers of protestors. It was the last surprise the campaign was to spring. The few who were into the secret knew they would not have much time to enact the script. The flabbergasted police would stand by only for a few minutes before pushing them back. Shekhar had even hired an extra portable video camera to capture that action.

The march began as a thick column from Tilak Marg and came winding down Connaught Place. No march to Parliament coming up from the Regal building ever went to the right. They all naturally turned left towards the Constitution Club or stopped just short of Patel Chowk. The police marched alongside complacent and inattentive.

A straw effigy with a hat of stars and stripes and 'Carbide' scrawled on it in big red letters passed from hand to hand from the middle of the demonstration to the head of the rally where Avidha, Suguna, Zintac, Mads, Hally, Sumitra and Nasreen walked together. As the line moved onto Patel Chowk on Parliament Street some protestors in the first few rows quickened their pace and turned into a lane on their right.

They marched briskly and stood before a building with plate glass doors. A small brass plate on the side of the door, almost unnoticeable, proclaimed it the head office of Union Carbide. The protest outside the Carbide office was the element of surprise today. They had planned to burn the effigy outside its doors.

Nobody later remembered how it happened or who began it all. In one moment the accumulated rage against the corporate house crystallized into a defiance of the law that had failed them. Someone stepped to the doors of the building and pushed. They were not locked, not even bolted from the inside – the corporation felt secure even amid the fury against it for weeks now.

The crowd pushed against the glass-fronted office.

'Carbide, *Bharat chhodo*,' a thundering slogan rippled through the wave bringing with it the power to crash the facade of indifference that faced them.

'Quit India,' said someone at the top of his voice.

In one single move the protestors rushed inside. They scattered into the rooms confronted by people typing, writing and carrying files. Avidha and Zintac walked into a room and into the petrified faces of three clerks, who scrambled to their feet. What were they doing here, inside this building where they did not belong? What were they to do now? They stood flummoxed. There was no plan to follow now. Her right arm swinging upwards with the fist waving into the high ceiling, Zintac screamed 'Carbide *murdabad*' into the terrified faces of the clerks.

People behind her took up the cue and began moving from room to room, shouting slogans. They did not touch any paper or file, they simply walked through the rooms raising slogans. A few press photographers chased them from room to room. Shekhar, taken aback by this new development, ran after them, his camera shaking in his unsteady hands.

In a trice the office was empty as the employees fled from a back door. The wave scattered into the maze of rooms, going from one to another, meeting no challenge to its occupation and finding nothing to do. Someone had dropped a pile of files and paper lay strewn on the floors, spilling out of file covers. Papers were stuck under rollers of typewriters. On one table a pen stand had been upset and Shahina watched as a ball point rolled down to the floor unhindered.

Someone said, 'Out, everyone, out.'

At that moment they heard the sound of glass shattering. Once. Then again, and again. All the protestors were now streaming towards the main door as if the sound of breaking glass heralded the end of the scene. The crowd that had dispersed was back in its form, like an amoeba pulling back its pseudopods to roll out into the street. They were brought up short in the lobby strewn with shards and watched transfixed as a stone came tracing a trajectory from outside, hit the glass pane and shattered another part of it. More shards joined the ones lying on the floor.

'Stop,' shouted Suguna as she ran out unmindful of the broken pieces of glass on the floor. Mads was standing outside, face contorted with fury. Nasreen was gnashing her teeth as Guddu by her side laughed and clapped gleefully. Three other women were waving their fists at the broken doors. One was almost frothing at the mouth. Mads was about to hurl another stone when Suguna pushed him back with all her might.

'Run,' said Sumitra stepping out of the office building as the first policeman came charging up the lane waving his lathi. The crowd stepped out gingerly trying not to step on the glass, crunching some of the smaller pieces under their feet.

Hally ran up behind Mads, threw his arms around his chest in a vice-like grip and began pulling him back, his hands flailing. The police had arrived in full force. The crowd got out of the building as Mads broke free but he was now hemmed in by a large group of protestors who had come into the lane to get them back onto Parliament Street.

'Someone check to see if everyone is out,' shouted Suguna to Nirmala who was running up the lane towards the office. She had not come into the lane with them despite being aware of the plan to hold a protest outside the office of Carbide.

'Get back, all of you,' shouted Nirmala and ran into the office building to check if any of the protestors remained inside. She came back within minutes. The office was strangely empty of human presence.

Outside the slogan shouting had stopped. All the slogans were over for the day.

The small group of protestors in the lane were still angry and trying desperately to shake off the arms pushing them towards the main road as the police surrounded them and began beating them. Guddu, separated from his mother, began to cry loudly as Nirmala pulled Nasreen away. Suguna scooped him up in her arms and began running towards Parliament Street. Strangely, even the street was now empty. The protestors were nowhere to be seen.

'Walk towards VP house,' someone was saying. The police had lined the road on both sides and were obviously waiting for reinforcements. '*Chalo*,' screamed a constable at Suguna, prodding her back with his lathi as she looked back to check if everyone had got out. She saw Hally coming up to her. 'Don't stop,' he said to her and grabbing her by the arm he began walking up to the other side of the road. This was well known territory for her. Her office was on the road that ran behind the Parliament Street.

Avidha and Zintac walked steadily towards the IENS building. 'Don't run. Walk confidently and if the police stop you, just say "Press". They won't touch us,' said Avidha to

Zintac, who kept turning to look if the others were following. The road was full of khaki uniforms. Guddu was beating his fists on Suguna's shoulders, arching his back, trying to get out of her grip. She struggled to hold onto him.

They emerged on Rafi Marg and into the huge crowd of protestors clashing with the police outside the VP House. The police was raining vicious blows on the protestors, not caring whom their lathis hit and where. Suguna's back ached with the weight of Guddu. She had thought of setting him down near her office but the police action made that impossible.

'This is just wonderful. Finally we make more news. No danger of being thrown onto the sixth page,' said Avidha to Zintac unsure whether to get inside her office building or join the protestors being thrashed by the police.

Suguna came up to them and told Avidha she was taking Guddu to her office and would bring him later to the house on Sikandra Road. 'Try getting the children into the IENS lawns,' she was saying when Zintac crossed the road to merge with the swirling crowd.

That was when Avidha spotted Mads, to one side of the crowd, lying on the ground curled up in a foetal position, hands covering his head in an ineffectual attempt to protect it from the lathis of two policemen who were beating him up mercilessly. He slithered on the road, sliding away from the cane of one only to run into the other's lathi. 'Stop,' screamed Avidha sprinting and trying to pull one of the policemen away. She tried tugging at his arm but he moved with the speed of lightning dragging her with him.

'Stop it, please,' she screamed trying to make herself heard in the roar of wails and screams. She began pleading with the policemen as Mads rolled on the road trying to duck the blows of the two constables who pounded him on the hips, spine and the head. Mads was trying to say something to her. She could not hear what it was. She did not know why they were paying special attention to beating him to a pulp. Avidha could not see anyone else singled out like this, only a general charge of the lathis as the police beat the crowd back although what they were beating them back from was not clear.

'Why are you beating him like this? You will split his head. He can die. Please stop,' she said repeatedly, her heart palpitating with fear. In response the constable raised his lathi aiming at the back of Mads' head. Avidha sprang up and clamped her teeth on the policeman's arm, biting him hard.

He spun round on her. 'What are you doing?' he shouted at her, rubbing the spot with his other hand.

'And what are you doing?' she screamed back. The other constable noticing his colleague's scuffle with the girl was distracted for a moment and Mads took advantage of the break in the beating to run for his life. Avidha knew it was now her turn to be thrashed. She turned to run away but the other constable yanked her back by her hair. She whelped in agony. Ajit, spotting this scene, rushed to her rescue.

'How dare you?' he asked the constable pushing him aside with grave authority.

'Do you know what she has done?' asked the policemen.

'I don't care. You have no right to touch women,' he said to him.

Avidha was now in the middle of the crowd where Latika was talking to a police officer, who seemed to be in charge, pleading with him to either let them go or arrest them. 'Stop this brutality and arrest us decently. Take us to the police station. You have no right to beat us,' she was saying. 'You probably don't know but today is International Women's Day,' she added for effect.

The officer looked distinctly unimpressed.

Harjit joined in her appeal as three blue police buses drove up the road and parked in front of them. Nirmala came up to them and dragged Harjit away. 'Are you two crazy?' she asked. 'There are women here with children. What if the police files cases against them? Do you understand the consequences? We don't want to be arrested. Ask the women to run away.'

She had been going around taking women aside and asking them to vanish but there was hardly anywhere to go. Some had run inside the lawns of the VP house but they were highly visible in their cheap nylon saris and their children in dirty brown and mustard-yellow sweaters. They did not belong here. Many did not know their way around and did not know how to get to the gurudwara that had been their shelter for two weeks now. Nirmala had asked them to assemble at the back of the building and wait there.

Harjit saw sense in Nirmala's argument. 'We can talk the police into letting them go once we are in the police station,' he said to her. But there was no time to argue things out. Events were now out of their control.

The posse of police that had surrounded the crowd now moved purposefully, cutting off possible exit routes, rounding them up and leading them into the waiting buses.

'We are being arrested,' said Latika as Nasreen came up to her, tears streaming down her cheeks. 'Please don't arrest me, I have lost my child,' she said to a constable who prodded her with his lathi. Nobody was listening to anyone. Zintac was in another bus with Avidha and they were craning out of the bus windows to look for Nasreen. They spotted her too late, as their bus began to move away.

They were herded into the compound of the police station on Parliament Street and when all of them were in, the iron gates clanged shut on them. A police constable came in and asked them to sit down on the floor quietly. 'I have to count all of you,' he told them.

'Don't give them your real names or addresses,' Harjit whispered to Sumitra. The whisper began to go round. It was tough for all of them to think up other names and most of them gave their real ones to the police. Harjit himself could not have hidden his identity.

Avidha made her way to Nasreen and told her Guddu was safe. Nasreen wiped her tears with her pallu and hugged her.

'I am so tired,' she said to Avidha.

A hush fell on the people in custody after a while and some began to doze off. After two hours of sullen silence Harjit went up to the iron gate and shook it. The chain that held the gates together with a padlock suspended from it rattled loudly, bringing a sub-inspector to the gate.

'You have not even given us tea,' complained Harjit. He knew that the police owed them that. In fact they owed them some snacks too. That was the rule. They had marched the whole day and everyone was thirsty and hungry.

'We have just called the Kanishka hotel for tea,' said the sub-inspector.

'Order some sandwiches too,' retorted Harjit.

They were let off after five in the afternoon charged with nothing more than violation of Section 144 that entailed a detention of a few hours or being taken to a place far from the site of the prohibited assembly and let off.

'You are under an obligation to drop us in your buses,' Harjit told the sub-inspector.

'When I want a refresher course I will come to you for training,' said the sub-inspector who seemed to specialize in sarcasm.

Most of the women from Bhopal went back to the gurudwara. Only Nasreen and Sumitra went to Sikandra Road with the others from Delhi to fetch Guddu. However, when they reached the house Suguna had not arrived. They sat in the lawn to wait for her. Sumitra was calmer today.

The moment Harjit reached home, he rushed to the kitchen to issue orders for tea and sent out a servant to fetch samosas. Mukta asked Nasreen if she knew about the plan to stone the office. She had marched up to the Carbide office but had refrained from entering the building.

'Was it planned?' Nasreen asked.

'Well, planned or not, was it right to do it? Should you have done it?'

'I don't know what happened,' she said. 'I was so angry when I saw that office. Those people killed us. We only threw a few stones at them,' said Sumitra.

Mukta sipped her tea. After a while she said, 'Imagine what could have happened. Suppose Guddu had been hit on the head?'

She immediately regretted the remark as Nasreen looked at her, eyes wide open with fear. 'I will never come to Delhi again, never. I will go away tomorrow, I will. Let Ali bhai be angry,' said Nasreen. She got up walked away towards the gate wiping her eyes with her *pallu*.

'Sorry, I didn't mean it,' said Mukta but Nasreen did not hear her.

'They killed us and you people are arguing whether we should have stoned their building. Do you people never get angry?' asked Sumitra looking at her with disgust.

'Listen, you don't seem to understand how serious this could have turned out to be. You could have been sent to jail. You would have been forced to appear in court every few months. You think that is easy?' said Mukta, suddenly angry that these two were unable to comprehend the seriousness of what they had done.

'That would have been a change from going to hospital every week,' said Sumitra, laughing derisively.

'The courts will let go of Carbide and put us in jail for throwing some stones?' asked Nasreen, infuriated at Mukta's insistence on telling them what consequences their actions could have had.

'True, they throw the law books only at us and not at Carbide,' said Mukta weakly.

Suguna arrived just then with Guddu walking by her side holding her hand. Nasreen rushed to him and hugging him began to cry. 'We won't stay here another day,' she said. Guddu now insisted on eating a samosa and took the chocolate from Suguna he had refused to eat in her office.

Chapter 19

AN IDEOLOGICAL BLOODBATH

The next evening there was an ideological bloodbath at the FOB meeting. The meeting was unusually large and acrimonious and began late. The room seemed too small and suffocating. Tempers spun out of control. The tension was thick.

Avidha was very late in arriving. The day before she had reported late to the office, only after the police had let them off. Another reporter was going through agency copies to file a story in case Avidha never got back. She had to face an irate Joshi, who told her she ought to learn to keep her distance from agitations.

'The paper pays you to write about them, not go slogan shouting with them. You want to do that, do it on your own time,' he told her.

Avidha had gone to office early to placate him and stayed

on till past the time of the FOB meeting. She had missed nothing but cacophony.

Mads sat on the step of the veranda nonchalantly rubbing some grass in his palm. 'Hey, let me bum a cancer stick,' he asked Shekhar and began to shake out the tobacco from the cigarette Shekhar handed him. Then he carefully mixed the cannabis into the tobacco and began stuffing the empty paper tube.

'Who planned this stone throwing? I want to know who did it,' Nirmala was saying, barely able to restrain her anger as she glared at Mads when Avidha arrived.

'Folks, let us call this off today and meet a few days later,' said Ajit in an attempt to calm everyone.

'I want to know who planned to throw those stones,' said Nirmala again, ignoring Ajit.

Zintac was surprised by her anger. A little stone throwing seemed to be quite in order to her considering what the people in Bhopal had suffered and how they had been betrayed not just by the corporation but by every arm of the state. Mukta had always found Nirmala wanting in respect for the law and was surprised that she was leading the opposition.

'Things can happen without being planned,' said Zintac.

'She wants to blame me,' said Mads to Zintac. Lighting up the joint he took a deep drag.

'She may be right,' said Suguna. 'The plan had been to stop in front of the Carbide office building for a few minutes. Who decided to walk in? We have a right to know who was behind this.'

'You people went in, I never did,' said Mads with an impish smile and winked at Zintac.

There was silence as they digested this assertion.

'And why did you not go in?' asked Hally enunciating each word slowly.

'Middle classes go inside offices, the poor always stay out. Thought you people would know at least this much.'

'Did you realize that there were women there? With children? Did it occur to you that someone could have got hurt?' continued Nirmala cutting in before Hally could respond.

Ajit adopted a reconciliatory approach to keep things from getting out of hand. 'Mads, think about it, man. Suppose one of the children had been hurt? Or crushed in the stampede?'

'And that would have been the first time people from Bhopal would have been killed, right?' said Mads, blowing smoke into Hally's face. 'Wouldn't it?'

'Shut up,' Hally hissed.

'I thought you were asking me to talk to you,' said the irrepressible Mads. 'I don't mind smoking a joint quietly.'

Suguna began to feel the undercurrent of old hatreds rearing their heads as ambitions clashed.

'Do you know Guddu was lost in that crowd? Separated from his mother. What if Suguna had not picked him up?' Hally asked Mads.

'Thank you, Suguna,' said Mads to her, tilting his head at her exaggeratedly. 'Did Nasreen thank you properly or not?'

Mukta flared up. 'How dare you make light of all this?'

Mads looked at her with amusement. 'Oh, spare me, you middle-class sissies. You people can't handle a bit of passion, can you? You have ganged up to read me a lecture in law and ethics? The police beat us every time we start a protest. What is new about that? Just because some of us got angry when we saw the Carbide office you will haul me over the coals? Why don't you go give this talk to the officials of Carbide? Ask them who planned the leak of the gas? Why don't you?'

He threw away the butt of the joint he had sucked dry and reached for water.

Nirmala said, 'Hello, mister manhood, everybody here has a right to know why people we walk with kept us in the dark. If anarchism is the chosen path it should have been made clear at the outset so people would know whether to join the group or not. So tell us all, who started the stone pelting? Did the women from Bhopal consent to your plan?'

'Have the women from Bhopal elected you their spokeswoman?' asked Mads.

'They haven't elected you either. We are here because we want to be. We decided to keep our plans from the police, not from each other. You were there in the meeting when this was decided,' said Hally.

'Are you saying I don't belong here?' asked Mads.

'By your own logic you don't. Nobody elected anybody here. The only thing that binds us is our volition, our confidence in each other,' replied Suguna losing her battle with her anger.

It was turning out to be an ugly fight between a compact group and the others began to feel sidelined. They watched veering to one side then accepting the strength of the other till vacillation became an unbearable burden. Zintac began to plead for calm. Ajit once again suggested postponing the meet.

Nirmala said, 'You delegitimized the struggle. We had been running a good campaign. It was beginning to have its impact. We were building pressure so well and now you have gone and given them a handle against us.'

'If you had kept up the pressure this would not have happened in the first place,' screamed Mads. 'That may not have occurred to you though.'

'Mads, we can't delegitimize the struggle,' said Mukta, 'We are asking for the law to be *implemented*. We are saying let those justices be punished because they bent the law to suit Carbide. What moral right do we have to do all this if we go breaking the law?'

'Don't talk to me about morals,' Mads shot back. 'I have no morals. You got proof of that yesterday, didn't you?'

'At least you have some sense of responsibility towards the survivors. Do you know how many criminal cases these women could have faced? They don't need more harassment. We formed a group to support you. And you did not take us into confidence. It is bound to make us angry. Is that so difficult for you to understand?' Mukta asked. She was trying to restore order.

Mads smiled derisively. 'Thank you for your great support. We are truly grateful. Don't know where we could have been without you,' he said.

Avidha, her head leaning against a pillar, was listening to the arguments silently, thinking of how the police had surrounded Mads and how she had bitten a policeman to save his head from being bashed in. Nobody seemed to be worried that he could have lost his life. A discussion on such niceties of the rules of campaign appeared totally out of place to her.

'What about the violence of Carbide? Can you see that? They should be going to prison, not we, because some of us lost our poise,' Avidha intervened.

That led to another uproar. Mukta told her the law was not based on her foolish notions of justice.

'The law is an ass as someone said. But intelligent people don't have to become asinine only because they practise law,' Suguna said her temper finally getting the better of her.

Mukta's hands began to shake. She got up and walked away towards the gate. Nobody here seemed to realize the grave trouble they had been in. She had adroitly slipped inside the VP House waiting for the police vans to leave, following them to the police station, and used all her persuasiveness and all kinds of legal and extra-legal threats to make sure the police did not book them for vandalism. She had told the DCP that his police had gone pulling women's hair and pawing them, that she could identify some of the constables who did it and was there to file charges of molestation. She had also told him that they had done it on International Women's Day and even though that made no difference to the law it would get them some extra bad press and she would ensure his superiors heard about it. Balagopal had curtly told her that someone had bitten a constable and she had snorted at him. 'Let us check out if the court will believe that. I hope you have a medical report to prove he was bitten.' She had bargained hard. And now Suguna, who had herself used Guddu as an excuse to run away from the police, was calling her an ass. What would happen if she turned around and made a charge of cowardice against her? It was against her principles to stoop so low and she stood by the gate fishing out a cigarette and lighting it with a trembling hand.

'Please, please, let us stop this bickering,' said Zintac, growing uncharacteristically tearful.

Nirmala was so caught up in her own fury she did not even notice Mukta's reaction. 'People of Bhopal don't lose their poise like this. Or they would have burnt down the Carbide factory the night after,' she was saying loudly. 'If we want

Carbide officials to go to prison we have to make sure we plan carefully, not hatch plots behind each other's backs. Those who want to act differently can stay out of this group. At least others won't have to face the consequences of their action.'

Hally looked at Ajit who threw up his hands and shook his head in resignation. 'Listen, everyone, you don't know how Mukta saved us from serious legal trouble. Let us stop this now and promise not to repeat this in future,' Hally said and got up to go over to Mukta. She did not even glance at him. She threw down her half-smoked cigarette and walked briskly out of the gate.

'The exodus begins,' said Mads, who had been watching her from the corner of his eye.

Hally came back and heard Mads. 'You wouldn't be here yakking like this if she hadn't saved you from going to prison. Learn to appreciate what people do for you.'

'Let her charge her fees,' said Mads in reply.

'Don't single him out,' said Avidha loudly. 'We now have to stand by him even if he planned it all, like you all think. The group can't let the authorities think we have cracks within.'

Harjit spoke for the first time. 'Avi is right. We must defend this in public. But here we must be clear what is allowed and not allowed in public protests. '

Getting up Nirmala said with a tone of finality, 'You discuss this whenever you want to. I am leaving this group.'

Suguna and Hally both turned to Nirmala to ask her to reconsider. Avidha stood up to run after Nirmala. 'Don't go, Nimmie,' she called after her but Nirmala did not turn to even look at her.

Ajit looked at Mads with unconcealed disgust. 'We can't have one man holding all of us to ransom. In future we stick to the plans we make. Is that clear?'

'Just tell me who is in charge here and I will obey,' said Mads, bowing exaggeratedly to the group.

Mukta had walked out of the FOB meeting because she could not endure being called an ass by someone like Suguna who in her view was not even a good journalist and had little to contribute to the campaign except as a housewife, supervising the cooking and reading proofs. She found the pride such people took in their absurd loyalties to their friends and lovers repulsive.

She went home feeling dejected and wanting to do nothing but sleep. The sliver of light shining under the closed door told her Vineeta was home. She had seen Vineeta looking extraordinarily excited after the incident at the Carbide office and join in the group being rounded up by the police. For her to not report to the FOB meeting on a day like this when so many things had to be sorted out was, to Mukta, a sign of her return to her post of the docile wife.

Vineeta opened the door looking quite happy but the moment she saw her expression she muttered something unintelligible, slunk into the kitchen and got her a glass of water. Mukta noticed the freshly changed sheets and the smell of food cooking on the stove and her head began to throb. She did not even touch the glass of water. Going into the bedroom she switched off the lights and lay down.

Vineeta had been meaning to ask her where she had been all the while they were inside the police station yesterday, and recount her experiences, but one look at Mukta's face, contorted with fury, shrivelled her up. She had also had a tiring day, cleaning the house neglected since the protest began and needing sleep and rest as much as Mukta did. And here was Mukta, not a word of thanks for her pains, behaving as if she had been lolling around in bed the whole day – and come to think of it why should she not if she felt like it, considering how much these people talked about being free to do what they wanted to all the time? They had no respect for women who took on the responsibility of housework even though they called them 'homemakers' and insisted all the time that language ought to be reformed, as if that changed their attitudes.

She rolled out the chapattis with clenched teeth. She banged the griddle on the stove every time she took it off the flame to flip the half-done chapatti and then banged it back on. Then she threw the rolling pin in the sink where it fell with a clatter.

Having finished the cooking she debated if she should call out to Mukta or simply store the food in the fridge and go to sleep on the couch. Then she asked herself why she had to sleep on the couch every time Mukta was angry. Why couldn't Mukta move out of the bed? She was herself surprised by the anger she felt and the deeper the silence around her grew the more she began to feel that her anger was justified.

Precisely at that moment Mukta screamed at her, 'Can we have some peace?'

'Why should you when I have none?' asked Vineeta screaming back at her. Then suddenly fearful of what she had done she sat down at the dining table and began to sob loudly. Mukta grit her teeth and came out of the bedroom.

'You want to throw things. Here let me help you throw them,' she said and picking up the table mats flung them into the kitchen. Then she looked around for something else to throw and finding nothing but books she kicked at the table.

It hurt her foot and she winced with pain. Then she kicked at the table again with renewed anger with the same foot. Even in her deepest of furies Mukta would never throw a book to the floor.

Vineeta ran into the bathroom and shut herself in. She washed her face for a long time while Mukta raved outside. When Mukta quietened she came out. Mukta was sitting at the table with a whisky and asked her with deceptive calm, 'Did you think I would murder you?'

Vineeta chose not to reply.

'When I ask you something you reply. Okay? You don't behave as if I don't exist,' Mukta screamed.

'You behave all the time as if I don't exist,' said Vineeta despite herself. 'I have learnt it from you.'

Mukta began to laugh all of a sudden. 'I am asinine. Don't learn from an ass, Viny. I am an ass.' She said it again and again. Then she downed her whisky and began to pour herself another drink.

Vineeta slipped into the bedroom and into bed as quietly as possible without being able to go to sleep. Mukta came in after a long time, stumbling all the way to the bed reeking of alcohol and fell onto the bed.

Chapter 20

PRIVATE LIVES

Prashant did not call Avidha even after the police crackdown. He could not have missed a news that had made the front pages of all the papers. Avidha waited. After two days she blinked.

'Hi,' she said to him, 'how've you been?'

'Busy.'

'Me too. We got nicely beaten by the police, two days back. I thought I may as well tell you I escaped unhurt,' she said.

'Good,' he said 'I didn't know you had such goons too in the campaign. That was a surprise...'

'They are not goons. Some people lost control. Doesn't mean they are goons...'

'...if you go stoning offices do you expect the police to stand around applauding you?'

'There are bigger goons in the government. The bureaucracy is a goon,' she said.

'We don't go around throwing stones at offices. Never heard of it,' he told her.

'No, of course not. Your job is to protect those offices. You don't break their windows. You only break lives. You break people's heads. I thought you were different. But you are also part of the machinery that protects the killers,' she said losing control.

'Is that all you know about me? Maybe you should reassess your feelings for me,' he said to her.

'You are right,' she said and banged down the phone on him. She felt good having done that to him after what he had done to her the last time. If he thought he was the only one who could show anger she would teach him she had the right and the capability to reciprocate the sentiment. She did not think of Mads as a goon, only a highly emotional protestor and the thought that someone she had been intimate with would call him names shamed and infuriated her. 'Bloody bureaucrat,' she muttered to herself.

Some days later Avidha got up feeling queasy. She was unable to drink her morning tea and lay in bed for long. She finally told Suguna she did not want to go to office. Suguna and she decided that eating out was not good for either of them and they would cook in the morning to come back to homemade food.

'You must learn, Avi, to cook some basic things, even if it is just khichri,' Suguna told her.

'Can Hally cook?' asked Avidha of her.

'I don't know,' said Suguna shortly.

'Hey, something wrong?' asked Avidha.

She was angry with Hally.

Suguna was so caught up in sorting out her own turmoil she did not take much notice of Avidha's sickness. She would get up in the morning and roam about listlessly on the terrace wishing she knew whether it was the hustle-bustle of work she missed or the company.

Then Hally had come round to see her in the office and the sight of him answered her question. Her face lit up and she rushed out to the canteen immediately, quickly disconnecting a call. Her happiness was wiped out a few moments later when, without even waiting for the tea to arrive, Hally asked her if she felt bad for calling Mukta asinine. Left to herself Suguna would soon have called Mukta to apologize but the fact that Hally had come to talk to her about it and not to meet her got her back up.

'Have you asked Mukta why she called Avi foolish?' she asked him.

Hally began telling her how Mukta had browbeaten the police. To Suguna it did not appear a great favour; everyone in the campaign did what they could. There was no need to feel grateful to each other all the time and she told Hally as much. Hally persisted in defending Mukta and said she had had the toughest time that day. 'Let me tell you, Mads had a tougher day. And Avi too,' she had said. Had the police filed a criminal case against her Avidha could have lost her job, though the press normally did not throw out reporters for getting into trouble with the police.

'All the more reason for you to appreciate what Mukta did for all of us,' Hally told her turning her argument to his advantage.

'Unlucky that Mukta is a lesbian,' she had said to that.

'I thought you had more sense,' he had replied and left.

She could not bring herself to forgive Hally for expressly coming to make her see how she had insulted Mukta. He should have trusted her more. She did not go to the FOB meeting that evening.

Three days later when Ajit proposed that Hally should talk to Nirmala to persuade her to come back Suguna pursed her lips and looked away. Hally had tried talking to her after the meeting but she told him shortly that Avidha was unwell and they had to leave early.

'I am loyal to my friends even if some people don't like it,' she had said to him.

Vineeta called Suguna one morning after Mukta had left and broke down on the phone. 'I am so scared, Suguna, I think that she has gone mad,' she said, unable to bear the stress. Suguna felt a cold shiver run down her spine. If there was one thing Suguna could not stand it was violence.

A sense of desolation overwhelmed Vineeta. 'In a marriage, you know, girls can go away to their parents. I have nobody to turn to,' she said.

This was the first time Vineeta had likened her relationship with Mukta to a marriage.

'Don't say that,' said Suguna. 'Come over to our place? It might help cool things down.'

Vineeta refused. Mukta would roast her alive if she discovered she had been talking to people about their fights.

'I wish I knew why she is behaving like this. Can you find out without telling her I spoke to you?'

Suguna told her how they had fought in the meeting. 'She is taking it out on you. Ask her to take on me if she dares,' Suguna told her.

Vineeta went numb and quickly put the receiver down not trusting herself to say another word.

Suguna called her back immediately. Vineeta guessed it was her and did not respond. She called again. This time Vineeta answered and told her coldly, 'I should never have told you all this and now I don't ever want to talk to you. Do you know Mukta knows enough to teach you all her life? You may think I don't know enough to assess her knowledge levels but everybody else says it too. If I knew what you had done I would never have called you.'

A distressed Suguna landed at her house that afternoon and tried talking to her but her unresponsiveness left her no window open.

'I have come here to explain myself and I will say my piece. After that the decision is yours,' Suguna told the downcast Vineeta. 'First, Mukta said Avi's notions are foolish. Avi is as committed as Mukta. I was angry with her for that and I hit back. I am also as loyal to my friends as you are and I thought you will understand why I behaved so badly with her. Not many understand such loyalties. I will apologize to Mukta. These things happen between friends and we can't break off with everyone only because they lost their cool sometime. You and I are close because we share this trait. If you don't understand my reasons, who will?'

Vineeta did not look up till Suguna left.

Despite her anger Vineeta was touched that Suguna had come rushing to make her explanations. That evening she told Mukta in a cold polite tone that she had something to tell her. 'Promise me you won't interrupt and you won't lose control. I can tolerate anything but your anger. It makes me feel so... as if... my very presence makes you angry... I feel life is worthless when you do it.'

Then she told her all about calling Suguna and her visit and her explanation.

'I know I am stupid. I should not have told Suguna anything. You may not believe this but even I feel hurt and lonely and you make me feel like that. If you had told me what happened I would never have spoken to her. I promise you I will not talk to Suguna again.'

Mukta looked at the newly emerging Vineeta with a mix of amazement and fear. The strength of her constancy and her self-flagellation as an offering to a love she felt unworthy of shook her. Her awareness that she had been taking out her anger on Vineeta because she was powerless was heightened by Vineeta's resigned tone.

Mukta hugged her and said, 'Don't forgive me, Viny. I may never improve if you did.'

As they lay in each other's arms Mukta told her she should forgive Suguna.

Hally had told her how he had tried to make Suguna apologize to her and she was struck by his sense of fairness. 'Some things,' Mukta told her, 'are best left to time. Maybe Suguna was very frustrated with the turn events took that day. She has been scolded enough, poor thing.'

Avidha's world was beginning to change.

She got up feeling sick every day but however much she tried to throw up she could not. Avidha did not tell Suguna that she had missed her periods and was now very worried.

Ever since they had begun sharing a flat their circadian rhythms had adjusted themselves in that mysterious way that women who live together experience and they had begun having their periods together.

She went to a doctor without telling Suguna and was asked to give in a sample of the first urine she passed in the morning for a pregnancy test. The next evening she went to collect the report. 'Positive,' it said.

The word sounded strange to her. It did not register for a long while. She walked back from the clinic of the doctor feeling as if she held someone else's report in her hand. She should have another test in another clinic. They do get it wrong sometimes, she told herself. She had an urge to talk to Prashant about it. She called him but could not bring herself to tell him on the phone. She asked to meet him. He said next week. He promised to call her but did not.

Chapter 21

BEING FRIENDS AGAIN

None of the volunteers had been as sorry to see the Bhopal people go back as Hally. He had gone to meet Suguna the next day hoping to persuade her to go for walks together in the morning. Dropping by at her office was not new for him but he felt shy and unsure that day. She belonged to a different world – where ideology had not made prejudice unfashionable and he did not know where he would find her standing when she discovered what he was. He had brought up her behaviour with Mukta as an excuse to have come seeking her. Their rapport was now in shambles.

Suguna was not given to strong words and had therefore been surprised by her own reaction to his criticism of her attitude to Mukta. After Vineeta had called to tell her the impact of her cutting words on Mukta she had sought out Mukta and told her how lucky she was to have someone as devoted as Vineeta.

'I did not really mean what I said to you that evening,' she said to her sincerely.

'Let us not talk about it,' replied Mukta feeling embarrassed by the oblique apology.

But with Hally the discomfort did not go away. She expected him to remain angry for a while but when he did not talk to her for days she began to feel exasperated. He could not be so daft as to miss the implications of a remark that smacked of jealousy.

That evening Ajit announced that a rally would be held at the end of March. He had persuaded the Supreme Challenger to address it and some people from Bhopal would arrive to attend it. Work began to be distributed and all heads turned in Hally and Suguna's direction for the trips to the press. Suguna thought of refusing but it had come to be seen as her work for the campaign and she would not let a personal disagreement prevent her from doing her job. Hally had no choice. It had always been his responsibility.

As they left the FOB meeting Hally fell in step with her and told her he had to talk to her about something. Avidha, who was walking with them to the bus stop, smiled at Suguna and said she would go home on her own and left them alone to walk up to Connaught Place.

'What is it?' asked Suguna, suddenly angry with him for his delayed response.

Hally was thrown by her stiffness. His words died on his lips. 'No harm in being friends,' he said, falling back on a tried and tested cliché.

'No harm in not being friends either,' she said. 'We can work together despite not being friends, can't we?' Suguna then told him that she had apologized to Mukta. 'I hope that makes you happy,' she told him. 'In case that is what you were going to remind me about.'

'I was only trying to keep the group from splintering,' he told her. 'I didn't know you were so touchy.'

'There was no need for you to intervene. Mukta and I could have sorted it out on our own.'

Hally gave a short laugh.

Suguna was enraged by it. 'You know something? You couldn't trust me to deal with this on my own. You think women can't negotiate anything on their own. It is so condescending.'

This had never occurred to Hally. 'I never saw it in that light,' he said honestly. 'You could have told me this. But you said I was defending Mukta because I had designs on her.'

'I got angry. So what?' she shrugged her shoulders. If he could not see that as a compliment she wasn't about to underline it.

Hally told her he had spent the last few years handling the small squabbles that NGOs got into. It was part of his job to smooth ruffled feathers and keep the work going.

'Good justification. It does not change the fact that you were condescending,' she told him. 'It is very difficult for men to apologize even when they are in the wrong. It is part of the male ego. It is part of the rules of patriarchy,' her voice growing louder with every word she spoke.

They were standing on the road having forgotten where they were headed.

'Attributing personal motives to me is not part of patriarchy, I guess. Luckily, Mukta is a confirmed woman lover or else I don't know how I would have proved to you that I was not attracted to her,' he said.

Suddenly Suguna began to laugh. His illogicality appealed to her in a way no amount of reasoning could have. 'You can be attracted to a lesbian even if she does not respond,' she told him. 'I personally find gay men very attractive.'

'You are really unfair,' said Hally, refusing to be deflected. 'I wish you would ask me straight away if someone attracts me. Like you did about Nirmala.'

Suguna told him she had asked about him and Nirmala only because she had been told about them.

'Let me tell you, I have worked with a lot of women and none of them has ever said I was condescending,' he said. At the last minute he prevented himself from saying even Nirmala had not found him so though she was among those most sensitive to such behaviour.

Suguna guessed what he had omitted. She shrugged her shoulders and said, 'I say what I feel. I don't care what others said or did not.'

The next morning they met as usual at the bus stop near her flat and walked all the way to Paharganj chatting about everything they saw on the way.

It was when they turned into the lane in which the press was that Hally paused, held Suguna's shoulders with both his hands and turning her towards himself, said, 'I feel like I want to be with you all the time. I haven't felt like that with anyone before.'

Overcome by his own audacity he abruptly let go of her shoulders and walked rapidly to the press. As they waited for the proof, he told her that if he had offended her she must forgive him.

'Do you think that would offend me?' she said.

He laughed and said, 'Don't know how to check your feelings. You sound so sensible all the time.'

'I know. I am very this-worldly,' she said. Then turning a brilliant smile on him she added, 'Send an application!' Her eyes danced with naughtiness.

'In triplicate?' he asked her.

'Yes,' she said and slid her notepad from her handbag and pushed it to him with a pen. He refused the pen and took out his own.

'Will you dictate, madam?' he asked.

She shook her head. The workers noticed the change in their manner and an old man smiled at his assistant and said, *'Kaam kar. Idhar udhar kya dekh raha hai.'*

'Dear Madam Sugunaji,' wrote Hally, 'I the undersigned am writing to inform you that I am feeling sick with emotions playing football with my heart. I am wanting information from your esteemed self if something like this happening to you also. The above mentioned emotions I am feeling for your esteemed self for few days now. So I am requesting to be given some emotions at your convenience. I am making this request herewith and hoping you will reply to the same. Please kindly respond at the earliest. Yours faithfully, Hally.'

Suguna read it and doubled up with laughter. She agreed to have tea for the first time in the press. She even asked for *mathri* for everyone. The old composer smiled and asked her mischievously if what 'sahib has just written had to be added to the leaflet'.

'No,' said Suguna sobering up and waking up to her surroundings.

Then pulling the sheet of paper on which Hally had written his 'application' she wrote on the margin, 'Request granted.'

Hally took it away from her and read it knowing fully well what she would have written. He looked at her joyfully and folding the letter began to put it in his pocket but she took it away.

'You will get a photocopy. The original remains in official file,' she said.

Chapter 22

A CHANCE LOST

Avidha was too tense to work or even attend FOB meetings but the rally, which was now scheduled for the end of March, kept her occupied. The public meeting was organized as a substitute for the meeting that could not be held on March 8 and some people had arrived from Bhopal to attend it, though not as many as the first phase of the campaign. The huge public meeting began around noon at the India Gate lawn off Rafi Marg.

As usual once Avidha arrived at the rally her own troubles retreated to the back of her mind. The hectic lobbying with some of the leaders was about to pay dividends and they were hopeful the leaders would go on record to support their stand against the settlement.

'Can't they change their minds once they are elected?' Avidha asked Ajit.

'That is their unquestioned privilege, my dear. But we have to make an effort,' he told her.

All the politicians who spoke at the rally committed themselves to supporting the cause of Bhopal. The Supreme Challenger, now widely expected to become the next PM, clearly said that the settlement was a national sell-out and he would remedy the injustice.

'The people of Bhopal are a very brave people, and the injustice done to them is worse than what happened in December 1984,' said the Supreme Challenger. 'I stand by you and we shall fight his injustice together. I give you my word. I will be your soldier fighting from the front,' he said to loud and tumultuous cheering.

None of them spelt out what exactly they would do.

Avidha was desperately hungry by the time she got back to office. She could hardly swallow anything in the mornings and when the nausea went down she could hardly stop eating. She reached her office too worried about her state to even think straight. She had expected to meet Nirmala at the rally but she had stayed away. She decided to go over to her place the next day to tell her all and seek advice.

Avidha called the canteen and ordered herself a samosa, a plate of hot gulab jamuns and tea. Her colleagues had begun to notice that the tea guzzler now drank very little tea and was always hungry. They were too scared to ask her about it. They were firebrands, those two, Suguna and Avidha, famous in the building for snapping if anything personal was even hinted at.

Joshi called her into his cabin – the glorified name given to the box partitioned off from the rest of the office space by plywood walls and a door with a glass pane in its centre. 'There is an invitation for a press conference tomorrow. Your beat,' he told her.

Avidha was about to excuse herself. She had planned to take the day off to meet Nirmala who lived in that godforsaken Mayur Vihar which she insisted on calling by its original name, Trilok Puri, revelling in the effort her middle-class friends put in to cover their discomfort at the idea of her living in a place adjoining a slum. It was infamous as the place where a large number of Sikhs had been slaughtered four years back.

'Please send someone else. I was planning to take the day off tomorrow. Wanted a little rest,' she said as she picked up the envelope. It was a press conference of the Health Minister at three in the afternoon, at Shastri Bhawan. This she had to attend. The chief was looking at her closely.

'I'll go,' she said with a weak smile

'I knew you would,' he said.

Avidha wondered what the old man meant. Did anyone suspect that her frequent visits to that ministry had some personal motivation too? Her samosa and gulab jamuns were cold when she got back to her table. The sight of the milky tea with a thin skin of cream rippling in the breeze the fan stirred up made her want to retch. A cold fear clutched at her heart. She wondered how she could be thinking of speeches when her own life was so uncertain, though why it should be so, why she should want to tell Prashant, she was not clear. In this day and age when girls used abortions as a substitute for contraception it made little sense to get so tense about an unwanted pregnancy. Avidha also knew the news would bring Prashant running to her and she asked herself if that was her motive, to exercise that power over him at least once.

She tucked the invitation to the press conference in her bag. There was no possibility of his being there but she could always walk into his office later. The minister had met the press only twice in the three years she had held the post and the press would be there in full force. She pushed away the plate offering the food to one of her colleagues and began to write her piece feeling happy.

He was actually there. His presence was a shock. He was too junior to be sharing the dais with the minister and stood impassively at the back, aloof and silent like a part of the furniture. Avidha sat with Suguna and smiled at Prashant who gave her a nod. She could hardly hear the minister's rambling about the state of the hospitals, the latest diagnostic tools imported for one of the government hospitals and the rising fear of AIDS.

As the press meet broke up and journalists surrounded the minister, Avidha deliberately walked up to Prashant with a wide smile, saying, 'Hello! How nice to see you here.'

His deadpan expression saved the day for him. 'Hello,' he said. Moving away from behind the minister he walked up to the other end of the room with her to be out of earshot.

'I left so many messages. You never called back,' she said to him even as the minister chatted with journalists.

One eye on the minister, he smiled at her. The sight of an officer feeding a line to a journalist in the presence of other journalists and top officials was quite unusual and this journalist had ignored the minister and the secretary totally.

'I was out,' he said trying to get away. 'I was going to call today.'

'Today? Why, you thought you wouldn't see me here?' she said waving at the press people clustered around the minister who was now looking at the two.

He began to pile a plate with sandwiches for her. 'I must talk to you,' she said ignoring the plate he held out to her. 'When can we meet?' insisted Avidha as she took the plate from him.

'Don't you want a word with the minister?' he asked her.

'No. I want a word with you,' she said.

'Later. I must go. We will talk later,' he said as he sidled away, smiling at his superior officers. Her face burning with humiliation, Avidha nearly left the room. Her friends were calling out to her though.

'What lead did you get?' asked a reporter smiling at her.

Avidha laughed. 'Only sandwiches,' she said. She heard their laughter and closed her eyes swallowing a bite then she moved up to the minister.

'These sandwiches are good,' she told the minister. 'Better than the food served in your government hospitals.'

The minister smiled at her brilliantly. 'That is meant for patients. That has to be healthy, not full of mayonnaise,' she told Avidha.

'Tell me,' she asked. 'How come you did not talk about the health problems of the gas survivors of Bhopal?'

Now the minister looked distinctly uncomfortable.

Avidha wished she had asked the question when the press conference was officially on.

'Why have you kept the ICMR reports on their condition a secret?' asked Avidha.

The minister glanced at the secretary, who nodded at Avidha.

'The government has the information and the government is providing them treatment. The research is meant to serve that purpose. We don't want the reports getting into the hands of those who can misuse the conclusions.'

'Like who...?' asked Avidha.

'You know that as well as we do. Let us not name any names,' replied the secretary turning to a senior journalist who wanted to know why it was so difficult to get a date for surgery in one of the referral hospitals. 'Hand over the details to my PA,' said the secretary.

She called his office from the information officer's desk. He had not got back. She went into the press room and began hammering out her report ignoring the dirty glances that some of the seniors gave her. Avidha rarely used this room. Her office was a few strides away. The old Remingtons here were mostly used by journalists with offices some distance away.

By five she had finished her story, got out of the building and stood at the gate wondering if she should really walk to Nirman Bhawan or call him first. Then gritting her teeth she began walking towards Nirman Bhawan thinking about ways of breaking the news to him. Should she tell him straight away or ask him what he would do if she were pregnant and take it from there? Would he blame her for having been careless about computing her dates? She had very regular periods and generally calculated which dates were safe but he was seldom with her then.

The sight of him had brought back the anguish that had gone down in the last few weeks and she asked herself if his stolid manner was an act he put on or was he truly the most unimaginative man on earth?

It occurred to her that never, not even in the first few months of heady romance, had he ever betrayed any weakness for her in public. He always sat sedately away from her at his office table and never played footsie with her.

'It will get you into trouble, won't it? It won't matter to me,' he would say to her.

He was in the office as she had guessed he would be. His secretary let her go in without checking first with the boss. He knew she had access. Avidha knew Prashant was too private to ask the secretary to fob off anyone he was suspected to be having an affair with and this way confirm the underling's suspicions.

Prashant smiled at her and offered her tea. She refused.

'Why? Had enough at the press conference?' he joked.

She should have told him then that he would have known if he had kept in touch, that she no longer wanted tea as much as food most of the time, that the child inside her made her eat endlessly, that she marvelled at how much that little clump of cells wanted to nourish itself.

'Why are you doing this? If you are tired of me, you should at least have the decency to tell me so,' she said without any preliminaries.

'What rot you talk. I told you I was out.'

'Where did you go? You could not even tell me you were going away.'

There it was again. Where did you go? Why did you go?

'I don't have to tell you everything,' he said.

His frown stung her eyes. 'Who is it?'

'Who?' he asked, perplexed.

'I think I know what is going on. So don't try to act innocent. Who is this woman you are seeing now?'

His face went rigid with anger.

'Tell me,' she persisted.

He looked at her, his face impassive as ever. Then getting up from his chair he said, 'I have to leave now. Bye, okay, bye.' As he opened the door he turned to her, mindful of the office staff outside, and added, 'Can I drop you anywhere?'

She nodded. 'Listen, I am sorry. About what I said. Sorry. But I must talk to you.' She was suddenly afraid that he would never talk to her again.

He kept walking without replying to her.

'There is something absolutely urgent that I have to tell you,' she said, driven to extreme anxiety.

'Not here,' he said.

She sat in his car as he drove out of the building and turned towards the India Gate lawns and further down to Rajpath. He was waiting for her to tell him whatever it was she had to say. She sat feeling wretched and wondering if there was indeed any reason for her to tell him anything. He went round the canopy with its empty space underneath and turned back on Rajpath.

Turning to her he said, 'Tell me what it is you have to say?'

'Don't you miss me?' she asked.

He looked away. He told her he had to go somewhere and would she tell him what it was she had to say to him?

She felt trapped in her own need for reassurance. She wouldn't tell him, this way. She would tell him only if he made one gesture, said one word that proved that he cared for her. 'It is over, isn't it?' she asked him.

'I am going to England,' he said irrelevantly.

'When?' she asked him. These trips don't get planned in a day and he had not even bothered telling her this till now.

'Next month,' he said. They rode in silence.

'For how long?' she asked hating herself.

Silence. He turned on Rafi Marg in the direction of her office.

'Where are you going?' she asked him.

'I thought you had to go back to office. I will drop you near the Press Club, okay?'

'Will you write to me?' she asked, feeling sick at the tone of pleading in her voice.

'I have other things to do too,' he said.

The words brought her anger and her confidence bounding back. 'Stop here, I can find my way,' she said.

He kept driving.

'Stop,' she screamed loudly. 'I said stop.'

He slammed on the brakes. She got out and banged the door of his car shut.

Chapter 23

WHY IMPEACH?

The power of Parliament to arraign a judge had never been used and if they succeeded in the inculpation of the justices, the campaign would win an unimaginable victory and breach the near-absolute immunity that justices enjoy. People were trying to impeach the justices of the Supreme Court by impudently camping outside their citadel, attributing extra-legal and even illegal motives to their verdict in a case that business and industry watched with as much avidity as the survivors. Their open inculpation and continuous diatribe against the institution had made a deep dent in the immunities the justices wallowed in.

Impeachment was the one word that captured the essence of the campaign and, as happens in such undertakings, most of the participants did not understand the implications of that word. They did not appreciate what it took to convert that word into action against those whose casual glances inspired awe, whose marginalia merited titles in classical languages, and whose words could grant life or death. They were caught in the seductive charm of its sound, the sizzling taste of it on their tongues and the excitement of chancing upon a permitted invective.

FOB was now confronted with the challenge to get its demands accepted. Denunciation was easy. Official repudiation of the settlement would take a legal political war. Ajit called a meeting of the war council to draw up the strategy.

Hally made a third, and uninvited, visit to Nirmala's house to draw her back into the vortex. 'You are behaving as if this campaign is the domain of Mads in which you will not set foot. It is so churlish,' he told her.

'If it is our domain, throw him out,' she had replied.

'You want Ajit to run this campaign, fine by me,' he said.

'The mode matters more than the people,' she said.

'The projectiles are already taking it over,' he said using one of her expressions.

Nirmala was averse to NGOs funded by aid agencies and said they reduced every campaign, every movement, every issue to a project. She called people in such NGOs 'projectiles' aimed at serious movements.

She rejoined the group despite her apprehensions.

Ajit had wanted to include only Nirmala and Mukta along with Ali and Mads in the strategy group. He told Hally as much who insisted on a more representative gathering.

'What is the point? Latika is neither here nor there, Zintac can't stomach the idea of a fight, Avi will be where Nims is and who else do you want? Suguna, I guess,' he said.

Eventually neither Ajit nor Hally could have his way. Mads refused to attend the meeting.

'Your agent provocateur has refused to come,' Ajit said when Nirmala arrived at his house.

'Leaving the compradors to work in peace,' she said laughing. 'Ajit, I wish you would not feed us so well. I don't know how to pay for it.' She could smell the lavish lunch he had organized.

'This is just fees for your professional advice,' he said. 'Food for ideas.'

'And drink for what?'

'Your sexy company,' he said, eyes twinkling.

It turned out to be a small group. Avidha could not get away for the day, Suguna had not been invited, and Mads had declined. Ali had arrived the day before and was occupying the guest room. He came down to the meeting looking rather glum and feeling feverish. Latika was the last to arrive and Ajit gave her a small packet telling her he had got it from Manali some time back and had completely forgotten to give it to her.

'Oh my! Best dope in the country,' she said, hugging Ajit and immediately rushing out into the backyard to smoke it.

Mukta strongly objected to addictions taking precedence and insisted on taking stock of the situation without waiting for Latika.

Ajit dragged out his report on the talks they had held with several MPs from the opposition who had all promised support without outlining the form it would take and hinting that a change in the government would suit them all. Latika came back, plonked herself on the sofa, placed a cushion on her lap and looked at Ajit with droopy eyelids.

'The Supreme Challenger is on our side. He is convinced

corruption has played a major role in this deal and that is his agenda, corruption in high places. We can count on him,' she said enunciating every word clearly.

'Surprise, surprise,' said Nirmala.

'Policymakers, as we know, have far too many motives and concerns. A judgment can be wrong but it can be convenient. If industry is penalized badly, foreign capital may leave the country,' said Hally averting the derailment Nirmala's snide remark had begun.

'Effectively, you are saying that whether the government changes or not, things will remain the same,' said Latika. Then turning to Ali she asked, '*Aap kya samajhte hain, kya karna chahiye?*'

'I have a headache,' Ali said.

'We have to find a way to make sure this settlement is not thrust down our throats. The government can do it despite the protests. They can wait for the dust to settle,' said Mukta. 'It needs to be officially rejected.'

'The only way open to us is to keep the pressure on. This must become a movement of workers and political parties supporting them must be forced to join the battle openly, clearly. It is a political issue and it needs a political solution,' said Nirmala.

'*Arre, woh kuch nahi karenge*. I have seen in Bhopal,' said Ali.

'I mean political in a broader sense, not related to political parties or elections alone. They are only part of politics. We need a different industrial policy, we need safety laws...'

'Can we focus on the settlement please?' asked Ajit, exasperated.

'Somebody tell me where is the money? Has Carbide paid up?' Ali asked.

'Yes,' said Mukta. 'The money is here in India, in the custody of the Supreme Court. If we don't challenge the settlement quickly they may start distributing it too.'

'You want to prevent it?' asked Ali.

'We want to increase the amount,' said Mukta.

'That can only be done by the court. It suits the government to let the judiciary take the flak. But we can't let the government think we are unaware of its collusion in the matter,' said Ajit.

'Are you suggesting we change the target of our assault?' asked Hally.

This is what Ajit did not like. Hally was always out to question his motives. 'I am only wondering where we take this campaign now. What do we do?' he asked, lips pursed.

'If the people refuse to take the compensation we can then have a people's repudiation of the settlement. We can do that. That will be so wonderful,' said Latika.

A long silence greeted this suggestion. They all looked at Ali for a response.

He shook his head.

'I think I will have a beer, Ajit,' said Nirmala.

Mukta was disgusted by that and the dope. Getting into an inebriated discussion was not her idea of addressing a serious issue.

'Be practical, Latika,' said Ajit and got up to open a bottle for Nirmala.

'We did have the "Boycott Eveready" campaign,' persisted Latika.

'Hah! How many boycotted it?' asked Hally. 'We don't have the organization to implement such things. People will not refuse to take compensation, and why should they?'

Latika smiled, 'Just an idea. So what else can we do?'

They were back to where they had begun from.

Ajit said they could hopefully depend on the Supreme Challenger. 'He is sincerely angry and he will do something, even if he does not do everything we hope,' he said. 'That is only fair. We must keep up the pressure on him and his politicians.'

'If you think those social quacks will fix this, I have nothing to say,' said Nirmala.

'Then *you* suggest something,' said Ajit, turning the tables on her. There was a heavy silence and Hally brought out beer for everyone. Ajit, bowing to necessity, asked Nirmala to outline her plan. She accepted the olive branch.

'It is not a plan, just some observations. Unless we make this a part of our larger struggle, go beyond Bhopal, we cannot truly slug this out. That we attracted large crowds has gone to our heads. This so-called support of the people? What exactly is it? People coming to rallies and listening to our speeches? And headlines in newspapers? It has no shape. We will soon have another crisis to capture the media's and the people's attention. Some politicians are already talking about avenging some imagined insult to national pride dealt four hundred years ago. They can't see the insults being heaped on the nation by such unscrupulous deals. We must force them to do something about this.'

Ajit sighed. Ali sipped his tea and asked aloud if he should take some medicine but Nirmala ignored him. They talked about the political situation for a while gradually turning to the factors that complicated the Bhopal case.

In their talks they had gathered that politicians saw Carbide as an industry that had aided the grand plan of the Green Revolution by producing pesticides. Few were willing to question the need for such industries whatever the amount and toxicity of the chemicals they brought into the country. The campaign had to contend with those arguments when it came to talking to policymakers. The priority of the Supreme Challenger and his cohorts could change if they were elected to run the country. Even the left parties had not played the active role expected of them in the case. How far they would go once they were adjuncts to the treasury benches was a moot point. The front's efforts to rope in the trade unions and the left parties into the battle had met with limited success. They came to make speeches but there was doubt if it would become an election issue.

'What we have to think about,' said Ajit, 'is how to get the survivors some money as interim relief. The government may change soon and we must put that on the agenda of the political front that may form the next government.'

'And we have to challenge the settlement legally,' said Mukta.

Nirmala glanced at Hally.

'We then have to prepare a lot of medical evidence to make sure the basis of the settlement is dealt a death blow. The government has done a very shoddy job. There are 16 categories of victims and even records have not been prepared properly. That has to be questioned. We need a lot of work,' said Nirmala.

'That can be done later, can't it?' asked Ajit. 'Do we have to go into details now?'

'It has to be done now, so whoever prepares the legal strategy knows about it. We have to, all of us, understand the significance of this part of evidence against Carbide,' said Nirmala. 'We must explain this to our MPs and all those top politicians you think are with us.'

Elections were due by the end of the year and they still had some months to lobby for support. They had no option now but to appeal to the judiciary and hope that the government would change.

It was a logical culmination of the way the battle had been defined. All hopes were pinned on the sense of the court and the sincerity of the people who were expected to be handed over the keys to South Block.

They knew that if every change in the government resulted in cancelled agreements entered into by the previous government, no government business would ever be conducted. Successive governments as a rule honoured treaties, agreements and contracts that their predecessors had signed.

Most agitations and campaigns demanded an enquiry or filed petitions. Participants of those agitations were then free to engage with the next crisis. Sometimes they asked for a change in the law and went home dissatisfied with assurances and some changes. This case did not allow for such solutions.

They spent more than an hour agonizing over how to bring about a complete reversal of the verdict.

Mukta proposed going back to the Supreme Court. 'The law is on our side, the arbitrators are not. We have to change that situation and we can use the law to do it,' she said.

'Maybe you could talk to Professor Thapar? You think he would join us?' asked Ajit. Professor Thapar, her former teacher and family friend, had written many small booklets dissecting important court judgments that had educated many outside the legal profession about the way courts worked and the flaws in their judgments.

They wanted three things from the court now: to get more money out of Carbide, to get criminal cases against its officials reinstituted and to revive Carbide's future liability. They could prove that the settlement order was so unjust it deserved to be liquidated. That was the easy part.

'Justice does not seem to have been the determining factor in the case till now. How will we address the motives of the court?' said Nirmala.

'Please, for once we have some definite scope of action and you...' began Ajit

'Ajit, such decisions are not made by law alone, you know that,' cut in Hally.

'That is where our demand for impeachment comes in,' said Mukta firmly. 'If the judges know that those who signed this settlement are to be dishonoured by Parliament they may not be influenced by other considerations.'

'It can also boomerang,' said Ajit. 'If the judges think they will be denounced by Parliament maybe they will simply sit on the petitions and we will lose the battle. The system is rather rotten.'

Nirmala flared up at that. 'It is very fashionable to say let us not blame anyone, the system is wrong. Well, the system does not run without people and the only way to make those people deliver is to make them pay for their neglect, their ignorance, their crimes.'

'Without the support of politicians we can't fight this fight,' said Latika.

'They are the ones who got us into this mess in the first place,' said Hally.

'At least the new hopeful for the prime minister's post is a man nobody can buy. That is a relief,' said Ajit trying to control the discussion.

'If you think one man can change everything, I can only pity you,' shot back Nirmala.

Even Hally thought she was being extreme. Other people had had the SC overturn its judgments.

'Did those judgments have any international financial implications? Did they involve millions of dollars? Did they involve asking a multinational to obey laws that the government won't enforce? What is wrong with you, Hally?' she asked.

'He probably does not want to adopt the Communist Manifesto,' said Latika giggling uncontrollably. 'He can't even trust those social quacks. Poor chap.'

Nirmala, at whom the comment was directed, asked her to take a nap.

'Some brains can't take the stress of ideas,' she told her and got up to open another beer.

Chapter 24

A FRIEND COMES KNOCKING

Nirmala had woken up to a bad day. Her phone was disconnected again for non-payment of the bill. There was no milk in the house, only one egg in the fridge, the bread was stale and a stray cat was mewing loudly outside her door for food. Nirmala had to give a talk on the Bhopal issue to doctors at AIIMS, from where she planned to go to the telephone department to pay her bill. She had no time to go to the market for milk. Nirmala gave the cat her egg.

'Sorry, I'll get milk, and fish too in the evening,' she promised, bending to scratch the cat under the ear. The cat gave her a disgusted look, grunted, turned her upraised tail and walked out the door majestically. It stopped short and dashed up the stairs towards the terrace instead of going down like it had planned to. Nirmala knew someone was coming up the stairs. She was about to shut her door when Avidha appeared on her doorstep.

'I called. Your phone is dead,' said Avidha.

'Disconnected,' said Nirmala.

'I must talk to you, Nimmie, I must. You have to help me. You don't know what a horrible time I am going through,' said Avidha without any preliminaries. She sat down on a chair and began to cry.

Nirmala was distressed that Avidha had chosen this day to unburden herself. She could not cancel her talk though she could postpone paying her phone bill. 'Come with me,' she said. 'After the lecture we can go somewhere and talk.'

By the time Nirmala finished her lecture Avidha had begun feeling her problems were faint compared to what was happening to Bhopalis and could not bring herself to talk about them.

She suggested a film. 'We can catch the three o'clock show.'

When they got out of the cinema hall Avidha was feeling normal. She said, 'I am so selfish. First I run away from you and when I am in trouble I turn to you.'

'The great Hobbes said that we are all selfish by nature,' said Nirmala to her.

'You are too good,' Avidha gushed.

'You are too dramatic,' said Nirmala. 'Let us celebrate the virtues of selfishness that have brought us together again. Let us get drunk and have something very bad to eat, even if it is not good for you.'

They bounded up the stairs to Rodeo, a Mexican food joint with saddles for bar stools and posters of old westerns on the walls, and ordered a jug of draught beer.

'Let us order those triangles,' said Nirmala. She never remembered the name, nachos.

They were both aware that Avidha was trying not to talk of what had brought her running to Nirmala that morning.

As Avidha poured out the beer into her glass Nirmala decided to break through the barrier.

'Should you be drinking?' she asked Avidha.

'Why?' asked Avidha her heart aflutter.

'Because you are pregnant,' said Nirmala.

Avidha closed her eyes, sat still for a minute, then looked at Nirmala with a steady gaze. 'How do you know? You haven't even felt my pulse. That is how doctors get to know in Hindi films.'

Nirmala took Avidha's wrist in her hand and with her thumb on her pulse, said, 'Have you informed the Ministry of Health?'

'What?' Avidha asked, startled.

'Under the rules they just framed, you have to inform the Ministry when you are pregnant, or how will it look after our reproductive health?' continued Nirmala.

So she even knew whose child she was pregnant with! Avidha gulped the beer and looked away at Clint Eastwood flashing a cocky smile from one of the posters.

'Have you told the concerned officer in the Ministry that he is going to father his second child? If second it is; there could be more,' continued Nirmala

'Why did you say that?' Avidha asked eyes growing moist.

'To hurt you. To get my revenge. I am sorry, Avi, but it hurt a lot, you know, when you wouldn't talk to me.'

They drank silently for a moment. 'I am a horrible woman,' said Nirmala. 'But have you told the man? Those are the rules of the game.'

'I am going to defy the rules,' said Avidha.

'You have already defied too many of them, girl,' said Nirmala.

Avidha marvelled at the timeless quality of old friendships. You could meet after years of awkwardness but within minutes you could carry on as if you had always been together. 'I have a confession to make,' said Avidha. 'I stopped talking to you because,' she waved her hand, 'I didn't want you to discourage me. You detest me, don't you?'

'You fell in love. Why would I detest you for that?'

'For falling in love with a married man. That is what you detest in me. Don't hold your punches, Nimmie, I can't stand that.'

'That is my rule, for myself. I can't stand the complications. They take up too much time. I have better things to do. Not everybody has so many things to do,' she said.

Avidha smiled. 'Oh, Nimmie, you are so full of yourself,' she said fondly. Her reason for staying away from Nirmala seemed so childish now that she threw back her head and laughed.

Nirmala smiled and poured herself some more beer. 'You know what? This affair of yours would have been worth it had you managed to get hold of the secret reports of the ICMR on Bhopal.'

Avidha said, 'I tried. Not too hard. I did not want to exploit the relationship.'

'Only be exploited!' retorted Nirmala. She looked at the dilated lids of Avidha and her tear-stained lashes. 'Sorry. I didn't want to hurt you, not this time.' She took her hand. 'If you think it is a secret you are too stupid. There is talk in the ministry. I have friends there.'

She had asked one of the women a few days back about the latest conquest of the 'resident Casanova' and had been told that he had found a journalist. The woman had described the journalist too. 'Dark, fattish, not even beautiful. But for him any sort will do. She must be giving him a lot of pleasure and publicity too,' she had told Nirmala who had kept her countenance with difficulty.

'He is quite notorious. Did you not know that?' Nirmala asked Avidha.

Avidha had to admit she had, though she pretended to herself that his reputation had been exaggerated, or that he had found the true love of his life in her. A part of her had wanted to be seduced by this man who had known many others. She told Nirmala how she had tried to break off, hoping all the time he would persuade her to change her mind and finally the loss of hope.

There was a heavy silence as both were lost in thought. Nirmala drained her glass and motioned to the waiter. 'We can't get the draught beer packed, can we?'

'Ma'am?' he asked, a puzzled frown on his face.

'Never mind. Please get these triangles packed and get the bill,' she said and taking Avidha's glass she downed it in three large gulps. 'I am inviting myself to your house. Pay the bill, will you? I am practically broke.'

Once they were home, Nirmala said, 'You never had any control, Avi. But you must stop blaming yourself. He has contributed his genes, and that gives him the right to know. Tell him. Even if you decide not to have the kid, tell him. He must know what he has done. Scare him a little. *Tell* him.'

This is what Avidha resented in Nirmala. She took charge and made her do things she did not really want to do. 'I hate him,' she said gnashing her teeth.

'Even that is a relationship,' said Nirmala unmoved. 'I know you will hate me but I must tell you something else too.

You must soon decide what you want to do. Do you want to continue with the pregnancy or...'

Avidha did not tell Nirmala that absurdly even now the child felt like a gift he had given her unknowingly. It was a part of him and she wanted to keep it. That was the real depth of her degradation but she did not have to tell her everything. Nobody, however intimate a friend, has a right to every corner of your being.

Chapter 25

A PETITION TO FILE

Vineeta was the first to learn about the strategy Professor Thapar had come up with. She had stood for three hours in the photocopier's shop, one of which was spent sitting out the power cut, getting over three dozen copies made of the thick sheaf of the petition Mukta had helped draft after long sessions with the professor and much research. 'We are going to file so many writ petitions in the Supreme Court against the settlement that the system will get clogged. They will have to revise the damned settlement then,' Mukta told her, trembling with excitement.

Vineeta paused in the middle of wiping the glass pane of the bookshelf. 'You mean the same court will upturn it? I can't believe this,' she said.

'You never appreciate what I do,' Mukta said.

The comfort of the last two weeks lay in tatters.

Vineeta resolved once again to never discuss Bhopal with her. Bhopal was inextricably linked with their relationship. But she brought it up again: 'Tell me, why do you have to file many petitions? One won't do?' she asked Mukta that night at dinner.

Mukta was impressed by the question. 'The SC can ignore one petition but if there are many identical ones it can't overlook them. This is a strategy to force the court to admit our petition and review it,' Mukta told her.

Vineeta found it illogical. If there was some legal point that could be raised why should it need several petitions to make the SC hear them? And if the SC did not want to review it why should it feel compelled to only because many people asked it to do so?

Harjit's veranda bloomed with *gurjari* dupattas and khadi kurtas once again. The FOB had slimmed down a lot since the people from Bhopal left and Hally had spent two days calling people up to tell them how important the cause was. Professor Thapar came to the meeting for the first time and was moved to see that the shock of the settlement had not worn off even after two months. The faces turned to him were full of the hope that he would tell them how the Supreme Court could have done what it had and how to fight back.

'I am very disappointed in the court. Dismayed,' said Professor Thapar.

Nirmala thought he talked as if his opinion mattered to the court. She watched the professor with great interest. The animated face, the nostrils flaring a little whenever he stressed a point, the hand waving – all brought conviction to every word he uttered. His face was not attractive and shorn of this mobility his features were unremarkable. Nirmala thought he actually believed things could be set right, and his belief was contagious. She was amazed at his conviction that he could make the court see reason, to teach the court some fine points of law like he taught his students. He could sway anyone today, she thought, and silently applauded Ajit for his choice of strategist. She sat back to examine the professor.

Professor Thapar became aware of the intense scrutiny he was being subjected to. He was used to the worshipful glances of the young and the inquisitive challenges of the more experienced women but had never been examined like a specimen in an anatomy class.

He looked at Nirmala directly. 'You have a question?'

'Not yet,' she said.

Ajit had had the petition circulated a week earlier and hoped for a thorough brainstorming session.

'Ask anything you want to. If we feel uncomfortable about anything in the petition we won't be able to defend it and we must be able to defend it to all those we are going to approach to become petitioners. We must swamp the court with petitions, making it impossible for the court to ignore us. So ask anything you want,' the professor said with an encouraging smile.

Thapar went through the main points in the petition. It said the court had no right to extinguish the rights of future generations; that it had given a meagre amount as compensation to victims; that the number of victims was much larger than the court may have been led to believe and that it was wrong to quash criminal proceedings against Carbide. The petition asked for the enhancement of the compensation amount and for the criminal cases to be reinstated. It also undertook to return the money Carbide had deposited if their charges against the company stood disproved.

'That doesn't sound good. Why do we have to say we shall return the money?' asked Suguna.

'That is only fair, isn't it?' asked Thapar. 'We have to proceed from an assumption of innocence, not from guilt. If they are proved innocent we should not penalize them. Suppose, for argument's sake, it turns out that Carbide was taking all necessary precautions, but a minor earthquake jolted the tank and it exploded? Can we hold it guilty?'

He smiled at them. Sagely. Reassuringly.

'Why are we going to this very court again when it let us down once? We have even asked for the justices to be impeached,' said Zintac.

Vineeta looked at her with interest. Did Mukta consider Zintac an idiot like her?

'We have talked about it at length – Ajit, Mukta and I. I can run through the arguments for you,' said Professor Thapar. He enjoyed addressing doubts. 'There is now a disruption in the relationship between the judiciary and the executive. There are obvious cracks in the system. The government is sitting pretty, letting the court take the blame. The court thinks that the executive misled it and made it do something very disreputable, dishonourable. The justices are feeling humiliated. You see, politicians can go to the press, address the public, make explanatory speeches in Parliament. What can the judges do? How can they explain to the people their reasons for the early conclusion of the case? Or how many considerations weighed with them? The economy of the country, the worsening condition of the poor victims, the government's lack of political will to take the case swiftly and decisively forward. The government told the judges that people were desperate only for money and would be eternally grateful to them if they got them early relief. Don't ask me how I know. I can't tell you that. But I know that is how the government persuaded the court. The judges are now very angry with the government. The court is now trying to find a way out of this quandary. It won't take the condemnation alone and why should it? We have to give the court an opportunity to extricate itself. We have to take advantage of this dislocation and there is a very good chance we can make the court hear us out and revise its own decision as much in our favour as in its own interest. It has been done before and it can be done again.'

Nirmala was unimpressed by what appeared to her a veiled and highly sophisticated defence of the judiciary. Is it easy to mislead experienced judges? A little glimpse of money must have helped it go up the wrong path, she thought.

'How can you say the judiciary and the executive are no longer friends?' asked Avidha. 'And what happens to our demand for impeachment?'

'Do you want to explain that, Mukta?' asked the professor, turning to his favourite student.

'No, sir! Not when you are at hand to make the explanations,' she replied. Thapar was a legend of sorts in the university and even students who did not do law sometimes attended his lectures.

Professor Thapar began expounding on the anguish the court felt after the deed had been done: 'Just look at the explanations being given out in the papers. The court obviously cannot explain its reasons now. It could have done that in a preface when it passed the order. A judge could have gone into the reasoning in the courtroom. The judges have complained in open court against the executive. One of the judges said that the court's name is being dragged through mud.'

Avidha, Hally and Mukta had indeed been present, in Court Number One, when one of the judges had suddenly burst out: 'People are saying all sorts of things against us on the streets. They are dragging the name of the court through mud. They are making charges against this court that we should never have lived to hear. What is the government doing to protect the dignity of the court? We are being abused by anybody and everybody. Slogans are being raised against us on the streets.' They had been thrilled to see tears in his eyes. The Attorney General had stood respectfully, head bowed, not wanting to witness this spectacle of a judge disturbed by what people were saying.

'Milord, I will draw the government's attention to this. I assure you, your lordship, the government will do everything possible to protect the dignity of the court,' he had said lamely.

Thapar told them that the court had enlisted the support of retired justices and eminent jurists who had written long articles in the newspapers explaining how the court was told the victims were dying, they could not wait any longer, the money settled upon was more than enough and that they would be remembered for all times for this act of mercy. 'Just read what a retired justice has written in the papers. He is speaking for the court, giving us the reasons of the court,' concluded Thapar.

Tea was brought in and some lit their cigarettes in relief. 'I am totally confused. We have not brought in any new arguments about the case. Why should the court reopen the question?' asked Hally as he poured out a cup for the professor.

'I like that question,' said Thapar who was feeling rather dispirited by the tame discussion they had had till now. 'We are not arguing a case against Carbide. We are challenging a decision of the court and we have pointed out why it should be overturned. We can raise all the issues you want during the course of the arguments. Is there anything specific you want to put in? Tell me.'

Hally looked at Nirmala. She remained silent. He then said that the medical categorization of the survivors was flawed and that should be questioned. 'It is not mentioned in the petition,' he pointed out.

Thapar nodded. 'You see, when we assert that the court had been misled we cover all such details. We don't have to list them all in the petition. We can raise them when we begin the arguments.'

'We have demanded the impeachment of the justices. We are now going back to the same court. How will we do it?' asked Avidha.

'You are seeing a contradiction where there is none,' said Thapar. This was one of the objections he had come prepared to handle. It was a very easy one too. 'Nothing prevents us from still seeking impeachment. Individual judges are to be impeached. The court as an institution is not to be impeached. It cannot be impeached. Indeed, we are seeking the impeachment of these justices only to save the hallowed institution from the disgrace they have brought upon it.'

Suddenly the gloom lifted. The road to justice was now clearly visible. Worried frowns turned to smiles. They began chatting, picking up bunches of the petition to take to their acquaintances to get them to become petitioners. 'What about all these rumours of bribes that the justices are supposed to have taken?' asked Hally. 'Do you have any definite information?'

Everybody stopped talking. The professor had many students in the court, lawyers and judges, and was sure to have a lot of information about what exactly had happened. Nobody expected him to be open about it. He surprised them.

'Yes,' said he. 'Those allegations of monetary inducement are true. Some got cash, some are to be paid in kind. The Chief Justice has been promised a stint at the International Court in The Hague. One has a lawyer-son in the US who will be cut into a top firm as a partner the moment the dust on this case settles. One got his own share of the spoils. There were five judges on the bench. I had known about three of them not being fully above board. But the other two? I am very surprised about them. They could not have let extraneous considerations influence them. I still want to think they have not. But I am told that the reputation of the fourth one is also compromised and I am truly shocked. The fifth has gone along out of the goodness of his heart. No two opinions there. He thought he was helping the victims get an early compensation. He thought he was doing a good turn to them. It happens. They too are human. He is the one who cried in open court.'

There was a pained silence as their doubts were confirmed and Avidha realized she had faintly hoped for a denial of the allegations. It all seemed so petty.

'Did they also quash all those criminal cases out of the goodness of their heart?' asked Ali. He usually kept so quiet in meetings that he was hardly ever noticed and always asked Hally or Ajit to explain things to him later, in Hindi.

That was a tricky question.

'That is where the court was out of line. Definitely out of line. You see, in the law they have this dilemma. Unless

247

the case is proven against Carbide the court cannot award compensation. Basically, a case has to be concluded or a verdict can't be passed. They had to conclude the case and they did it this way. Let Carbide off instead of waiting for say, 10 or 20 years for the case to be proven. Then probably Carbide would have found reasons to challenge it in the US. How long could everyone wait, 20 or 30 years? Or more? Such prolonged delay in getting justice would defeat the very purpose of the exercise.

'In such a situation the only way to grant the compensation was to quash all criminal cases and conclude the case. The court must have thought financial penalty is the worst punishment for a corporation. After all a corporation cannot be sent to prison. Even if some officers are sentenced what purpose of justice will that serve? They were only obeying senior officers, they had no motive to kill people. That is how the government must have argued before the judges. The three who obviously had pecuniary considerations must have then persuaded the other two.'

Now Avidha began to feel seriously uneasy but could not place her finger on it. Nirmala began to find Thapar even more fascinating. Had he been there on that bench in the Supreme Court he would have given a very good justification for the settlement. He was here though, on the side of the campaigners.

'On what grounds are we demanding enhancement of compensation?' asked Nirmala wanting to bring him back to the problem of omitting the categorization of victims in the petition. It did not go down well.

'Would they have awarded such a paltry sum had an American been killed? Is the life of an Indian less valuable than an American's? Is that not reason enough to ask for more?' asked Latika, agitated beyond measure.

Thapar smiled. 'That is not how courts award compensation,' he said. But nobody was listening to him. The discussion on the value of the life of an Indian and that of an American continued unabated for a while.

Finally Professor Thapar turned to Latika and said, 'She wanted to ask something else. Before I answer your question,' he said to Nirmala, 'we must look at the way the compensation amount was calculated. We can bring up all the arguments you find necessary to raise in the course of the case. We can tell the court how it was misled about the numbers of victims, the condition of victims and also the earning capacity of the victims, which forms the basis of calculating the amount of compensation normally.

'Let me tell you that the court was aware that the numbers of the victims may exceed the figure the government had given it. The settlement order clearly says that if the numbers of victims is larger the Government of India should make up any deficit in compensation. We must drive that point in and ask Carbide to make up the deficit.'

'This is terrible,' said Suguna. 'You are saying the people of India were ordered to pay for injuries inflicted by a multinational company on the people of India for nothing more important than corporate profits!'

'Sad, yes, very sad, but there it is. We shall bring up all this in court,' said Thapar. 'But don't forget that the government was also part owner of the UCIL factory. So we have a contradiction here too. The government is vicariously guilty and is also representing the victims.'

'If they were experimenting with chemical weapons, it is even more ironical that the court has asked the people of India to pay for having been made the guinea pig,' said Hally.

The assembly turned glum again. Tea cups were being piled back on trays and comments on this incredibly unjust system began to flow.

'Why don't we demand that the court should never be allowed to quash criminal proceedings?' asked Suguna. Ajit shook his head in dismay.

'We cannot. We should not,' Ajit said. 'It is an important power the court has. If it did not have any such power many of us would not have cases against us quashed. Even now many people arrested in Bhopal for staging a demonstration are facing criminal charges. We want this court to quash the cases against them, don't we?'

Ali now asked if the criminal cases filed against him and some others could be quashed now.

'Not if we are repudiating the settlement. The court would probably do it tomorrow if we asked, but we are not asking for it,' said Latika. 'Sorry, we have to continue to fight.'

To her surprise Vineeta enjoyed that evening's discussion. 'Did he teach you in college?' she asked awestruck by Professor Thapar's performance. 'You are so lucky to have had such a good teacher.'

Mukta was not feeling so lucky now. She had a vague feeling of unease and would not have been able to explain her reasons had she been asked to do so.

Chapter 26

AN EARLIER CASE

Ali and Latika were both embroiled in the same case. They had been part of a demonstration outside the Vidhan Sabha in Bhopal in which Mads and some others had suddenly started pelting stones at the car of a minister who was driving past and vanished. The police had beaten up the scattering demonstrators and arrested 11 people, most of them from Delhi, two from Mumbai. Arshad Ali was the only one from Bhopal to be arrested. Several criminal charges were slapped on them.

Ali knew the names of all the four people apart from Mads who had stoned the minister's convoy. He was too proud to deny involvement or reveal the names. He would never squeal on his comrades even if he disapproved of what they did. He had taken the charge and had learnt to keep his distance from Mads in protest demonstrations. It was difficult to carry on any campaign without the involvement of Mads in

Bhopal and Ali grudgingly respected him for his intelligence and his acute perception. Except for his tendency to get out of hand sometime, Mads was a good agitator, he knew the latest developments in the ongoing case, had a wealth of information and a wide network of professionals. He had a charm that was hard to resist but Ali did not trust him and could not do without him either.

Mads had neither come to see them in prison nor made any efforts to get them bail. After friends from Delhi arrived to bail them out, Latika alone had gone to Mads spoiling for a fight.

Mads had responded calmly, 'Why should I have bailed you out? Are you not adults able to look after yourselves? The poor go through such troubles every day. Who helps them? They have no resources like you people do.'

Latika had been left speechless. She had found this attitude of nonchalance quite sexy.

'Let the bloody middle class get a taste of state power!' He had continued. 'They will forget all that jargon they use all the time, long and polite words and civil language. Yuck!' Then he made an extra-sweet *nimbu* sherbet for her and offered her a joint.

As she sipped at the drink he continued to disparage them as the fence-sitting middle class that makes noises within legal boundaries and 'suckles at the teats of power'. It was good for them to undergo some suffering and learn what it means to live like the poor, with no law on their side, with the police always treating them with suspicion, clanking them in prison for things they had never done.

This point of view struck her rather forcefully. She was thrilled that she had seen the inside of a prison. It was like a red badge of courage and honour, like a medal conferred on her. She was an academic of sorts. Her future prospects did not depend on the outcome of the criminal case. The case would only add to her allure. In fact the only thing that did matter to her was the seizure of her passport. She managed to seek permission of the court to leave the country when she wanted to but it was very tiresome. But it added to her stature at NGO conferences abroad where she was introduced as a brave campaigner facing criminal charges in a case known the world over like Hiroshima, the Bhopal gas disaster. A case in which to be seen standing against Carbide was a matter of pride. To have the state filing a case against you was even better. Mads had indeed done her a favour!

Once the group came back to Delhi they held a discussion on their experience in Ajit's house who had organized their bail. The whole group was furious with Mads.

'I had not consented to the act. I was not a participant in that act of stone throwing. Now my future is at stake. I can be sentenced for something I did not even do. I don't want to go to prison. Call me a coward if you want to but that is how I feel,' Rakesh Nigam, the most articulate of the group and the most agitated one, had said.

No amount of arguing or pledges of support to fight their case by the Delhi group convinced Rakesh to join the struggle again. The other boys too had turned their backs on the campaign.

'Sometimes, things go wrong. You can't walk away because of that,' Hally had argued. 'Suppose there had been no stone throwing and still the police had arrested you? What would be your reaction?'

'You don't understand, do you?' Rakesh had asked, flaring up. 'I am not scared of prison. But I won't go to prison for something I did not do. I would have if those people who threw the stones had stood by their actions. They ran away. They let us suffer for what we had not done, what we had not approved of, what we had not even been told about. Is this ethical? Is this right? If this is what the people in the movement can do to you, what right do they have to point fingers at the state? The state is supposed to be oppressive. But why are you like them? I am against this attitude of using people as if we are cannon fodder.'

Hally had not understood this insistence on being informed about each and every action. 'It happens,' he said, 'perhaps they had not planned to throw stones, perhaps it happened in a moment of anger.'

'Why did they run away then?' asked Rakesh, his eyes boiling over with rage. 'Since you have appointed yourself their spokesman perhaps you can enlighten us.'

Hally got angry too. 'They ran away because they should have. Why get into the police dragnet if you can escape it? I don't think there is much glory in doing that. Forgive me but I am no Gandhian. You could have run away too. Why did you stand around to be arrested? You see the inside of a prison for a few days and you chicken out,' he shouted back.

'That is the point,' Rakesh said wagging a finger in his face, 'we could not have run away because we did not know stones were to be thrown. We were at the back, in a crowd of people jostling and running. We heard some noise, we did not know what had happened. We did not know what to do. We did not even know Bhopal well enough to know which way to run and which fence to jump. If you call that chickening out, yes, we chickened out and I have no intentions of talking to you.'

'I don't want to talk to your kind at all,' Hally had told him.

All the other members of the group had looked at Hally with unconcealed hostility. Only Latika said that she did not mind the case. 'It is part of the struggle. We take the credit for the campaign, we also share the blame. I have no complaints,' she said.

The wagging of the finger, like a schoolteacher trying to teach an errant boy some good manners, really got to Hally. He had had enough of such people talking about volition and choice. Millions have no choice and these people want choice even in a struggle. He had stormed out vowing never to talk to Rakesh again.

Ajit had always kept in touch with them keeping abreast of the case that had not moved much. Every few months they had to go to Bhopal to appear before the magistrate. It was expensive. Rakesh was used to saying that he hoped the case would drag on for 30 years. 'At least in my youth I will be a free man,' he used to joke.

After the settlement was announced Rakesh had called Ajit to check for details. He attended the first meeting at the Law Institute with three others of the group that had taken to calling itself 'the criminals'. They refused to join the protests but they were still available to work for the campaign, doing research and preparing briefs, anything that did not involve going out on the street

Latika had earned Hally's respect because she had not deserted the campaign on the streets.

Mads was not bothered that they had lost some activists. He was sure they would have left for some other reason. The middle class always did; they found jobs and deserted movements, they started families and blamed the spouse for their inability to stay on in the movement or they went abroad for studies. 'This way at least they got an aftertaste of their deviation into the movement. They will never be rid of that aftertaste,' he had said to Latika.

After Mads had repeated his stone throwing act outside the Carbide office Hally had begun to see some strength in the objections of the 'criminals'.

Chapter 27

AVIDHA WRITES TWO LETTERS

After her outpouring to Nirmala, Avidha curiously felt more anguish than less. She procrastinated, finding refuge in doing nothing, lying in bed listening to Begum Akhtar and Mehdi Hassan. She began to comprehend Nirmala's admonishment that aesthetic appreciation of old poetry should not be allowed to shape one's emotions.

The distraction of the campaign was now over. The petitions were being taken around to intellectuals to sign so that they had at least hundreds to file if not thousands. The agitation had now moved into the comfort of drawing rooms.

Nirmala had asked her a few times whether she had written to Prashant. One morning she got up, her heart racing away, for she had recalled that he was about to leave for England and she must write soon. She stared at the blank sheet not knowing how to begin. His words came back to her. 'I have other things to do too.'

She wrote a letter, crying most of the time while writing it. *'Why did you have to hurt me so much? I have always known I am nowhere on your list of priorities. I had nearly stopped fooling myself that I meant more than a passing fancy, one among many and not even a particularly favoured one... so why did you have to point that out to me?*

'I know it is my fault. I gave you the power to hurt me when I opened the folds of my heart and gave you access to all the feelings burnt into them. I even deciphered them for you, the fool that I am. I told you things I had never told anyone before.

'What hurt me was your unequivocal statement that you have other things to do too... yes... yes, of course.

'And as usual you probably phrased it inaccurately. You have other things to do first, my dear. Avidha does not exist for you till you choose to bring her into existence! But I exist independent of you and your desires and your indifference too. I shall never impose that existence on you now, never again. Good bye.'

The next day she read it again and realized she had forgotten to tell him about her pregnancy. She was ashamed of the grovelling tone of the letter. She tore it up.

She decided to write another letter, this time in the office where the bustle would keep her from slipping into the morass of self pity. She wrote it in fits and starts and on top of the sheet she wrote 'pregnancy' to remind herself that she must not forget to put that information in.

To her dismay that too became another long litany.

'It has always fallen to the lot of men to prove to women how foolish they are. So be it with me too. I am not writing to you to thank you for teaching me how foolish I am. I am writing to tell you something else,' she began. She thought she was doing well.

'Listen, Prashant, I am pregnant. I should have told you this before but I took a long time to decide whether to tell you or not.

I would have told you earlier, had you asked me gently what I wanted the day I came to meet you after the press conference. I would not have asked you to take on the responsibility of the child. I would never have asked the impossible of you. But how would you know? You thought I was selfish, for there is no other kind you know. Selfish people do not have the imagination to extend beyond themselves and know another kind. Yes, look bored and turn your face away.

'*You have done that already, turned away. You got what you wanted. In fact that has been the nature of whatever it was between us. You made your demands, you didn't stop to think whether I could give it to you, but I did. Always. Whatever it cost me.*'

Now she began to get carried away.

'*Do you remember the first time we had gone out? I don't think so. I do because that is the day I should have realized how much I meant to you. To put it more accurately, I should have known I meant very little to you. I had spent the whole day on a bag of peanuts working at a furious pace to finish and be able to meet you on time. I could have asked you to meet me two hours later but I did not. I arrived on time and stood by the roadside waiting for you. It had begun to drizzle. You came more than an hour late, not bothered about the woman who stood in the rain on the side of a nearly deserted road braving the curious and frank stares of passers-by, walking up and down the roadside, to avoid being shown money by paunchy men on scooters offering to buy her body.*

'*It happened every time we went out. Once you even told me on the phone, "I may be a little late but you will naturally wait!"*

'*I swallowed all those humiliations because I lost my heart to you. It is not your fault. You did not ask for it. You did not want it. For that innocence of yours I forgive you. I forgive you not in the flush of some victory I have won over my feelings today, out of the generosity of my heart in a moment of triumph. I do not forgive you because I cannot hold you to anything. Also, I forgive you not because of a gift that is growing inside me, a gift you did not intend on giving me.*

'I forgive you in the bitterness of my defeat so that I am free of any emotion for you. I shall not spare you one shred of my emotions, rancour, anger, despair. Nothing. You have no right to any part of me, least of all my emotions. I am finally free of you.

'I disown you. I disown you completely. Therefore this child is not yours. It is mine and mine alone. You did not want it. You have no claim on something you did not want.

'You may as well ask why I am telling you about the pregnancy if I reject you like this. I am telling you because someday I may have to tell my child about you and then I do not want you to deny your miserable contribution to my child's existence. I tell you so that you know.'

She had taken two days to write the letter cutting out many portions and shortening it from the long epistle it had been to begin with. In her heart she thanked Nirmala for having made her write it. The writing of the letter rid her of the baggage of many unresolved feelings.

In the morning feeling strong and at peace she got up early and went out to the terrace to water the cactus. The cactus looked as if a spider's web had caught in one of its thorns. Avidha bent down and realized it was more like a piece of cotton wool wrapped around a thorn on one side of the head of the cactus. She showed it to Suguna who peered at it closely touching it with a tentative finger.

'There is no semul cotton blowing yet, Avi. It could be a flower.'

'If that is a flower of this cactus I don't want it,' replied Avidha.

That evening Avidha showed the letter to Nirmala and even asked her to edit it. Nirmala refused to read it. After much persuasion she did but made no comment.

Avidha now wanted to send the letter to Prashant and her only regret was she would not be able to see his expression when he read it. She said as much to Nirmala.

'The best thing to do would be to go and give it to him personally to make sure he reads it,' Avidha said.

Nirmala smiled to think that Avidha had mistaken emotional exhaustion for detachment and that his reaction still mattered to her.

The thorn on the cactus began to grow and looked like an ear bud now. Avidha and Suguna watched it fascinatedly and watered it very carefully making sure the cotton did not get wet.

Chapter 28

AVIDHA GETS ADVICE

By the second week of April word was out that Avidha was pregnant. It spread through the circle like the yellow-green threads of mimosa blossoms. Avidha had told Suguna when she came home one night to find her gorging on mutton pulao. 'You will grow very fat soon,' Suguna said. 'You have begun eating a lot.'

Taking Suguna's hand into her own Avidha said, 'I am pregnant.'

'I suspected as much,' said Suguna.

What Avidha liked best about Suguna was her capability of keeping away even when she was in the same room. Silence with Suguna was usually a companionable one. She did not pry. She never crossed the line that demarcated individual space like some intimate friends did. Strangely, it was the incurious nature of Suguna that Avidha had begun finding unable to live with. Having a secret nobody wants to find out about is not thrilling at all.

With the cooling of Prashant's ardour she began to think of Suguna as a very cold person. She had not forgotten that Suguna had sat by her side on those terrible nights when she could not stop crying but that now appeared to her as a concession to form rather than genuine concern. Now she was saying she had suspected the pregnancy all the time. Avidha felt she could not talk to her anymore. She went to her room, switched off the lights and went to bed without shutting her eyes.

Suguna sensed the withdrawal but did not voice her hurt.

Avidha, in a despondent mood, told Vineeta and soon the news leaked. There was much speculation about who the guy was. After some discreet and open enquiries and long chat sessions on the phone and in the coffee house it was ascertained that he did not belong to 'the circle'. They concluded that he was not only a rank outsider but seemed to be a rather cussed one at that. Was he married? Would he marry her? Would they live together? The fact that nobody knew a thing about him signalled to them that poor Avidha had been ditched. 'She deserves sympathy,' they said, smacking their lips to suppress their smiles.

The campaign had slackened by then, the public meetings were over, more than a hundred identical petitions were being filed diligently in the Supreme Court, some signed by dozens as petitioners. FOB meetings were now held thrice a week and the attendance had dropped drastically.

Latika was the first in the FOB to mention her condition to her. They were going through files ticking off the names of all the people whose signatures they had obtained on the petition. 'Sometimes one tends to be carried away. You gave in to an impulse. I can understand. Women hardly have any negotiation powers,' Latika told her, giving her a sympathetically wise nod that made Avidha want to box her teeth in.

'I wasn't negotiating a business contract with him,' she said to her acidly. 'This is a relationship you are talking about, not a market.'

Latika shrugged eloquently. 'This is the language that makes women weak,' she said. 'You invest so much in a relationship and look what you get? Only trouble and tension. You must learn that relationships are as ruthless as the marketplace. But the point is what you want to do now. You should do it soon, go to a doctor. I can come with you if you feel awkward going on your own.'

Avidha refused to respond. Latika told everyone how she had tried to help, 'but she isn't listening to sense'.

One morning as she watered the cactus Suguna called out to Avidha excitedly to come out and see how the thorn with the cotton wrapping on the cactus had changed. It had grown tall and looked like a miniature candy floss. It had begun to look quite pretty like a fuzzy mast stuck in the side of the cactus.

'Our very own pregnant cactus!' Suguna said.

Avidha looked away and walked to the door to pick up the newspapers.

When Suguna brought the tea to her Avidha was standing on the terrace staring into the distance. Suguna caught hold of her hand and took her inside.

Sitting her down on the bed she said, 'Avi, I want to talk to you about your pregnancy.'

Suguna waited for her to respond but Avidha sat so still she found it very difficult to proceed. She beat about for a while trying to get through to Avidha and finally provoked a response only when she offered to go with her to any hospital for an abortion. Avidha told her she had not yet decided whether she wanted to abort.

'You have to think this thing through, Avi,' said Suguna firmly. 'Your life hangs in the balance here.'

Avidha found it strange that Suguna was talking about her life when the unborn child's life was being weighed against institutions and morality it had no connection with and that now seemed to her against the natural order of things. She gave her a thin smile.

'Think of the money you will need to bring up a child properly,' Suguna said repressing her annoyance.

Money, Avidha told her, would not decide things in her life.

'You can lose your job, darling. In an ideal world you could have done what you chose to, not in this one,' Suguna told her.

'If we go along with what the world wants, how will it change?' Avidha asked.

Suguna told her rhetoric did not change reality.

Avidha said, 'You know, Suguna, it is these small compromises we make in the name of practical considerations that keeps the status quo undisturbed. Eventually people like you turn out to be on the side of convention.'

'And your defiance will change the world, will it?' Suguna asked.

Mukta made things worse with her abrupt manner. In her view the theory of equal responsibility did not hold good in the matter of pregnancy in which men should bear more responsibility because they had less physical burden to cope with.

She called Avidha one night to tell her she should not pay an exploitative male the ultimate compliment of carrying his genes in her womb and must reclaim her freedom by rejecting everything that belonged to him.

'Just leave me alone,' Avidha screamed at her and replaced the receiver without waiting for a response.

Shekhar came by two days later. He was the most qualified among them to talk about the travails of child care, being a father. He shot up to the second-floor flat without a thought to spare for Mrs Kapoor. Avidha asked him if the landlady had seen him.

'Balls to her,' he said.

He made himself comfortable on the floor of her room on a durrie, pulled out a matchbox from his hip pocket, extracted a small shiny packet of aluminium foil from it and pinching a small piece of something sticky and black wrapped in it began telling her what he had come to tell her.

'Hey, we are friends so I guess you don't mind my barging in like this. I came to talk to you, man,' he began.

'Woman,' corrected Avidha automatically.

'Huh, woman, you dunno what you getting into. Thought I'd tell you what I been through.' He refused tea or *nimbu pani*, declared they would have lunch together and began rolling the tiny piece of sticky black paste between thumb and finger. 'What is that?' asked Avidha who had never seen something like it before.

'Dope,' said Shekhar and reclined a little more against the cushion propped against the wall. 'Charas, you know,' he explained. Avidha asked him to go out on the terrace to smoke, then petrified that the landlady may smell it asked him to stay put inside the room though the acrid smoke brought her gorge rising.

Shekhar had a slightly jowly, bottom-heavy face. He kept it covered with a short curly beard that made him look very attractive with luscious pink lips peering out of his dark beard. He had beautifully wide eyes with dopey eyelids drooped like shutters half down on a shiny window. It gave him a drowsy look.

He launched forth into the gory details of childcare in his usual lethargic manner. The way he sounded, having a child was a punishment that only the stoutest of people could bear. He talked of nappies, the stuff inside them, sleepless nights, standing in long queues for vaccines and other drudgery.

'You think it is cute having a baby? Let me tell you, woman, even breastfeeding isn't what they show you in pictures. It takes half an hour to just prepare for it. You got to have hot water ready and sterilised napkins and you have to wipe the mound before sticking it into the baby's mouth. Make a man prepare the boob for feeding and he will never look at another pair again.'

'How nice your daughter will feel when she knows all this. I am sure you regret having had her,' Avidha said with some asperity.

She had hoped Shekhar would take offence at her words and leave. Instead he said, 'I don't regret the kid. Not saying don't have the kid. Your kid, your call,' he concluded.

'Have you quit smoking?' he asked her as he lit a normal cigarette, putting her on the mat.

She had not. 'It'd be a good side-effect if you quit,' he told her.

'Thanks,' said Avidha derisively. 'That is the only positive thing you have said about pregnancy.'

'I never talked of pregnancy. Till the brat is inside, it is good. It is when they come outside that they create problems,' said Shekhar unperturbed.

Avidha knew Shekhar only slightly and had always been fascinated by his laid-back ways and dreamy looks. Close up he seemed to be someone quite different. For all his sleepy looks the man was rather alert.

'You know the best side-effect of pregnancy?' Shekhar continued, blowing smoke in a thick column from between his full pink lips into her face, deliberately it seemed to her, and leaning close to her.

She sat in front of him transfixed, dying to light up herself. She was about to borrow his cigarette for a drag when she heard with disbelief what he had to say.

'The sex. Best side-effect. Safest to have sex when you are pregnant. Can't get pregnant again, what? Ha, ha ha!'

Avidha was unsure how to react. 'So what do you say? Feel in the mood?' He flung the words at her casually.

She was caught by so much surprise even her humiliation took time to surface.

'No,' she said mechanically.

'Just thought I'd check. No problems. Think about it till we have lunch. We can roll later,' he said.

'There is nothing here for lunch,' she said to him.

What the hell was wrong with her, she should boot him out. She shook herself wriggling her shoulders. 'Shekhar, leave,' she told him springing up from the durrie. 'Just leave,' she said again.

He shrugged. 'Never thought you were stuffy,' he said to her, raising his eyelids from his half-shuttered eyes. His irises glinted in the sunlight as if with anger.

She shut the door and screamed loudly, collapsing on her knees, beating her clenched fists on her thighs and kept screaming till tears streamed down her cheeks and she broke down completely.

Chapter 29

A LUCKY DAY

'This has to be my lucky day,' thought Hally as he walked up the lane towards their house. There was a power cut and Suguna's landlady would not see him. He had been told to be especially careful of that. If anyone were outside in the yard he was to simply walk past and watch from a distance till the coast was clear. The leafy avenue looked deserted. He stood before the house unsure where the stairs were. Then he noticed the door left ajar. He pushed it diffidently, saw the staircase and suddenly it was lit. The power was back.

He climbed softly up the stairs. After the first-floor landing the staircase was unlit. The stairs continued up turning left leading to the barsati.

The door that led onto the terrace was closed. A candle, looking quite freshly lit, stood outside the door. He thought even practical women had quaint notions of lighting a staircase with a single candle. He rang the bell. She seemed to be in no hurry to let him in.

He looked down to snuff out the candle and noticed that it was stuck in a small earthen bowl that weighed down a red envelope. 'Welcome. The door is open,' read the small card. He smiled, pushed the door, blew out the candle, and crossed the small expanse of bare terrace to the square block divided into two rooms that stood perched in the middle.

'What a perfect invitation to a burglar or a rapist,' he said, waving the envelope.

'Which one are you?' asked Suguna.

'Both,' he said, not being able to see her expression even though his eyes were now used to darkness. He stood still, taking in the mesmerizing effect of the light and looked up to check what fancy chandelier made up this play of light and shade. She had used an old basket made of iron wires, the kind that in his house was used to store eggs. The wire cage was woven in places with black and gold thread. Hally knew what it was: a *kalabattu*. At the centre of the table a clutch of lighted candles was stuck on a tawa over which she had placed the glass bowl of an old hurricane lamp.

Hally suddenly felt awkward as Suguna busied herself with their drinks and placed them on the table on two opposite sides. He picked up his glass and as she made a move to pick up her own he walked across the table. She turned to him.

'Suguna,' he said, 'Suguna.'

'What?' she asked, breathless.

'Just wanted to say... your name. It has such a nice sound. Rather unusual.'

'I don't like it,' she said.

'I do,' he said.

'What else do you like?'

'That's what I came here to check out. And you? What do you like in me?' he asked, tracing the collar of her T-shirt and bending to kiss her throat.

'I like the applications you write,' she said.

He threw back his head and laughed.

'Avi loved it,' continued Suguna.

Hally was put out. 'So you show your private letters to people?'

He looked away.

The spell was broken. They chatted desultorily till Suguna asked him if he was truly angry.

'Hurt,' he said placing a finger on his chest.

'I can rub it away,' she said placing her lips where his finger had been.

He pulled her into his arms and they began to wrestle with each other. Soon they were kissing tenderly, then hungrily, and then they forgot to kiss as they stared into each other's eyes.

They finished the drink over an hour later in bed where he took the glasses to her.

In the morning Hally asked her if he should leave before her help arrived. Neither of them had slept.

'No, you can be here officially as if you have just arrived. Dress up properly,' she told him. He had to put his shoes on.

'I am afraid I'll go to sleep soon,' he told her. They decided to check that later.

They stood in the small kitchen getting into each other's way and turning to kiss. It took them a long time to cook their omelettes. Just as Suguna flipped the second one onto a plate the help arrived.

'Tell me about yourself,' she said getting all formal with him and carrying the plates onto the table.

'There is not much to tell. I was doing my MA from JNU when they threw me out in my final year. Rusticated.'

'Really!' Suguna sat up a little straighter, alert and curious. 'Why did they do that?'

'There had been some discrimination against a Dalit student and we had this long agitation. One day I said in a speech that had we been violent the authorities would have heard our complaint. Only because we sat holding a non-violent dharna nobody paid us attention. I even said we could be driven to violence if our complaint went unheard. An enquiry was ordered. The enquiry committee made very adverse remarks on my role in the agitation. Then the authorities threw me out.'

Suguna was struck by the very short narration. 'Why didn't you deny it?'

'I will never deny what I said. Besides I knew they would throw me out anyway,' he said. He finished his omelette. 'You see, I have a lot of courage.'

The help came in just then, having finished the dishes, to sweep the rooms.

They got out onto the terrace with their mugs of tea.

'Why would they have thrown you out anyway?' she asked picking up the conversation from where he had left it.

'Because I am a Dalit,' he said looking straight at her. 'You didn't know that?' he asked when she did not say anything. How had he neglected to tell her that?

'No, I did not,' Suguna said simply. 'You know, you were thrown out because of your threat to use violence. Not because of your caste.'

'Listen,' he said, leaning forward angry with himself, 'that is what everybody says to me. Lots of frustrated students make threats but the university thinks about the impact that

drastic actions like rustication can have on their careers. They
don't easily throw students out like this. I know they don't
unless the student is one they never wanted in the university.
And they don't want Dalits in higher education.'

'So you think,' she insisted.

'That is what I know,' he said vehemently.

'That is belief,' she said. 'How can I argue with such strong
beliefs? What evidence do you have?'

He stared out at the gulmohar with its vermilion-tipped
buds and took a deep breath.

In his first year he had been part of a group opposing the
internal emergency that was determined to not let the prime
minister come to the university. He was at the forefront of
the agitators and when the cavalcade was close the group had
begun hurling stones at the policemen standing guard. The
cavalcade turned away. There had been an enquiry but the
authorities were lenient. 'Boys will be boys,' they said and let
all of them off with a stern warning not wanting to destroy
their future prospects.

He told her about it. 'When I was actually violent, they
tolerated it. When I merely threatened violence they showed
me the door. Can't you see why?'

'But JNU is dominated by leftists,' said Suguna amazed.

'Janeyu you mean?' Hally began to feel that the conversation
must end now. 'I must tell you that is what we called JNU in
those days. We said Marxists came here to have their *janeyu
sanskar*!'

They laughed.

'Your turn now, tell me about yourself,' he said as she
placed the mugs on the terrace wall.

'My life has not been so adventurous. Dad and mom are
both academics. My mother is a Kannadiga and my father

is from UP. So you see, we had a most liberal casteless atmosphere in the family. My three brothers and I lived happily with our parents in a number of houses all over the city moving from one rented place to another. Then I moved out.'

'Do they belong to different castes?' he asked.

'Not really. They are both Brahmins. But from different regions, which is considered as bad, you know.'

He stopped himself from commenting on that.

They carried the mugs to the kitchen. The woman who had come to clean the house was leaving. They got back to the room having bolted the door on the terrace.

'I am trying not to think of many things,' he said honestly. Then holding her by the shoulders he said, 'Suguna, I must ask this. I must. Does it matter to you? My being a Dalit?'

'Do I sound like it matters to me?' she asked surprised by the intensity of his tone.

'You are saying it without even thinking about it. Please think about it and let me know. Take your time,' he said.

He left soon afterwards. Suguna could not sleep after that, thinking why their first tryst had to take this turn. She did not like the idea that she would have to be under test all the time, trying to prove her sincerity.

Chapter 30

HALLY SUFFERS

Hally was born, like all children, without clothes and a name but with an unshakable identity and the burden of shame it thrust upon him. For his mother he was a sparkling diamond in her drab existence surrounded by squalor, stench, soot and filth that she kept washing and mopping away only for them to return with a persistence she could not beat, only match with her insistence to clean it out of her courtyard. She named him Heera, a diamond, for he also brought her the pride of becoming at last a '*ladkori*', the mother of a son, after three daughters.

He went to school, literally walking on land consecrated by the dead buried years ago with full religious rituals and headstones. His ancestors had removed those headstones – overcoming the fear of reprisals from the gods – to claim the land from the dead. The spirits of those uprooted dead occasionally visited the women in the neighbourhood demanding retribution. It was for women to tie coloured threads on the *mazars* and feed the djinns and pay the agents who drove away such rambling souls with their hard-earned coins. They gave food to mendicants and lit incense sticks on stone slabs smeared with vermilion to ward off the evil eyes of those spirits whose subterranean homes they had demolished.

Every day Hally walked to school through those layers of shame, repentance and appeasement of souls and the curses sent to people's heads, kicking the lemons smeared with vermilion out of the way. He walked passing many identities on the way – the *gudadiwalas* who sat outside homes as miserable as his, taking advantage of the daylight to stitch together torn scraps of sheets into duvets; book binders laying thick layers of glue that they lifted from pots in which they had just boiled powdered arrowroot; the flower sellers with their hands buried in mounds of marigold petals, weaving bright yellow and fragrant white garlands of jasmine.

He walked past lanes overseen by the low roofs of house on both sides, and the towering thick-stemmed trees. Neem, peepul and mangoes grew lush with the nourishment they sucked from the kitchen waste dumped on their roots and the dead interred there. He walked through mornings filled with smoke rising from the *angeethis* made of small tin buckets and dragged outside into the lanes on which women cooked rotis, taking in the aroma of frying garlic and onions, watching women grinding cumin and red chillies on stone slabs stained yellow with the turmeric pulverized on them for years, withdrawn and lonely, feeling different and wanting to be one of them. He always stood to stare at the heaps of bright marigolds, their bright yellow and orange colours arresting his child's eyes. The lanes were full of their children playing *gulli danda* and marbles and abusing each other with gusto. If they had any bloom in their lives it went unnoticed like the tiny blooms of the neem hidden in the dark recesses of the branches, too tiny to be seen, smelt or touched. The trees and the people all were rooted to the place and bore fruit before anyone even noticed that they had had flowers.

There was fecundity all around bringing with it the coarse language of sex and bias. People threatened to get inside the genitals of each other's mothers and sisters so constantly that nobody ever took offence. It was the ordinary everyday communication of people born to work and reproduce. Fecundity and work were the realities of life as he saw it and he hated that life with the hatred of the deprived.

All round him the mornings were stuffed with work. The boiling and sticking of glue on thick cardboard covers, of stitching together printed sheets, of heaping dung and patting them into cakes to be slapped onto walls as dark ornaments to dry, of long sharp needles being run through the soft sepals of marigolds.

His pride fought with the sense of perfidy at the alienation and difference his school thrust upon him. The school with its science labs and its system of announcing the names of students who had scholarships, not for having topped the class, but for having been born to particular castes, invited and excluded him. The days the teacher announced the names of the boys who were to get the *vazeefa* were days he wished he could sink into the ground or become invisible. He never understood why the *vazeefa* could not be given discreetly. His classmates who made paper boats and played marbles with him smirked at him. He was a bitter child, quick to take offence. That is why one of his friends had named him *hala*, poison, the friend for whom he deciphered the difficult to understand verses of Surdas and the writings of Dwivedi and who regularly borrowed his notes. He kept his bitterness locked up inside him, quietly bending his head to books at home and not making too many friends, trying not to bring many friends home, though most of his classmates lived in the neighbourhood in equally filthy surroundings but with wider lanes and in houses with bigger rooms.

He clambered onto the ramparts of the fort his history teacher had told him was Prithviraj Chauhan's fort as he walked back from school loath to return to the house, desperate to escape the drabness of his existence, running away from the class teacher's look of veiled contempt. He had done nothing to earn that contempt. He was, if anything, a good student, better than most. It was his birth, the womb he came from that the teacher had contempt for. His child's diction had no words to express these feelings. He felt cheated and angry and had an intense desire to run away. He hid and watched people streaming into the mosque on Fridays, sitting on the fort's wide rampart and dreaming of the time when he would live in a house as high as this wall of the fort. He would be rich one day, yes, he would, and he would live in a big house and never would he be ashamed of inviting anyone home. Ambition took vague shape in his mind. One day he would be a doctor treating that same teacher, old and decrepit and pleading with his old student to save his life and begging his forgiveness for the shabby way he had treated him. Another day he would imagine himself a lawyer saving the teacher's bounder of a son from a charge of murder and the old man touching his feet with gratitude.

His family had tried hard to shake off the stigma. They had forsaken traditional skills and learnt new ones, given up making shoes as if the profession brought shame. Giving up the expertise in telling the leather of a kid from that of the buffalo to learn how to stitch clothes and tell the difference between linen and cotton, his father and his two uncles struggled to find a foothold in the business for years, bringing home less money and much talk about rising up the ladder. They had looked up to education as the panacea that would rid them of the burden they had carried down the ages. By the time Hally passed out of high school his ambition had changed. His father expected him to join the civil service, nothing less. He was the family's hope. When he was in college his dying father had said to him that he must do well in his exams, he must become an IAS officer. He must lead the family into a better life. That hope shone from the eyes about to give up their light.

'Do you trust me?' he had asked his father.

His father had nodded with a smile. That smile stayed with him as a blessing. The only one he would have in a long life full of turmoil.

College had begun to change many things for Hally as he understood that education was not the ladder that could lead him out of the pit of shame Hinduism had cast him into. He was exposed to Marxism and began to see the world with new eyes and made new friends with serious long faces for whom a smile was akin to betrayal of the cause they espoused. They had finely chiselled definitions and always expected reality to fit their theory and grew confused when the world displayed its independence. He was hypnotized by their innocent belief that they would soon make a revolution and their readiness to lay down their lives for that change. Like many of his generation he had cut his political teeth on the internal emergency that had officially outlawed freedom, engaged in the raging debates on constitutional guarantees, always aware that there was one constitutional guarantee nobody wanted to talk of, the one that prohibited segregation and the idea of impurity at birth that was honoured mostly in the breach. His romantic friends did not even know that here, in this very city, people lived in lanes neatly demarcated for different castes and the lower rungs of that ladder went deep into a pit in which he was born. He joined the underground resistance with an ardour that provided a vent to a lot of the accumulated bitterness of his existence. He was aware all the time that the talk centred around what the state could do, did not do, how it could be made to do. It never peered into the way people violated the rights of other people on a daily basis with the sanction of religion and tradition that even his comrades appeared to condone.

His brief association with a small underground left party had however left him disillusioned. He realized that there was little or no space for his experience in the party. They preferred to dismiss caste as one of those problems of the superstructure that would go away automatically once the fundamentals of the system changed.

'Then why is it that even rich *chamars* are not treated as equals by rich upper-caste people?' he had once asked of a party senior.

'Comrade,' said the senior to him, 'it is this system that distorts people. Once the whole system is changed then you will see it will all change.'

He did not want to join the civil service anymore. He had developed ambitions of teaching college students and moulding young minds. That was the way towards progress, he was convinced.

It was when a student in JNU complained of caste bias in the marking of his papers that Hally had finally confronted the fact that for the leftists caste meant just an inconvenient question they had no intentions of addressing. They had refused to join the agitation, all his arguments countered with, 'This is not a class issue. We can't get sidetracked into dealing with problems of the superstructure. Class struggle is what we must concentrate on.'

He had cut his own swathe and was soon out of the university. His dream of teaching college students was over and he had taken any odd job that came his way as his mother waited patiently for the son to join the civil service, till he had had to tell her that he would never be what they had thought he would become. 'I am going to do greater things,' he told her. He had no idea what greater things he could do. He had joined a trade union, to begin with, as a research assistant helping them edit their magazine and had despaired of doing anything more meaningful on that job.

From being ashamed and bitter to being angry he had come a long way, resolving his dilemmas on his own and eventually conquering his feeling of shame and discomfort to such an extent that he could even laugh at some of its aspects and make jokes about it. He had come to accept his caste and the fact that he would have to prove himself more efficient than others to be considered equally good. He had seen the women's movement articulate this reality with great interest. 'Our conditions are so similar,' he had thought. 'But this movement too does not want to look at caste.'

Frustrated and with a sense of futility he wondered if he could use the skills he had picked up from his father to start a business. He knew enough about clothes and their cuts to launch a brand of readymade shirts. It would be hard work and not something he would enjoy. The shop his father and uncle owned was still around. He could use the space, hire a few tailors and begin something not very expensive. His uncle may even help him out. He had seriously begun considering the idea of borrowing some money and starting an enterprise to make readymade shirts when the Bhopal gas disaster took place. Moved by it he too had joined the volunteers who had rushed to Bhopal, his plans forgotten. He had been forced to leave his opposition to foreign funds as he desperately looked for a job.

He had met Nirmala and grown really close to her. She had given up the allure of medical practice in favour of questioning the way it was practised. He shared her poverty, in her case not something she could not avoid, and her aversion to Marxists.

He had once asked her, 'What do you have against Marxism?'

'The fact that it does not have good practitioners,' she had replied.

His affair with Nirmala had ended as abruptly as it had begun. Nirmala had been honest with him from the first day and told him not to hope for anything long term. 'My work comes first. Don't tell me we can work together, and live together. It does not work in this imperfect world,' she had told him. Sometime later she had told him, 'Let us stop this while it is good. We are both enjoying ourselves too much!' He did not pretend to understand, but he had retreated gracefully.

With Suguna it seemed to be different. It had grown slowly on him and there had been no intense intellectual talk; only a small spell of working together and yet he knew that if she now walked out of his life it would take him a long time to recover.

'What a fool I am,' Hally thought. He could not imagine what had made him insist that Suguna think coolly about whether his caste mattered to her. He did not know if it was the distrust of the upper castes that was in his bones, his only inheritance that he was loath to give up that made him do it or some need for reassurance. If he could not transcend his caste roots how did he expect others to do it?

He remembered how she had asked him what he really wanted to do in life. He had told her he wanted to have a house on a hill 'in which we can both grow our own vegetables'.

Instead of being thrilled she had pointed out that he had not even checked whether she wanted to go live with him in the hills. 'You simply presumed I would want to.' Could they have a normal relationship with their acute awareness of their positions as members of discriminated categories? Then he laughed. When would definitions change? As Avidha had asked who would change them if everyone simply went along with the accepted?

Ever since that morning he had left her house he had been berating himself. She had not come to the last two meetings. He wanted to go to her house, hold her in his arms and tell her nothing mattered when they were together and that is how he wanted it. He stood in the veranda of Harjit's house waiting to see if she would come today. He would have to go in soon for the meeting was about to begin. 'Oh, God, please make her come today,' he prayed under his breath and stopped short at that. He could not believe that he, a staunch atheist, had just called upon God for help.

Suguna walked in. 'Hi!' she said cheerily to him. All his tension vanished and came back.

'How have you been?' she asked.

'Fine,' he said falling back on convention.

'Really? I thought you wouldn't have been fine,' she replied. He was startled and reassured.

'You are so bad,' she continued. 'You did not even call to check why I hadn't come.'

Absurdly, he thought she was trying to soften the impact of her decision to break up.

'Tell me... now...' he stammered.

'I won't,' she said turning back with a pout. She was stunned to see the impact of her words on him. She liked her power over him and the exquisite torture she was meting out to him and walked nonchalantly into the room to greet the others.

Suguna and Hally walked to CP later.

'You know I thought hard about it,' she told him. 'Very hard. And yes, it makes a difference.'

His world was shattered.

'Because you are not free of it,' she continued, oblivious of his reaction.

He looked at her vacantly. He had not even heard what she had said.

She looked perplexed that he was so cold. He looked away.

'Don't you agree?' she asked perplexed.

'What?' he asked.

'Don't you see it?' She held his hand. 'If you are not free of the burden of your past I will have to deal with it all the time and that will make a difference.'

He hugged her there on the road making passers-by pause. A loud whistle and a catcall reminded them they were on a street in Delhi.

Chapter 31

AVIDHA TELLS PRASHANT

Avidha thought it strange that all her friends knew about her condition and yet the man who was responsible for it was blissfully unaware. She asked herself why should he have a pleasant holiday in England?

She wrote a two-line letter for him.

'P, I am pregnant. Thought I would let you know. A.'

She put it in an envelope and went to his office after having called to check that he was in. She had to wait two days before he was available. She went in, placed the envelope on his table, and told him, 'I only want you to read this. I am leaving.' She turned and left.

Prashant opened the envelope wearily.

He stared down at the two sentences not believing them.

'I don't know how many people she is going to bed with,' was his first thought and he immediately felt ashamed. He knew had there been another she would not be so obsessed with him. She would not have told him about her condition had he not been the father. A heavy weight of responsibility descended on his brain. In a flash the consequences dawned. If his wife found out, she would end the marriage. What would his son have to say about it? He was old enough to understand such things. He immediately dialled Avidha's number. He finally got her on his fourth attempt. He had to meet her. He had to. If possible now. At this moment.

Avidha felt the power she had acquired with her pregnancy. She made an excuse to not meet him that day.

He called immediately after she put down the receiver. He had to meet her. Had she forgotten? He was leaving for England in four days. They must discuss this.

'Have you forgotten that I have work? I can't leave the office before eight,' she told him.

'I will pick you up at eight then,' he said.

She met him outside the Rail Bhawan 20 minutes after eight. He was waiting for her when she got there. 'My fortune changes,' she thought. 'Too late for me to enjoy it.'

He took her to a restaurant in Lodhi Garden that was secluded enough for them to have a private conversation. He looked concerned and very worried.

'I am sorry for what happened,' he told her.

Avidha suddenly felt that she had misunderstood him all along. He was not such a selfish guy after all.

'This will be a major problem,' he told her.

'For you?' she asked.

He knew enough to sidestep that. He also did not wish to create any problems for her. He was actually concerned as much for her as for himself. He did not want to feel responsible for destroying her future. She was young. She could find someone else. Her whole future was at stake here and he knew she was foolish enough to stake it first and think about it later.

'For you. As well,' he began to talk to her about the loss of face she would suffer. 'You must get rid of it. Okay?' he told her.

'You are worried that I may tell your wife,' she asked clutching at her abdomen. 'That if this comes out, it will destroy your marriage?' she asked him.

'Yes, I am,' he told her. 'I would be lying to you if I said no. But believe me I am more worried about you. It does not reflect so much on men as it does on women. It will create more problems for you. Won't it?'

He was right of course.

She hung her head and said she needed time to think.

'What do you need to think about?' he was annoyed. Was she going to have a child only to exercise some power on him? He did not know how close he was to the truth. For the first time Avidha had discovered he would come running to meet her at midnight, if necessary, only because of her condition. She did not know whether to thank that bundle of cells inside her for bringing him to her or to hate it for having more power than her.

'I don't know if I want to kill the child,' she said deliberately using the word 'kill'.

He looked astonished. He said she was being stupid. 'It is not as if we planned this. We did not. So let us please put this behind us,' he said to her. 'Avi, if you are worried about the money I can help you. I can. I mean you can go to a private facility too. Please don't worry about the money. Let me handle that part at least. That is the least I can do.'

He wanted to ask for details. When did she discover it? Why did she not tell him? He did not ask. He could work that out himself. There was very little time for her to make the decision. She must do it fast. 'Be sensible,' he told her.

He dropped her close to her house looking as sick with worry as he was when he met her. 'Let me know by tomorrow. I will worry,' he told her.

'I may take more time to decide,' she said with an imperceptible smile.

He got angry. Did she not know he was going away?

'Why should your convenience decide everything in my life?' she asked flaring up.

He calmed down. 'Okay, take your time,' he said. 'How much time do you have to get this done legally?'

Even if it was a little beyond the legally stipulated time he could help. No problems. He was quite well placed for that. In fact, placed in the right ministry. 'I will be away for two weeks,' he told her. Something he had not told her the day she asked him.

She felt emotionally exhausted. She had no energy to think.

'Give me your address. I will write to you,' she said.

He could not do that. So he was not going on his own. 'So much for being worried about me,' she thought.

'The letter may reach after I have left. I am there only for two weeks,' he told her. 'I will call you.'

He did. Twice in one week.

The second time he grew annoyed. 'Why are you being so stubborn?' he asked her. 'If you decide not to abort just remember I will have nothing to do with it. Nothing. You are on your own there.'

She put down the receiver and felt empty. She sat at her desk feeling like an outsider watching herself, devoid of thought and emotion. He had finally set her free with those uncompromising words of his, 'I have nothing to do with it.'

With that disownment he had made the unborn child hers alone. Now it was up to her to decide whether it had a future or not.

She was curiously no longer distressed. Her brain began to function as if the cells had awoken after a coma. There was no hurry to decide anything, her brain told her. She knew she would sleep very well tonight.

She opened the door to Suguna's office and called her out. 'His concern for me is conditional, you do what I expect you to do or it is good bye. That is his attitude.'

Suguna was struck by the change in her demeanour. 'Avi, does it not hurt you?'

'I am beyond hurt now. He has lost the power to hurt me. Suguna, I am so happy today. I belong to myself again,' she said.

Chapter 32

THE CACTUS BLOOMS

Avidha had an important decision to make and she knew there was little time now. If she wanted an abortion she needed to have it within a week. She had spent the night at Nirmala's to be free to think. In this quiet place where few buses came and there were not more than two cars to be seen in the neighbourhood Avidha felt like she was transported out of Delhi. Nirmala's house overlooked a marsh that spread out from a long and shimmering lake. They had taken many walks around this lake and it was one of her favourite haunts in the city.

She walked to the gate keeping close to the tall iron fence on the road littered with the faded orange petals of the gulmohar. The amaltas swung its bunches of pale green buds overhead. Birds were busy building nests, the air was full of their mating calls. She walked slowly past the marsh in which tall eucalyptus crackled their brittle leaves and shed scabs of silvery bark. She strolled up to the far corner of the large lake and sat down on a fallen acacia close to the lake, startling a water hen that jumped into the water cackling to itself like an irritable housewife annoyed by salesmen knocking on her door. Avidha watched life go on around her, as if she and her pains did not exist.

Bulbuls trilled, robins whistled and a koel cooed to his mate. Then she heard the brain fever bird join in, its voice rising slowly from a low pitch to a maddeningly high note and thought how it was like the man who had brought her to this pass, abrupt, sudden and killing.

She thought about the time she had met Prashant and how in a short space he had gone from being another face in the corridor to being a face she could kill for and how it must now once again be made to feel like a stranger's face. The nights she had spent with him were not an illusion, neither were the mornings when she had yearned for his touch, reached out to him, trying to hold his impatient self inside her and how she had finally been forced to give up. She knew she would never go on a walk with him again, his hand around her waist, never be able to have him when she wanted, never be able to call out to him for help. She had always known this but somehow she had managed to hope that it would happen someday. Did her subconscious leap up to repulse him the moment she found life unbearable without him? Is that how she had lost him forever? She could not answer that. All she knew was he had been there, but he was gone now and his memories brought neither pain nor joy. They did not even feel like an old movie she would want to watch again. It no longer mattered whether he saw that as a loss of privilege or good riddance to bad rubbish. She did not want him. The only decision she had to make was about the growth inside her and what to do with it.

Was she prepared to shrug off the burden of thousands of years of acculturation to be free again and decide what she wanted without bothering what others would say or expect of her? Was she ready to give up the familiar life, redefine all relations with one unretractable step to claim that freedom she had incessantly talked about? Could she do it? Could she live alone, coming back to a crying child and paid help, coping with the everyday grind of life without the support or the facility of consulting another adult, possibly, for the rest of her life? Was she prepared to answer the million questions that would be asked by friends and extended family and one day by her own child? Would she become bitter to everyone whom she could not or would not want to answer?

Once again she was surrounded by questions and no one was there to answer them. She got up and walked a little distance and then sat down on a bench. She could not run away from her doubts. They were part of her and she had to arrive at a decision soon, not by default and procrastination but by understanding herself.

Her turmoil was complete. She felt as if she had sullied her life, filled it with the scum of unnecessary emotions and romanticism. She sat still watching the web of dry and rotting leaves of water hyacinth float by like an island. A mallard sailed into view like a majestic double-decker boat, wriggling the ridiculously small black curl in its tail at her. The lake, she thought, was not clear and uncluttered. Yet the mallard lived in it, finding food. Clear ponds, she realized do not feed, they have no lives.

Avidha knew what she had to do.

Nirmala was sprawled in bed, a newspaper fluttering in her hands. 'Nimmie, I have decided. I will have the baby. A straight life is not for me,' she said.

Her mother was surprised to see her in the morning. Did she have a day off?

Avidha told her she had something important to tell her. Sushila remembered how she had come in one evening as if she was about to share some confidence and had not told her much. Once again she knew whatever Avidha had come to tell her was not good news.

Avidha sat silent for a long while watching her mother change cushion covers. She had rehearsed the scene many times in her mind but now when she was sitting across her mother, busy with her chores, somehow all those scenes seemed inadequate and inappropriate. The only way to do this was to blurt it out or she would never be able to get it off her chest.

'I am pregnant,' she told her mother.

Sushila's face was inscrutable. She sat stunned, as if she had not heard her.

'Will he marry you?' she asked after a long moment.

'No,' said Avidha, not volunteering any more information.

Avidha sat looking at the floor and had a fleeting glimpse of the yellow border of a sari moving towards her. She looked up. Her mother slapped her. 'How dare you come and tell me this? I wish I had never had a daughter. I wish you had died in childhood,' she said.

Avidha had expected many things but not this slap. Her mother had never beaten her, never hit her.

'Who is it?' she asked when Avidha held her silence.

'How does that matter?' Avidha said angrily.

'Do you know who it is? Or don't you know even that much?' asked Sushila.

Stung by the taunt Avidha got up and left.

'Never come back to my house again,' spat her mother from behind.

This woman is my mother. She thinks I am a slut. She thinks I don't even know who put his genes inside me, Avidha thought, her blood boiling. She does not care what is happening to me. She does not care what I feel, how I feel. She does not want to know if I feel betrayed and lonely and sad. All she is bothered about is that precious name of her family and the disgrace I brought to it. She does not love me as I am, only what I could have been. Is this what they call a mother's love? Unconditional love, my foot. No love is unconditional. They all love the image they have of you. You dare alter that image and all love is dead. Instantly.

She went home and told the wall what she wished she could scream in her mother's face: 'I will never tell you who it is. I know, but I won't tell you. That is your punishment. You never wanted to know me, you only wanted me to be what you think a good girl should be. You made me so insecure. You gave me no confidence in myself. You are to be blamed for this. This is all your fault, your fault.'

Her father came to see her the next morning. He looked very disturbed. He was very fond of his daughter. She shared his weakness for literature and they had spent many evenings arguing about characters in novels. Now his daughter had become like a character from one, he thought. Suguna tactfully left for work soon after he arrived.

'Your mother told me,' he said.

She wanted to ask him exactly what words her mother had used. Had she simply reported the fact as if even pronouncing those words about her daughter contaminated her tongue and she would use as few words as possible or had she used many adjectives? Had he blamed her for it? Had she blamed him for it? Had they argued and fought or had they both kept quiet?

Instead she looked down at the floor waiting for him to go on. They sat in her room.

'Tell me who it is. Maybe I can talk to him,' he said.

Avidha was driven to tears. How small he feels, she thought, only because she had done something he thought was wrong. He felt he must set it right even if it meant pleading with a stranger on her behalf.

'No point, Baba,' she said. She nearly told him who it was but the memory of her mother's slap came back to her. Her cheek burnt with shame.

He kept looking at her with his beseeching eyes. Unable to meet that gaze she looked back at the floor.

'What did I do wrong? What was wrong in your upbringing for you to bring such disgrace to the family?' he asked her. 'We are such an old family.'

That was one of the burdens she had been trying to shake off ever since she was a child. That was one of the things he did wrong, placing the burden of a family on her shoulders that she did not want.

'Very old family,' he said again.

She swallowed her tears. In her view all families were old. 'The fact that we exist is proof that we had ancestors and only because the names of some families are not on land records or in the records of the *pandas* of Banaras or Gaya does not mean these families sprang up yesterday, freshly evolved from apes,' she was used to saying. It then flashed upon her that they expected such things to happen to families consigned to the lower castes, whom they saw as immoral and promiscuous. The bias shamed her on his behalf. Where was his logical side? She loved her father and his pain communicated to her. She could not live by the rules he had. That tormented her too.

'Can't something be done?' he asked her.

'What?' she asked him

'These days doctors do so many things.'

Dear old daddy! She felt like hugging him. He would not even mention the word abortion. He only wanted to be rid of the proof of her actions. Was it her mother's belated idea of saving the family from disgrace? If there is no proof does that mean the act had not been performed? What hurt him more? The fact that she had slept with a man she was not married to? Or any man who did not want to marry her? Or the idea that there may be more than one man in her life? Or that she was going to have a baby without being married?

'I don't want to do it,' she said to him, tears coursing down her cheeks.

Is that what he would have wanted had one of his students been pregnant by him? He would be shocked to learn she knew about his affairs; she also knew he would have taken them to the hospital himself to get rid of the foetus. She wanted to know how men like him reacted when they knew they were responsible for having put a girl in what they euphemistically called 'trouble'. Would he tell her how he would have reacted if she asked him now? How do even highly educated people like him explain their double standards to themselves?

'I will write to Kaustubh. He could find you some job in Canada. You could go away. Nobody will know,' he said to her having digested her decision to have the baby.

That was plan number two then, hide her from people who know the 'old' family and that would make it all right.

'I don't want to go to Canada,' she told him, then went to the kitchen to make him a cup of tea.

He sipped the tea reluctantly as if now even a glass of water she touched would be polluted. 'You cannot come to our house. Never. Your mother says so. And she is right,' he said.

Right, blame Mother for the decision. Could he not stand up and tell his wife she would come and meet him and if she, the wife, disapproved she could go away somewhere while Avidha was visiting?

The thought that her child would possibly never know what it meant to have grandparents hurt her more than their rejection of her.

'Yes, Baba, I understand,' she said.

He asked her softly to think about it.

Avidha went down with him when he left and they ran into Mrs Kapoor who was returning from one of her satsangs. She introduced her father. Mrs Kapoor asked him in for tea. He refused. She told him what a very helpful daughter he had. 'So independent. Like girls should be today. You must be very proud of her,' she said to him. He smiled at her.

On the way to the market to find an auto he turned to her and said, 'What will she say when she hears of this? She won't say I should be proud of you then.'

Unable to resist anymore, Avidha took hold of his hand. He stopped. She said to him, 'Baba, I used to be very proud of you.'

Her brother called her in office two weeks later to tell her he stood by her. 'I am sure you have thought about what you are doing. I know you can't talk from the office. Avi, if you want to come here, you are welcome. You have a home here. You can come for a holiday if you wish. If you want to migrate that is another cup of tea, not so easy. Ma and Baba won't stand by you. I hope you don't blame them. They are too old to change now. But believe me, I am with you. And your baby will have a loving uncle, always. I will come meet you around Christmas. You must call me to tell me whether I have a niece or a nephew. So I can buy suitable presents.'

She put down the phone and began to sob. However much she thought she could do without a family it still mattered to her that her brother stood by her. Never before had she felt so lonely.

Avidha soon realized that her 'liberated' friends were much worse than her parents. They had begun making decisions on her behalf as if by the only act of not taking precautions to avoid pregnancy she had suddenly become irresponsible in everything,

Mukta was very angry with Avidha for going ahead with her pregnancy and deciding not to involve the man in it. 'Tell me who he is and I will send him a legal notice,' Mukta told her. She told her the least he could do was pay her child support. She would drag him to court to make him do it. 'If he wants to keep this a secret, a legal notice alone will bring him to his knees. He will settle. He will probably pay more than what the court may grant just to make sure his wife does not know.'

Avidha told her it smacked of blackmail.

'Why do you insist on protecting that cad? He has his fun and leaves you holding the baby! Literally in this case. He must pay for it.'

That is exactly what Avidha did not want. For him to feel it was his duty to do anything for her or her child. If it were his wish, his pleasure to own the child, to love, she would willingly take any help he gave her and understand his reasons for not being able to do more. 'I don't like duty, it smacks of sacrifice and sanctimony,' she said. 'You won't understand.'

She knew her pregnancy had become a topic of conversation everywhere. Once she walked into the FOB meeting and suddenly everyone fell silent and she knew they had been discussing her. She felt awful.

Suguna kept at her with her enumeration of all the problems of bringing up a child on her own. She was afraid her paper could throw her out on grounds of moral turpitude. It was doubtful if even the union would fight on her behalf. Some women's groups would but what use would such a fight be? If it went to court the decision would likely come after her child had grown up and found a job on the bench.

'Think of the expenses,' Suguna said to her. Their salaries had never seemed meagre to them but they did not even have decent savings. Children were expensive luxuries. They needed doctors and formulas and toys and they grew out of their clothes so soon.

The challenges seemed insurmountable. Avidha would lose face in the building that housed her office among all those male reporters and seniors who now treated her with some modicum of respect. If Shekhar could behave the way he did what would be the attitude of those stuffed shirts who looked down on women influenced by 'women's lib' as immoral? Everybody was advising her to 'get rid of it'.

Only Nirmala did not argue with her. And only Vineeta was thrilled for Avidha.

Chapter 33

SHEDDING BAGGAGE

Avidha wrote a long piece on the legal challenge to the settlement and like all other pieces on Bhopal it went in for clearance by her chief.

Joshi called her into his chamber and asked her to revise her article. 'How can you praise such an anti-national act?' he asked angrily.

The paper had consistently supported the campaign and suddenly her chief wanted her to condemn the writ petitions. He told her that people who said that the money already taken from Carbide should be returned could not be considered national.

'That is not what the petition says,' she said to him. 'It says if Carbide is found not guilty...'

'So you think there is a chance it may not be guilty? That is anti-national.'

ANJALI DESHPANDE

'We can't presume guilt or innocence. That is not our job...' she began and was cut off mid-sentence by Joshi who flew into a rage. 'Don't try to teach me things. You are playing into the hands of those agents of Carbide. I thought you had more sense.'

She tried to make him see her point but Joshi would pay no heed. 'They paid up. That is proof of their guilt,' he told her. 'And now you go and say we'll return the money...'

'They may pay without admitting guilt. See, all the cases were quashed. It could be cheaper for them to pay their way out...'

'I won't publish this rot,' he told her and threw the article in her face. It fluttered to the ground.

Avidha stood up shaking with anger.

'You think being fair and rational is anti-national? Are you telling me that all those people who signed this petition are anti-national?' She named several famous people including former diplomats, historians, economists, sociologists and journalists.

'Tell me who can't Carbide buy?' asked Joshi bristling with rage at her defiance.

'You tell me how much Carbide paid you,' she shot back.

'You dare... me... they need... not... even try,' he said stammering in his fury.

'So you sold yourself without even being paid for it,' she screamed back.

'Shut up and get out,' screamed Joshi.

She walked out into the staring faces of her colleagues who immediately surrounded her to ask what had happened. They were thoroughly enjoying themselves. She went straight to Suguna's office and told her what had happened.

'Call the top dog,' she said.

Avidha's editor-in-chief was an old communist based in Bhopal who had insisted on importing Avidha to cover the disaster when it took place in 1984. He had told her he did not trust his local reporters to do a good job. 'They are either in cahoots with the local politicians or simply too foolish to understand such a big case,' he had told her frankly. That had made Avidha quite unpopular among her colleagues.

'I am sure to lose my job,' said Avidha. 'After this the old bugger won't stand my pregnancy. He will throw me out. Maybe I should simply drop that story.'

But she called the chief editor.

The old man listened to her patiently and laughed when she told him what Joshi had said. 'Who, by the way, devised the strategy?' he asked her.

When he heard about Professor Thapar the old man started laughing even more. 'The rumour is if our super-clean politician becomes prime minister, Thapar will be made the head of the Law Commission,' he told her.

'Really?' she asked. 'Sir, but what about my piece?'

'Go tell Joshi that Thapar's father had once been invited to tea by Nehru. They were both barristers and they talked about how most people don't understand that every criminal has a right to defence. That will convince him that Thapar is a nationalist. He is such a fool. I will call him. '

Avidha began to laugh. 'Is it true?' she asked him. 'Did Nehru really ask him to tea?'

'I don't think so,' said the editor. 'But does Joshi know that? In our country myths are history. Nationalism is *surya namaskar*, bow to the rising sun! You don't worry. I will talk to Joshi. I will tell him that exposing anti-nationals is the duty of the press and you are doing a great service to the nation.' He laughed loud and hard.

Her article was cleared from Bhopal. It made Joshi hate her even more.

That evening Nirmala dropped by to tell her that she had to make another trip to Bihar and would be away for at least a month. She had come down to hand her a set of keys to her house so she could have a place to go to and be on her own if she ever felt like it.

'I want to ask you a favour,' said Avidha. 'Will you help me get rid of some of the things that I now find very disturbing?'

Avidha took her home and gave her two books of poetry and a pair of silver earrings that Prashant had given her. 'Please get rid of them for me. Dump them, give them away, sell them, do anything but make sure I don't see them again. They remind me of him. He wanted me to cut the little one out of my body. I am throwing him out of my mind,' she said and began to cry.

After a while she wiped her tears.

Nirmala gave her a smile. 'I want you to know that I will help you bring up the kid.'

'You don't...'

Nirmala cut her short. 'What is the point of saying people should have the right to choose if you can't provide them the support they need? I am not doing you a favour. I am doing it for my principles. We can share a house or we can stay close to each other's but, Avi, you are not alone.'

Avidha wiped her tears and hugged her close. Then turning back to the cupboard she said, 'There is something else.'

She pulled out the coverlet she had embroidered from the bottom of the cupboard. 'I made this for him. Isn't it ghastly?'

Nirmala opened it to look at it. 'It is rather pretty. Avi, I wish you had learnt some patience. That is what it takes to do anything well.'

Nirmala left soon afterwards. 'We must hold a party to celebrate your decision,' said Nirmala as she and Avidha walked to the bus stop.

Chapter 34

THE DRY STICK!

Mukta was, once again, preparing a dossier on the Bhopal case, this time for politicians, putting together arguments to demonstrate how the Supreme Court had used its wide ranging powers to strike a blow at the rights of people.

'We do not know the process by which they arrived at this awful settlement,' she said to Nirmala. 'That is what must be found out. Who is responsible? Politics and commerce usually decide how the law should be bent and twisted out of shape.'

Nirmala laughed at her. 'We shall never have that drama of impeachment we are so keen to stage. I feel sorry for you.'

The long hours they spent with each other had brought them closer and Mukta sometimes found herself wishing Nirmala was not straight. Then she would feel guilty for having betrayed Vineeta in her thoughts and be extra good to her. Vineeta put down the change she could see in Mukta to the intellectual gratification that Nirmala provided her.

Mukta finally came up with a draft after Nirmala had left for Bihar. Ajit read it with great care and asked her to revise it. 'Why do you have to ask how the court arrived at the decision? Just leave it at what the court did. That speaks for itself,' he said to her.

'I have put in all the laws that it overlooked. But the most important question is why. *Why* did it do it?'

'They thought they were doing the victims a good turn,' said Ajit.

'How can a justice think he is doing the murdered a good turn by letting off a murderer?' asked Mukta.

'We have to presume,' said Ajit patiently. 'All this talk of Carbide being a murderer is just talk. We can't prove it.'

'We have no evidence because the process of getting to the evidence was sabotaged by this very settlement. Or CBI could have gone to the US and found that UCC was responsible for the design and who knows what else. We had a chance. We lost it.'

Ajit squirmed. He did not know how political players would respond to it. In his talks with some of them they seemed unconvinced that impeachment was called for in this case. 'Don't go for an overkill,' a rather astute politician had told him.

'What does the Supreme Challenger say?' asked Mukta.

'That is the problem. He says nothing,' said Ajit. He thought he should take her along to some of these meetings and she could verbally brief them about things they did not dare put down in writing. 'He can at least find out. Should I put down all that is being said outside the court about its motives?' she asked Ajit. 'So he is convinced about the need for impeachment?'

Ajit immediately discarded his decision to involve her in discussions with the politicians. He was not sure if her idea about including the talk of corruption in the dossier was such a good one. 'We can't put rumours in an official briefing. We will tell the leaders verbally,' he said.

'There is no need to tell them,' said Mukta, getting angry. 'They know how the court functions better than us.' She got up to leave. 'You do what you want to do with it. Cut out anything, add anything, it doesn't matter to me.'

'You must understand, Mukta, that politics will decide everything.'

'That is why we have to bring it out in the open. Make it impossible for politicians to ignore the talk about the motives of the justices. We have been saying it in our speeches.'

Ajit got angry too. 'What are you cribbing about? We said many things in our speeches, and the court kept quiet.'

'Precisely. You know why? Because the court was ashamed that it had done such a thing. We must not let it forget. We must make Parliament get us the answer. Why did the court do it? Why did the government do it? As the sole representative of the people,' Mukta was screaming now, 'it went to the United States as a sovereign plaintiff and lost the case in India over which it has sovereign rights. Why? How? That is the most important question for us.'

'I don't want to handle hysterics,' flung back Ajit.

Mukta picked up her bag and left.

'These bloody women,' he screamed at his wife. 'These three women will be the death of me. As if that Nirmala was not enough. That Avidha has been saying all kinds of things in her speeches. Now this one is thrusting her agenda. Who the hell wants impeachment? Who cares? What will we gain by it?'

Avidha, Suguna and Hally sat on the terrace sharing a plate of namkeen and drinking tall glasses of *nimbu pani*. Initially, Avidha had tried to come home late from work, to give Suguna and Hally some time on their own – he did not spend every night there but he did drop by very often. It was Suguna who had brought it up with her one afternoon. 'Do you run away only because he is coming over?' she asked her.

'Guilty,' admitted Avidha

'It is your home, too, Avi, you come and go as you please,' she said. 'And I know Hally does not mind having you around.'

'No man ever objected to a harem,' Hally had said pulling a serious face. After that Avidha became a part of their world. They spent most evenings together, mostly at home but also at Mandi House where they went to watch plays, and in Harjit's house, where the meetings of FOB were now held infrequently.

One evening Mrs Kapoor had come upstairs to find Hally there. He had got up to greet her respectfully and told her they all worked together and he came there often to discuss work. Next time he came by he had first gone to meet Mrs Kapoor and found her sitting in front of a TV, its screen full of snow. Mrs Kapoor had told him how nobody managed to repair anything in the neighbourhood and how her only companion, the TV, was probably now lost to her forever. Hally took the TV away the next day and got it repaired in

Paharganj for half the amount the old woman had paid for repairs earlier and won her over completely.

'Let Mrs Kapoor discover I am a *chamar* and then let us see how she reacts,' Hally said, as they sipped their drinks.

'I will tell her tomorrow!' Avidha said to him, laughing. 'At least Suguna and I will have time to ourselves like we used to before you came along making sheep's eyes at her.'

Hally laughed, then looked at her astutely. 'Miss him sometimes?'

Even though she had convinced herself that she was free of Prashant her appetite for his memories still seemed to be going strong and she made a conscious attempt to throttle them.

'Yes,' she admitted to him. 'I do, sometimes.'

'You never want to tell us who he is, do you?' he asked.

She told them. 'I was crazy about him. I did not want him to lose anything, his family, his child, nothing and yet be mine,' she said calmly.

'Who is he? Do we know him by any chance?' asked Suguna.

'You may know him. We are on the same beat. Prashant Mishra.'

'That dry stick!' exclaimed Suguna involuntarily.

Dry stick?

'With the overhanging face?' Suguna continued.

Avidha looked away. That is one more thing she would have to bear, people commenting on her bad taste.

All of a sudden the call bell began pealing urgently.

Mukta made her entry, destroying their Saturday evening peace.

'I am going to quit FOB,' said Mukta ignoring the glass of water Suguna had fetched her and the stool Avidha pushed at her.

After half an hour Mukta had cooled down enough to report on her fight with Ajit.

'But we already know how it happened and why,' said Hally.

'You don't listen to anyone, do you? I am not saying I want the answer. I am saying the answer must be put on record. For the people of India.'

That night, Suguna and Hally, yet to fall asleep, heard what sounded like loud and dry sobs from Avidha's room. Suguna rushed in to check on her.

'I just remembered what you said about his face. You are right! It does hang,' said Avidha doubling up with laughter.

By the time Nirmala returned from Bihar FOB meetings had become so irregular they had to be convened specially and people had to be cajoled and shamed into attending them. Those not involved in working out the legal strategy had begun to feel redundant. Only a few worked regularly on the issue. Mukta, despite her threats to walk out, had to keep her commitment to help out in the court case and only the court could now decide when she would be free of it, if ever.

Rains, slush, waterlogging, everything added to their reasons for not attending. Zintac's father was unwell; Latika was in Switzerland to give talks on Bhopal; Avidha and Suguna were now caught up in following politicians and their interminable talks of alliances and management of contradictions.

At the end of July Avidha reminded Nirmala that she had promised her a party to celebrate her pregnancy.

'They do it traditionally in the fifth month, don't they?' asked Nirmala.

They were in Harjit's house attending a small meeting. Harjit overheard them and insisted on throwing the party.

'Brilliant,' said Ajit to Nirmala. 'What an inspiration to get everyone back.'

'This is a party, not an FOB meeting in disguise,' said Nirmala annoyed with him. 'Or I would have made you pay for it.'

'A project nobody will fund,' said Ajit.

They got together in Harjit's house, a full house of FOB and some others, to get drunk and dance and gorge on delicious food. But Harjit had planned a little ritual to launch the party. He had festooned the little gazebo in his backyard with marigold garlands and took his place behind a round table with a silver bowl of punch and glasses on it. He poured out ruby-coloured punch in small crystal goblets and stood up to make a toast.

'Avidha, our comrade, you are the bravest of girls I have known. There is nothing great about having a child because the whole family wants you to have one. It is great and courageous to have a child when the family is opposed to it. I want to tell Avidha that we are her family and this child will have many aunts and uncles and could've had some grandparents too but nobody among us will agree to be recognized as so old, even an old fogey like me. This I say is the true form of democracy. Let the moral majority rot in its cesspool of abusive traditions. This house is for those who defy, not those who bow and scrape. To the charming Avidha I say, "*Avidha, tum aage badho, hum tumhare saath hain!*"'

Then picking up one of the glasses of punch he said, 'To Avidha plus one.'

Harjit hugged Avidha and handed her a box wrapped in green silk.

The wrapping turned out to be a sari. Inside was a big square box. Sitting in three deep hollows in it on cream satin lining was a silver bowl, flanked with two small silver glasses and two silver spoons. 'Make sure you put the silver spoons in the baby's mouth,' said Harjit.

Avidha was overwhelmed. She handed Harjit the sari saying, 'Keep the wrapper. I take what you gave to the child.'

'Traditionally, the wrapper goes with the gift. Nimmie told me women are given a green sari when they are five months pregnant,' said Harjit. 'You can get it changed if you don't like the colour.'

'Thank you, Avi, for teaching Harjit the value of tradition,' said Hally.

Avidha was embarrassed and raised her glass to her lip. She had had a few sips when Mukta took away her glass and said the 'plus one does not need to drink'.

That led to a fierce argument with Nirmala saying that Avidha could have a little wine. 'That is why we are having wine punch here. Harjit could easily have given us Scotch,' she said.

Latika said she had seen enough doctors misusing their degrees but she was surprised that finally Nirmala had joined their ranks.

Mukta said with a bitter laugh, 'So I am now the evil mother-in-law only because I say pregnant women shouldn't drink.' She got up and left the garden to go towards the house.

Vineeta came running after Mukta. 'Don't go away, please. Avidha may feel bad,' she said to Mukta.

'I am only going to the loo,' said Mukta. Abashed Vineeta went back to her glass of punch and joined Avidha before she noticed Ajit walking up to her.

'I guess now you will make me *gond ke laddoo*,' said Avidha to Vineeta, reaching out a hand to Ajit.

'I don't know how to make them. I wish I could ask my mother, but you know I can't.'

Avidha gave her a tight smile. 'We are both in the same boat, I can't ask Ma anything either,' she said and quickly turned away, walking towards the gazebo.

Finding himself alone with Vineeta, Ajit turned to her and abruptly said, 'I forgive you.'

Vineeta was stupefied. She moved away from him before Mukta could get back. Walking around the beds in the garden she tried to control her agitation. What did he have to forgive her for? Ajit followed her.

'We must behave normally,' he said to her.

She looked back flustered, automatically checking for Mukta. 'I don't know why you are saying you forgive me. I didn't do anything bad to you,' she said.

Ajit smiled and went back to chat up Avidha.

'Avi, just make sure you have a daughter,' said Zintac loudly, her glass raised high. 'Remember your landlady's rule. No boys!'

That woke up Avidha to a problem she had not even thought of.

Chapter 35

A FRIEND MAKES HER CHOICE

Convention lives like a virus in the brain, dormant in presumptions. Only a confrontation with the proscribed challenges it into existence. It was Avidha's pregnancy that forced Suguna to examine her own easy truce with accepted norms.

When Avidha and Suguna had decided to share a flat they had discussed everything threadbare from who will do what to how to share the household expenses and duties. After they moved in many of the rules had fallen by the wayside but they coped. What they had never discussed was what if one of them decided to have a child presuming marriage would precede such an event. Now Avidha had presented her with a situation that destabilized her comfortable life. If Avidha thought, in her Hindi film-influenced way, that she could fade out in one scene and appear in the next with a baby in her arms, *pallu* on her head and her best friend by her side, she was being unreal and unfair. Suguna began resenting her assumptions and the additional load of work it necessitated.

'I must talk to her,' she told herself and every day she postponed it. Some days they arrived too tired. Some days, Avidha was in one of her moods, lost in herself. There seemed to be no right time to bring up the subject.

One hot humid morning in August Avidha suddenly clutched at her stomach and said, 'You know I felt something.'

Suguna was petrified. She thought she was going to miscarry. 'Let us go to a doctor,' she said trying not to panic.

'No, silly. It felt like something kicked at me. Very slight. Do you think it is the baby kicking me?' asked Avidha.

Suguna decided that she could no longer postpone her discussion. 'Tomorrow,' she told herself. 'I can't spoil her first day of feeling the child's kick for sure.'

She got her chance when Avidha returned from UP, the hotbed of the electoral contest, having covered political rallies of the Supreme Challenger. Hally, a regular visitor when she was away, had cooked enough mutton the evening before to last them the next day. Avidha was delighted. To come back to delicious food, a friend to chin with, what else could a woman want? Life was good.

She put on her favourite cassette of Khusro's poems. '*Sab sakhiyan ke paas piya hai, mera piya se milne ko jiyara tarase,*' she hummed with the singer, shaking her head slowly.

'Lucknow was not so muggy,' said Avidha when Suguna brought in a plate of salad with peanuts.

She began telling her about the massive turnouts at the rallies. 'The government will change for sure,' she said. Suguna did not want to discuss elections. She was looking for an opening to broach the subject that had been bothering her. Avidha, munching on peanuts, began asking her about news of FOB. 'I have been feeling so guilty, not having gone to any of the meetings. Any idea what is going on?'

Then Avidha told her how one of the more important leaders in the Supreme Challenger's camp had said in his speech that the corruption in a defence deal was not an ordinary incidence of corruption like that in the supply and purchase of rice for ration shops. 'I think corruption in a rice deal is far more important for people. It affects the poor directly. These politicians are such hypocrites. Corruption is only an electoral plank. I don't think the Supreme Challenger is serious about fighting corruption. They may not help our cause either. All these deals Ajit is cutting with them may be just eyewash.'

'Avi,' said Suguna cutting her short, 'will you blame me if I bring up some practical things?'

'I would mind if you did not talk practical,' said Avidha. 'You won't be yourself then.'

'I have been thinking about what Mrs Kapoor will have to say when she realizes you are pregnant. She will throw us out.'

Avidha's pregnancy was now beginning to show though she had taken to wearing oversized kurtas to hide the bulge.

'It has been at the back of my mind ever since Baba came here and told me she would look down on me. Should we start looking for another flat?'

Suguna realized that Avidha had assumed they would always be together and began to feel unfriendly. She had rehearsed the piece many times but all the nice prefatory speeches now fled her memory. 'That is another thing I wanted to talk about. This is difficult to say, you know, Avi, so I will say it outright. I am very fond of you. I feel beastly saying this. I don't know how to say it, but Avi, I have to tell you. I am not up to bringing up a child. Even living with one in the same house.'

Avidha's blank stare filled her with remorse.

'Please don't misunderstand me. I dare say I will love the kid a lot. But I think we will have to find separate flats. Our flats can be next to each other's. We can have our own pads and be together too.' She looked uncertainly at Avidha.

There was a long silence in the room. Unable to bear it anymore Suguna said, 'Please, don't take it too hard. Please say something.'

Avidha gulped down the gin and poured herself another one.

'Should you be drinking so much?' asked Suguna.

'How does it matter to you?' asked Avidha.

'I was afraid of this, you know, that you will misunderstand. What would you have done in my place, tell me,' Suguna said, trying hard to get through to her.

'I understand. And you don't have to make the effort of moving into a flat close to mine,' said Avidha.

She went into her own room. It felt cold in there as if no living thing had ever passed through it. They had somehow got into this habit of spending more time in Suguna's room even when Hally was around cracking jokes getting into involved discussions, sometimes being deliberately provocative with each other. It now felt more lived in and cosier.

'I am truly alone now,' thought Avidha as she sat on her bed shivering despite the heat. Why had she made Suguna and Hally her substitute family? She and Suguna had only agreed to share a flat, not a life. Would Suguna have reacted like this had her sister been pregnant? She must have talked this out with Hally and he must have left it to her to handle this. She had thought Hally was different but he turned out to be just like the others. Men! They are all the same. All these months she had tried to overcome the wound Prashant had given her and when she was nearly healed Suguna had dealt her another blow. All those oldies are right when they say friends can never be family, she thought disconsolately.

Suguna came in and sat next to her. 'Talk to me, Avi. Don't make me more miserable than I already am,' she said.

Avidha could not believe that she was blaming her for making her miserable. Everyone blames me, she thought, and began to cry softly. Then burying her face in her hands she wept openly. Suguna felt a few tears course down her own cheeks.

'Just leave me alone. And don't feel miserable. You are not responsible for what I have done to myself,' Avidha told her after a while.

Avidha discovered the next day that Joshi had cut out the portion from her article in which she had related what the leader had said about the rice deal. When she asked him why, he told her reporters had no right to question the editor. This led to another showdown.

She argued that they had a duty to inform people that the Supreme Challenger was after all not so serious about fighting corruption, it was only an electoral plank.

'All politicians are scoundrels. They are also incredibly stupid,' he told her. 'I have pointed out to the leader that he must not go saying such things. That is enough.'

Avidha said she did not get information for him to drive his private bargains with politicians.

'How dare you talk to me like this?' he asked her. 'I will drive as many bargains as I want to. Go complain to your sugar daddy.' He meant the editor-in-chief who, he knew, this time would be on his side. They were all supporting the Supreme Challenger and hoping he would finally end the monopoly of one party and one family in national politics.

'You think your stupid articles make a difference to people? You are too pompous,' he told her. 'I will be very happy to take you off the beat. Now get out.'

Joshi had largely supported her idealism but these days he continually criticized everything she did or did not do. Avidha thought it was her now-obvious pregnancy that made him critical of her. It could also be a ploy to make her quit the job. She was thankful that he had not openly brought up the issue with her.

She had kept it to herself but some of the junior political leaders had asked her, with meaningful smiles, why she had not invited them to her wedding. She had till now managed to keep a straight face and tell them she did not discuss her private life with anyone. She felt the frankly curious looks they directed at her everywhere she went and knew that her press card shielded her from their dirty remarks. She swallowed the insult and told Joshi coldly that she had the guts to practise what she said and he did the bidding of others.

'The day people like you come to respect me I will know I have truly betrayed my creed,' she said.

Chapter 36

A SEVERE DILEMMA

Hally was facing one of the severest dilemmas of his life. He had just left the house of a former ambassador who had served in many countries. He had had two meetings with the venerable man on the Bhopal issue.

The first time they had met the old man had asked Hally, 'If you are going to the court once again for a review of the settlement order, should you not drop that impeachment demand of yours?'

Hally vehemently said that they could not and would not.

The old man smiled tolerantly. 'Seems a little out of place to me. Why annoy them if they are going to sit in judgment again?'

Soon enough the demand for impeachment vanished from their leaflets. Professor Thapar came to one of the FOB meetings and told the group that they had mounted enough pressure on the court and must now concentrate their fire on the executive. He was very persuasive.

'What is the need to ask for the impeachment of the justices in every meeting? It is excessive and we must take care to not push the court beyond a point,' said Professor Thapar.

The meeting had discussed it for over an hour. Nirmala, Hally and Avidha were in the minority who disagreed. Mukta and Vineeta were then taking a vacation in Manali.

'In effect we are giving up the demand for impeachment, are we?' asked Hally.

'No. Look at it sensibly. This government is not going to accept the demand. We will have to wait till the new government is elected. We have made the demand. It is on record. We can shelve it for a while, can we not?' asked Professor Thapar.

'Sounds sensible,' said Suguna.

Most members of the meeting veered round to his viewpoint.

After a few weeks the retired diplomat had called to tell Hally he had spoken to some of his old colleagues and friends and a statement was ready that could be released to the press. Would Hally care to collect it?

That was the statement Hally now held in his hand and had to take it to Ajit to discuss it before they presented it to the FOB meeting. Mads and Ali were again in Delhi to check out the possibility of securing interim relief. As Mads put it, 'May as well get something before we get nothing.'

Hally walked out of the air-conditioned study of the old diplomat without making a single comment on their statement. He felt like a charlatan when he thanked the old man for his support. He could trace back the dilution of his principles to his fatal decision to work for Ajit. The day he gave up his opposition to foreign funds for political work he made a compromise that had led him to this day when he considered himself to have become a part of the problem.

The FOB meeting was being held after a long interval. Mads came in and stretching himself on the sofa laid his head in Latika's lap who began to run her fingers through his unkempt hair unmindful of the interested looks of the company gathered in the room.

'You know, Zintac, we have had a love letter, hand-delivered by our very special messenger, Ajit Khanna,' said Mads, waving a sheet at her. Hally had given him a copy of the statement minutes before and Mads had guessed that it was Ajit's stratagem to keep the press interested.

Nirmala looked at him with disgust and continued to read the minutes register to check how far down the road the campaign had hurtled. They had not even recorded the minutes in the last two months. Avidha and Suguna generally handled the responsibility of keeping records and Avidha had steadfastly refused to do so after a while. None of the men ever volunteered to jot down the minutes. 'Another extension of women's household work,' Suguna called it. 'Keep all the *hisaab*.'

'Do you want to read it?' asked Mads, waving the sheet at Nirmala. 'You will truly enjoy it.' Finding no response from her he said to Latika, 'Will you read it out to us?'

'Mads, sit up. We are to have a meeting,' said Ajit entering the room.

'Go ahead,' said Mads provocatively, 'is this sexy scene disturbing your concentration?'

More people began arriving. Mads kept lying on the sofa till Hally came, looked around for a place to sit and pushed up Mads's feet to make space for himself.

'Don't touch my feet, I am yet to attain sainthood,' said Mads.

Everybody laughed. Hally did not even smile. Mads sat up and placed the statement on the table with a flourish.

'Ajit has got us a beautiful gift. A love letter from all the eminent people of this country,' he said. 'Please somebody read it out.'

'Why don't you do it?' asked Harjit.

'My English is not good,' said Mads with mock seriousness. 'There are many long words in it. I have read it several times but I have not understood it'

The letter was handed to Avidha to read.

It was titled 'Statement of Eminent Persons' and had been signed by 33 people: academics, former bureaucrats, two former ambassadors and sundry advisors to the government, famous people whose names appeared in news columns and editorials and whose articles on everything from scarcity to foreign policy made the editorial pages regularly, and who advised the government on everything from insanity to insanitation.

These persons had expressed 'strong disapprobation' of the settlement which they said had compromised the sovereignty of 'this great nation of Gandhi and Nehru'. They went on to say that the time had come for people with a sense of 'patriotic duty and responsibility' to stand up and be counted, and to rise to the occasion and speak in one voice. It reminded the nation that Nehru had called factories the 'temples of Modern India' and his successors had defiled those temples by letting 'rampant profiteering' to be installed as the presiding deity. 'The nation must stand up and correct the course, the nation must act as one to go back to the ideals of the founding fathers of our great country and fight the desecration of these temples to ensure that compassion flows out of them instead of killer gasses.'

It concluded with, 'We must all contribute and raise Rs 705 crores and hand it over to the government so that it can immediately start disbursal of compensation to the unfortunate victims and send a strong and clear message to Carbide and the government that India does not stand before them as a beggar but a sovereign plaintiff demanding justice. Only such strong and unambiguous action can send an unequivocal message to the Government of India that money does not matter, justice matters, profits do not matter, people matter. This rich country can raise any amount and even though her denizens are poor they are generous of heart and strong of will. The strong arrive at no compromises. They seek and get justice.'

There was a moment's silence after Avidha put down the sheet.

'What pompous asses they are,' said Avidha to Nirmala in a low, almost inaudible, tone, 'imagine actually giving themselves the title of "eminent persons"! The only saving grace is they haven't opened the statement with "we the undersigned eminent persons..."'

'You know, Avidha, these people have been making themselves counted for years now,' said Mads wondering what remark she had made. 'Every few years the government does something to give them the opportunity to count themselves.'

'And their count never goes up. Was there any cheque with that statement?' asked Mukta, joining in the sarcasm.

'The time has come for us to open a bank account,' said Nirmala.

'Actually, it is not such a bad idea. Why don't we

concentrate on raising the amount? If people only gave ten rupees each we could raise this so easily,' said Latika.

Nirmala raised her eyebrows eloquently.

'Who will put in all that work?' asked Suguna. Did she even realize the magnitude of the effort? Convincing millions of people to donate ten rupees, the handing out of so many receipts and the handling of those funds?

'Haley bhai, I think they are saying the right thing,' said Arshad Ali once Avidha had roughly translated the statement for him. 'We don't need their cash compensation. Can these people raise that amount and start some kind of enterprise to help these survivors find easy work to do? They can also help us to find markets for the things we can then make. That is what we need.'

'You are not supposed to ask such relevant questions,' said Mads, mightily impressed by Ali's intervention.

'I must say, Mads, it is a love letter like you said and it must be kept like one. Wrapped in scented cloth and treasured in a sandalwood box,' said Suguna.

Ajit had expected some criticism of the move but not this amount of ridicule. He now decided to put a stop to it. 'Not everybody has to be out on the streets with us. They can help from where they are. These people's sentiments are sincere. We must keep their interest alive.'

'I would have had more respect for their intentions had they been weighed down by some cheques,' said Hally.

That surprised Ajit. He knew Hally's leanings and enjoyed a good mental wrestle with him, but he had seldom used such strong words to directly condemn anything Ajit had done in public. There was some protocol to holding a job after all. It signalled to Ajit that Hally had finally made up his mind to quit his organization. He was not too sorry about it.

'Their intentions are good,' persisted Ajit.

'Good intentions do not change the world,' said Nirmala to him. 'They never did. Good intentions alone are not enough.'

There was an uncomfortable silence and Harjit stepped in. He had fixed many appointments with some of these eminent persons and accompanied Ajit and Hally to meetings with seven of them. He found their cool, distant demeanour, their measured tones, their old-world language and the harking back to some imagined glorious past ludicrous. Once he had enough to dine on for a week he had stopped going to these meetings.

'I have a proposal,' Harjit said. 'Let us all hold the next meeting at the house of the former his excellency the ex-ambassador who is the first one to have signed this letter. There we can discuss the modalities of raising and managing the funds.'

Ajit pursed his lips and held his silence only because he was enraged beyond endurance. It was all right for these people to make fun of the statement but did they know anything about the subtler ways of building pressure on the government? They protested everything but did they have any suggestions for an alternative? They had not even been able to come up with a proper plan for interim relief that they had been mulling over for weeks now. Ajit thought it was most unfortunate that when attendance in meetings went down these radicals were the ones who stayed put.

'We need these people to keep writing articles and raising these issues in their clubs and parties. That is how peer pressure is built. You guys don't seem to appreciate what we have done...' Latika was saying.

Ajit did not wait for her to finish.

'I am off. You people plan your insurrection,' he said.

Chapter 37

A NEW MOTIF

Nirmala was waiting for a call from a JNU professor who had acquired a flat in Patparganj that she thought Avidha could rent. Avidha had been flitting from one friend's flat to another. This unsettling over and above the turmoil of pregnancy had brought her close to a breakdown and Nirmala now had to think clearly how much and what she owed her friend. She had asked Avidha several times to move in with her but she insisted on renting a flat of her own.

'I don't want to be a burden to another friend,' she told Nirmala.

'Come when it suits you, tragedy queen,' said Nirmala to her.

She had taken out the appliqué-work bedsheet Avidha had made and began adding a small intricately embroidered scorpion with jewelled eyes to its zodiac theme. She quickly hid it in the cupboard when Avidha arrived in the evening with Zintac. Hally, Avidha told her, had brought Zintac with him to her office. He wanted her intervention in the misunderstanding she had had with Suguna. Avidha had not returned to her flat after that evening when Suguna had distanced herself from her decision to have the baby. Avidha told Nirmala that Hally had told her that he was not part of Suguna's decision. 'He says I should recognize others' right to live as they choose,' said Avidha. 'As if I don't understand that much.'

'You are being too touchy,' Nirmala told Avidha as she spooned coffee into the filter.

The anger Avidha felt for Hally had subsided a little but she still felt abandoned. She was politely distant with him despite Zintac trying to bring about a rapprochement.

Zintac sighed. 'You know, there are so many big things we are making compromises on, how can we simply up and leave friends because of minor misunderstandings? We will all be so lonely.'

Before Avidha could take issue, Nirmala asked Zintac what she was hinting at.

'Money, my love, money. I sure would like to see crores being raised by FOB. I would love to handle it. Never seen so much money in my life,' she said in her usual irreverent manner.

Zintac disliked the task of counting pennies and noting down every detail as treasurer of the group but she did it diligently, like she painstakingly edited badly-shot films. It was work and she never shied from it.

'Maybe,' she said, 'we should go to the US to raise funds. Go where Carbide is based? Is it West Virginia? We are more likely to get that kind of money there.'

For all her reputation as the most non-serious character in this whole gang of do-gooders she sure hit the bull's eye, thought Nirmala, looking at her with new interest.

'Why didn't you say so? In the meeting?' she asked her.

'So many people were pouncing on the statement I thought they would all think I was making fun of it too,' she said.

They began to talk about FOB over coffee and where the campaign was headed and how long they would remain in the group. Nirmala said Avidha did not have to think much about it. 'Let the baby come, it will make all the decisions for her,' she said laughing.

'In the last 10 years I have been part of many campaigns,' said Zintac, 'There are only those 300 people with long faces who get together and say the same things to each other. They keep raising the same slogans too. "*Abhi to yeh angdai hai, aage aur ladai hai.*" If they were more accurate they would say, "*Abhi to yeh angdai hai, aage aur angdai hai, angdai hi angdai hai.*"'

Nirmala laughed too.

'Who named you Zintac?'

'I am a brand,' said Zintac. Taking off her scarf that she had used as a thick ribbon to tie her hair, she stepped in front of Nirmala, spreading it before her said, 'Your donation for the struggle to seek justice in the Bhopal case, ma'am.'

Nirmala dropped a rupee coin in it.

'To this the people of the United States of America add 470 million dollars. Thank you,' she said tying up the rupee in one corner of the scarf and tying her hair with the scarf again.

'What did you study in college, Zintac? I mean what was your discipline?' said Nirmala pressing further.

'Never had any,' Zintac laughed. Then noticing Nirmala's slightly creased forehead added, 'Political Science. I graduated with that and then I went and joined a mass communications institute to learn how to make films. I will never have the funds to make one though.'

Nirmala thought she should have landed the job of documenting the campaign instead of Shekhar Singh and said so. 'Shekhar is doing a good job. He is a friend,' replied Zintac without any rancour. 'I am truly serious about this. I don't mind having more money in the kitty. We are now down to three thousand four hundred and thirteen rupees and seventy-five paise only. Do you know it is their money, the money of those funding agencies of the US and other countries that has kept our campaign going? That keeps most of our campaigns going.'

'Does it? I thought we took no funds for this one,' said a startled Avidha.

'Not directly, no. We tried to keep it free of the contamination of foreign funds for people like you. To respect your scruples. Indirectly, it is their money, the money of the funding agencies. Those who donated large chunks of money to the campaign are people who work on fancy salaries for NGOs funded by those agencies. We use their cars, their typewriters, their stationary, their offices and their money too. A lot of these people present the bills for travel to their organizations. You see they are being paid allowances to attend meetings.'

'You don't say so...' said Avidha shocked.

'You do know a lot,' said Nirmala

'Treasurers do...' said Zintac smiling at her mischievously.

'They really are the forensic scientists of any enterprise, are they not?' said Nirmala.

'So tell me, is our campaign free of the contamination of foreign funds or not?' asked Avidha.

'The forensic evidence says it is not,' said Nirmala. 'I knew the projectile invasion would win eventually.'

Avidha and Zintac looked at her questioningly.

'These people like Ajit. Petty traders of peoples' issues. Converting all struggles and agitations into neat projects and getting them funded by aid groups. I call them projectiles. Without people like us their shops would shut down.'

Zintac smiled sadly.

'Frankly, we are as guilty as them, perhaps more. We do their work for free. We give them legitimacy. We lend them credibility,' said Nirmala after a while.

'You never said this before,' said Avidha.

Nirmala stared into the dregs of her coffee.

Hally had access to all the forensic evidence and he had diagnosed his illness. Three days after the meeting he told Ajit he wanted to discuss something important with him and Ajit invited him to dinner. He would rather hear Hally resign over an intimate drink than in his office through an official letter. That would have to come but he reduced it to a mere formality.

They were on their second beer when Hally told him he had decided to quit his job. Ajit was not surprised but he felt bad all the same for losing such an able assistant.

'I have been such an opportunist, Ajit. Taking on this job and working on issues as if I could not work for them in a purely voluntary capacity,' Hally said to him.

'You are too harsh on yourself, Hally. Not taking advantage of an opportunity is foolish.'

Hally laughed aloud. 'Stop it, stop trying to confuse me. Those two are not the same thing. You know perfectly well, opportunism means not going beyond a point in the struggle. It is to go beyond that point that I am leaving.'

Ajit raised an eyebrow at him and asked him if he had another job offer, in a trade union perhaps, that suited his ideology more. Hally told him he had nothing definite in mind. He could look for a job or go into trading.

'I will never again mix my political work with my livelihood needs – that much I am sure of. I won't be paid by some foreign agency to work in agitations, reducing people's issues to projects.'

Ajit laughed at that and said he hoped Hally would be able to stick to his resolution. 'You know, Hally, funding agencies really love your type. The sharper your condemnation, the greater their interest in you. After all, it is not friends you need to buy. You need to buy enemies. And someday I am sure your price in that market will be very high.'

Hally laughed too. 'Ajit, I do hope I will never be up for sale. You think everyone can be bought, don't you?'

Ajit did not think everyone could be bought. He knew most people could be confused and that was better than buying.

'I do hope there will be no hard feelings, Hally. And you will come to FOB meetings too,' Ajit said.

Hally smiled back at him. 'I am not in the campaign because of this job. It goes beyond that for me. In fact it is to be true to the campaign that I am quitting this job.'

Ajit nodded. This is what he had always liked in Hally and it would be tough to find a replacement for him. He told Hally to carry on with the job till he found a replacement but Hally was in no mood to oblige him.

At dinner Ajit told Kamini the loss he was just about to suffer. 'This fellow has chosen his conscience above a friend. I feel let down,' he said.

Kamini told him to follow Hally in his creed if he could not bear the loss or stop playacting. To Hally she said, 'Keep in touch with me even if you can't stand him.'

Chapter 38

BRAIN FEVER

It had rained the night before and the earth was sending
up rancid vapours. As Mukta walked up the leafy avenue
on the Mall Road in the university area she could smell
her own sweat, which ran in thin rivulets down her legs and
between her breasts. She wished she could have got home
and had a bath before coming on this errand but her work in
court had ended late. The auto driver had refused to venture
inside these lonely lanes where he would find no passengers.
She wiped the sweat from her face. Suddenly the high-pitched
call of a bird rent the oppressive afternoon. 'Whither whither,'
it appeared to say endlessly, its sound reaching for a higher
octave till it stopped in the middle of the highest octave.

A furry grey hawk swooped down in front of her on
the metalled road, gave her a malevolent look and picked
up a worm scurrying to escape its boiling burrow. Mukta

stopped mid-stride. The bird flew back to the branch of an overhanging acacia where its red-eyed mate flung its cruelly curved beak upwards to the sky and let out the same plaintive call again, *kyun, kyun, kyun, kyun*, why, why, whither, till Mukta could not bear to think of how it would stop just as it reached a crescendo. She broke into a run as if pursued by a demon. The birdcall followed her. She sprinted to the house and rang the bell insistently seeking refuge inside her professor's house.

Professor Thapar stepped out onto the veranda. 'The door is open, Mukta. It always is, in the day. Have you forgotten?' He looked at her strained face and the widely dilated eyes. 'Are you unwell?' he asked.

The bird called again.

'That bird... some strange hawk,' said Mukta turning in the direction of the garden. Has the bird followed me like an ill omen, she thought.

'That is the *papiha*,' he said, amused. Nobody was scared of a bird. 'The British have a strange superstition about this bird. They think it calls "brain fever" and if you hear it call it brings on a brain fever.' He laughed. 'We are more sensible. We identify it with the call of love.'

So this was the bird of Hindi film songs and Hindi poetry! Why is it thought to be romantic? Why on earth would those Hindi poets sing so many paeans to this bird as if it was some heart-broken lover? The call now sounded to her like 'brain fever' and she thought the British were right, it was an evil one, this bird with its spiteful eyes.

Mrs Thapar came out and hugged her and took her inside chattering all the while.

'It has been such a long time since you came by. Very busy lawyer you have become,' she complained affectionately. She remarked on how thin Mukta had grown, all because she insisted on living alone and must be living on bread and eggs. She must get proper food. She got her *muthiyas* to munch on with a tall glass of freshly made lemon sherbet, sweet and cold. She also fetched a jar of pickled mangoes and promised to pack her stuffed karelas and paranthas for the night. She asked after 'your friend Vineeta' and wanted to know when 'that girl would finish her course and go back to Bhopal'. The Thapars were family friends and Mrs Thapar wanted to know all about her brothers and her mother too.

Professor Thapar pulled out his chair from under his worktable with a definiteness that signalled to his wife that she must leave them alone. Mukta darted him a grateful look. Lying about Vineeta had begun to nibble away at her self-esteem.

'You should someday come to see *me*,' said Mrs Thapar, 'and we won't let him interrupt us.'

The cool interiors of the room helped Mukta regain her composure. She began with the arguments for the court first. She went through the bases the law provided for calculating damages to life and limb and they talked about how ill-equipped the law was to assess damage to health in a case like this one.

'We must challenge the categorization of victims that the government has done,' she said to Thapar. 'I have here the fresh analysis of what little data we have. We must ask the court to give us the reports of the research the ICMR has done. Without that our analysis is incomplete.'

Professor Thapar nodded thoughtfully.

'Do you really think it is necessary?' he asked. 'We can challenge the settlement on many other grounds.'

'Sir, we have those arguments too. But the only way to get the court to order more compensation is to prove that the government underestimated the amount because its categorization was faulty. Some long-term impacts of the gas have been placed in the class of temporary injuries. There are many such errors.'

'Tough,' he said.

Mukta was annoyed. 'We can do it. The ones who will suffer long-term effects of the gas are so many more than the government has made us believe.'

'We shall think about it,' said Thapar.

'The money is very important, sir,' said Mukta. 'The civil liability is as important as the criminal liability.'

'Sure, the money is important. Exceedingly important. But we have a precedent. The SC has itself ruled that the capacity to pay of the accused has to be taken into account and the compensation has to be commensurate with that capacity to pay. Carbide has enormous capacity to pay.'

'We are using it. The categorization will add to the substance of our argument,' said Mukta. She was painfully aware that the 'capacity to pay' argument could be challenged and Carbide would do it. Why was Professor Thapar being so resistant to the categorization argument?

She was silenced however by his next sentence, 'Get on with the other arguments, Mukta. I am meeting Cawasjee and his associates tomorrow. They have made their own preparations and let me see what they have laid out.'

She felt vaguely uncomfortable. Mrs Thapar called from inside to ask if they wanted coffee or tea. She began to sense her uneasiness congealing into the unexplained anger that had begun to live inside her. Her throat was dry. She could do with another glass of Mrs Thapar's strong, sweet lemon sherbet.

She began pulling out the brief for the politicians from her bulging file. Professor Thapar told her there was a strong possibility they could get the new government to pay interim relief. Mukta was amazed by his conviction that the government would definitely change. Her interest in politics was low and she was not sure those going for the jugular of the ruling party would actually manage to slit it.

'I must say, sir, that we should ask these politicians to put in the demand for impeachment of the justices on their manifestos,' she said.

Thapar threw back his head and laughed. 'You can't be so naïve, Mukta,' he said. 'Who reads manifestos nowadays and who remembers them? They are not worth the paper they are written on, like someone said about international treaties. Who had said it? Hitler?'

Mukta joined in his laughter weakly. 'Still, that way we have something on record. Manifestos record promises.'

'We have their speeches on record, though there is nothing to prevent them from going back on their promises. Politicians! They are all a bunch of renegades,' he said.

A servant brought in coffee for the professor and more sherbet for her.

Mukta drank the cool drink greedily. Finding her voice she began to argue earnestly. 'We have to pin the blame, sir, we cannot let the court think it can get away with such a shameful thing. We must try.'

'Why is impeachment so important, Mukta?' asked Professor Thapar leaning towards her and moving aside two books lying on the table between them.

'For justice,' she said.

'How will impeachment get you justice?'

'It will send a strong signal to the bench that such things will not be tolerated,' she said.

'Who will you impeach, Mukta? Those politicians and officials whom Carbide financed? Do you know how many politicians and their wives went shopping in New York letting Carbide pay for everything? Will you impeach all those officials who went inside the factory to inspect it and filed reports saying everything was fine because they charged hefty fees for every faulty gauge, every malfunctioning meter they found? Those doctors who floated theories that people did not die of the gas, they died because they were already ill and dying, and fudged the records? They were all too busy counting the money they got in return for favourable reports. Will you impeach those economists and planners who tell us we need factories like Carbide for our development? That entire class that uses people's poverty as an excuse to allow industry to pollute the environment and then uses pollution as an excuse to keep people away from resources?

'This Parliament did not bother to pass any law to protect our environment. It did not pass any law to protect our people from the toxic materials used in such factories. This Parliament did not even pass a law to cover just such an accident when the trade union kept warning them that something like this was waiting to happen. Mukta, you want this Parliament to arraign a few judges? What will you achieve? Nothing. The court alone was not involved in this. It was used as a medium.'

'Then they don't deserve to be on the bench,' she said doggedly, 'they must be punished.'

Professor Thapar sat silent for a long while.

'Don't lose your focus, Mukta,' he continued when she did not say anything. 'You are a lawyer and your job is to get the best for your client. The gas victims are your client. Get what you can for them. The rest is rhetoric.'

Even though she had lost some of the awe for her former teacher she felt inadequate and unable to argue further. Yet, she was convinced that she was right in wanting to go ahead with the demand that so many had raised in that first meeting on the settlement. Was that anger all wrong and useless? What use is anger at injustice if time will dull its edges? If everybody were to sit back and say, the case is too old now, there is no need to hold anyone accountable, it is useless to make a charge and bring the accused to trial, would not the entire edifice of justice collapse? He would have a response ready to silence her. That was the hallmark of a great legal brain – it could argue on any side.

'This was one of the demands of the campaign. The first demand. We have to fight to get the demand fulfilled,' she said.

'Who remembers demands made in the heat of the moment?' he said. 'Do you know how many MPs will be needed to even move a motion for impeachment? At least 100 members of the Lok Sabha or 50 of the Rajya Sabha. We need a majority in both Houses of Parliament to pass the motion. It will have to cut across party lines and I don't think we have so many MPs on our side.'

So now he was dredging up practical difficulties to weigh on his side.

'That is why, sir, we must get the political parties to put it on their manifestos. The new government will have enough MPs to get a motion moved. We can at least try... we cannot give up without trying. Even if the motion is defeated in the Parliament, we will have signalled something. We will have fought our way through to some distance.'

Professor Thapar waved his hands in dismissal and shook his head.

'How much can we expect a new PM to do? How many enemies can he make? It is not practical.'

Mukta wanted to give up arguing. Everywhere it was the same. Avidha had told her how Thapar could be made head of the Law Commission if the government changed. Everyone has a price, she thought, and felt betrayed. He had just called the politicians renegades and that description could fit him as well. It was probably not the proffered post but his conviction that stood in the way. She would never know.

She made a last attempt to plead again. 'Sir, the system can survive this. The system actually needs to punish errant office-holders, to survive, to pose as fair. The system is above individuals. We can try making our MPs understand this.'

Professor Thapar leaned back in his chair. 'The talk, Mukta, is that Carbide has paid enough to the ruling party to finance its election campaign. I am sure you know that the counsel for UCIL is an important member of the ruling party. He is running for Parliament this time and from a seat considered safe for the party. It won't be possible. Let us leave it at that.'

Mukta felt dismayed. 'We cannot accept defeat even before we have begun to fight. We must fight. We must,' she said, evoking no response.

They sat together for a while. Mukta was aware that the discussion was over. She must leave now. She stood up. Thapar called to his wife that Mukta was leaving.

'Memories of injustice have a strange way of haunting history, sir. They surface generations later in much distorted forms. We must not let such memories build up. We must fight as best as we can,' she said. 'We must try even if we don't win. Think about it, sir.'

She left the house with the lingering feel of Mrs Thapar's hugs and the jar of pickle. She refused the offered lift till a point where she could find an auto. The evening was setting in. As she stepped out into the darkening garden the brainfever bird called again.

Chapter 39

WHOSE MONEY IS IT?

By the time general elections were announced much had changed in Avidha's life. She had shifted into the JNU professor's flat who knew she was unmarried and was about to have a child. She packed her bookcase with care and took it to her parents' house when she carried her stuff in the tempo to her new flat. Her mother did not even open the door for her. She left the bookcase on the doorstep peeping in to see if her father was around.

Avidha did not like the Patparganj area where buildings were coming up all around her. She was surrounded by dust and bricks and the noise of construction. The sight of the little babies of workers lying on sacks of cement and heaps of sand crying disconsolately was so dispiriting she spent most of her time away from the flat.

She had sought legal advice from Mukta on asking for maternity leave.

'There is nothing in the law that says you have to be married to get maternity leave. If the office refuses we shall take them to court,' Mukta had told her.

Avidha had applied for maternity leave and to her surprise it was sanctioned without the office raising any furore about it. She did not know that the editor-in-chief had stood by her firmly. He had called her to congratulate her and even asked her to send him sweets but he made no comments about her marital status. He did not quite approve of what she did but she was a good journalist and he did not want to lose her.

The election campaign kept her on her toes and she was petrified she may go into labour in the middle of a road trip but Joshi had refused to take her off the beat. Even political leaders had begun to sympathize with her plight.

Joshi found her unacceptably immoral. Now she was asking to be excused from out-station trips. If she was so daring as to become an unwed mother she also had to prove that she could be a good professional despite the problems her own actions had got her into. He thought she was taking her freedom to write bold pieces for the paper too far by living up to her theories. Every time he saw her he was outraged. He sent her on as many trips as possible to avoid seeing her among other things. He told her he was understaffed and if she wanted to have long holidays to enjoy her pregnancy she should have become a clerk and not a reporter. She was free to resign. He enjoyed telling her that.

B.L. Joshi, like most journalists, continually cribbed about the superficial nature of journalism, nurtured ambitions of writing novels, had written some short stories in Hindi and was acquainted with her literary critic father.

He told her that her father had been prophetic in giving her that name.

'Not conforming to any form, are you? That is what Avidha means. No genre,' he told her.

In the last stage of her pregnancy Avidha shifted to Nirmala's flat and kept asking how she would know when it was time to go to the hospital. They were still to decide whether they should share Nirmala's flat and save money or keep their own spaces intact.

In the middle of November Ajit called a FOB meeting on interim relief.

The party of the Supreme Challenger had agreed to consider giving interim relief to the survivors if they won.

'This is a breakthrough. We must have a plan ready to submit to them when they come to power,' he said.

They cheered loudly. Even Nirmala was impressed enough to tell Ajit he had indeed done a good job. Avidha attended the meeting determined this would be her last before childbirth.

The first thing they had to think of was how much money would they need for this. 'The High Court has already calculated that for us. Rs 350 crore. We should ask for that sum,' said Mukta. 'I don't know why we need a longer meeting or a plan.'

'We need a plan to decide how to distribute the money,' said Latika. She was jubilant. She had been with the Supreme Challenger when he had nodded his serious head and said, 'The people cannot wait. Governments can. Why can the government not give them some compensation, and take it from Carbide later? It can be done.' For a man who spoke very little this was as good as a promise.

'Will this money be deducted from their final compensation amount?' asked Avidha.

'Yes,' said Ajit.

Nirmala wanted to know now what happened if Carbide did not have to pay. 'Don't forget that is what we have said in the petition. If we lose the case we shall return the money. So what happens if we lose the case?' she said.

Ajit told her they would talk to the government about such an eventuality. He had never worked very closely with Nirmala before this campaign and he now found her becoming hard to tolerate. She never seemed to forget any detail.

'The settlement says the government must make up the deficit and that will help us then,' he said, hoping Mukta would not start objecting now.

Ajit then outlined the scheme he and Latika had in mind. The government, he said, would set aside a sum and all the survivors, every individual, would get Rs 400 a month. Nirmala was the first to react.

'Give them a lump sum. Every family has some permanently injured, some dead, some with lesser degree of injuries. All of them can be given a minimum amount depending on how much the government is willing to pay out and be done with it.'

'That will never do,' said Latika. 'They will spend the sum on marriages and dowry. The men will probably use all of it on booze.'

The meeting broke into a furious discussion. Latika said the survivors needed the money for medicines, which was the *raison d'être* of the interim relief scheme. Avidha agreed.

'What tells you, Avi, that the men won't drink away the money if they get a small amount every month?' Hally asked.

It dawned on Avidha that it would probably be very tough

to spend all the money on liquor if they got a large amount. 'You have a point there,' she said.

Latika pointed out once again that there were other things it could be squandered on like marriages.

'Stop being patronizing,' shouted Nirmala. 'It is their money. Who are we to decide their priorities?'

'Do we have the authority to tell our rich what they should do with their money? Why are we doing this to the survivors then? They paid for it with their lives, their health. Let them do what they want,' said Hally completing what Nirmala had begun to say and could not because of her fury.

Nirmala and Hally were heavily outnumbered. Latika and Ajit said they were responsible for getting the relief and making sure it was used properly.

'Are you their guardians?' asked Nirmala who found their attitude pompous and insufferable.

'We certainly have to act like that,' said Ajit, miffed at her tone.

'Like the government of India did? Became their parents and then took away their rights?' said Hally.

Avidha began to feel acutely uncomfortable. Her back was hurting and she leaned back on the sofa, asking Zintac to fetch her a cushion, to support her back.

'Let's leave,' said Nirmala to her.

Ajit asked if they needed his car. They said they would take an auto and Zintac went to look for one. Harjit was not home and his car was not around either.

Hally came out with Avidha and said, 'At least something good will happen this year.' He and Suguna were now living together in the same old *barsati*.

'What did you tell Mrs Kapoor? That you were testing out Suguna to see if she would make a good daughter-in-law?'

Hally laughed. 'We told her we married in court. She invited us to dinner and gave Suguna a sari as a gift.'

The auto arrived and Hally and Suguna supported Avidha to get up from the chair. 'I am tired of this,' said Avidha. 'I can't even walk properly.'

'Is travelling in an auto safe for her?' Suguna asked Nirmala.

'Nothing is safe,' said Nirmala, 'everything is safe. It depends on how you look at it.'

The auto drove off.

In the auto Nirmala turned on Avidha with fury. 'I told you I didn't want to come to this meeting. I can't stand this patronizing attitude. And you are becoming as bad as them.'

'Nimmie, my back hurts,' said Avidha.

'Shut up,' said Nirmala seething with rage. 'Hundred and thousands of women have babies and you ask to be pampered every minute.'

Avidha turned her face away.

'Can we make do with *ande ki bhujiya* and bread tonight?' asked Nirmala when they got home.

Avidha said she would make paranthas to go with the eggs. She had rolled out the first parantha when she felt a slight pain in her spine. She had had false alarms a few days before so she turned the gas off and went to lie down on the bed. The pain subsided gradually. She went back to the kitchen and had just managed to cook the parantha and roll out the next one when the spasm shot into her spine again. Unable to keep standing, she once again turned the gas off and went to lie down. Nirmala noticed her this time and came in to the bedroom to check.

'I have this pain in the back,' said Avidha. 'It came on, went away. Now it is back. It will go away, don't worry.'

'We must call the cab,' said Nirmala. She began dialling the taxi stand number.

The taxi arrived half an hour later. Nirmala began packing an overnight bag. 'Trust her to go into labour at night,' she thought, as she put in a change of clothes for both of them, towels and a sweater in a bag. In the end she opened her cupboard, picked up the coverlet Avidha had made and she had added her own motifs to and stuffed it in the bag.

By the time they reached AIIMS Avidha had begun screaming in pain. As she got inside the hospital she felt the rush of warm water flowing down her thighs. She turned to Nirmala and said, 'I must go to the bathroom. You don't know what I have done.'

'The water broke, don't worry, nothing to be embarrassed about,' said Nirmala.

Within minutes Avidha was screaming loud enough to deafen Nirmala.

Nirmala spent an awful night with Avidha abusing her in between her screams of agony. She sat with Avidha till a little girl the colour of honey pushed her way into the world in the wee hours of the morning.

Nirmala was the first to hold her in her arms and kiss her moist forehead.

A little while later she lifted the coverlet from her bag, folded it so that the patch in the middle would show clearly and wrapped it around the child over the hospital sheet and took her to Avidha.

349

Chapter 40

DOUBTS AND DECISIONS

The FOB's fondest hope, that the government would change, came true that winter. The new prime minister was sworn in on the eve of the fifth anniversary of the gas disaster and there were many small celebrations to welcome the change.

Bank accounts were being opened for all survivors for interim relief.

'Now we can hope that the settlement will be overturned. I feel so happy!' Avidha said.

This was the first time Avidha had spoken of anything other than the child and the exercises needed to bring her back into shape. A little girl of just a few pounds had dropped into her life and taken over every inch of space. Her clothes lay scattered all over the house, she decided when others would get up and when they could sleep. Avidha was always tired and irritable.

Prashant had hoped that Avidha had decided against having the child. He had been shocked to see her looking rather swollen in the corridor of his office one day. He did not even recover enough to nod to her when she came to face him. She threw a cheery 'hello' at him as she passed by. He went to his chamber and waited for her to come, absolutely confident that she would. She did not. That was in September. He did not see her again. By mid-December he thought of checking on her.

One morning he called her home number, that he had in his diary and that he had never used before. He got Suguna who told him Avidha did not live there anymore and asked for his name. He disconnected. Suguna guessed who it was and called Avidha.

Nirmala did not like Prashant's interest in the child. That afternoon, as they sat with the child in the balcony of Avidha's flat soaking up the sun and munching on peanuts, Avidha asked, 'What does he want now?'

They had just decided that Avidha should move in with Nirmala. Prashant could now upset those plans.

'Probably only wants to know whether it is a boy or a girl. Call him. Put him out of his agony,' said Nirmala.

Avidha went out on a leisurely walk in the park. It was the migratory season and crowds of pintails and shovellers were feeding in the lake. There were hundreds of birds in the lake now and however stealthily she approached they seemed to sense her presence and moved away towards the far shore. She watched them describing circles in the lake and taking short flights.

Evening began to fall and the sun painted the waters in many shades of orange. She got up with a firm resolution. It was time to call Prashant. He may already have left the office. If his secretary picked it up she would replace the receiver. She suddenly did not want to talk to Prashant. She was at peace.

She went to Nirmala's house and called him. Prashant picked up the phone.

'You called?' she asked. 'What was it you called about?'

Prashant was taken aback by the brusque tone of her voice. 'Just like that,' he said. 'You all right? Had the baby?'

'I am fine. My baby is fine,' she said

'A son or a daughter?' he asked.

'How does that matter?' she asked.

'Thought I should find out. The father should know at least that much.'

'I never said she was yours. I just said I was pregnant. That is all I said.'

She was right.

'So you had a daughter. I thought because you told me that... well, you did seem to say...' he stammered.

'Is that what you thought? That I told you because it was yours? You see I wasn't sure whose it was so I told all the three men in my life that I was pregnant. Don't worry. '

There was silence at the other end.

'Is that all? Anything else you want to talk about?' she asked

'I don't... well...' said Prashant. He had no talent for thinking fast in such unexpected situations.

'Hey, it is okay! Such misunderstandings happen. Goodbye,' she said and put down the receiver.

Prashant knew she was lying but a lingering doubt began to crawl in his brain like a worm. He was not used to being laughed at, and that too by a woman who could have been, and had been, his slave for all her intellectual strength. He knew he could try to discover the truth but the consequences could be devastating either way, whether she turned out to be a liar or not. Nailing her lie was not in his interest. He sat in the office late into the night ignoring the phone and the files on his desk.

Chapter 41

A SURPRISE VISITOR

Avidha was washing the baby's clothes when the doorbell rang. She was not expecting anyone and did not even want anyone to come in after the emotionally harrowing time she had had. She opened the door prepared to send away the salesman for water purifiers and was so taken aback to see Mads at her doorstep she even forgot to invite him inside.

He breezed into the room, dumped his bag on the floor, slung the *jhola* on a chair, looked around the house complained that he could not hear the child, and found her in the bedroom, fast asleep.

'She is so beautiful! Does she take after the guy?' he asked.

'Thanks for being so honest,' said Avidha laughing. She felt very happy.

'I shall wait till she wakes up,' he declared. 'Meanwhile we can have some adult talk and something to drink.'

Within minutes he had made the house his own. He peeped into the fridge, stalked into the kitchen, opened tins and bottles. She seemed to have no vegetables. Did she at least have rice? Without a word to her he ran down and came back half an hour later with a plastic bag laden with potatoes, peas, tomatoes, cucumbers and lettuce.

Then he got down to making lemon sherbet. Handing her a glass he plonked the bag of peas on the table and began shelling them. Avidha sat near him feeling redundant and in the way. Mads kept up a running commentary on the plum postings some of their 'campaigners' had got. Thapar was now heading the Law Commission and Cawasjee was the Attorney General.

Avidha knew about it. The day their counsel had been named the Attorney General had been one of acute anxiety for FOB. They did not want to lose him. He had made his conflict of interest clear to the government and declared that in the Bhopal case he would be on the side of the petitioners. He would not take the job if the government opposed the petitioners. The government had assured him that it would throw its weight behind the petitions challenging the settlement. That had led to the strongest assurance they had yet got. The Law Minister had issued a statement to say that the government was opposed to the settlement leading to endless phone calls among the FOB members whose hearts swelled with pride at the principled stand Cawasjee had taken.

Avidha had called Cawasjee to congratulate him and he had told her all this. She told Mads how much she appreciated his sense of professional ethics.

'Great to be able to have ethics. It is greater to have food,' he said, annoying her. She did not like him so much anymore.

The child woke up crying loudly and forgetting the peas, Mads picked her up and felt her wet nappy, changed her and handed her to Avidha to feed her. Afterwards he rocked her till she fell asleep.

Then he cooked a delicious meal and they ate taking turns to sit by the child who got up just when the food was on the table.

'You know, Avi, I will never forget what you did for me that day to save me from the police,' he said suddenly. 'You are foolish and romantic like I used to be.'

Avidha began to think he was not as bad as he was made out to be.

He told her Ajit had thrown a party and he had drunk himself silly 'only to get away from all that talk of interim relief'.

'Ajit is damned pleased,' he said between mouthfuls of rice.

'And you?' she asked.

Mads told her nothing pleased him as she must have discovered by now.

'So you are here to discuss interim relief with officials,' she asked him.

'There is no point in discussing anything with officials,' he told her. 'The government will do what it wants to do.'

Avidha told him not to denigrate all the effort FOB had put in to wrangle interim relief for survivors.

'That money belongs to survivors,' said Mads waving a fork at her. 'Government coffers are full of the dollars Carbide gave us. It can claim to have sufficient hard currency reserves.

The people of Bhopal have earned a lot for the government. How does it matter if a few pennies are given to them?'

'You are an ingrate,' she said.

'Only the weak are grateful.'

'Only deviants are thankless,' she retorted.

He laughed. 'Doesn't take much to recognize your own type!' he said. 'But when I look into my conscience I won't feel guilty.'

'So will I. Not guilty,' she said defiantly.

'Your conscience is too anaemic. You go to three demonstrations and it is satisfied. It would in fact be gluttony for you,' he said derisively.

She was used to his abrasive manner but familiarity is no palliative for hurt. He finished eating and stepped out into the balcony to smoke. She began to fold the baby's clothes to pack and resolved to steer clear of the Bhopal issue. He came back into the room standing with his hands resting on his hips. She could feel his rage seeping out of his stiff form.

'You know what I have against people like you? Your bloody smugness,' he told her. 'You people are worse than Carbide.'

'Yes, of course,' she said, provoked into responding. 'We tolerate people like you and that must certainly make us worse.'

'Such barbs never bother me,' he told her with derisive calm. 'I have nothing against Carbide and the government or the court. They are not my friends. They don't hurt me. I don't let them. It is people like you who stabbed me truly well. Just look at the way you let us down. You walk in and out of the movement when it suits you – for however long it suits you. The survivors have no choice. They survived without your interim relief and they will survive what the court will eventually do to them. You are the ones who actually sold us out.'

'How dare you...' Avidha stammered. She had been called many things in life but nobody had ever questioned her commitment.

'You did. You people. You built your careers. You even got funds to participate in our struggles. And you feel you have done something very glorious. Sorry, but we don't exist to supply you material for your glory. You sold us to international seminars and to journals. You sell everything we have. Our experience, our diseases, therapies, cures, our hopes, our disappointments. You sell our lives. You are worse than Carbide. At least it is openly an enemy. You are an enemy that is difficult to recognize. I tried, you know, to smash that conceit of yours. But no amount of stone-throwing can smash that complacence. You people protect yourselves rather well.'

Avidha walked into the bedroom to check on the child and did not get back for a long time. When she came out, he had folded all the clothes. She told him she was tired and needed rest.

'Right, throw me out. You know, Avi, sometimes you people help the government look compassionate. That is what you are doing with the new government. Avi, you are very infantile and the outcome of this case will hurt you. It is not my job to protect you from the hurt. I want you hurt. Sometimes only a deep thrust can wake you up.'

'Is that why you came here?' she asked aghast. 'To tell me I needed to get hurt?'

'I told you I came here to meet the kid. I like meeting children. They are the only innocent people in the world.

After animals, I mean. Animals are the most innocent and they stay that way. Kids grow up to become you and Ajit.'

'I want to sleep now. Goodbye,' she said tersely.

'I got a gift, for the child,' he said.

He opened his bag and brought out a small kaleidoscope. It looked handmade, a rough octagonal tube pasted over with gaily painted paper. 'Thank you,' she said softly.

Mads took out an envelope and tiptoeing into the bedroom placed it on the child. 'You know, the moment she can hold it she will shred it,' he said, gazing at the child affectionately. 'Children are the original anarchists.'

Avidha did not want Mads giving the child any money; he had so little. She took up the envelope, went out and placed it on his bag.

Mads followed her and laughed in an undertone, with disdain. 'You think there is money in it? How conventional do you think I am?'

He extracted a sheet of paper from the envelope and waved it at her.

'It is a poem for her,' he said. 'You must keep it very safe and give it to her when she is old enough to read and understand it.'

It was handwritten on pink paper and signed. She inserted it back in the envelope and impulsively hugged him.

Mads wrested himself away. 'Don't teach her to look to the left and right and go down the straight road. That road leads into the maws of status quo. All of you will be digested in it and turn to shit,' he told her.

'That is so gross,' she said offended.

'Life is gross. Don't tell me you haven't noticed. Grow up.'

Chapter 42

THE DISSENTERS

In early March Ajit convened what he called a 'full general body meeting' of FOB at the Law Institute. He called everybody at least twice telling them a crucial decision had to be made and they must find time for the meeting. He went to Nirmala's house to invite her and Avidha and meet the child for the first time.

'It is imperative that you two come,' he said.

'There lies my categorical imperative,' said Avidha, pointing to her child sucking on a rattle. Everything Avidha did nowadays was measured against the simple test of the little mite's comfort. All her assertions of freedom were wiped out.

'What is so important about this meeting?' asked Nirmala.

Ajit shook his head. 'If I told you, you wouldn't come,' he said.

Avidha had by then shifted in with Nirmala. It surprised everyone that she had agreed to share her inviolate space with a child, who is nothing less than a tyrant. The child was nearly four months old and Avidha had used up all the leave she had. She and Nirmala were not sure they wanted to take the child to a long and serious meeting and had nearly decided that Nirmala would attend it alone when Vineeta offered to babysit. She came the evening before with Mukta.

'You know, Viny wanted to adopt this child,' said Mukta watching the expertise with which Vineeta was trying to make the baby burp. 'I have to keep reminding her the child is not hers.'

Of all their friends, Vineeta was the only one who made regular trips to their place and helped out even with the filthiest part of childcare that even Nirmala refused to do.

'What is Ajit so agitated about?' asked Nirmala.

'Has to be about arguments on the petition. What else?' said Mukta.

The child burped and gurgled. Half an hour later Vineeta was happily showing a letter to Avidha. It was from Ali. 'My first letter from Bhopal,' she said.

It was a brief letter and Ali had told her that he had found out the name of the big red flowers she had asked about. They were called African Tulips. 'Sad, it is not a nicer name. Or we could have given that name to our little one,' said Vineeta. The child still did not have a name.

Once again the hall in the Law Institute was packed like it had been just over a year ago. Ajit roamed around greeting people and gently complaining of their neglect of the cause.

At last he sat down on the dais running a hand through his hair, looked around to see if everyone he expected had come and began to clear his throat. The conversations on the sidelines died down and Hally got up to close the door to the room.

'I have an announcement to make. Then we have a decision to make,' Ajit began. He licked his lips nervously. A hush fell on the room.

'I have heard from the Attorney General. From Cawasjee, I mean,' said Ajit. 'He says we should not bring up medical categorization in our arguments in the case. The government will support our petition so maybe it is not so important after all...'

To Suguna it seemed such a tame thing to call such a large group meeting for.

'Has the government filed an affidavit in the court to say it rejects the settlement?' Mukta asked.

'No,' said Ajit. 'No, but Cawasjee has told the court that the government is on our side.'

Some of them began to clap when they heard this.

Mukta stood up and asked, 'Why are you clapping?'

The cheering and the noise died down.

'It is not enough,' said Mukta. 'The government is the sole representative of the gas victims. It must take a clear stand. It must file an affidavit. Otherwise its stand has no meaning.'

'Come on, you know the government can't put this in writing. It cannot throw out what the earlier government did. Why ask for the impossible? Is it not enough that our own counsel is now Attorney General? That he is arguing in our favour?' asked Latika.

Mukta's hostility made it very difficult for Ajit to continue. He swallowed. He appreciated what Mukta said, and he did

362

not want to be charged ever with having done anything without consulting them. That would render the basis of their questioning the settlement contradictory and meaningless. It would erase the difference between him and the government whom they had steadfastly accused of acting behind the survivors' backs.

'The Attorney General has asked me to get back to him about it. I have to consult all of you for that. He has said that we must give up the question of categorization of the victims in the arguments. That is what the government obviously wants. Otherwise we will probably lose the support of the government in the case.'

Most of them did not understand why it was such a major question. It was good of Ajit, very good of him, to ask them to come over and to consult them when they were no longer so active in the case but why was this question so important?

'On what basis will they increase the compensation amount then?' asked Nirmala.

Ajit smiled at her. 'I don't know, Nimmie. I am only asking you what to do now.'

'You are asking us?' said Mukta flaring up. 'When I pressed for so many things you people told me politics will decide everything. Now what voice do people like me have? But thank you, Ajit, thank you for letting me know what is going on. At least now I know first-hand how this system works. Thank you for continuing my education.' She stormed out of the meeting without looking back.

The meeting broke into a babble. Everybody began speaking at the same time.

'This is what I call democracy in action. Everyone talks, nobody listens,' said Harjit. 'Can we behave like decent people and talk one at a time?'

It took some time for people to quieten. Ajit looked at Hally hoping he would get Mukta back but Hally shook his head.

'Why do you need our consent?' asked Nirmala.

'I don't,' said Ajit, his face stiff with anger.

'If they can overturn the settlement without bringing this medical thing in, what is the problem?' asked Harjit.

Ajit remained silent, letting the discussion take its own divergent courses, not lending it any direction.

'I say, man, leave it to the experts. That guy standing up in court, Cawasjee, he is our man, right? This seems like so much consultation for nothing,' said Shekhar.

'Wait, I want to understand this. Does this mean that the court may not overturn the settlement?' asked Avidha.

'No,' said Ajit unable to keep quiet. 'We have so many other arguments to pursue in the case.'

'Tell me,' said Nirmala sweetly, 'if I say we reject the Attorney General's advice and insist on raising the matter of faulty classification in court will you agree with me?'

'This has to be decided by a majority vote,' said Ajit.

'Justice,' Nirmala said leaning forward, 'justice is not some lost treasure to be excavated from within cracks in the system. It has to be the outcome of reasoning based on fact and placing those facts in the context of power and the exercise of power. Categorization is an absolute must. It is the only basis on which the settlement can be reviewed properly.'

There was silence in the room as those present digested her statement made in a slow deliberate tone.

'I am sure Cawasjee knows enough law. And Professor Thapar too. They both agree this is how it should be,' said Ajit.

'The Law Minister has openly stated that if the process of arriving at the settlement is revealed it will affect the dignity of the court,' said Suguna. 'That is political pressure. It is a threat to the court, isn't it? So what are we getting anxious about?'

'That is not an official threat. The official threat would have been a motion to impeach. We raised that demand and we dropped it,' said Hally who had been silently listening to the discussion till now. 'That is what Mukta is angry about.'

'Impeachment is not possible. Besides, it will only anger the court. It won't get us anything,' said Latika.

Nirmala looked at Latika with exasperation.

'We are not discussing impeachment. So stop talking about it,' said Ajit, trying to control the discussion. 'This way we'll get nowhere.'

'Which is where we have got after a whole year of trying to get somewhere. The majority is not even listening to us, so record our dissent and let us put a full stop here,' said Hally and got up to leave.

Suguna pulled at his hand and made him sit back again. 'Don't be extreme. The new government is not so bad after all. They have made a financial commitment to us. They will provide interim relief. They will get the settlement revised. You wait and see.'

Hally got up from the chair again. 'Don't pull me down with you. We cannot let practical things govern everything.'

'Has anyone asked Ali and Mads?' asked Avidha waking up.

Hally stopped on his way to the door.

Ajit had asked Mads and Ali both to attend this meeting. 'If you people think that what you decide now will make any difference to the case, take a jump, Ajit,' Mads had told him. 'We will hack our own course.'

Ali was unwell and painfully confused. He wanted to know if that would change the outcome of the case.

'I don't know,' Ajit had told him honestly. 'But I trust the man, he was our counsel and he is a good one, in fact one of the best.'

'Then do what you want to do,' Ali told him. 'I trust you people.'

Ajit told the meeting that he had Ali's consent to do what he wanted to and Mads had told him he had nothing to say on the issue.

'So where do you stand, Ajit?' asked Avidha.

'I think that this whole question of medical classification is being exaggerated. We can think of that when we come to distributing the amount of compensation. Why bring it up now?'

They continued to argue for over an hour. Nirmala wanted to know if they thought enhancement of the compensation amount was not important. That led to another furore with Latika protesting that she had had enough of this constant questioning of their motives.

Ajit eventually put a stop to the discussion saying it was late and they must vote.

Hally vehemently opposed the voting and said Ajit should have let them know of the Attorney General's request when he called the meeting. 'Everybody could then have had the time to think it over. What is the hurry to vote? We can get together for a vote a few days later.' He still stood by the door and made no move to find a seat or step out.

Ajit said he knew the members would not come back to vote on the motion later, which was why he had to have the vote today.

'Get up, Avidha, let's leave. We have lost the case,' said Nirmala to her.

Avidha shook her head still deep in thought.

The question was put to vote. The decision was almost unanimous. The issue of categorization was not to be raised at all. Suguna voted with the overwhelming majority.

'I am too confused. I don't think I want to vote on this one,' said Harjit. For once in his life he had not been able to make up his mind.

Nirmala and Hally kept quiet till Ajit had counted the hands raised in favour of his proposal.

Then Nirmala said, 'Write it down that we voted against you.'

'Sure,' said Ajit and turned to Avidha. 'How about you, Avi?'

Nirmala left the room. Hally kept standing near the door, leaning against the wall.

The decision had been made and one more vote against the proposal would make no difference but Ajit was wondering if Avidha would vote with him.

Avidha recalled the warning Mads had given her about the outcome of the case. She was not sure how it could affect the case. She was beginning to feel uneasy that Ajit had categorically refused to give them time to think.

Why was Ajit deciding so many things?

'Why can't you give us time to think, Ajit?' she asked.

'Take your time,' said Ajit. 'You can vote by phone, Avi.'

She laughed. 'To everyone, give time to everyone. Discard this vote,' she said.

Ajit shook his head. 'You know we won't be able to get such a big gathering again. Avidha, all of the members of FOB are no longer so active. You know that.'

That brought her thoughts into focus. Why did Ajit want these inactive members to vote when he had been having small group meetings to decide strategies till now? Why did he need all these people who had lost track of the details of the case to vote at this juncture? Only to be able to assert that he had sought consent? So this was hegemony!

Once again she blamed herself for not having been able to see the manner in which he had wrested the leadership of the campaign and sidelined those who had lent it its sharpness. She now remembered how Mukta and Nirmala had fought to have their arguments included in the briefs, and how they had always been in a minority. She thought of Hally's futile attempts to bolster their arguments and how he finally had to give up his job. They had all been made irrelevant to the struggle. That is why perhaps they could see the impending failure of the struggle.

Avidha looked at Suguna. Only a year ago they were together, carefree, both a little concerned, a little confused about the Bhopal case. Today Suguna appeared to be clear about how far she would go and in which direction. She would probably build an oppressively successful career. Avidha gave Hally a rueful smile. She herself seemed to lose friends because of her romantic insistence to have all or none. She would never be pragmatic.

Her face flushed with anger, she stood up.

'I know it makes no difference,' she said to Ajit. 'I vote against the proposal.'

Ajit smiled a tiny, imperceptible smile.

Hally opened the door and they left together. Mukta and Nirmala were sitting on the steps waiting for her and they sat down next to them. She felt as if she had just lost many friends and had come to be part of a small family.

'I feel so terrible,' she said to Mukta. 'I will be so happy if you are proved wrong.'

'Nothing will make me happier. But I am afraid the verdict is now a foregone conclusion,' said Mukta. 'You know how it makes me feel? That Vineeta was probably right. Going back to the same court? What sense did it make?'

'Except that the court will once again take the flak!' said Hally with a laugh.

'Another crack in the system,' laughed Nirmala.

They walked together to the main road and stood under a streetlamp, waiting for an auto, their shadows shrinking around their feet. It was cold and beyond that small pool of light the world was dark.